Child *of the* Forest

Daughter of the KGB

S. D. SHADDEN

ISBN 978-1-0980-4285-1 (paperback)
ISBN 978-1-0980-4587-6 (hardcover)
ISBN 978-1-0980-4286-8 (digital)

Copyright © 2020 by S. D. Shadden

All rights reserved. No part of this publication may be reproduced, distributed, or transmitted in any form or by any means, including photocopying, recording, or other electronic or mechanical methods without the prior written permission of the publisher. For permission requests, solicit the publisher via the address below.

Christian Faith Publishing, Inc.
832 Park Avenue
Meadville, PA 16335
www.christianfaithpublishing.com

This novel is a work of fiction. Although the story draws on the historical record, the characters, incidents, and conversations are invented.

Most Scriptures taken from the New King James Version. Copyright © 1982 by Thomas Nelson, Inc. Used by permission. All rights reserved.

Printed in the United States of America

August 26, 2023
To Pauline,
May this novel take you on a special journey, one that inspires you as the characters inspired me. God Bless you.
S. D. Shadden

> To those who must dwell in the shadows so
> that others may live in the light

If you do not know the trees, you may be lost in the forest; but if you do not know the stories, you may be lost in life.
—Siberian proverb

PROLOGUE

KGB Colonel Viktor Kurgan sat hunched over his wooden desk; the harsh glow from his lamp cast his large shadow against the wall of his private office. On his massive desk, a tall stack of files bore a wide red stripe running diagonally from corner to corner, looking as if their tan throats had been cut by an executioner's blade. Each file had been red-flagged: "Requires Special Attention."

Colonel Kurgan, the most secretive man in one of the world's most secret organizations, methodically investigated each file—searching, but not finding. As he reached for each file with his long curved fingers, the shadow on the wall resembled a wolf's fangs, devouring each file, along with the unfortunate person listed within. This dark image was only appropriate since with his piercing gray eyes, premature gray hair, and merciless demeanor, he had acquired the nickname "the Gray Wolf."

Near the bottom of the stack, the Gray Wolf smiled and pushed the other files aside. Extracted from the heart of the folder, he held a sheet of paper, a letter, a desperate person's plea. The colonel underlined a name using his black fountain pen and wrote a notation beside the name in his trademark blood-red ink.

With satisfaction, Kurgan stamped the outside of this special file "Top Secret" and placed it in his personal safe, just behind his desk. It was well past midnight, but his efforts might someday produce what he so eagerly desired: a malleable young disciplined candidate—one to be made into Kurgan's "own image."

Colonel Viktor Kurgan, the Gray Wolf, spymaster of the Soviet KGB, believed that he had finally discovered this elusive person; he had found the perfect assassin.

The name underlined and the notation written in blood-red ink was "*Anya Ruslanova*—Siberia—child of the forest." This is her story.

PART 1

The Forest

*From the womb of the morning, you
have the dew of your youth.*
—Psalms 110:3

CHAPTER 1

"Anya, come here. Look at this track and tell me what you think." Aleksandre Ruslanov (Sasha to his friends) stepped to the side of a large track in the snow so that his daughter could see. His blonde-haired, blue-eyed daughter knelt beside him.

Both were draped in heavy furs to such a degree that they looked like upright animals. Their furs provided not only warmth but life itself: the animals provided the furs so that Sasha and his family could live. The Ruslanovs never forgot that sacrifice. They revered wildlife and considered them a neighbor and a friend.

Sasha obtained furs during the long Siberian winter. He hunted and fished for the remainder of the year. The furs provided his only income. The hunting and fishing put food on the table.

Sasha and his small family lived a simple life with few luxuries. Most of the money from his furs purchased more cartridges. The remainder bought a few basic staples: salt, tea, flour, and some vegetable seeds. Once a year, he managed to barter for a few gifts for his wife and daughter. Sasha bought nothing for himself. If he needed something, he made it.

Anya was careful not to bump her father's rifle while examining the track. The old single-shot rifle was her father's most treasured possession. It was a bit heavy, but it was very solid and incredibly accurate. It was an heirloom, passed down for three generations, beginning with Sasha's grandfather. It was more than a rifle—it was an emblem of the Ruslanov family.

Anya gazed at the track clearly outlined in the snow. The enormous print dwarfed her eleven-year-old hand when she inserted it into the track. "Papa, the front paws are different. The right track has a gap on the side."

"Anya, you have sharp eyes. One footprint can reveal an entire life. This is from an old male tiger. Look at the size and depth of the print. He was injured many years ago, probably from fighting. His right paw is missing part of one toe. See the pad and then four toes. Each toe will have a claw with two addition dewclaws on the front feet. The dewclaws are very sharp since they never touch the ground. They are used to better hold an animal when the tiger kills with his four large front teeth. I have seen this track many times over the years. This forest is part of his large territory. He roams over three hundred kilometers. There have not been many wolves or small bears in this area all winter. He is the reason they left. They fear him. This is his country for this winter. We will leave him alone. The forest is big enough for all of us."

Sasha and Anya continued their hunt. Anya easily kept pace with her father. She was large for her age: from her father, she bore his solid frame and height; from her mother, she was blessed with a pretty Slavic face, thick blonde hair, and blue eyes. Anya's striking eyes were described by the forest people as "more blue than the sky—brighter than the sun." Anyone who saw them never forgot them. Those same eyes were searching now for a lynx.

Since early morning, Sasha and Anya had been stalking the large male lynx. The appearance of the tiger had forced the lynx to backtrack to a nearby streambed. Both predators were close; their presence felt but not seen. Anya loved this stage of the hunt and these special moments: being with her father, the woods, the animals, new discoveries every day.

Sasha taught Anya all he knew about his way of life. Sasha believed in the hunt. He did not trap or use snares. The only God he knew was the God of creation. In this creation, Sasha saw order and precision. Hunting for specific animals seemed a natural way to preserve this order and a way of life.

His hunting method took more time, but it never depopulated an area of a certain group of animals. Sasha knew every animal had its place. If one species was totally eliminated, the natural order was upset, and other animals would also leave. Sasha also did not have to be tied to following a trapline. If a storm appeared, he could wait out the storm in their warm cabin rather than worry whether trapped animals were starving or freezing to death.

Sasha was a hunter, but he loved and appreciated wildlife. They provided his family with food, clothing, and a small income. Other trappers made more money in the beginning, but Sasha felt he could live in this forest forever. His code as a simple one: respect and harmony.

The Ruslanov family had lived this lifestyle for several generations. They were attracted to the Sikhote Alin Mountains because of the region's microclimate, which provided for a variety of trees and wildlife (much more than the colder tundra in the north or the more humid southeastern regions closer to the sea).

Over one hundred years ago, the Ruslanov family settled in this large valley in the midst of the forest. At that time, no one held a paper with a legal title; but the other settlers respected all homestead boundaries, particularly for those who had come first. There was plenty of land, and it only made sense: if everyone trapped the same area, the game would soon be gone.

There was little competition to live in this steep, rugged country with no roads. The closest settlement was called Vladimir's Store. It was not even a village—just a simple outpost for trading furs. It still took several days of walking over rough terrain to reach the outpost. City dwellers and the logging industry stayed away—there were easier ways to make a living—and certainly less lonely. Anya and her family knew no other life. They believed they lived in paradise.

An hour later, Anya and Sasha found the lynx at the top of a narrow ravine. It had killed a large white rabbit, and it was cautiously feasting. After a few bites, it lifted its head and scanned the area before continuing to eat. This was the largest lynx Anya had ever seen, and its light-colored winter coat was prime and full.

Sasha handed the rifle to his daughter. "Anya, it is time. This animal is for you. With his fur, I can buy you more books."

"But, Papa, I have only shot rabbits and small game. What if I miss or just wound it?"

"Daughter, remember what I told you: from the side, shoot it behind the ear. At a distance, aim at the shoulder to hit the heart and lungs. If it faces you, shoot in the center of the chest. If a dangerous animal charges you, have courage, concentrate, aim carefully—and wait. The clear shot will come. You will sense it. When the animal is almost upon you, shoot it in the eye. It will strike the brain and die before reaching you. You only have one shot. It must count. Listen to the inner voice that whispers, *Now is the time*."

Anya took the rifle and rested it on a log. The lynx could not smell, hear, or see them in the brush with the wind blowing away their scent. The lynx kept bobbing his head while eating, tearing at the flesh. Anya decided to wait until he lifted his head one more time to scan the area. It was a risk. The rabbit was almost consumed. If the lynx suddenly left, they would not get another shot for that day.

The lynx slowly lifted his head and looked to the right and to the left. He was a magnificent creature, standing on a boulder at the top of the ravine with the forest in the background—a prince of all he surveyed. Anya would remember this stately image for the rest of her life.

The sound of the rifle shot surprised Anya. She had instinctively pulled the trigger just as the lynx raised his head. The lynx fell on the top of the boulder, the bullet hitting him behind his left ear. He died instantly, as if struck by a bolt of lightning. Sasha looked at his daughter with pride; it was one of the finest shots he had ever seen.

Anya quickly reloaded the old rifle. She remembered her father's words: "After a shot, wait patiently and approach with caution. Never assume, daughter. The wounded are always the most dangerous—whether man or beast."

Anya walked quietly toward the outstretched animal. Sasha followed behind her. He let her carry the rifle in order for her to complete the task, to make the full circle as a hunter, to appreciate the animal's sacrifice. Anya nudged the lynx with her rifle. When it did not move, she respectfully knelt beside it and stroked its soft fur.

Sasha gazed down at the two together and said, "Anya, thank this creature for your books. Thank him for his life. Thank the God of creation for your clean shot and for this animal's quiet death. Let's take him home."

Anya savored the moment. She stood erect and cradled the rifle across her left arm. Raising her eyes to the clear blue sky, she scanned the horizon just as the lynx at her feet had done only moments ago. The entire vista before her was beautiful and massive—the woodlands stretched endlessly beyond the horizon to the sea. A feather of her blonde hair flew across her cheek and danced in the breeze. Her heart still raced from the hunt, but her soul felt a perfect peace. This land, this life—for her, there could be no other. In every fiber of her being, she knew, *This is where I belong.*

CHAPTER 2

The winter fur season was coming to a close. This year's bounty had been an especially good one, and Sasha felt blessed. In a few months, he would gather the fine finished furs and take them down the mountain.

Going "down the mountain" required an arduous trek that took several days. Sasha had a special pack made of light saplings lashed together by sinew strips. His *L*-shaped pack formed two ninety-degree angles; one side fit against his back while the bottom part faced outward behind him. The furs were folded to fit the open pack with the heaviest furs at the bottom. A rope on each side of the pack held them securely together from top to bottom. When traveling, Sasha wore a soft leather strap at the top of the pack across his forehead and buckled a wide leather belt at his waist. The load was always heavy but well balanced for the long journey.

The task was made easier since Sasha knew that there was no other way to get down the mountain. He never complained. These furs meant another year of survival for Sasha and his family. Also, it was his only way to get books for Anya, to help her, to advance her education. Sasha could not give much—but he gave all that he had.

CHAPTER 3

The spring thaw came early, and soon the ground was firm enough for Sasha to make his rendezvous down to Vladimir's Store. Anya and Sonya helped him to put on his heavy pack and to adjust the load. He carried his rifle on a leather sling over his right shoulder.

Sasha turned and held his wife's hand while looking at the ivory ring on her finger. "I hate to leave you both here alone—you know that."

Sonya nodded her head but avoided looking into his eyes. Handing him a small parcel of food, Sonya replied, "Yes, my love, I know. But what is to be done about it? This is our life."

"Anya, take care of your mother. I have to take the rifle. I left a sharp double-bladed axe by the door. Maybe someday we can get another rifle." Anya knew that they could barely afford ammunition for one firearm; purchasing another for her was only a dream—but a nice one.

Sasha bent slightly and kissed the women on each of their cheeks. Anya took his left hand and walked beside him. Sonya stayed on the cabin porch. The small cabin was Sonya's emotional anchor. It was too painful to walk beside him, to release him, to feel his presence leave her. Sonya realized that every time he walked out of the door, it might be the last time she would ever see him. It was wild country with wild men and wild beasts; sometimes it was hard to tell them apart.

Near a stream that flowed near the cabin, Sasha released Anya's hand. "Daughter, it's time for you to go back. Mind your mother and help her while I'm gone. I know I can count on you. I'll try to be back in a week. Count the sunrise seven times. On the eighth dawn, I hope to be standing on our porch." He stroked her hair, looked at the rising sun, turned east-southeast, and walked away.

Anya sat next to the rippling water amidst yellow wildflowers. She watched her handsome father, with his strong build and auburn-brown hair, cover the ground with each long stride. She did not take her sparkling blue eyes off his image until he disappeared from her sight. The sun was just barely over the horizon—the first dawn of seven, then look for him on the eighth. She knew he would return, just as he had said; her father always kept his word. Anya tossed a wildflower with seven yellow petals into the ice-cold water. It floated east-southeast, as if trailing her father, until it also ran toward the sun and beyond her sight.

CHAPTER 4

It was a beautiful day for a new journey. The grass was already turning dark green, and the wildflowers flourished everywhere—a field of color completely surrounding him. The birds had returned, and their presence always lifted his heart. The Siberian summers were brief but a welcome relief from the long cold winters. Sasha accepted both in his easygoing way; each season carried its own blessing.

In good conditions, it was generally a three-day walk to Vladimir's trading post. Sasha's first destination was a trapper's cabin. He hoped to arrive before nightfall. This was his closest neighbor, and the trapper always welcomed his unannounced visits. The conversation alone was a delight for a single trapper, who seldom saw another soul in his country. Sasha's visit was the highlight of this lonely trapper's year.

The second day brought Sasha to a location he called "the Springs." It was a large pool of ice-cold water created by a tall waterfall. It was a refreshing break to what was the longest day of the trek.

By the third day, Sashing neared the edge of the forest, where an extensive plain stretched below. The climate was more temperate in this area. There were four seasons, but the winters were milder than the high-mountain forests where Sasha dwelled. One of his best friends lived in this area, a farmer named Dmitri.

Dmitri was a squat red-headed man with a bristly red beard that looked as if it were on fire. His powerful arms and barrel chest reminded Sasha of a forest bear. Sasha always hoped that those bear-like arms never grasped him, for Dmitri was known for his temper, making him a short-fused keg of dynamite.

Dmitri farmed on this plain. He needed the grasslands for his modest herd of dairy cattle, two horses, and several chickens. He had a massive garden and a small hayfield for winter forage. His main income was derived from selling cream, butter, eggs, and an excellent round of cheese. These products, along with his summer garden, provided him with a sufficient income to live alone without the constraints of the communist farm quotas. For the communists, he was too far away and too insignificant to bother with. Dmitri liked it that way.

Dmitri used his horses to carry his farm products to Vladimir's Store, and he leased them to trappers who needed assistance for their final journey to the trading post. He also stored trade goods in his small barn if the trappers required several trips to take their items home. These services came at a price, but not for Sasha.

Sasha made his way down into the plain. He was already smiling when he spotted Dmitri hoeing weeds in his garden. Dmitri chopped as if every weed were an insult to his perfect garden, as if to remonstrate, *How dare they trespass!* Dmitri felt that they needed a good lesson: *Take that! And that! And that!* The farmer was so focused that he did not see Sasha lower his heavy pack and quietly walk up behind the chopping fanatic.

"Poor plants," said Sasha, "and such violence from a man who claims to be a farmer."

Dmitri leaped forward like a frightened toad and wheeled with his hoe into a fighting stance. When he recognized Sasha, he threw his hoe into the air and rushed back to hug Sasha. Dmitri's head rested just above Sasha's stomach; such was the difference in height.

"I... I ought to wrestle that worthless rifle from you and shoot you for a scare like that!" Dmitri shouted. "No wonder you're such a good hunter—you're the perfect sneak. Now what did I do with that hoe? Oh well, let the chickens eat it. Come into my humble home. I just made a round of cheese, and it is quite good, if I say so myself. Sasha, Sasha, you have come just in time. Tomorrow we will take the products of our hard-earned labor to that lazy Vladimir and skin the conniving scoundrel this time. Come to me and let me kiss your cheek in greeting—better yet, find my hoe. Hoes cost money, kisses are free. Don't dawdle, Sasha, come into the house."

And they talked as only friends can do—the whole night through.

CHAPTER 5

Anya and Sonya turned over the dark earth one shovelful at a time. It was a beautiful spring day to be outside enjoying the weather and each other's company. The work was hard but satisfying. They were planting vegetable seeds. Flowers growing around the cabin would be nice, but that cost money. Besides, there were plenty of wildflowers all about them.

The harvest from their garden sustained them for the entire year. The Siberian summer had a short growing season, but the increased sunlight from their northern latitude allowed the garden to flourish.

Sonya stopped a moment and rubbed her back. Her braided blonde hair fell to the middle of her slender back. She glanced an Anya, who was still working the soil, and smiled when she realized that Anya was almost as tall as she. Sonya looked at her hands, no longer soft but still feminine. She caressed her full red skirt, faded and patched. Perhaps it would last until autumn; it would have to—it was all she had.

Living on the mountain was the only life Sonya had known. She was the daughter of a trapper's family who once lived northwest of the Ruslanov homestead. Her parents' land was even harder in which to make a living than here. Both her parents were gone. They died like most mountain people: hard times and hard work. She felt blessed to be where she now lived: content with her home, her family, her life.

She picked up the shovel and began working again. She missed Sasha. He only left them once a year; still it seemed an eternity.

Sonya first met Sasha at Vladimir's Store, the same place where he was probably selling his furs at that moment. She smiled when she remembered her first impression of him. Sasha was tall and muscular, even at age sixteen. His dark-auburn hair and kind blue eyes made him stand out among others his age. She liked his polite, easygoing manner. It signified to her a quiet strength.

After their first meeting, Sasha spent the summer walking for an entire day each way to see Sonya at her homestead. They were dutifully chaperoned. Most conversations were by a nearby stream. It was sweet, it was innocent, it was a woodland love. They married at the end of the summer.

The marriage ceremony for these two sixteen-year-olds was attended by only their parents. Neither the bride nor the groom had siblings, and there were no other living relatives. The simple service was conducted by the two fathers; no one else was available. Still it was special to the six people gathered around a fireplace with Sonya's silver cross as an ornament and her mother's old Bible as their centerpiece.

Sonya and Sasha Ruslanov started their new life together with a new cabin built by both families, an old rifle, one small silver cross, one double-edged axe, two cooking pots, and many hopes and dreams of a good life together. Fondly, Sonya glanced at her wedding band, a beautiful piece of carved, polished ivory, handmade by Sasha. She had worn it every day of her life since she was sixteen. It looked elegant on her lovely slim hand. She would not trade it for all the gold and diamonds in Russia.

Sonya continued to smile as she looked at her pretty daughter, diligently working the soil in the sun. She prayed that Anya would someday find her own "Sasha"—one worthy of a woman's dreams.

CHAPTER 6

Sasha and Dmitri tied the weary horses to the hitching post and water trough outside Vladimir's Store. They quickly unloaded the saddle packs and loosened the cinches to rest the horses' backs. They placed their goods against the storefront on the large wooden deck, which faced east to gather the morning sun.

The few residents liked to call it a village, but it really resembled a glorified trading post, with a small government office down the street. Its location at a crossroad kept the place alive. Trappers referred to it by many names: the trading post, the crossroads, Vladimir's Store, or simply Vladimir's. Whatever they called it, Vladimir owned it, and ran it well.

The trading post made most of its money exchanging furs for supplies. The furs were freighted by wagon to a railhead and then sent south to a factory near Vladivostok. Vladimir's saloon was the only legal establishment to serve alcohol in the region. His store-saloon also held the only post office. He even held funds for locals, trappers, and the small government office—all kept in his large black safe—for a small fee. Eventually, all roads led to Vladimir's, and he managed his monopoly skillfully. Business was always good, and he made sure it stayed that way.

Vladimir was tall, olive-skinned, with salt-and-pepper black hair (still mostly pepper), sporting a well-trimmed dark slender mustache. His bright brown eyes radiated warmth, intelligence, and a touch of orneriness. He had never met a stranger, and he knew everyone and everything about everyone. No one needed a newspaper—just go ask Vladimir.

Vladimir saw Sasha and Dmitri through his large storefront window. He wiped his hands on a white rag, opened his arms wide, and exclaimed, "Welcome, welcome. Look, a warrior and a criminal—I know not which man is which, but we need both in a civilized society! Come, have some of my excellent vodka, get drunk, and let me steal all your trade goods!"

Dmitri and Sasha entered the small dark saloon to socialize with Vladimir and a few hapless trappers. Dmitri ordered some of Vladimir's "excellent vodka." Sasha always believed his nondescript vodka could scald the hair off a dog's back. Instead, Sasha ordered a mug of Vladimir's "excellent" watered-down beer, but only one—every beer meant less for his wife and child.

Sitting in a corner near the only window of the saloon, a trapper poured himself another glass of vodka from a nearly empty bottle. His eyes were dark and glassy. His coal-black hair was pushed over his ears like a pair of raven's wings. His fur cap and vest had bald spots, as if his garments suffered from terminal mange. Raising his glass to Sasha and Dmitri, he smiled, showing his crooked yellow teeth. The new visitors acknowledged his salute and raised their glasses, but did not join him. His name was Chekov, and his reputation and appearance closely resembled that of a shedding snake.

Chekov tottered to their table and plopped down into a chair, uninvited. "Always good to see old friends. Sasha, Dmitri—it has been so long. Where have you been?"

"Unlike you, Chekov, we have been working," Dmitri retorted. Dmitri always hoped Chekov would drink himself to death before they would meet again, but Chekov had the insides of a steel trap.

"And you, Sasha, how is your wife and little—?"

"My daughter, Anya, she's almost twelve," Sasha replied.

"Sasha, it is so fortunate that we meet today. Only yesterday, you came to my mind. I believe we could make a fortune as partners in that high valley of yours. What do you say?"

"I already have two partners. Their names are Sonya and Anya. I need no others."

"No, no, no, you miss my point. With your tracking skills and my large number of traps, we could share the work and split the profits. It would be a gold mine."

It was none of Dmitri's business, but he could not hold his tongue. "Yes, Chekov, but when the gold is all gone, all that is left of a mine is a large empty hole in the ground—something like the country you have completely trapped out of existence. Isn't that so?"

Chekov gripped the bottle with his nicotine-stained fingers. He wanted to break the bottle into Dmitri's all-knowing mouth. Instead, he smiled and replied, "Well, yes, I have been busy as usual, but I'm always on the lookout for a new opportunity—with an old friend. Think about it, Sasha." With great effort, Chekov staggered back to his table to finish his bottle of vodka before ordering another.

Vladimir broke the tension by popping his head around the corner of the saloon and mocked, "If you two cheap Tartars are not going to drink all of my fine liquor at one sitting, then come outside and show me what you brought so that I can seize it for as little money as possible!"

Dmitri and Sasha followed Vladimir, who marched like a Soviet general with a large piece of canvas under his arm. "Sasha, reload the horses and tie them in the shade of this tree. Dmitri, help me spread this canvas on the ground," ordered the "general."

When every item was placed on the canvas, Vladimir examined each fur with a smile while stroking the thick soft surface with his hand. "Sasha, these are the finest furs that I have ever seen. This lynx pelt takes the prize—extraordinary!"

Sasha proudly explained, "Anya shot that lynx, one shot behind the ear. The lynx is hers."

Vladimir never took his eyes off the exquisite and valuable fur. "I don't believe it. Dmitri, take one side of this pelt and raise it toward the sun." Both men lifted the lynx hide high into the air, as if they were offering a sacrifice to a Siberian sun god.

Dmitri smirked and said, "What do you think now, you disbelieving, heathen scoundrel? Not one bullet hole anywhere?"

"What I think, Reverend Dmitri, is that I do not want to make Sasha or his daughter mad at me. One shot. Amazing and so beautiful! Well done, Sasha. I'll take the whole lot. Once you get your supplies, we will settle the amount, and then I will skin both of you, as usual. Now, Dmitri, what did you bring me—rat poison?"

"No need, Vlady, your 'excellent vodka' could kill man or beast with a single dosage. However, I did bring these. Perhaps your rats will like them." With a wry smile, Dmitri laid on the canvas sheet several large discs of his homemade cheese. He also placed a dozen jars of butter and thick cream next to them. Finally, he presented a large basket of carefully wrapped eggs.

Vladimir raised his arms into the air and exclaimed, "Eggs, eggs, another miracle! How did you get them down in one piece? These are more valuable than gold! Dmitri, if you were not so short and ugly, I… I would simply kiss you!"

"Spare me the kisses, just open wide your purse and fill my hand with your silver, you thieving rascal."

"Sasha, I am going to ignore this vile man. Here is the key to my storage shed. Put your furs on this canvas—far to the left, away from the other pelts. Please put the lynx on top and cover them carefully. I will store them properly later this evening. As for you, farmer Dmitri, let's all have a slice of your delicious cheese with some black bread and a glass of my wonderful beverages."

"The Last Supper, eh?" Dmitri retorted. "Oh well, I'll even drink poison—if it's free."

Sasha grinned and stooped to gather the furs off the canvas. Dmitri and Vladimir had traded insults for years; but underneath it all, there was a deep, affectionate trust. He knew they would be the first to defend each other, if trouble ever came their way.

Vladimir could not resist holding the lynx fur up to get another look at it while Sasha and Dmitri gathered the fruit of their hard-earned labor—a Siberian transaction on a beautiful, early summer day: each man content with his life, his work, his friendships. Vladimir's statement was true: yes, it was a type of "miracle."

Sitting by the window in his dark squalid corner, Chekov watched Vladimir hold the prime lynx pelt into the air. If that was a sample of what was in Sasha's pristine valley, Chekov thought, then he, Chekov, whom he considered the best of all the Siberian trappers, planned to get some of it—no matter what he had to do. "One person does not deserve all the luck," he murmured. Chekov downed his glass of vodka in a single gulp and snarled at the bartender. "Bring another bottle."

CHAPTER 7

"Sasha, now that this exquisite meal of black bread, outstanding beverages, and someone's overpriced cheese is finished, we might as well settle accounts," Vladimir suggested. He glanced at Dmitri and continued, "I know what you want, old skinflint—money, money, and more money. I'll get you next time when you come for supplies."

"Some of us work for a living and can feed ourselves," Dmitri helpfully replied.

Ignoring Dmitri, Vladimir called Sasha over to his counter. "Sasha, you have cartridges, salt, flour, vegetable seeds, needles, thread, candle wax, wicks, and what is this—soft cloth?"

"It's for Sonya," Sasha said.

"Really! I didn't think it was for Dmitri—a feed sack would do for him. Sasha, this is beautiful: dark navy blue with red roses and a burgundy trim. An excellent choice, my friend, the best I have! In fact, if you like flowers, I have something very special."

"Why do I always get nervous when you have 'something special' to offer?" Dmitri remarked.

"Silence, my simple fool. This is beyond your small mind. Sasha, look at this. There is nothing like it within a thousand kilometers. Let me read the package, 'Tulipa Uniflora': Siberian tulips."

"Who did you steal that from?" Dmitri asked. "Those aren't from around here."

"If you must know, nosey man, I got them from a sailor whose ship was berthed at Vladivostok. I don't know where he got them, but they were a present for his wife. When he got here, he discovered that his wife had left him for another man. He was very angry with her. However, he had been gone for two years—that might have had something to do with it. In any case, angry people make angry deals. I traded him tulip bulbs for excellent vodka—a wonderful exchange, and everyone was happy. Sasha, there is nothing to it. Plant them when you get home, and next spring, Anya and Sonya will have the finest flowers on the mountain. What do you say?"

Sasha picked up the package off the counter and carefully examined it, turning it over in his large calloused hands. "Thank you for thinking of us, Vladimir, but we can't eat this, and the mountain provides thousands of wildflowers. The cloth and books will have to make do."

"Oh yes, the books!" Vladimir hurried to his storeroom directly behind him and returned with a small canvas sack full of books. He carefully placed each book on his wide wooden counter. "Let's see, what treasures we have here? Just as you ordered: one very heavy medical book, a book on Russian literature, a couple of children's books, and the best for last—Tolstoy's *Anna Karenina* and *The Cossack*. Beautiful, aren't they?"

Sasha lowered his eyes and said, "Vladimir, many thanks for getting these, but what I ordered was a medical book and one child's book for Anya. I can't afford the rest of these, but thank you all the same."

"Sasha, I am beginning to believe that you are even more of a tightwad than farmer Dmitri over there. Look at these: *Krokodile* (*The Crocodile*) by Kourney Chukovsky and illustrated by the famous Nikolai Remizov. Here's another: *Zagadki* (*Riddles*) by Samuil Marshak and look at these wonderful drawings by that famous painter Kuzma Petrov-Vodkin. Tolstoy's *The Cossack*, I got for you, and *Anna Karenina* for Anya and Sonya. These came all the way from Moscow by train to Vladivostok, and then by wagon to my little counter. Six months, Sasha! Six months to get these!"

"What does a child need with crocodiles and riddles in Siberia?" questioned Dmitri.

"Because she is a child!" Vladimir replied with a slight edge in his voice. Looking at Sasha, he continued, "You said that she took the lynx. These books are worth more to her than any fur or temporary treasure. Let's make an investment—let's invest in her!"

Sasha fingered the books and looked at the pretty drawings. Vladimir had gone to a lot of trouble, and they were beautiful. With regret, he said, "I'll take the medical book, one child's book, and one book by this Tolstoy. I can't do any more. Sorry, Vladimir."

Vladimir did not want to shame Sasha. He knew Sasha to be a proud man and that it was hard for him to turn down the books for his daughter. Life on the mountain was meager and hard—sacrifices had to be made.

"All right, all right, Sasha, you drive a hard bargain. I must admit that I got a little carried away with your order. By the way, when is Anya's birthday?"

Sasha's cheeks turned bright red, and he looked away from the men toward the store window. He hated to admit that he did not know the exact date when his daughter was born; he had no clocks or calendars. He only knew that Anya was born in the late spring to early summer. The wildflowers were just beginning to bloom.

"She will be twelve in a few weeks." That was close enough.

"Very well, my hard-set mountain man. You pay for three books. The *Krokodile* is for Anya's birthday, and *Anna Karenina* is for your pretty wife's anniversary and because she has to put up with you. Don't argue. They are my gifts, and this is the only day that I will be generous to anyone for the rest of the year."

Sasha smiled and knew that he was beaten. He took Vladimir's hand and clasped it with both of his own. "Thank you, friend. They will enjoy your presents. You are a good man."

Dmitri shook his head and burst out, "Oh, don't tell him that! It will only go to his head. He probably stole those books from that poor drunken sailor, along with those flower seeds."

"They are tulip bulbs, not little seeds. You should know that, farmer Dmitri—oh, why do I explain? Sasha, what do I order for next year? I won't get so carried away this time."

"Anya needs another book on mathematics, Russian grammar, and a good novel of some kind. Vladimir, you decide. You know best. I trust you."

Sasha's words warmed Vladimir's heart. For once in his life, the silver-tongued trader was momentarily speechless. However, he recovered quickly.

"It shall be done, Sasha, no matter the distance or the expense. They will be waiting for her next year." Vladimir started waiving his hands toward the door. "Now you two go to the saloon and get out of here. I have to pack all these goods, and I'm tired of both of you. Go drink several bottles of my excellent brew and let me get to work."

Neither man ventured into the saloon, but when they stepped outside to check on the horses, Vladimir began to arrange Sasha's supplies. Vladimir held the vegetable seeds in one hand and the package of tulip bulbs in the other hand. He looked at both and proclaimed, "Seeds for the body, tulips for the soul!" He looked at the books in front of him and quietly said, "And with these, dear Sasha, we plant a harvest for the future." Vladimir wrapped the tulip bulbs in the soft navy cloth patterned with the red roses and hid them near the bottom of the pack, carefully placing the books and the other supplies around them. He smiled and looked out of his window at the two men watering the horses while thinking of Anya. Indeed, he was already looking forward to next year's "harvest."

CHAPTER 8

"Sasha, stay a few more days. I have plenty of food, and conversation is good for the soul," Dmitri said at his farm on the border between the woodlands and the plains.

"Thank you, but no. I must get back to my family. I have been gone too long as it is."

"Then do me this favor, Sasha. Take that bay horse and let him carry your supplies, at least to the springs. It will save an entire day. The horse is old, and he knows that trail better than either of us. Unload at the springs, take off his halter, and attach it to the packsaddle. Then just turn him loose. He can see better than any human at night. He will trot the entire way and be home before sunrise. He is a wise horse. You be wise as well. Use him and hurry home to your loved ones."

Sasha did not want to abuse Dmitri's friendship. However, the horse would probably be safe from injury or thieves. Sasha seldom saw anyone on the trails. It did make sense to use the horse.

"Dmitri, what if someone steals him on his return?"

"Then, Sasha, I will tell Vladimir to give me back my horse, or I will hang him. Honestly, friend, no one will touch that old rogue. I can barely catch him when he thinks there is work to be done. Take him. You know I am right."

Sasha and Dmitri loaded the bay, dividing the supplies equally by weight on each side of the animal. Dmitri loaned Sasha his best packsaddle and panniers for the trip up the mountain. They shook hands and hugged each other with affection. With teary eyes, they bade each other farewell, knowing their paths would not cross for another year.

"Go well, friend Sasha!"

"Stay well, friend Dmitri!"

The sun poked its head above the horizon, and both men knew it was time to part. Sasha took the rope on the halter, and he and the bay started up the trail. At the top of the rise, Sasha gave the horse a brief rest to catch his wind, and Sasha looked down at the valley below. He waved one more time to Dmitri, who was still in the same spot that Sasha had left him—a faithful sentry watching over a friend.

The day was so pleasant that Sasha made excellent time: a dry trail, beautiful sunshine, no wind, and not a cloud in the sky. Dmitri had been correct: the bay horse was a godsend. The "old rogue," as Dmitri called him, was surefooted and carried the load well. At every break, Sasha checked the cinch and the ropes on the packsaddle. It fit the bay perfectly; the load never shifted.

Sasha could walk as fast as the horse, and they arrived at the springs by the late afternoon. The springs was actually a pool of water that held the runoff of a small waterfall. It was an oasis in the forest: wildflowers circled the pool, and the waterfall freshened the air with a cool mist.

Sasha unloaded the panniers of his precious supplies and placed the packsaddle near a large tree. He bathed the bay's back with an old rag soaked with the crisp water from the pool. Sasha hobbled the bay's front feet and allowed the horse to eat the luscious grass near the pool while he prepared a fire and a makeshift camp for the night.

When the bay's back had dried, he saddled the horse with the packsaddle and removed the hobbles. He stroked the horse's neck and said, "Be safe, old friend. You served me well. Be nice to Dmitri."

Sasha placed a pair of fur mittens that he had made into the pannier and latched it shut. The mittens would keep Dmitri warm this winter. He turned the bay to the trail. The horse pitched its ears forward, nickered softly, and trotted down the slope until it was out of sight.

That night, Sasha sat by a warm fire with the soothing sound of the waterfall behind him. He could see the stars peeking through the massive limbs of the tree. Dmitri insisted that he take along some chicken, bread, and cheese for the trip. Sasha could ask for nothing more: a warm fire, a generous meal, cool water, a waterfall to sing him to sleep underneath a clear sky full of stars. Lying on a bed of evergreen needles, underneath the fine old tree, Sasha draped a fur cape over his weary limbs. His last thought for the passing day was, *If God lives in heaven, it must be just like this.*

CHAPTER 9

Sasha saw the family homestead from a distance. A thin line of smoke wafted from the cabin's chimney, spiraling upward into the sky. Sonya and Anya were inside having a nice meal, he reasoned. To the left of the cabin, the dark brown earth had been prepared, needing only a few seeds to begin the growing cycle again: new life to sustain others. Sasha surveyed the homey scene, and tears formed in the corners of his eyes. He felt blessed beyond measure—a sense of peace and warmth for his family and their simple way of life.

Anya heard his footsteps first and flung open the cabin door to greet him. She ran and leaped into his arms. Even with a heavy pack and with a rifle on his shoulders, he easily carried her weight—the mountain was a man, the man a mountain.

Sonya watched from the doorway the pretty scene unfolding before her: the two people she loved most in the world in each other's arms. She approached Sasha, kissed his cheek, and helped him remove the heavy pack from his weary shoulders. Anya retrieved the rifle, and she noticed, as usual, it was oiled and cleaned.

After finishing a hearty meal together, it was time to unload the pack. Anya could barely restrain her excitement. This was the most wonderful moment of the year: special treats that would have to last a year. This was better than Christmas.

Christmas for the Ruslanov family was celebrated sometime in December when they found and shot a fat deer. It was a pleasant day, but not necessarily a certain time, just an event to exchange homemade gifts. The yearly event of unloading the pack was, to Anya, the discovery of buried treasure.

"For my lovely wife, new cloth with needles and matching thread."

"Sasha, it is so beautiful. I love the colors. I love everything about it." She hugged his neck and whispered in his ear, "Most of all, I love you."

Sasha kissed Sonya's forehead and paused to glance at his anxious daughter. She could barely keep still.

"Anya, your lynx bought several books." One by one, Sasha handed each book to Anya. With each book, he could see her excitement growing; her eyes were aglow with each new "nugget of gold."

"Papa, where did you find so many?"

"At Vladimir's Store. He outdid himself this time. Oh, before I forget, this book, *Anna Karenina* by Tolstoy, is for you, Sonya, and this book called *The Krokodile,* is for you, Anya. They are presents from Vladimir. Next year we are all making the trip down the mountain, and you can both thank him. Sonya, don't you agree? Anya is old enough to make the trip. She needs to spread her wings and meet new friends."

Sonya caressed the cover of the book with a beaming smile on her face. "Yes, it would be a nice trip for all of us. I would like to see Vladimir and Dmitri again. Anya is strong enough. She will probably leave the two of us behind. We may have to tie a rope on her to keep her with us. Next spring, we will share something special together."

While Sasha continued to unload the various supplies from the white canvas sack, Sonya spread her cherished new cloth on the table in order to better view its pretty colors. In the middle of the cloth, she discovered the tulip bulbs. "Sasha, what is this?"

Sasha shook his head and smiled. "Vladimir called them Siberian tulips. He bought them from a sailor who came from Vladivostok. I don't understand this. I told him I could not afford them. Maybe Dmitri is right. That Vladimir is a crafty devil."

"I think he is a crafty angel!" Sonya said. "This is a gift we can all enjoy!"

That afternoon, three happy people planted all the vegetable seeds in their small garden. With six busy hands, the prepared ground was soon covered and ready for the spring rains.

For the remainder of the afternoon, Anya lay on an old fur skin in the sunshine on a grassy knoll, next to the rushing stream, surrounded by wildflowers and her new books. The fur felt warm on her stomach, and her long blonde hair fell down her back in a single braid. She glanced behind her and saw her mother planting the tulips around the edge of the cabin, where the flowers would receive the most sunshine. Her mother softly hummed a tune while she worked—the complete vision of contentment. Her father sat on the porch cleaning his rifle: always a sign that he would be hunting tomorrow.

Anya realized that this was the happiest day of her life, lying in sun at her special place, reading her books in the midst of beautiful wildflowers next to a rushing stream, being near those she loved. Life could not get any better, she thought. Rolling on her back, she opened a book and said, "Well, Mr. *Krokodile*, what do you have in store for me today?"

Chapter 10

The passage of summer to autumn comes quickly in Siberia. Autumn displays its special charm: the beautiful colors, the garden harvest, the fresh scent of the crisp air. But in the wind, there is always the faint whisper, *Winter is coming...winter is coming.*

Sasha and Anya spent the summer and autumn fishing, hunting, and helping Sonya with their productive garden. The meat had been dried and the vegetables preserved for the long winter ahead. There was a chill in the air.

The first light snowfall had come and gone. Sasha now took Anya with him on every hunt. She was twelve and strong for her age. She had a keen eye for tracking, and she never missed a shot when Sasha gave her the rifle. She embodied in heart, mind, and soul a new creature of the forest. She and the spirit of the wild country that she roamed had become one.

With the arrival of winter, the furs became heavier and more valuable. With two sets of eyes and hands, the work of acquiring and tanning the skins was more productive and enjoyable.

"Sonya, with my new helper, this may be our best year yet," Sasha said.

Anya smiled and looked up from the reading of her medical book. She read it every evening.

Anya liked the art of helping things to heal. During the summer, she had mended the wing of a small bird and cared for it until it could fly again. A young rabbit had a broken leg, and Anya cured it as well. The rabbit became so tame that she made it her pet, until the arrival of winter. One day it just left—such was nature in the wild.

Hunting was a way of life, and for Anya's family, their very survival. However, Anya also loved to watch injured creatures recover, to become whole again. She had never met a doctor, but she harbored the dream of being one someday. After completing her studies, she wanted to return home to help others since there was not a doctor anywhere in the region to meet the medical needs of the mountain people. It would probably never come to pass, but it was always nice to dream.

At the crossroads of our decisions, a single step can determine a family's destiny and life. Sasha could sense the weather as readily as Anya could read her medical book. Anya saw her father preparing to leave for the hunt. She placed her book on her small bed and put on her fur boots and coat. Her thick blonde hair fell on each side of her white fur hat.

"Anya, I would like for you to stay with your mother today. She is not feeling well. I want you to keep the fire going for her so that she does not have to go outside for more wood. Please cook her a broth and watch over her."

Anya did not complain. She removed her furs and handed her father his rifle.

Sasha hugged and kissed Anya and Sonya. He said, "We're running low on fresh meat. I won't be long. I'll be near the rock where Anya shot her lynx. A storm is coming. It will soon be very cold. I can feel it coming."

Sasha shouldered his rifle, waved goodbye to those he loved, and closed the door behind him. Winter had come.

CHAPTER 11

As the sun was going down, Anya stood on the cabin's porch in the fading light, hoping to glimpse the towering figure of her father walking toward his home. This had never happened before, especially with a winter storm brewing in the north. The air was definitely getting colder. She could feel the wind biting her cheek.

Anya gathered more wood and tried to stay busy. Neither she nor her mother wanted to admit that something was wrong, but a gnawing fear seized them. Why did he not come? Where was he? Was he safe? Was he injured?

Anya knew there was no man alive who could take better care of himself in the forest than her father, but the Siberian cold favored no one when its icy fingers held them in its grasp. She wanted to leave and search for him at once. However, it would be impossible to find his tracks in the coming darkness, and it would be dangerous for her as well. She had to be patient. She must wait.

Anya and her mother ate silently. Her mother was trying to be brave, but Anya could see the growing fear and concern in her mother's eyes. Her mother was wearing a navy-blue skirt with red roses and a burgundy hem circling the garment. It lightened Anya's heart when she remembered the warm summer day that her father had presented the cloth to her mother. Now that seemed very long ago—almost another lifetime.

"Rest, Anya, it is time for bed. Your father would not want us to worry. He can take care of himself. He knows those woods like the back of his hand. Sleep well. Tomorrow will be a long day."

Anya draped her fur blanket over her shoulders, but both knew that sleep would escape them throughout this long night.

Sonya took a small silver cross off the fireplace mantle. It was her prized possession. It had been her grandmother's, passed to her mother; now it was hers. The cross and an old Bible that her mother had given to her were the only remnants of her Russian Orthodox faith. Holding the cross was a small gesture; still it sustained her.

Anya watched her mother bow her worried head, kiss the silver cross, and then place it back in its sacred spot on the mantle. Anya closed her eyes and prayed to the only God she knew, "God of the forest, be with my father. Tomorrow—be with me."

CHAPTER 12

Anya placed more wood on the dying embers in the fireplace. She quickly dressed in the darkness. When the sun dawned, she had to be ready at first light. She made one last trip to the woodpile, stacking the wood near the fireplace so that her mother would not have to suffer the cold. Her mother was still not feeling well, and Anya wanted her to stay close to the fire.

"Anya, I want to go with you, but I would only slow you down. I don't have my strength back. Here are some dried meat, bread, and a small canteen of water. Take the hatchet that we use to split kindling. You may need to make a fire to warm you and your father. The hatchet and your knife will be your only protection. God forbid you will need either one. Anya—find your father."

"Don't worry, Mother. I will find him, I promise. I will bring him back."

Anya placed the food and water in a small canvas pack. She tied a pair of snowshoes and two pieces of rope on each side of the pack. The hatchet was thrust into a broad leather belt next to her knife. Both weapons rested comfortably by her side in case they were needed.

Anya put the pack on her back. It was not heavy. She would have to travel at a fast pace. Standing on the porch and looking at the cloudy sky, she knew there would be no warmth for this day.

"Don't worry, Mother. Stay by the fire. I'll be safe—I'll be fine." She kissed her mother's cheek and jogged toward the mountain trail.

Racing along the firm trail, she knew her first destination would be the rocky ravine where she had shot the lynx. Her father had said that he would be hunting near that outcropping. She covered her mouth and nose with a scarf to protect her face and lungs from the icy wind. She simply had to hurry. The light passed quickly during this time of the year. She had to help bring her father home or to make a camp for them before darkness fell. Without a fire, they would never survive the plunging cold of the night.

She made it to the ravine by midmorning. The scent of snow was in the air. A few flakes had fluttered on her cheek throughout the trek. More would be coming.

As she approached the rocky ledge, she found her father's footprints in the snow. This lifted her spirit, and she increased her pace, even though the trail was becoming quite steep. "Maybe he took shelter on the side of the large rock out of the wind?" she reasoned.

Her next discovery chilled her blood. From the side of the ravine, new tracks emerged, which followed directly behind her father's footprints. Something was following him. Anya knelt closely to the ground and carefully examined the new spoor. The tracks were enormous. She placed her hand inside the print. The right paw was slightly different than the left paw. Anya jumped to her feet and ran up the trail with all her might.

CHAPTER 13

Anya immediately recognized the paw prints. It had been two years since she had seen them with her father. The old tiger had returned.

Anya ran slightly bent over so that she could better view the ground. A light snowflake occasionally touched her shoulder. Soon it would be heavier and cover the trail, along with any hope of finding her father. Anya's burning lungs cried out for rest, but there was no time to waste. The distance between the tiger's tracks and her father's footprints was getting closer to each other as she proceeded up the trail.

Perhaps the tiger was just curious. Wild animals often follow unusual tracks or a scent to discover its source. A large male bear had followed Sasha and Anya up a canyon for over an hour last spring. The bear's curiosity cost him his life. Sasha shot him behind the left ear when the bear stood on his back legs to scent the air. Maybe it would be the same for this tiger?

An hour later, Anya turned a sharp bend and walked into a large circle of upturned snow. There had been a ferocious struggle—black blood lay frozen on the side of a rock. Was it the tiger's blood or her father's? She searched the area to find more answers.

At the base of a tree, she found Sasha's rifle. Examining it, she found that nothing was damaged, but it had four claw marks equally spaced on the wooden stock of the rifle. Sasha would never have left his rifle behind. He might not be dead, but he was certainly in grave danger.

Anya took a small twig and rammed it down the barrel of the gun to remove any trapped snow. She ejected the shell and examined it. It was fresh and had not been fired. It was too cloudy to inspect the barrel for dirt or snow, so she pointed the barrel down and forcefully blew warm breath through the empty chamber to clear any debris. Anya wiped the cartridge on her dry shirt under her coat and reloaded the rifle.

There was a long streak of blood leading up the increasingly steep and narrow trail. One rifle, one bullet, one shot—would soon determine the fate of her father and her own destiny. As Anya followed the crimson blood trail with the rifle in her hands, it began to snow.

CHAPTER 14

The snow began to cover the trail of blood. Anya could still see indentations in the snow that led to an elevated entrance on the side of a cliff. Without the tracks, it would have been almost impossible to see the cave.

Anya tested the wind. It was blowing in her face. The tiger would not be able to detect her scent. Slowly, she proceeded toward the dark entrance at the base of the cliff. The tracks ended there. It was the tiger's lair. She had to get the tiger out of the cave to discover whether her father was still alive.

Anya reflected upon Sasha's lesson about tigers. He taught her that their hearing was their strongest sense. Quietly, Anya found a position near the opening of the cave but at a bend in the trail. If the tiger charged, it would have to slow momentarily to turn toward her. Anya rested the rifle on a rock that partly shielded her body. She calmed herself and remembered her father's words: "Daughter, if a dangerous animal charges you, have courage, concentrate, aim carefully, and wait. The clear shot will come, and you will know it. When it is almost upon you, shoot it in the eye. You have one shot. It must count. Listen to the inner voice that whispers, *Now is the time.*"

Anya snapped a branch and threw a rock into the entrance of the lair. Deep within the entrails of the abyss, she heard a gathering storm, a low menacing rumble, a growling echo of rolling thunder. It was as if the cave itself roared through its dark forbidding mouth, *I am here, I am fierce, I am coming.*

CHAPTER 15

Anya sighted the rifle at the opening of the cave. She could only hope that there was not another exit, but due to the shape of the rocky slope, it seemed unlikely. The snow swirled around her with the wind. It hampered her visibility, and now the wind carried her scent to the tiger.

Anya moved to her left into the shadow of a rock outcropping at the bend of the trail. If she did not have a clear shot when he emerged from the entrance, she hoped that this position might give her a few precious seconds to adjust, should the tiger suddenly charge without warning.

The tiger moved with stealth like a strong current in a river: not seen but felt nonetheless. In order not to be seen, the old hunter moved next to the side of the cave and avoided the direct sunlight streaming into the mouth of his lair. He crouched momentarily to allow his yellow eyes to adjust to the slanted rays of the sun, just beyond his reach. He smelled the human scent in the wind and knew it came directly in front of him. The tiger sensed his attack would have to be fast and powerful. When game could not be killed by stealth, his roar and quick speed caused fear, confusion, and hesitation. A few seconds were all that he needed to make the kill.

Like an athlete at the starter's block, the tiger crouched low, digging his paws into the dirt floor. Every muscle of his body was tensed and wound like a taunt spring. When he caught the human scent again, the tiger sprang through the opening from darkness to light, like a meteor across the night sky. All of his senses were intensely focused to detect any sound or movement, to direct his charge, to force its source into his jaws.

The tiger's charge was so sudden that Anya was caught off guard. She had hoped that the tiger would pause and scan the area as the lynx had. This would have given her just a split second for a clear shot. Now she saw a stripped blur racing toward her.

Anya refocused and made herself breath slowly. Everything seemed to be moving so quickly—there was no time. For such a large animal, the tiger made a small target in her gunsight. He was running low to the ground, his head bouncing up and down with no apparent pattern. *How can any animal run so fast?* Anya felt her throat tighten. *One shot. How? Where? When to shoot?*

Daughter…have courage, concentrate, aim carefully, and wait. Listen to the inner voice that whispers, Now is the time.

Papa, help me. Help me now.

The tiger rushed upon her. Instead of taking the bend in the trail, the tiger leaped over the rock where Anya was hiding. As the tiger sprang into the air, he roared with such intensity that Anya felt the air vibrate on her face. Anya aimed at the tiger's left eye. She could see his yellow teeth.

This is the time, Anya—now—now!

A shot rang out and covered the valley, echoing from stone to stone and tree to tree. Its message, as old as time itself, carried by an ancient voice: *Life has fled. Come and see. Blood soaks the ground and cries out to me. Come and see…come and see.*

CHAPTER 16

Anya sat on the ground with her back resting against a rock. Sasha's rifle lay next to her; smoke rose from the barrel as if it were a dying breath. Part of the tiger's tail encircled Anya's feet, appearing as if a striped snake had simply gone to sleep.

Anya breathed heavily, trying to clear her head. The tiger's force had knocked the breath out of her. She reached inside her coat and touched her right side. When she withdrew her hand, her palm was red with blood. She could feel a warm trickle dripping down her body.

The old tiger had made only one mistake: had he attacked from the bend of the trail, he would have had Anya trapped with no escape from her alcove. Leaping over the rock gave Anya a fleeting second for a straight shot to his exposed left eye. The tiger lashed out in his death throes and struck Anya, knocking her against the rock, but already—life was fleeing him. Anya's heavy fur coat and vest absorbed most of the blow, but the tiger's claws grazed her side and lower ribs. Examining the wound would have to wait.

Anya braced herself with her back against the rock and raised herself over the lifeless tiger. Her legs trembled, but there was a certain peace about the scene. Sasha had believed that this was also the tiger's territory and had said, "We will leave him alone. The forest is big enough for all of us." As Anya looked down at the large tiger with its beautiful markings, she softly whispered, "Not quite big enough today, Papa, not today."

Anya lifted the tiger's heavy right paw and retrieved Sasha's rifle. She saw the odd shape of the paw and her fresh blood on his claws. She did not have another bullet. Her father would give her more ammunition, once she found him. Clenching her teeth, she embraced the rifle and ran up the trail. Her side hurt, but there was nothing for it. Endure, search—find him.

The dark mouth of the cave loomed before her. Its irresistible pull beckoned, driving her forward, as if it were saying, *Come, Anya, come to me. Venture into my jaws. Search deeply within my bowels. But know this, fair child, on the day that you dare to enter—you will never leave the same.*

CHAPTER 17

Anya crouched on one knee and peered into the opening of the tiger's lair. Her heart was beating so fast that she breathed deeply several times to slow her pace and to clear her mind. The hair on her arms and head seemed to be standing on end. A sudden shiver raced down her back. Her side still throbbed, but she hoped the pain would heighten her awareness. She felt a sense of dread, not wanting to enter yet knowing that it had to be done. She had to know if her father was in there or lying somewhere nearby wounded and bleeding. The snow was coming down harder. The sun was about to go down.

This is the time, Anya. Go. This is the time.

Anya held the rifle in front of her. Without ammunition, it was little better than a club. Still, just having it in her hands gave her confidence. After a few steps, she waited for her eyes to adjust to the darkness. The cave was surprisingly large. She could walk upright with just a slight tilt of her head. She heard the trickling of water toward the back of the hollow formation, where there must be a spring. The air was dank and musty with the pungent smell of cats and bones. The tiger had lived here for years. This was an old cave with many secrets.

Anya proceeded deeper into the lair while trying to utilize all the sunlight possible behind her. Step by step, it was an eerie venture into the abyss.

"Papa, Papa, are you here? Can you hear me? It's Anya. Speak to me."

Anya walked a few more steps and found her answer. A shaft of light reflected off the wall of the cave to display a man's hand, clenched in defiance but severed nonetheless. Anya ran only to stumble and fall upon a pile of flesh and bones that had once been her father.

Moments before, the cave had echoed the thundering roar of the tiger who ferociously challenged the world. Now it emitted the wail of something wild and forsaken: the cry of the broken, the haunting sound of a shredded soul.

CHAPTER 18

Anya wept until she could weep no more. In a daze, she dragged what was left of her father into the fading light. The grisly task emptied what few emotions she had left. There was not much left of him, just a few tissues holding the bones together on his large frame. She saw two puncture marks at the base of his skull. Also, the neck vertebrae had been broken. At least, she thought, he died instantly; he would have felt only a sudden flash of pain.

Anya knew it had been an ambush. The two sets of tracks revealed the entire story. The tiger must have caught her father's scent at the ravine and backtracked Sasha until the tiger closed the distance. With the wind covering most of the sound, the tiger would only have had to make one leap from cover to attack Sasha from behind. The end would have come quickly. The powerful tiger easily dragged Sasha into his lair.

The air grew colder, and the snow was gathering near the cave entrance. Anya wiped the tears off her cheeks with the back of her hand. She stood over what remained of her father and said, "I can cry and die, or I can make preparations to survive this storm. Papa, we are going to leave this cave together, or we are both going to die next to each other. I promised Mother I would bring you home—and I will."

Anya found Sasha's belt that carried his knife and more ammunition. By instinct, she loaded the rifle, but she kept the shell casing that carried the bullet which killed the tiger. She kissed the casing and reverently put it into her vest pocket.

"Father, this is for you and for all that you taught me. Your wisdom saved my life. I will never forget this—never."

Anya unsheathed her father's knife and walked out of the mouth of the cave toward the fallen tiger. The tiger who killed her father would now be required to save her life.

Anya brushed the snow off the big cat. His body was still warm. She stroked his thick fur and said, "Tiger of the forest, my father said that there was enough room here for all of us, but you decided otherwise. My father would not have touched you, but I will. Today you lose your beautiful, warm coat. From this day forward, it is mine."

She skinned the tiger in record time. Her father's knife was exceptionally sharp, and she had much experience dressing smaller animals. The head, tail, and paws were left intact with the hide. The pelt was still quite heavy, even separated from the carcass. She draped the large hide over her shoulders and tied the two front paws together, each resting over her chest. Dragging her trophy across the snow, she left a bloody winding trail, just as the tiger had done to her father. The tiger's head bounced on the back of her neck. She could feel his teeth graze her shoulder. It was too much.

Anya tossed the cape onto the snow, grabbed the tiger's right ear, and with one fierce slash of her father's knife, she decapitated the predator. His head fell between her feet. His one eye seemed to be fixed on her, his face still with a snarl.

With determination in her fiery blue eyes, she returned the tiger's deadly gaze and spoke to him, "Tiger, I need food. Mine is gone. My father fed you—you will feed me." Anya pulled the hatchet from her belt and grasped Sasha's bloody knife in her other hand. She walked back to the long muscular body surrounded by red-stained snow. Then she began her work.

Anya returned to the tiger's lair. At the mouth of the cave, the ebbing light shrouded her silhouette. The dying sun captured a primordial scene: the tiger's striped coat encased Anya's body, his front paws hung tied together across her chest, his claws caked reddish brown with her dried blood. Anya's moist, silvery breath escaped from under the fur cape and slowly rose to the ceiling. In Anya's left hand, she carried the tiger's severed head by his long front teeth. In her bloodstained right hand, she held the tiger's still warm heart.

CHAPTER 19

Anya looked over her shoulder and, for a moment, pondered the setting sun. The next few hours would determine whether she survived the freezing night and the coming blizzard. She piled her heavy load against the side of the cave and went to a fallen tree near the entrance. The sharp hatchet easily chopped through the dead limbs. The exertion took her mind off what had occurred in the cave, yet her side still hurt, and she could feel the blood seeping into the waistband of her fur trousers.

She made a circle of stones to contain a fire and to heat the rocks. The dry limbs were stacked around the firepit. The wood would eventually dry as the night passed. There were plenty of twigs and dried leaves to start the fire. Sasha had taught her to build a fire with flint and steel. It was one of his first lessons. He had told her, "Daughter, a fire means life." Tonight she knew he was right.

Soon a nice fire was blazing. The wood dried quickly and gave enough light for Anya to inspect and clean her wounds. She was not only concerned with her loss of blood but, even more, the danger of blood poisoning from the bacteria in any animal's mouth or claws. She placed a metal cup full of snow on a flat rock near the fire. She did not trust the water at the back of the cave; it might be contaminated. And without a lantern, she could fall and injure herself. A broken bone would be fatal in this cold.

She washed the four red stripes across her side with the melted snow as best as she could and tightly wrapped a strip of her shirt around her waist, hoping the pressure would help stop the bleeding. She knew that she would carry the scars for the rest of her life. Scars were the least of her concerns at the moment—she had to block the increasingly frigid wind; the temperature was continuing to fall.

Anya found Sasha's pack. The side of it was ripped, but inside she found two tarps. Sasha carried the tarps to wrap skins or meat to keep them clean. With the smaller canvas, she reverently covered her father's remains. She had to turn her head while placing the wilderness shroud over him; it sickened her and made her angry at the same time. She arranged the larger canvas at the entrance of the cave to help deflect the wind by tying the large canvas to two stout saplings, jamming the makeshift structure against the stone walls and the earthen floor. It would work, unless the smoke drove her out of the cave.

Anya hoped there was enough natural ventilation to carry the smoke out of the cave. To test this, she tossed a small green limb onto the fire. To her relief, the smoke floated upward and toward the back of the cave. She reasoned there must be a small opening or fissure to draw the smoke like a chimney. She stoked the fire and realized how tired and weak she felt. The search, the fight, the loss of blood, the preparations, and the emotional loss were taking their toll. She needed food. She needed rest.

Anya spread the tiger's luxurious cape on the ground near the fire. Its thick fur felt warm on her legs. It would preserve her for the long night ahead—and so would his meat. She stabbed a long stick through the center of the heart and rested the stick on a rock over the fire. The flames lightly touched the heart, and she could hear the meat sizzle, as if in protest for its violent treatment.

The tiger's severed head and two paws covered her lap. The tiger's teeth were yellow and worn; he was a very old tiger. Perhaps that was the reason he had attacked Sasha: her father was easier game, in the tiger's domain, near his lair. The claws were large and had seen much use; however, the two dewclaws, positioned higher on the paws, were still quite sharp. Anya took Sasha's knife and extracted all ten claws, placing them in a small leather bag, which she hung around her neck.

Grasping the tiger's massive head, she drew it to her, touching her forehead against his. Eye to eye, she stared into the tiger's face. One eye was gone from Anya's bullet slicing through it—bloody and vacant—much the way Anya felt at that moment. The tiger's remaining yellow eye reflected the flame of the fire—glowing, as if to challenge her still.

"Eye for an eye, old tiger. You killed my father. Now I will take the weapons you used on him, eat your heart, and take your kingly robe as a payment and a remembrance. The forest was big enough for all of us. Time to pay."

Anya squeezed the tiger's awesome head between her knees while staring at his yellow piercing eye, as if the tiger's fierce gaze penetrated deeply into the recesses of her secret heart. With Sasha's knife, she deliberately began removing the four large yellow-stained fangs which had killed her father—and vanquished her soul.

CHAPTER 20

About the time Anya was fighting for her life with the tiger, Sonya stood on the cabin porch and worried about her daughter. Anya should have returned by this time. In a few hours, it would be dark, and the weather was turning colder. There was the scent of snow in the air.

Sonya felt her feverish forehead. She still did not feel well, but her daughter's life might be at stake. She promised herself that she would not go far. Perhaps a lantern shining at the base of the trail could guide Sasha and Anya home. She had to try.

Sonya dressed in her only fur coat. It was long and very warm. She did not have fur trousers like Anya and Sasha since she did not hunt anymore. Her thick blue skirt with red roses and a burgundy trim, along with her woolen leggings and fur-lined boots, should be warm enough for just a few hours. She put a new candle in their only lantern and tied a rope on the head of an axe, which she carried across her back. A small satchel contained a meager supply of bread, water, and a flint and steel with some dry tender, in case they were needed.

As Sonya put on her fur hat, a few snowflakes fell on her shoulders. She adjusted the satchel, lantern, and axe and proceeded toward the mountain-valley trail. The crisp air felt soothing to her hot face. The light snow did not mean much this time of the year. It would be spring in another month or so. In this late winter season, there was the occasional blizzard, but it seemed too cold to snow very much. Perhaps the cold would drive Anya and Sasha down from the mountain. Perhaps the lantern would draw her family home. Perhaps it was not too late.

Sonya looked back at their humble homestead. There was candlelight in the window, and the smoke from the chimney signaled warmth and happiness. It was a simple existence, but it was theirs, and the three of them had built it with their own hands. She was proud of her home and family. Now her only desire was to have them safely beside her.

The snow was not deep, and Sonya made good time until she reached the base of the valley. The trail at this point gradually became steeper. Sonya looked over her shoulder. She could barely see the small yellow glow in the cabin's window. The sun was about to set; it would be dark in another hour. "Maybe just a little farther," she thought. "I know this part of the trail well enough." Within a short distance, a heavy snow began to fall.

Sonya walked until the snow covered the trail. She stopped to catch her breath, then called out, "Anya, Sasha—do you hear me? Come to me." Only silence.

She decided to wait a short while longer, and then she would have no choice but to return home. It was time to light the lantern. The wind had increased and seemed to slice her face. There was a large rock ahead where she could get out of the wind to light the candle in the lantern. As she approached the rock, she transferred the satchel to her left shoulder. What Sonya could not see was that just before the rock, the snow covered a depression next to a ravine. She was looking in the satchel when her left foot fell through the snow and lodged between two boulders. She felt the ankle bone snap when she landed on her side. Worse yet, the satchel slid down the ravine and out of sight.

Sonya wiped the tears off her cheeks and lay quietly in the snow for a few minutes. "I have to think clearly," she repeated to herself. She realized the changing weather signaled a blizzard. The mountain held no mercy—even for the wounded.

Sonya tried to stand but fell again. She still had the axe. She had to make a shelter until Anya and Sasha came down the trail to help her. Slowly she crawled to the rock to escape the wind and driving snow. At the base of the rock, she dug with the axe until she found a few sticks. With these, she tied a crude splint on each side of her ankle. Using the axe as a crutch, she walked a few steps and chopped the lower evergreen branches from a tree next to the rock. Sonya hobbled back to the rock and spread the branches like a green fan around her. The rock and branches would deflect the wind and some of the drifting snow, but it would not deter the cold.

Darkness had come, and the temperature was dropping as fast as her satchel had gone over the ravine—the flint and steel with it. Sonya sat and drew her legs under her heavy coat. She made herself as small as possible to conserve her body's heat. She was exhausted, and it was difficult not to fall asleep. Her eyelids seemed so heavy. Fight the cold. She decided to think warm thoughts: the candlelight in the window, the fire in the cabin, the smoke from the chimney—the love she felt for her family.

Her head began to sink. So tired. *Surely, Anya and Sasha will pass this way? They will find me. Think warm thoughts.* The bitter wind howled its approval. An icy hand gripped its fingers around her body. *Warm thoughts...see them soon.*

CHAPTER 21

Anya awoke when rays of the sun touched her face. She was next to the fire, wrapped in the tiger's warm cape. The fire and the thick fur had kept her alive throughout the freezing night. Anya felt as if she were encased in a fury cocoon since the fresh hide had frozen around her. She worked her arm out of the stiff hide and tossed the remaining wood into the firepit. The red coals soon ignited the dry wood, and the skin became more flexible as it thawed.

The blizzard was over, and she could see snow piled against the sides of the large canvas at the cave's entrance. Anya could better see the inside of the lair in the early morning light. Her father's prone figure lay nearby. The canvas shroud still covered him.

Anya warmed herself by the fire and prepared herself for the long day that lay ahead. She knew she would have to battle the thick snow and the heavy burden of two warriors: her father's remains and the tiger's fur—neither could be left behind.

As she took down the canvas tarp and the two saplings at the cave's entrance, a plan formed in her mind: she could evenly distribute the weight by making a travois: tying the canvas to the saplings, enabling her to drag the load behind her. Most of the weight would rest on the ground rather than on her back and shoulders.

Her next task was something no child should have to do: She took her father's pack and placed his smaller bones, which the tiger had scattered on the hard dirt floor, into the pack. Her hands trembled as she carefully searched around her father's corpse. Several of the bones were gnawed and broken, but she eventually gathered them all. With several pieces of rope, she bound the smaller canvas around Sasha—to protect his body, to protect her soul.

Anya pulled the travois next to Sasha. She placed the tiger skin on the canvas and gently lifted Sasha onto his striped coffin. She lashed Sasha's pack to the top of the travois, shouldered her rifle, wrapped a rope around her arms and shoulders, and began her long journey home.

As she approached the mouth of the cave, Anya looked back into the lair. Out of respect, she had placed the tiger's head on a small fan of evergreen branches. The bloody paws were placed in front of the head. From a distance, it appeared as if the tiger were on his belly, resting his head on his paws and looking outward at anyone daring to enter his domain.

Anya could not help but stare into the tiger's yellow eye. From the fire, a small flame spiked above the dying embers. The flame danced in the tiger's glaring eye and made it glow. It was as if the tiger still challenged her, even from death, crying out, *You took my life, my weapons, and even my heart—but my spirit remains. We have traded scars and mingled blood. You may leave my lair, but I will never leave you, forever stalking the recesses of your heart, mind, body, and soul. Go now—but the flame within my eye will burn within you.*

Anya shuddered and turned away. She lifted her head to the sun and felt it caress her face. Dawn called to her, *Time to leave the darkness of this lair, time to enter the light of a new day, time to go to the home you love.* Tightening her snowshoes, shouldering her rifle, stepping out of a tomb—into a veil of light—Anya pulled the travois onto the snowy trail.

"Father, we are going home. I promised Mother I would bring you back—and I will. You always took care of me. Now I will take care of you."

A tender girl entered a dark cave to find her father. A young woman emerged into the light to find a new destiny. The travois, which carried two warriors, glided silently behind her.

CHAPTER 22

The sunlight sparkled on the fresh snow, bidding its welcome to a new white world. Siberia seemed to be like that, thought Anya: one dark night, it can almost kill you; the next morning, glitter and enchant you—like a fairytale world.

Anya came to the bend in the trail where she and the tiger had fought their fierce duel. The tiger's skinned body lay completely covered in a mound of snow. Anya thought that this was appropriate for such an old tiger of the forest: a tomb on a battlefield, the snow—a blanket for the dead.

The snow was not as deep as she had expected. The wind had blown much of it into drifts on the sides of the mountain. After a few hours, she removed her snowshoes and tied them to the travois. She retied the knots holding Sasha to the tiger skin and canvas. Anya increased her pace. She planned to reach the cabin by nightfall. It would be so good to see her mother.

As Anya broke trail through the snow, she pondered what she would tell her mother about the last twenty-four hours. How could she adequately describe the death of her father, the fight with the tiger, the boneyard of the tiger's lair? Her mother was strong, and her mother knew the dangers of the mountain. Still, what to say? How could she comfort her mother?

The lower Anya descended, the faster she walked. The snow was not as heavy, and she was making excellent time. At this speed, she would be home a few hours before the sun set. The Siberian days were getting a little longer as spring approached, but not by much. Tired and hungry, Anya pressed onward.

She stopped to take a rest at a familiar spot. She recognized the large boulder where she had shot the lynx, standing on the rock as he had scanned the surrounding area. Anya looked at Sasha covered by the canvas on the travois.

"Remember, Papa? Remember the day? You handed me this rifle. You gave me the confidence I needed. Give me strength now and for the days ahead."

When Anya turned to place the tug rope across her arms and shoulders, a light breeze raised a tuft of fur hidden in some branches at the base of the rock. Anya dropped the travois and quickly shouldered her rifle. She aimed at the furry object, but she could not recognize what it was. Cautiously, she took a few steps toward it with the rifle ready to fire. The wind blew again, and one of the branches fell on the ground. Just below the fur, Anya spotted a dark-blue background with a red rose framed by the evergreen branches. "No, no, no!" she screamed. "Please, not you—not again!"

Anya rushed to her mother and desperately knocked the snow off Sonya's stiff body. Anya shook her mother's shoulders and called out to her, "Momma, wake up. It's me, Anya. I'm back. I have Papa—just as I said I would. Please talk to me. I'm back… I'm back."

CHAPTER 23

Anya held her mother for a long time. Perhaps she hoped that new warmth would transfer life into the body of her mother. Perhaps she knew it would be the last time that they would ever cling to each other. Perhaps she just could not let go.

Anya rocked her mother gently in her arms. Sonya's face looked like a porcelain doll's, with closed eyes that had just gone to sleep. Rocking back and forth, Anya described her ordeal on the mountain: the tiger, the cold, the horrors in the cave. Anya begged for forgiveness for leaving her mother alone. She also scolded Sonya for leaving the warm cabin and for freezing next to a rock on a merciless mountain. Anya reset the splint. Maybe that would help her mother down the mountain. *Yes, that would help.*

"Now, Momma, we have to get home before nightfall. It will get cold again tonight. This time, stay in the cabin. Please, stay in the cabin."

When Anya tried to help her mother stand, the veil lifted, and the blue vase shattered on the stone floor of Anya's mind. Sonya remained in her curled position, as stiff as the tiger's body up on the mountain.

Silence wrapped its cold arms around Anya. She wanted to cry, but tears would not come. She wanted to scream, but her words had died. The shattered vase was not to be mended. Her mother would never plant tulips again.

With the strength given to those who no longer care, Anya lifted her frozen mother and placed her on the travois next to her father. She looked at her parents lying beside each other on a bed of striped fur. She wanted to crawl between them and once again hear laughter and stories—to feel their warmth, maybe even to receive a tickle on her stomach from days not so long ago. Anya placed a hand on her aching side; now she had claw marks across her ribs and scars running the length of her heart, mind, and soul.

Silently, as if in a trance, Anya slung the rifle over her back, lifted the travois rope across her weary shoulders, and trudged down the long snow-drenched trail—a trail that led to a dark cabin window in which the light of a candle had slowly burned away.

CHAPTER 24

By the time Anya reached the cabin, an orange half-moon was rising. A few of the brightest stars began to appear. The night chill settled over all.

Anya staggered to the storage shed adjacent to the cabin where Sasha stored his hides. It was really just a modified lean-to attached to the cabin structure, with a large preparation table for cleaning and tanning pelts and several shelves overhead.

Anya rested the travois on the side of the table. She could see her breath rising in the moonlight. Blue shadows entered the doorway, shrouding them all. Her strength was spent; she could do no more. Her parents would have to rest here together until morning. It was already well below freezing, and it would get steadily colder as the night passed.

She had to use the rifle as a crutch to steady herself. If she fainted before reaching the cabin, she knew that she would be joining her parents in their frozen tomb. Her hands trembled when she opened the cabin door. For a moment, she had to cling to the doorway for fear of falling. The cabin looked the same as she had left it. Only thirty-six hours had passed, but she felt as if it had been a lifetime. The dark cabin affected her in an unsettling way: cold and alone, Anya felt lost in the only world she had ever known.

There was a small loaf of bread on the table. Anya tore off a large piece of bread and ate it slowly, savoring every bite. Thankfully, there was plenty of wood and kindling next to the fireplace. Within minutes, Anya had a roaring fire before her. The ice on her coat and boots melted, and steam rose off her body, as if ghostly spirits had been released. She covered herself with a fur blanket and lay near the crackling fire. She was too exhausted to even remove her coat and climb into her bed. Her hands were still shaking when she placed the last piece of bread into her mouth. Before she could finish her simple meal, she passed out on the cabin floor—dead to the world in a world now dead to her.

Chapter 25

Anya awoke the next morning when the rays of the sun filled the cabin. The fire had gone out, but a few hot coals and some dry kindling soon brought it back to life. She sat at the worn wooden table and renewed her strength with more bread and some dried meat.

While eating, Anya assessed her situation: There was plenty of food to last throughout the remaining winter. There would be no more hunting trips, except for some small game for fresh meat. Sasha's winter season had been successful, and although there were not as many pelts, all were of very high quality.

Anya thought of her parents still on the travois in the fur shed. She wanted to bury them and put them finally at rest, but the ground was frozen hard as iron. In another month, the spring thaw would allow this task.

Reluctantly, Anya went to the door of the shed. She pressed her forehead against the door and closed her eyes. She felt a sense of dread and loneliness. Anya told herself, *This must be done. Be strong. Honor them.*

As Anya entered, a shaft of soft morning light lingered across the couple on the tiger skin. In some ways, it was a quiet, touching scene: both were finally together again. She caressed her mother's cheek. Sonya still looked as if she had just gone to sleep.

For now, the large flat table in the fur shed would have to be their mausoleum. Anya lifted her father and placed him on the table.

For such a big man, how light he seemed; the tiger had seen to that. She placed his pack, containing his smaller bones, at the head of the table. Anya had to struggle to place her mother next to Sasha. Her mother's frozen body made her easier to handle; nevertheless, it was an unpleasant task.

Gently, she wrapped her mother in a clean canvas. Placing her hands on her parents, she said, "Rest now, loved ones. Spring is on its way. I will take care of you. The winter is passing. Rest and wait."

Anya dismantled the travois. Cutting the saplings in half and with a thin strap of leather, she formed a cross for each of her parents. Reverently, she placed a cross on each of their frozen bodies. Carrying the tiger skin, she walked to the doorway, glancing back at her parents one last time. As she slowly closed the door, the rays of light faded from within the shed while creating shadows into the aching depths of Anya's heart.

CHAPTER 26

Anya held the stiff tiger skin and brushed its luxurious fur. If sold, it would bring a great price, but another part of her wanted to keep it as a remembrance. In any case, it would have to be finished and tanned to be of any value.

She hung the large skin on the side of the lean-to facing the sun. The pelt covered most of the shed. Anya had learned from Sasha not to nail a hide and make holes in it but to lash it against a wall or table. Sasha's furs always brought a premium, and Anya determined that this trophy would be the same. She was glad to have the work; it kept her hands busy and her mind occupied on more positive things.

She found Sasha's tools in a wooden chest under his bed. Sasha had only a few tools, but he kept them sharp, and he took good care of them. Next to the toolbox was a smaller wooden box containing ammunition. She also found a large sealed jar which contained a tanning solution, "the recipe" handed down for several generations.

Anya sprinkled the raw side of the pelt with water. The sun and the water loosened any remaining flesh. She began the arduous task of carefully scrapping the hide. Eventually, it would become smooth and clean. Once the tanning mixture was worked into the skin, both sides of the pelt would be as soft as a kitten's coat.

The bright warm sun fell on Anya's back. It comforted her: the work and the warmth lifted her spirit. While scraping the massive skin, she began to realize that the sun and the tiger would be her only companions for the trying days ahead.

CHAPTER 27

Anya labored week after week on the tiger skin until it felt like velvet in her hands. The soft pelt gave her confidence and strength: by day, it became her striped bedspread; by night, a thick cloak that covered her—a protection from the cold and loneliness that surrounded her.

Each day the sun dawned earlier and set later than before. It still froze every night, but soon it would be spring. The food supply was low but adequate. Her parents were still "asleep," sealed in their frigid tomb.

One day, while chopping wood, Anya noticed thin green shoots raising their delicate heads above the ground. The snow had melted, and the heat from the sun and earth had called them from their winter sleep. Anya smiled and remembered the happy day when Sasha returned and brought books, supplies, blue cloth with red roses and burgundy trim, and most of all—Siberian tulips.

Anya leaned on the axe and said in a sweet voice, "Hello, tulips, remember me? My father carried you to us. My mother brought you to life. Finally, you show up for a visit. It's about time!"

The words "It's about time" lingered in her mind. Anya looked into the light-blue sky and turned her face toward the sun. She pressed the toe of her boot into the dark soil and knew, *Yes, it is time.*

Anya stood at the door of the shed for just a moment to build her courage for what she had to do. She touched her forehead against the rough wooden lintel and quietly said, "God, whoever, whatever, you may be—please, help me now." She removed the woodblocks and pressed rags from around the edges of the door; it had been sealed all winter. Anya's hand trembled when she opened the door. A blast of cold air struck her face, as if it were leaping toward the sunlight. There was a faint, musty smell inside the shed, but it was not wretched as she had feared. A pick and a shovel was now all she required.

Anya went to her favorite hideaway by the stream. It was here where she lounged on that pleasant, sunny day reading her new book *The Krokodile*. She remembered watching her mother plant the precious tulips and her father cleaning his rifle. Yes, this shady knoll would be their final resting place.

The ground was still hard, but the pick and shovel did their work. By the end of the day, Anya had the two graves prepared. She left a space between her parents. Someday she would join them, resting peacefully between the two people she loved.

Anya lined the graves with oilskin canvas. She could not allow her parents to just lie in the dirt. She used a wooden wheelbarrow to transport each parent to the grave site. Placing two ropes under their legs and shoulders, she slowly lowered each into their canvas abode.

Leaning over Sonya, Anya placed on her mother's heart the only treasure her mother had ever owned: the silver cross from her ancestors. For Sasha, she placed the spent brass cartridge, which she had fired to kill the tiger, on the center of his chest. She then arranged the tiger's four large teeth—north, south, east, and west—around the cartridge until it formed a yellow cross. Placing a fine soft pelt over each face, she reverently draped the oilcloth over them—a wilderness shroud—knowing she would never see them again.

Anya gave them the only requiem she knew:

"Father, Mother, I have done all I can for you. Already I miss you. I must now live for all three of us. I don't know how… I don't even know if I can. Kind Father, may your God of the forest and creation give me your wisdom and your strength. Beloved Mother, may your God of life and love give me something to live for, to help me in the days ahead. Someday I will join both of you. Wait for me… wait for me."

By the time Anya filled the graves with the dark earth and hammered the sapling crosses at the head of the graves to mark them, the sun was going down. Anya dried her cheeks and looked at the dying sun. Something had also died in her. From that day forward, no one ever saw her cry again.

CHAPTER 28

Spring arrived in its dazzling way: everything seemed alive and full of life. Sonya's tulips were in full bloom—a row of yellow maidens swaying in the breeze in a rhythmic dance. Every time Anya saw the tulips, it reminded her of her parents. She smelled them and felt their delicate yellow petals; their fragrance always made her smile. Vladimir's gift had indeed become a joy and a delight.

Anya wondered what Vladimir and Dmitri were really like. Sasha had described them in detail. He often laughed when he retold their sharp, witty arguments. Anya remembered sitting by the fire and seeing her mother smile as Sasha became more animated, swinging his large arms or frowning to imitate Vladimir or Dmitri.

Anya knew she would be meeting them in a matter of days. Her supplies were almost gone, and she needed to sell last year's harvest of furs in order to survive and continue living on the mountain. She sat at the table and traced the journey with her finger on a crude map that Sasha had drawn. Sasha, ever the planner, made the map in case he became sick or injured and Sonya needed help or supplies. The trail was clearly marked with landmarks at every major turn. Anya was not really worried; the weather was warm, the ground now green and firm. It would be a new adventure, and Anya wanted to be away from the cabin and the constant reminder of two fresh graves, if only for a short while. She needed to talk to people, to see some new country, and to actually meet "old friends" that she knew only in her mind.

There were still two duties to finish before she could leave: Sasha's special *L*-shaped pack had to be loaded with the furs, and the tiger's cape had to be considered. Anya could not part with the tiger skin. It meant more to her than any amount of money. This season's furs were prime pelts, so money would not be a problem for supplies. The cape was too large and heavy to take with her. She could just leave it behind. Theft had never been a problem. The cabin door did not even have a lock. Anya could only remember one visitor in her entire life, but what an unsavory visitor he had been. What if he returned?

She could not recall his name. He was thin with dark hair and very crooked yellow teeth. His breath reeked with the smell of vodka or some strong drink. His bloodshot eyes kept scanning the cabin while he talked with Sasha. He particularly fixed his eyes on her mother's silver cross on the mantle. He and her father did not have an argument, but neither could they agree on some matter. Sasha did not invite him to stay overnight, which would have been customary. The visitor took the hint that it was time for him to leave. As he left, his crooked smile said everything: this is a man not to be trusted. Anya felt the tension leave when the stranger closed the door.

If he ever returned, he would certainly steal the valuable pelt. Anya decided to dig one more grave.

****

The shed contained a large iron trunk once belonging to Sasha's grandfather. Sasha used the trunk to store his best furs. It was lined with an especially thick canvas, and the lid had a very tight seal. Anya placed inside the trunk the tiger skin, her mother's Bible, and a jar that contained the tiger's claws. She withdrew three claws to keep for herself. Upon sealing the lid and seams with wax and lead, she draped the last of the oilskins over the trunk to protect it from the soil and moisture. She could get new canvas at Vladimir's Store.

After digging a shallow hole between her parents' graves, Anya lowered the trunk into the opening and topped it with dirt. When finished, it looked as if a small child had been buried between her parents. Anya thought, in many ways, it was true.

That evening, beside a roaring fire, Anya took the three tiger claws and formed a necklace. She wrapped the base of the largest claw and the two sharp dewclaws with a band of thin leather. The claws were then attached to a leather thong, the largest claw centered between the two dewclaws. It looked striking around her neck: the contrast of the downturned yellow claws and the dark leather against her fair skin highlighted her blonde hair and sparkling eyes and seemed to make her face glow. She touched the necklace and looked at herself in a crude hand mirror. This would be her talisman and a source of strength—her anchor of remembrance when upon life's stormy seas.

The next morning, just before sunrise, Anya stood at the doorway and took one last look at all the familiar things within the cabin that she called "home." With hesitation, she walked away and slowly closed the door.

She made a final stop at her parents' gravesite and placed a small bouquet of yellow tulips on each mound, including the "tiger's grave," as she liked to call it. She paused for a moment and listened to the laughter of the rushing stream. It flooded her heart and mind with warm memories.

Anya glanced at the map, shouldered the pack of furs, and stood with her father's rifle in her right hand. The sun was just lifting its fiery head above the horizon. Its rising centered on a particular saddle between two mountains. Every year of her life, her parents had knelt beside her, pointed at the rising sun, and declared, "Anya, on this day, you entered the world. Mark the location, mark the sun. This is your special day." They would then kiss her cheek and take her small hand to help her point at the saddle to face the sun.

Anya stood facing the sun and pointed directly between the two mountains. She said, "Yes, my parents, today I enter a new world. I am alone, but not afraid. From this day forward, the three of us are one."

Unknown to anyone on earth except for one young girl, dawn had just heralded Anya's day of birth. Anya faced the morning light and began her journey. She celebrated her birthday with the sun—she was thirteen years old.

CHAPTER 29

Anya was tall and strong for a thirteen-year-old, but the heavy pack took its toll. Her shoulders ached, and she sometimes staggered under the load. It had been a hard journey, taking her longer than she had expected. Her food supply had not lasted, not eating for over a day. Fatigue and hunger were making her stop even more along the way to catch her breath.

Late in the afternoon, Anya approached a tidy little farm and spotted a short, portly man with a full red beard carrying a pail of milk. She glanced at Sasha's map and exclaimed to herself, "That has to be Dmitri!"

Dmitri saw the lone figure walking toward him, but he did not know the trapper, thinking, "Such a small man to carry such a heavy load of furs." As the stranger drew nearer, Dmitri placed the bucket on the ground and walked to greet him. Dmitri was shocked to discover that it was not a man but a young girl.

Anya spoke first, "Sir, may I trouble you for a drink of water? My canteen ran dry back on the trail after leaving the springs."

"Of course, dear child, let me help you with that pack. Let's place it against this tree. You look exhausted. Come to my well. I am blessed with excellent water on my farm."

Dmitri recognized Sasha's rifle. He also noticed four long grooves across its wooden stock. Dmitri felt a tight knot in his stomach. Something was wrong—Sasha would never sell that rifle.

Dmitri settled the pack and said, "I know another who has a rifle similar to yours. His name is Sasha Ruslanov. You wouldn't happen to know him, would you?"

Anya put down the water dipper and replied, "Yes, he was my father."

*****

Anya sat at Dmitri's table and ate a welcome meal of bread, cheese, and fresh milk. She told Dmitri about all that had happened since that fateful day when she had braved a storm to find her father.

As Anya told her story, Dmitri stood with his back to her and looked out of a window. He could not bear to face her, afraid his emotions would give way, only to break down crying. His old friend was gone—Sasha's brave daughter eating at his table. A tiger. A storm. Sasha was such a good hunter and man of the woods. How could this happen? Poor Sonya frozen to death. How could this child survive on that lonely and harsh mountain? What would be her future?

Dmitri quickly wiped a few stray tears off his red cheeks. "Anya, rest here for now and rebuild your strength. We will use my horses to carry your furs to Vladimir's Store. I don't know how you made it through the winter and down the mountain. You certainly come from sturdy stock. Your parents would be proud of you. Rest now, my child. We will see Vladimir in a few days. He's a crafty old reptile, but he is also wise. He loved your parents, and his advice will be good. Whatever happens, this will always be your home, for as long as you desire."

Anya smiled and said, "Thank you, Dmitri. Father told me that you are a kind man. I will return to my parents and to our cabin. My home is in the forest and on the mountain. That is where I belong. However, I look forward to meeting Vladimir. I brought him something."

Anya reached into her vest and handed Dmitri a small book entitled *The Krokodile*. In the center of the book, there lay a pressed yellow Siberian tulip.

Dmitri held the delicate yellow flower in his thick calloused hands, and with trembling shoulders, he began to weep.

CHAPTER 30

Vladimir immediately recognized Anya when she stepped through the doorway of his store and stood beside Dmitri. She looked so much like her mother with her thick blonde hair and her bright-blue eyes. She was taller than Vladimir had imagined but, without a doubt, the daughter of Sonya and Sasha.

Vladimir had never told anyone, but he had hoped to marry Sonya. He spent time with her when she came to the store every year, but when she met Sasha, her heart was opened, and no one else could enter. Vladimir always regarded Anya as the daughter that he never had.

Vladimir came from behind the counter. With outstretched arms, he hugged Anya and kissed her on each cheek. "You must be Anya. Dear girl, what are you doing in the company of this rogue? Sasha tolerated him, but you and your mother must surely have better tastes."

"Don't listen to him," Dmitri replied. "He is probably full of his excellent vodka again. Don't ever drink the stuff. It has been known to melt bark off trees."

"Ignore him, Anya. We all do. By the way, where are your parents? Sasha mentioned that all three of you would come to see me this year. Those two lovebirds should be here by now. Don't tell me, dear girl, you came alone?"

Dmitri walked over and gently placed his hand on Vladimir's shoulder. "Sit down, Vladimir. You may need some of that vodka. Listen to her."

Anya told Vladimir about her struggles. When he learned about the deaths of her parents, he was visibly shaken. He slumped in his chair and covered his face with his hands.

"Dmitri, I think I will have that drink. Ask the bartender for the 'special bottle.' He will know what that means. It is a little different brand."

Chekov sat in his favorite corner by the window. He saw Dmitri rush to the bar and then carry an expensive bottle of vodka back to the adjoining room. Always the opportunist, he weaved between the chairs and tables and decided to invite himself to the party. As he approached the doorway from the shadows, he saw Vladimir talking to a slender young girl who was standing over Vladimir, stroking his hair. Chekov watched as Vladimir took a stiff drink of vodka, looked upon the girl's face, and exclaimed, "Anya, I just can't believe your parents are dead! Poor Sonya! Poor Sasha!"

Chekov smiled and stepped backward, away from the doorway into the darkness of the bar. He left through the bar's back door and hurried down the muddy street. This was information the district commissar needed to know—a report that would change everyone's life.

****

District Commissar Lepan sat with his feet on the top of his large scarred desk. He was admiring his tall black spit-shined boots. His assistant, Petrov, kept them in perfect condition, along with all the paperwork that endlessly arrived from Vladivostok and Moscow. Lepan's long black leather coat with red hammer-and-sickle insignias on the lapels, his tall boots, and his thick fur hat were the emblems of his authority; he cherished each of them. The leather coat was too light for real warmth, but no one else had anything like it. Fear and respect were more important to him than being cold on occasion.

Lepan was tall and heavy. He enjoyed towering over smaller men and imposing his will on others. He had joined the Communist Party as soon as possible when he saw which way the political wind was blowing. The party gave him this wilderness outpost as a reward, but he felt that he should have received something more worthy—at least Vladivostok. The fact that he was lazy and incompetent never registered in his self-absorbed mind.

Chekov slammed the office door behind him and told the lean blonde-haired assistant, "I need to see Commissar Lepan right now! It's important!"

The overworked aide looked over his shoulder through the doorway. Lepan was still admiring his boots. "He's very busy. Let me ask him. Comrade Commissar, a man would like to speak with you. He says it's urgent."

Lepan grumbled to himself and settled his heavy feet behind his desk. "Fine, Petrov, send him in."

Chekov quickly closed the door behind him and stood in front of Lepan's desk. "Commissar, a young girl has lost her parents. It is a sad case. Having no other relatives, she must live alone in the mountains. She is one of the forest people. Without your kind assistance, I fear she might starve."

"Chekov, I pay you for political information. Surely she has some friends who can care for her. Why this frothing at the mouth? How old is she?"

"She's large for her age—maybe twelve, thirteen, hard to say. Besides being an orphan, she has a load of valuable furs: sable, ermine, fox—a fortune. I saw them at Vladimir's. The area where she lives is full of this treasure." Chekov could see that Lepan was interested. "If her family's claim was abandoned and she became a ward of the state, then I would do the work, and you, comrade, would get half of the profits. You claim the child, I'll claim the land. She is still at the store. Once she leaves, you will never find her in those mountains. I suggest you hurry."

Lepan leapt to his feet and grabbed his hat and coat. "Yes, this may need investigating. Petrov, get in here. Tell Petrov the family's name. I'll need their file."

Chekov shouted over his shoulder, "Ruslanov: Aleksandre, Sonya. The daughter's name is Anya." He ignored Petrov and hurried to open the door for the commissar, his new "comrade," and the "protector of the people." Carrying a thin folder, Chekov followed at a respectful distance while Commissar Lepan hurried down the street, ignoring the dark mud sloshing on his black boots.

CHAPTER 31

Anya spread all her new books on the counter. Her innocent joy gave some comfort to Vladimir and Dmitri. Vladimir was extremely pleased that she enjoyed the selections he had chosen for her.

Lepan and Chekov entered the front door of the store. The small bell attached at the top of the door rang and announced their presence. All the previous smiles vanished, as if the high-pitched bell rang a warning. Lepan smiled and nodded a greeting to everyone in the room. Chekov could not take his eyes off the beautiful pile of furs stacked high in the corner.

"Greetings to all," Lepan said. "It has come to my attention that there may be a need of assistance to one of the many charges in my district. Health and safety are always important matters." Lepan opened a discolored file and held a yellow sheet of paper close to his face. He said, "This file contains three names: Aleksandre, Sonya, and Anya Ruslanov. No other relatives are listed. Tell me, child, where are your parents? This is only a formality. I always insist on accurate records."

"My parents are not here. They died this winter, but I am capable, and I live on our property."

"Well, well, all alone," replied Lepan. "That certainly changes things. We can't have a young girl starving in the mountains. We must also think of your education."

Dmitri bristled like a cornered lynx. "What do you mean 'alone'? She is welcome to stay at my farm for as long as is necessary. Those are books on the counter, not dolls. She has all the help she needs."

Vladimir squeezed Dmitri's shoulder to silence him. He stepped forward with outstretched hands. "Comrade Commissar, these things have happened before. You know that we always take care of our own. Dmitri and I will legally become her guardians. I guarantee that she will have the best of tutors."

Lepan nodded and placed the faded sheet into his folder. "Very noble indeed. However, she cannot be tramping back and forth to that isolated cabin. You know how hard the winters can be there. You two are just old bachelors: a farmer and a saloon keeper. You know nothing about raising and educating children. This is not suitable."

Vladimir shrugged his shoulders and replied, "Comrade Commissar, then let us compromise. I know of a fine boarding school in Vladivostok. Several people from this region have sent their children to this school during the winter. I will personally pay for her schooling, and she can spend her summers between Dmitri's farm and her family's cabin on the mountain. It is very pleasant there in the summer. It would be almost a holiday. This way, she receives an excellent education, and she retains her family's homestead. She will always be escorted by Dmitri or by me and thus never be alone—the best of all worlds, Commissar."

Lepan knew it was a reasonable solution, and so did everyone else. Chekov saw Lepan's hesitation and a fortune slipping through his fingers. Chekov whispered into Lepan's ear, "Remember, Commissar, utilization of state resources—health and safety."

Lepan stiffened and said, "The government cannot allow this valuable property to simply become a holiday house for an orphaned child. I have superiors in which I have to answer. Simply not acceptable."

"Please let me keep our home!" Anya pleaded. "I am grown now, and I have already lived there this winter. With both of my friends' help, I will be fine. Don't do this to me—don't take away everything I love!"

Lepan turned his head away from her and gave his verdict, "You are far from being grown, and sadly, there is no 'our home' at present—only you. You must now come with me for your health and safety as a ward of the state. Chekov, gather her things. They will be inventoried and placed in safekeeping for her."

The cornered lynx had had enough. Dmitri rushed forward, his hand raising the blade of his large knife from its sheath.

"Chekov, touch that girl or her property, and I will gut you like a fish."

Vladimir quickly grabbed Dmitri's powerful wrist and stepped between the two. "Commissar Lepan, where will she be going?"

"The girl will come with me, and tomorrow she will be escorted to the State Child Services Bureau at Vladivostok, until this can be settled. It shouldn't take long. They have the authority to place her where the state thinks will be in her best interest. She will remain in my custody for the time being. She must come now. We wouldn't want a runaway roaming those vast mountains, would we?"

Vladimir snatched a piece of paper from his cluttered desk. He coldly stared at Lepan and said, "Commissar, let her stay at my home tonight. You have no facilities for a young girl. This signed paper will act as a security bond, stating that she will be here, whenever you say. If she does not appear, for any reason, this entire establishment will be forfeited to the government. Dmitri will sign as a witness."

Lepan knew Vladimir was right while secretly hoping the girl would flee to the mountains. He could confiscate her property, get Vladimir's profitable enterprise to manage for the government, and skim money from both properties. With Chekov's cut from the furs, he would be a rich man in just a few years. Also, he did not want the inconvenience of this young girl.

"Very well," Lepan conceded. "Tomorrow, here, at 5:00 a.m. The trip is a long one. Chekov, the furs and the rifle."

Anya stepped forward and said, "The furs have already been sold. Take the money. The rifle is a gift from my father to Dmitri. It is his now. I will be here tomorrow." Anya placed the money on the counter and handed Sasha's rifle to Dmitri. Dmitri cradled the rifle in his arms and glared at Chekov, daring him to try and take it. No one dared.

"It's just an old single-shot cannon." Chekov sneered. "Not worth the trouble. Let's go."

Vladimir handed the money and the signed document to Lepan.

"Commissar, all state business concluded. I'll let you see yourselves out. Chekov, you might want to take your business elsewhere." Vladimir looked over his shoulder at Dmitri. "For state health and safety. We wouldn't want anything to happen to you, would we?"

****

Early the next morning, Vladimir lit three lanterns and placed them beside Anya and Dmitri. The store window emitted a faint glow against the darkness waiting outside.

"Anya, listen carefully—we don't have much time. Dmitri is going with you to Vladivostok. We won't take no for an answer. Once there, he will present this letter to the authorities for a request for guardianship. I am also including a small pouch of money to ease their decision. Regardless of what they decide, I am contacting an old friend in Moscow. He is a man with influence. We served together in the army. He owes me a favor. I saved his life at Stalingrad. Your release to us will be that favor. This may take some time. Anya, do not lose hope."

The bell over the door rang even louder in the still morning air. Anya jumped a little at its high-pitched sound. She was nervous about what lay ahead, but she tried to hide it from the others. She knew they were doing their best, but a sense of dread gripped her heart.

Assistant Petrov stood inside the doorway in his best uniform. He carried a sidearm in a battered leather holster across his left hip, connected to a worn strap across his chest and shoulder. A leather pouch on his right shoulder completed the ensemble.

"Comrade Petrov, where is our fearless leader Commissar Lepan?" Vladimir asked.

"He's asleep. He felt that this was a simple assignment, and he is much too busy to leave at this time. I have all the necessary documents in this pouch."

"In other words, the lazy dog cannot be bothered with a long trip to Vladivostok," Dmitri said. "So much for the 'health and safety' of the citizenry."

Vladimir smiled and countered, "Dmitri, Dmitri, don't be so harsh to our young friend. Comrade Petrov is correct. Such a simple task needs only his expert skills."

"Thank you, comrade," said Petrov. "We should be leaving. My cousin, in the wagon outside, will take us to the railway spur. We will signal the train to stop and then proceed to Vladivostok."

"Comrade Petrov, one last thing," Vladimir said. "Our good friend Dmitri will be going with you and Anya. I have some supplies that I need. Dmitri will accompany you and pay for any expenses that Anya may incur."

"But Commissar Lepan said that only the girl and I were to go. I must seek his permission."

Vladimir's smile vanished. He spoke in a low tone, "Petrov, he is going, just as I said. If you refuse this simple request, I will be forced to contact Moscow and report the frivolous waste of state funds by you, dear comrade. I am offering private funds for all expenses—that includes you and your cousin."

Vladimir slid a small leather bag down the long counter. It settled next to Petrov's elbow. "Just a thank-you for all your hard work on such a dark morning with everyone's eyes quietly closed in sleep."

The silence hung in the air as if a heavy cloud had descended from on high. Petrov looked at three stony faces and their piercing eyes—an uncertain rabbit surrounded by wolves.

Petrov quickly put the bag into his overcoat pocket and said, "Yes, yes, company would be welcome. No need to trouble anyone. Since I do all the accounting, your contribution will greatly aid the citizenry and the state. Now we must be going."

Vladimir hugged Anya tightly and kissed her cheek. His sudden tears ran down the side of her slender neck. Dmitri patted his shoulder. "Don't worry, Vlady. I will watch over her like a hawk. You have my word."

In the crisp morning air, Vladimir could hear the creaking of the old wagon, even as it passed out of sight. Forever it would be etched in his memory: the sight of a young blonde-haired girl in a weathered wagon bravely waiving farewell—but with abject fear in her eyes. He sat at his small cluttered desk looking down at the scuffed wooden floor, his hands shielding his grieving eyes. The prime furs were still piled in the corner. Sasha's rifle symbolically rested against them: the rifle, the furs, the man. A new bolt of lavender cloth lay on a shelf—a special order as a gift for Sonya. Anya's books remained in neat stacks on the counter. All about him, so full of memories, so empty of life. What Vladimir failed to see in his sorrow was a thin yellow tulip that had fallen from Anya's favorite book, *The Krokodile*. It lay on the dusty floor at the edge of the counter near the door—soiled and torn, crushed under the foul treads of hardened men.

CHAPTER 32

Petrov pulled the rope, raising a large red metal disk on a slender pole. He tied the rope at the base of the pole and joined Anya and Dmitri in a crude wooden shelter. The chipped red disk needed repainting, but Petrov hoped the train engineer would be able to see the signal in time to stop for them. This rural track eventually reached the main line that led to Vladivostok, often called "the End of the Line."

In the gray before dawn, they heard the train before they saw the column of smoke in the sky. Anya had never seen a train. She was curious as to how fast it would travel. Petrov led the way and showed the conductor the commissar's letter, stating this was a party on official business. The conductor found them seats near the front. Anya was required to sit between Petrov and Dmitri.

When the train gained its steam, Anya was amazed at the speed everything passed before her. She saw more landscape in a single day than she had in her entire life. However, after several stops, the novelty ended, and fatigue settled over her. Dmitri put his arm around her, and she rested her head on his broad shoulder. The train had a rocking motion, and between a man in uniform and a farmer who loved her, the iron rocking chair lulled her to sleep as they charged downward to the End of the Line.

****

CHILD OF THE FOREST

The Trans-Siberian Railroad ends in Vladivostok. Anya truly had reached the End of the Line. As they approached the large rail station, on a slight rise, Anya saw that the city spread clear to the sea. She had never seen a city. She had never seen the sea. She had never imagined that there was such a place, with so many buildings, with so many people scurrying in every direction. It was as if she had entered another world.

Anya exited the train into a swirl of other travelers. She felt stiff and weary from the long journey. She decided that it was easier to work two days on the mountain than to take a long trip by train. Dmitri took her hand so that she would not get lost in the crowd.

Petrov called to both, "Don't get separated. Follow me."

Anya only hoped that Petrov's words would come true: "Don't get separated." Anya looked at Dmitri with sad blue eyes. Her lower lip trembled, and with a quivering voice, she beseeched him, "Dmitri, I want to go home." Dmitri gently squeezed her hand and turned his head away from her. He quickly brushed a tear off his weathered cheek. Two lonely figures followed a man in uniform, walked hand in hand through an arched doorway, and entered the jaws of the city.

****

The State Child Services Bureau was a gray concrete building within walking distance of the railway station. In typical Stalinesque architecture, it was utilitarian, drab, and tasteless. In the middle of the building were two massive doors. The second floor had only two windows facing the street. When the lights were on and the two doors were opened, it looked as if one were entering the mouth of a dead man's skull. Anya gripped Dmitri's hand tighter as she entered "the skull."

Petrov handed his papers to a male secretary who resembled a turtle, with his half-closed eyes and a physique wider than his chair. After glancing at the papers, he motioned with his head toward a row of chairs without saying a word. Petrov asked Anya and Dmitri to take a seat, and he prepared himself for the long wait. Anya never released Dmitri's hand.

Two hours later, they were escorted into the dim office of a Child Services caseworker. Since there were only two chairs, Petrov stood near the door. A man in his fifties with short-cropped gray hair that seemed to bristle in every direction sat behind a cheap metal desk piled high with various forms. He appeared to be hiding from the world between two tall white pillars of paper. He reminded Anya of a weasel she had shot in the forest.

"District Commissar Lepan—never heard of him. However, this case seems pretty straightforward: parents dead, no relatives, orphaned child."

Dmitri interjected, "Comrade, what is not so straightforward is that another friend of the family and I are willing to be her guardians, to support her financially, and to pay for her education. Why should the state bear this burden when close friends are willing to step forward?"

"Is your first name Dmitri and the other man is Vladimir?"

Dmitri nodded in reply. "I'm afraid the district commissar has written in his report that the two of you are unfit as guardians and has directed us to enter the child under protective services as a ward of the state. We have the final say, but any guardians are investigated and approved by the district commissar where the child will live. You see the problem, don't you?"

Dmitri looked back at Petrov and asked, "Comrade, could we speak with you alone for a moment?"

Petrov took the hint and stood outside the office door. He knew what was going to happen, and he did not want to witness it in any case.

Dmitri patted his pockets as if he were looking for something. He emptied his pockets of a money pouch and a few papers and placed them on the metal desk. Dmitri pushed the money a little closer to the caseworker with his elbow while he continued his supposedly absent-minded search. Finally, he said, "Oh well, it was just a paper. Perhaps I left it on the train." Dmitri and the official stared at the money on the desk. Dmitri raised his eyes and looked straight into the man's face. "Comrade, we all admire your compassion and hard work. Talk is cheap—appreciation is not."

The official thought for a moment, leaned forward, and whispered, "Comrade Dmitri, I would love to accept your fine 'appreciation,' but you have to understand the system. These district commissars run their territory like a little fiefdom. I don't understand this case. Most commissars would gladly let a child remain with other family members, neighbors, or friends. Something smells rotten here, but I cannot just overrule his investigation and recommendations without proof. Bring me that proof and your 'appreciation,' and I will reconsider your guardianship request." The official straightened his back and stared at the doorway. He raised his chin and said, "Until that time, she must be supervised and protected as a citizen ward of the state."

Dmitri lowered his head and knew that he was defeated. He muttered under his breath, "Understand the system—what system? Whose system? Certainly not for us."

The official wanted to end the uncomfortable interview as soon as possible. He snapped his fingers and said, "Petrov, you there, Petrov, come in here. Take the child to this address. A driver will be waiting outside. Give the resident this paper. I'll phone ahead to let them know you are coming."

Anya was smart enough to sense that something was not quite right, but she was not worldly enough to recognize the rancid scent of deceit.

CHAPTER 33

The faded-green staff car drove slowly to the outskirts of Vladivostok. It stopped on a quiet street with few cars, but many trees lining the sidewalks. The gray overcast sky matched the mood of the occupants.

In the middle of the block stood a fortress-like structure surrounded by tall gray cinderblock walls. The only redeeming feature was a domed copula at the center of the building with a partially covered cross at the top of the dome. The compound had once been a pretty convent, but it had been converted not as a place of worship but as a warehouse for children: "the People's Orphanage."

The cross was to have been removed, but the workmen discovered that to do so would damage the delicate dome, making the roof leak. Stalin's ever-pragmatic engineers solved the problem by simply attaching a large red star to the crossbeams of the cross. It was such an odd configuration that it became a landmark. Anyone asking directions for the orphanage was told by the locals, "Follow the star."

Petrov led the way to the massive wooden door of the orphanage. There was a large tarnished brass ring held in the mouth of a brass lion's head in the center of the dark weathered door. He raised the ring and let it fall three times. Each time it struck the brass plate, it reminded him of a firing squad he had witnessed during the war: the metallic ring and then the sickening thud against fearful men and new corpses. Petrov now felt the echo of each brass blow on his own chest.

The heavy door opened slowly. A fierce-looking woman in a black dress with pallid skin, raven-black hair, and a small bun tightly wound on the back of her head barked at them, "What do you want?"

Petrov handed her the admission papers and gestured with his hand toward Anya.

Anya still clung to Dmitri, but in her right hand, she gripped the tiger-claw necklace. When the harsh-looking woman stared at her and screamed, "Don't just stand there—get in!" a small drop of blood dropped from her clenched fist onto her white fur coat. The tiger's claw had pierced her again.

The matron saw Anya grasping something in her hand. She snarled, "Don't try and hide a crucifix. They are not allowed here. Give it to me."

A sudden calm came over Anya. She released Dmitri's hand and stared directly into the matron's scornful face with a flash of lightning in her bright-blue eyes. Anya spread her hand to reveal a bloody palm and three tiger claws. She turned her back to the matron and calmly said, "Dmitri, keep this necklace and Papa's rifle for me. Someday I will return for them." She placed the bloody claws into his hand and gently kissed his cheek. Ignoring the matron, she walked through the open door into what she considered a living hell. She had once entered a tiger's lair and had overcome—she was determined to survive this Soviet cave as well.

Dmitri watched Anya's silhouette fade away as the matron slammed the door in his face. Dmitri grasped the brass ring and hammered it over and over, but no one returned. Finally, his strength gave out, and he slid with his face against the weathered wooden door—the long splinters slashed his face as he dropped onto the stone entrance. A bright-red streak ran down the length of the door, as if the brass lion's mouth was spitting blood to mingle with a wounded man's tears.

Petrov walked over to Dmitri and tried to help him get up onto his feet, but Dmitri would not be moved—he only wept with his face against the door. Petrov reached into his overcoat and dropped Vladimir's leather money pouch onto the stone floor in front of

Dmitri and quietly walked away. Petrov was not a religious man, but even he had heard of the one called "Judas."

Petrov walked down the stone steps and looked up into the gray sky. He motioned for the driver, sighed with exhaustion, and prepared himself for the long journey ahead. Getting into the faded car, he said, "Railway station, please." Petrov looked out of the streaked car window at the dome above and felt that he was not following the star but that the red star would not stop following him as they silently drove away to the terminus station known as the End of the Line.

PART 2

The Orphanage

*We have become orphans and waifs,
our mothers are like widows.*
—Lamentations 5:3
(after the fall of Jerusalem)

CHAPTER 34

Anya walked along a narrow portico with ornate columns spaced four steps apart. The *L*-shaped portico framed a small courtyard. In the center of the courtyard, there stood what was once an elegant fountain. The sound of bubbling water had vanished long ago. Anya thought that the fountain symbolized the orphanage in its entirety: alone and neglected; the water flowed no more.

Anya walked over and touched the fountain. Its surface was dry and rough; several brown leaves fluttered in the basin. Holding on to the edge of the fountain, she looked up and discovered she could view the gray sky. She determined this spot would be her center: no matter how difficult things became, her world would have to revolve around this fountain. Here, she could stand and visualize a world without walls. The sky would not always be gray.

The heavy door slammed, and Anya flinched as its thunder echoed around the portico. The matron placed a heavy steel bar across the back of the door and locked the ancient door with a large skeleton key attached to a ring on her belt. When the matron walked, the large key jingled against several other keys on the ring—the hollow chorus of captivity.

The matron snatched a slender wooden stick about the diameter of a working man's thumb that had been hidden inside, leaning against the old door's rusty hinges. The matron did not want Petrov and Dmitri to see her swagger stick dangling ominously from a leather thong around her wrist. Now she wanted Anya to see her baton of authority. She pointed the well-used rod at Anya and shouted, "Mountain girl, I'll only tell you once: *never* turn your back to me, and you will *always* address me as Head Matron. The other female wardens will be Comrade Matron. The director's formal title is Director Krimloviche, or as he likes to be called informally by the children, Uncle K." The matron smirked at her "Uncle K" assertion and sneered at Anya. The matron's half-smile seemed more sinister to Anya than the woman's small black eyes could ever portray.

"The rules are simple: follow them without question—or suffer. Now follow me."

Anya caressed the lip of the fountain and softly whispered, "I'll be back." Walking behind the haughty matron, Anya observed the profile of the shapeless black dress and the tight, tidy bun on the back of the stern woman's head. The matron's keys rattled on her belt, and her short, quick steps sounded like rapid pistol shots fired into the cold stone floor.

Behind them could be heard the forceful thumping of the brass ringer held in place through the mouth of a lion. It raged over and over, striking against the outer door until it too—like the fountain—faded away and flowed no more.

Chapter 35

Dmitri staggered into Vladimir's Store pale, gaunt, exhausted. Shocked by the dark circles under Dmitri's eyes and the brown scabs on the side of his face, Vladimir rushed to Dmitri and sat him on the closest chair. The once jaunty, robust farmer just stared at the wall. His demeanor was like that of a man who was the only survivor of a ship wrecked upon the high seas.

"We've lost her, Vladimir. I failed her. They have sealed her in a giant tomb. She's dead to us—gone. I plan to make two others dead in her place." Dmitri raised his head and stared at Vladimir with glassy eyes. "Where's the rifle she left? I need it now. I remember leaving it here someplace. Where did I put it?"

Vladimir knew that Dmitri was not bluffing. He had never seen him like this. He preferred the cocky, satirical old rascal of a farmer to the ghost of a man who now sat before him. Vladimir knelt and draped his arm across Dmitri's shoulders.

"Dmitri, Dmitri, look at me. Anya is not dead—just delayed. I want you to read this message. Take it in your hand...that's it. I wrote to my old friend in Moscow. It is his response. Remember, I told you about him. Dmitri, look at me. It's a telegram I just received today by special courier. They only do that for important people or in special cases. See, Anya is both important and special now. Go ahead and read it to me."

Dmitri's shoulders began to shake and he shouted, "Vladimir, did you sell her rifle, Sasha's rifle? Because if you did, I will have to punish you as well! You know that, don't you?"

Vladimir realized he was next to a live volcano. The ground was shaking, and soon an explosion would send hot bubbling lava in a fierce wrath against Chekov and Lepan.

"No, no, no, Dmitri. I wrapped the rifle in an oilcloth and safely locked it away. I would never sell something like that. Don't be foolish. Let me read to you—pay attention, crazy farmer."

> Vladimir—Good to hear from you—Received information on girl—Contacted Vladivostok—Placed Red-Flag status on name and case—Any new events reported directly to me—Appealed guardianship—Patience—System takes time—Best to you—Colonel Viktor Kurgan—Moscow Center.

"Dmitri, listen, things are moving. Rest here a few days. Become your spiteful self, and I will kick you out and send you home. I hired two men to care for your farm, so don't worry about a thing. Come, lie down on this cot next to my desk. I'm going to get you some food."

Vladimir helped Dmitri to the cot and covered him with a blanket. Dmitri fell into a deep sleep the instant his head touched the pillow, and he dreamed of a young girl, gray walls, and two evil men hanging from a tree.

Chapter 36

"Everyone wears a uniform here. Put your hat and clothes on that bench," the head matron said to Anya. "They will be returned to you when you leave, if they still fit."

Anya folded her lovely fur clothing and put on the "uniform," which was, in reality, just a cotton flour-sack dress with three holes cut in it for the head and arms dyed a muddy-brown color to better cover any future stains. She noticed it was old and threadbare; she could only imagine what it would be like in the winter wearing this thin garment.

"I would like to keep my boots," Anya said. "I don't see any shoes here."

The matron pointed her stick at Anya. "There aren't any shoes for a good reason. It's summer—you don't need them. You won't be pampered here, mountain girl. Don't ask questions. Do as you are told. Follow me."

Anya tried to get her bearings as she walked behind the matron on the cold stone floor. There had been many additions to the old convent; however, there did not appear to be any coordinated logic to the renovations. Whenever they needed more space, they just added a new wing of rooms, each jutting off in another direction from the original chapel complex. With the chapel dome in the center and arms protruding in all directions, Anya smiled when it reminded her of a strange octopus.

Anya noticed that one entire wing was the eating area. Long wooden tables with backless benches ran the entire length of the room with an aisle in the center. The only decoration was a large picture of Stalin hung on the chipped concrete wall. The tabletops and floor were stained but reasonably clean. Anya later learned that all the work in the dining area was done by the children, except for the cooking of the food.

The last leg of the "octopus" was the sleeping area. A small metal bed with a stained mattress, a blanket, and a pillow was Anya's new home.

"Remember the number on the bed," the matron said. "This is where you are expected to be every night when we do a head count. If you are not at your station at that exact time, you will be punished. I'll only tell you once. Here is a broom. Sweep the entire area. You might as well be useful. I have other duties to attend to rather than babysit you."

Anya felt as if she were sweeping the surface of the moon, that she now lived on a different planet—a world in which joy, kindness, and respect had vanished long ago. She looked down at her stained flour-sack smock and at her bare feet shuffling against the hard stone floor. A slow anger swelled inside her. This was wrong. Everything she loved had been torn from her: her home, her loving family, her friends, her dignity, her dreams. She swept harder and faster across the uneven floor until the head of the broom snapped at its base.

Anya received her first beating on her first day for her first assignment at the orphanage. What Anya did not know was that her fine fur clothing was sold on the black market before the sun went down.

****

Anya sat in the infirmary while the other children ate their evening meal. The orphanage's medical facility was a small room with a crude narrow table, a couple of chairs, and several empty shelves. A small white medicine cabinet hung on a wall near the door. The red stripes on her back and legs reminded her of her battle with the tiger—a struggle she had won.

A woman entered the room and approached Anya. Anya tensed, expecting the worst. The tall slender matron smiled at her, took a small key which hung around her neck, and opened the medicine cabinet to remove a jar of ointment.

Still smiling, she asked, "What is your name, dear? You must be new. I've never seen you."

"My name is Anya. I just arrived today. Are you a nurse?"

"Yes, I was trained as a nurse, but I am also now a seamstress, cook's assistant, children's helper, chief errand girl, and last but not least, comrade matron of this popular institution. Are you impressed?"

Anya felt her sense of fun, and she smiled for the first time in several days. "With so many impressive titles, what should I call you?"

"My official title is Comrade Matron Elena, but when we are alone, just Elena will do. The little girls call me Sister. Take your pick. Better to address me as Comrade Matron when in front of the head matron or Comrade Matron Svelte. Have you met Svelte?"

"Is she the short, stocky woman with reddish-brown hair who carries a sharp stick? If so, I think we've met." Anya slightly raised her brown smock to reveal the red welts and the black bruises on the back of her legs and hips. One wild stroke had slashed the skin near the four scars on her side.

Sister Lena turned her head in disgust. "Lord, have mercy. What did you do to deserve this, child?"

"I broke a broom while sweeping. The head matron called it 'vandalism of state property.' She and Svelte took turns with their sticks."

"Anya, what about these four marks along your side and ribs? Surely, they did not do that to you?"

"No, Sister. They are injuries from another place, another life, which now seems far away."

"Anya, have you had anything to eat? Supper is almost over, and I assure you there will not be a scrap of food left."

"I don't remember. I think I had some bread and cheese on the train with my friend Dmitri."

"Well, in that case, Anya, we will elegantly dine together. Munch on this bread and sliver of meat while I put you back together again."

Sister Elena gently rubbed the ointment across the many welts and bruises. She took her time to clean and bandage the wound on Anya's side. The kind matron wanted Anya to finish the entire meal—the only food Elena was to have that day.

Elena smiled and hummed a jaunty tune while she worked. Her kind hazel eyes brightly danced with the music. Anya ate the meager meal and looked at the woman's lovely chestnut hair and thought she saw a ray of light that penetrated even the depths of hell.

****

Sister Elena escorted Anya to the sleeping hall. Anya was pleasantly surprised to find that she now had a longer bed. "Is this mine?" she asked. "It's the same number but a larger bed."

"Yes, I had Sergei put some longer rails and a slightly longer mattress here for you. You are much too tall for that other bed. I'm afraid it is just as narrow. We use the same metal headboards, just longer or shorter rails. I hope you don't mind, but I placed several of the smaller girls and their beds around yours. It makes them feel more secure."

"No, I don't mind. I will help them all I can. So it is just girls that live here?"

Elena straightened the sheets on the bed and replied, "Yes, we have a very small staff. We don't have the facilities or the people to accommodate both. There is an orphanage for boys on the other side of the city."

"Sister, I will stop asking so many questions, but you mentioned Sergei. How many people work here?"

"You will like Sergei. He is a kind old soul. He does maintenance and yardwork for us. There is a cook, Ursula, who does the best she can on a limited budget. You have met the three matrons. Finally, there is the director and his young assistant. I'm afraid the children do the cleaning and sewing, but we will get to that another day."

Elena draped a square cloth at the foot of Anya's bed and tucked the corners under the mattress so that the ointment would remain on Anya's legs and not stain her mattress. When Elena finished, Anya sat on her bed and gazed at the cavernous room lined wall to wall with beds of various lengths, most much shorter than hers. Her warm bed at the cabin, lined with soft furs, seemed further away than ever. Never had she missed her home and her parents more than sitting on the flimsy bed in what she considered a human warehouse.

Elena saw the sadness in Anya's eyes. She touched Anya's shoulder and said, "I know this is hard for you, and it seems very harsh and strange. I lost my parents when I was even younger than you. Look at all these small beds—so have many others. Be thankful that you had your parents longer than these poor children. This place is not much, but believe me, there are worse places than this. Rest now. The other girls will join you soon."

Elena kissed the top of Anya's head and waved to her as she left the hall. It made Anya feel warm. It was the first affection she had received from another woman since her mother kissed her goodbye on that fateful morning when she left to find her father. Anya watched Elena leave and softly whispered, "There are worse places than here, Sister…simply because they don't have you."

CHAPTER 37

Anywhere creatures gather, a pecking order reins, particularly within institutions. Anya soon learned that her new surroundings were a reflection of her experiences in the wild regions of the forest: the strongest predators ruled over the weakest prey.

The director of the orphanage (Uncle K) ruled over the head matron, who in turn ordered the other matrons according to their duties, who then relied on the older girls to assist the younger children. The cook, Ursula, and gentle old Sergei generally were left alone to do their duties and to ask for help when needed. Being new, Anya knew she would have to establish her place in this new wilderness.

It seemed odd to Anya that there were so few "older girls." Most of the children were from ages four to ten. She later discovered when a girl turned sixteen, she was released from the orphanage to begin work in one of the many factories around the city or to apprentice as a seamstress.

The orphanage's workday began early, starting with "cleanup time" and then a simple breakfast. After breakfast, basic academic classes occupied the rest of the morning, taught by retired school teachers recruited by the ever-concerned Sister Elena. The only vocational training was sewing, and all the girls were required to work every afternoon in this endeavor. After supper, the children cleaned the dining hall, with concentrated cleaning every weekend since the teachers were absent. There was never any real free time.

In any system, there are gaps in the schedule. Anya found solace by going to the fountain—her sacred spot—just to look up into the sky. It calmed her and reminded her that there was a world outside, beyond the gray walls that surrounded her.

One day, while standing at the fountain, Anya heard the most beautiful singing. It was coming from under the portico. A young girl about Anya's age swept the stone pavement. She also was a "new girl," arriving just a few days after Anya. She had the uncommon name of Esmeralda.

Esmeralda was not as tall as Anya, but she had bright brown eyes and dark hair with a lovely olive complexion. She was quite pretty and, like Anya, looked older than her age. The head matron rudely referred to her as "the little gypsy."

While Anya chaffed at being confined, Esmeralda seemed to just flow with the system like an unseen current in a river. Nothing seemed to upset her. Anya followed her sweet music as Esmeralda swept her way around the portico.

Old Sergei also heard the music, and he stepped out of his workshop just to listen. He motioned for Anya to come to him, and with a wide smile, he exclaimed, "That child has the voice of an angel. No songbird in a tree could sing better. I noticed you like the old fountain. It's a nice spot to rest and think."

"Why doesn't it work, Sergei? Is there no water for it?"

"Oh, child, there's plenty of water, but no pump that works. There is a metal plate by the cobblestones, but I am too old and too tall to crawl into it."

"My name is Anya. I'm new here. What if I slipped inside there, and you told me what to do? I'm pretty good with my hands. My papa taught me. He could make or fix anything."

"Honey, I bet he could at that. Well, let's-give-it-a-try! If anyone asks what you have been doing, just tell them I asked for your help. If there's any trouble, I'll back your words—since it happens to be true. Take this light. I'll lift the plate, and you scamper like a little squirrel, telling me what you see."

Anya's heart lightened, looking forward to the challenge. She always loved helping her father. Sergei could not replace her father; but he was a man who cared—that was more than enough.

The crawlspace was tight even for Anya. She soon found herself under the fountain amidst a curtain of cobwebs. She brushed them away and found a square box with corroded copper wires.

"Sergei, I think I've found it. The wires are all green and rusty. What do I do?"

Sergei excitedly searched in his battered toolbox and handed Anya a stiff wire brush. "Anya, brush the wires as hard as you can, especially where they connect to the pump. Keep your hands on the wooden handle and don't touch the wires. I don't want my little squirrel to get a jolt and singe her hair. In fact, put your hair down the back of your dress, just to be safe. Go ahead, let's see what happens."

Anya felt the joy of being useful. She scrubbed the cables until she finally saw a spark from the main outlet. "Sergei, I think we are almost there. It's sparking and hissing at me."

"Well, what do you know, Anya! The old girl is still alive and scolding us for years of being ignored! Here are some pliers. Carefully open the cap at the end of the pump and pour this can of water into it. It will prime the pump. Listen now—stay away from those wires and don't touch anything with your wet hands."

Through great effort, the brittle metal cap finally turned, and Anya finished her task. She asked, "What now, Sergei?"

"Anya, clean the cap with the brush and screw it back on the pump. Try to keep any rust from falling into the pump. When you come out, don't touch those wires with your hands or feet. Easy now. Be careful."

Anya emerged with a happy grin on her face. Sergei helped her through the small opening, and he replaced the metal plate. He was also smiling, and he said, "Well, Anya, let's see what kind of mechanic you are. Come to the shed, and we will flip a switch and see if she sings."

Just inside the shed, a small electrical switch was connected to the wall at eye level. Sergei dramatically waved his arm at the box. He looked at Anya with a twinkle in his gray eyes and said, "My lady, now that it has juice, give it a whirl and let's see if it works. Make sure your hands are dry and push up that lever. You have the honors."

Anya rubbed her hands on her thin brown smock, and with eager eyes, she pushed the lever upward. They heard a loud humming sound, and then the fountain seemed to cough and sputter. A thin stream of rust-colored water shot into the air, as if it were spitting at the sky. One by one, the small openings of the fountain spurted water until the humming stopped and a cascade of water arched into the air and began to fill the basin.

Anya and Sergei could not contain their excitement; both ran to the fountain. They dipped their hands into the water to rejoice, to prove to themselves that it was indeed real. Anya always kept the fountain clean, and soon the basin filled with pure, sparkling water, slowly draining back into the pump to spring forth again.

Sergei fondly looked at Anya and touched her wet hand with his calloused fingers. With a tender voice, he said, "Anya, your father would be proud of you. You brought the lost back to life."

Anya and Sergei stood beside each other, facing the fountain, mesmerized by its crystal voice—which, like Esmeralda, drew forth joy and life from every breath of its new song.

****

The head matron was upset about the fountain, not that the water flowed again but that she had not given permission for the project. Sergei kept his word and reminded her that the director allowed the older girls to help him when requested. Sergei was a kind man, but his fixed gaze at the head matron firmly signaled that an argument with him, in the presence of the director, would be a battle lost. Sergei helpfully replied, "I've shown the director the new fountain. He was delighted."

The angry matron decided to bide her time and to make both Sergei and his little helper pay for their disrespect, particularly the upstart mountain girl.

"Get to the sewing room, mountain girl!" the matron shouted. "Comrade Matron Elena will show you what to do." The matron left in a huff, her yellow stick dangling from the leather strap on her wrist.

The sewing room was in the rotunda of the old chapel, the religious symbols carried away years ago. Broad tables were arranged in semicircles; each half-circle contained children of similar ages and skills.

Sister Elena smiled at Anya and pointed to a seat next to Esmeralda. This particular group had the more difficult task of making shirts. Anya's mother had taught her basic sewing skills, but nothing like this. Anya found it tedious.

Esmeralda, happy as usual, hummed a quiet tune and finished seam after seam. When she finally finished a shirt, it was a work of art. Esmeralda gave the shirt to Sister Elena, who bragged on the perfect garment while stroking Esmeralda's lovely brown hair. Esmeralda regained her seat and, still humming, began anew.

Anya hated the sewing, but she enjoyed gazing at the architecture of the quaint chapel. The domed ceiling gave the room a grand, open feeling. Beneath the dome, there was a complete circle of stained glass windows, each depicting a biblical scene. Anya was amazed at their intricate beauty and how the refracted sunlight colored the entire room. The fountain and the chapel made her feel free.

Talking was not allowed when the head matron and Comrade Svelte occasionally made their presence known, but Sister Elena used a lighter touch. She knew the girls did not get much free time and that they needed the companionship. She allowed conversation in hushed tones so long as the work progressed.

The head matron knew this violation occurred when she was not present, but she did not press the matter. It was Elena's show—let her deal with it. She and Svelte did not want to be bothered with the mundane supervision of a sewing class. They were more concerned with the finished product. Their black-market contacts always had ready cash available, especially for the fine shirts and trousers the older girls made.

The head matron had convinced Director Krimloviche that the sewing class was needed for the poor girls so that they would have some viable skills when they left the orphanage. Besides, the extra income could help with constant expenses. The director agreed and obtained permission from the State Child Services Bureau—after all, it would save them money, the Bureau reasoned.

When the money began to accumulate, the director took the lion's share, the matrons got a healthy portion, and the orphanage received a trickle. Clever accounting and the explanation that the children's crude work did not bring much covered most of their scheme. Sister Elena was always a troublesome concern: she refused her "share" except when she absolutely had to buy medicine and supplies for the infirmary. Elena was not going to let the girls suffer. They had earned the money; it should be used for them, she reasoned. Since most of the funds for her precious medicine came from black-market profits, the three conspirators felt safe that she would be equally incriminated if she were to speak out of turn to the authorities.

While Sister Elena was pleasantly working with the little girls, who were sewing borders on white table napkins, Anya whispered to Esmeralda, "Does it seem strange to you that here we are working with this nice cloth, yet we are wearing stained brown rags?"

Esmeralda moved closer to Anya while never letting her clever brown eyes stray from looking at the chapel doorway. "I'm new here, Anya, but I've noticed that every day the head matron has a different piece of jewelry on her hand or on her dress, that Comrade Matron Svelte often has the smell of vodka on her breath, and that dear Uncle K spends most of his time upstairs in his office with his pretty assistant. I would guess there is a little trading going on, but what do I know? I'm just the little gypsy girl."

Anya looked up at the stained glass window that elegantly displayed Jesus driving the crooked money-changers from the temple with a whip. Anya continued working, but she decided that those who had desecrated this beautiful chapel and made it a den of thieves also needed the lash of His whip.

CHAPTER 38

Anya and Esmeralda eventually found their places as being the "new girls" at the orphanage. The natural pecking order always seems to find a way. When one of the girls of the orphanage desired sympathy or someone to uplift her spirit, she went to Esmeralda. However, if she needed protection, Anya became her sword and shield.

Anya could not stand a bully, regardless of her size or age. She would warn an offender once. For any future violations, the offender found herself sprawled across the hard stone floor. One penalty was generally all it took. Anya's life in the forest had made her fast and strong—bully beware.

Sister Elena knew about this new transformation of roles, and she did not interfere. She could not be everywhere for a kind touch or a protective gesture. Esmeralda always made time for others, and she had an unlimited reserve for mercy. Anya never went too far in her efforts to be the "great protector." The other matrons could care less, so long as there was peace and order. They expected a certain pecking order and encouraged it. There were no complaints from the other girls, for then all those involved would have to go before the head matron, and no one wanted that. Consequently, a certain peace descended upon the orphanage.

Another change in Anya's duties had a lasting effect. During a sewing class, two young girls bumped into each other and fell: one hurting her arm, the other her knee. Without hesitation, Anya helped them up and led them to the infirmary. Sister Elena followed closely behind them. Once in the infirmary, Anya began cleaning their wounds and searching for bandages. Elena smiled and recognized Anya's medical skills. Taking a key from around her neck, Elena opened the medicine cabinet. She instructed Anya as to the correct medications, but she allowed Anya to do the work.

"Anya, for some time I have needed an assistant. Overseeing the medical station, the sewing classes, and helping in the kitchen is too much—there is just not enough of me to go around. The other matrons seem preoccupied with other matters. How would you like to be my assistant?"

Anya's eyes brightened, and she exclaimed, "I would love it, Sister Elena! I've always wanted to know about medicine. I once had a medical book, and I studied it every day. Besides, it is one thing to sew a pair of leather moccasins and quite another to tailor a shirt. My heart is not into it. May I start today?"

Sister Elena winked at Anya and pointed at the bandaged children. "It looks like to me, young doctor, you already have. Let's get back to the sewing class. After supper, we will go see the director."

****

Anya and Sister Elena walked up a wide outside staircase leading to the second story of the original convent, where the nuns used to reside. Several smaller rooms had been renovated to form four living quarters and an expansive office at the end of the covered open-aired hallway. There were flower boxes outside each window, with the doors and windows all facing the courtyard and the fountain below. From this vantage point, Anya could see that the chapel, living quarters, and the courtyard had been connected and must have been quite a pretty place before the drab appendages were constructed.

When they reached the top of the wide staircase, Anya asked, "Sister Elena, do you live here?"

"Yes, Anya, my room is here in front of the staircase so that I can get to the infirmary without disturbing the others. When there is a sick child, I often spend more time sleeping on a cot in the infirmary than up here. I can check on them throughout the night, one of the many reasons I need an assistant."

"Does all the staff live here?"

"No, Anya, just the head matron, the director, his assistant, and myself. The head matron lives in the room at the far end of the hall to your left. My room is next. The assistant's room is next to mine, and the director has the apartment next to hers, which adjoins the large office at the end of the hall on your right. Ursula and Sergei live nearby. Svelte takes the bus from town. We have an appointment in ten minutes. Let's not be late."

Elena softly knocked on the director's large ornate door. A striking slender young woman opened the door and escorted them into the office.

"Anya, this is Sofia, the director's assistant, and this is Comrade Director Krimloviche."

"Come, come, everyone sit down. Let's be comfortable," the director said. "Well, Anya, one of our new girls and already desiring more responsibilities—most commendable."

The director rattled on in good cheer. He was a nervous sort who never seemed to know what to do with his hands. Even sitting at his desk, Anya could tell he was a large, stocky man with muscular arms and a barrel chest. She thought him massive enough to be a wrestler. He had dark thinning hair, which he combed straight back, and a neatly trimmed black beard. But it was his eyes that disturbed Anya: even though he was smiling and talking in a cheery voice, his eyes never moved from staring at her. Anya had seen this focused look many times in the forest: when a predator had finally settled on its prey.

****

The meeting did not last long. The director did all the talking, and he readily agreed that Sister Elena needed help. It was agreed that Anya would help in the kitchen when she was not needed in the infirmary.

Sofia sat in a large leather chair at the side of the room and simply observed the meeting. She never took any notes, just elegantly nodding her head when the director glanced at her and announced his decision. Anya kept glancing at Sofia. She was the most beautiful woman Anya had ever seen, with her blue-black hair, hazel eyes, and smooth, creamy complexion. Anya watched every graceful gesture that she made. Anya had heard stories about the aristocracy of Russia, but until today, she had never met one. It was nothing tangible; it was just there. This aura surrounded them like a gentle flowing breeze—you knew it, and so did they.

The director escorted Sister Elena and Anya to the door. Sofia remained seated.

"I'm glad we had this chat. Comrade Elena, keep up your good work, and, Anya, help her all that you can. Feel free to call me Uncle K. Many of the children do."

Anya walked with Sister Elena away from the office toward the staircase. Elena was smiling, obviously pleased with the outcome of the meeting. Anya looked back over her shoulder and noticed that the director watched them the entire length of the hallway. He too was smiling, and his eyes never left Anya.

CHAPTER 39

The next morning, Sister Elena introduced Anya to Ursula, the cook. It was a quiet Saturday. Since there were no classes and no patients in the infirmary, Elena asked Anya to spend the entire day with Ursula.

"Anya, this is Ursula. She is an excellent cook—you can learn a great deal from her. Ursula, Anya is to be your helper when she is not in classes or assisting me in the infirmary. She is a good worker. Well, I must be on my way to supervise the younger girls. I will return to help you with lunch."

"Come over here and let me look at you, child. I don't bite," teased Ursula. "You don't have much meat on your bones, but you're a tall sprout. Anya, I only have three rules: be clean, put things back exactly where you found them, and don't waste anything—that's it. Follow those three rules, and we will get along fine. I was told that you came from a mountain region, so you must know how to use a knife. Come over here and chop these vegetables for a nice stew we are going to have for lunch. Be careful and don't chop off any fingers, or they will be the main course in the stew." Ursula smiled and handed Anya a large butcher knife.

Anya immediately liked Ursula. She was a natural grandmother, the sort of person Anya had never known. Anya's grandparents had all passed away when she was just a baby. Ursula looked like a grandmother with her white curly hair that stuck out in every direction from underneath her bright red kerchief. She was a big-boned, heavyset woman but surprisingly quick in her movements.

Ursula hummed while she worked. She took a sprinkle of this, a handful of that, and put it in the stew; no cookbook was needed. Anya perceived that Ursula had been cooking all of her life and that she enjoyed being an excellent cook and sharing her food with others.

"Anya, let's taste this witch's brew. Test this broth. What does it need?"

Anya sipped from the wooden spoon and replied, "Just a little more salt, but not too much. Some pepper and a touch of garlic, if you have any."

"Anya, I'll make a cook of you yet. I have some salt and pepper next to me. Slice a little of that garlic. We're lucky to have it."

Anya enjoyed feeling useful and being a partner in something worth doing well. She liked the warm kitchen and Ursula's professional but easygoing manner. Yes, she could learn a great deal here with Ursula.

"Ursula, what should I call you when the head matron is around?"

"Call me anything but lazy." Ursula chuckled. "Ursula is fine. The head matron doesn't come in here very often. This is my kitchen, and it is not wise to argue with someone who has a meat cleaver in her hand. Except for Elena, I've worked here longer than anyone, so I generally get my way."

"Sister Elena has been here that long!" exclaimed Anya.

"Well, deary, I'm not quite as old as Ivan the Terrible, but close. Elena came here as a young girl when this was still a convent. Her mother died when she was just a few years old. Her father owned a shipping firm here in Vladivostok. She had a nanny for several years until one day her father went to Moscow and never returned. Personally, I think the Bolsheviks wanted his company, so they made him disappear. He must have known something was about to happen. He had the nuns take Elena before he left for Moscow. Elena never saw him again."

Anya paused to absorb what she had just heard. She turned toward Ursula and asked, "When did you come here?"

"I came here when the Communists closed the convent to make it an orphanage. They put the nuns on trial and shipped them to a gulag in Northern Siberia. Elena was still young, and the nuns had given her medical training. She was useful, so they allowed her to stay. She became the first orphan here. I came right after that since there was no one to cook after the nuns were sent away."

Anya became quiet and continued her work. Her thoughts led her to kind Sister Elena, who had been without a parent most of her life. Anya did not like her situation in Vladivostok, but she was beginning to realize that others had suffered as much, if not more, than she had. At least she had known her parents until she was thirteen. It was also a comfort to know where they were buried—not for them to just disappear, never to be seen again.

"Ursula, I don't mean to gossip—"

"Gossip, why not? What's a quiet kitchen for if not to talk? What's on your mind, girl?"

"Yesterday, I met Sofia, the director's assistant. She looked older than the rest of us but still young. Is she an orphan, or does she work here on the staff?"

"Oh my, Queen Sofia! She is both an orphan, and she works here. She has been here a couple of years. She originally lived in Moscow. Her father was a diplomat of some note, something to do with economic things, money, I don't know. Rumor is that he had the courage to tell Stalin the collective farms would not produce enough food and would lower the economy or some fancy words like that. Stalin executed him as a traitor, exiled his wife to the gulag, and transferred Sofia from a nice school in Moscow to this orphanage. Stalin made an example of her family—don't disagree, or else."

"I noticed she is very pretty," Anya replied.

"Yes, she is. Bring those vegetables over here, honey. The director also noticed that, and she soon became his assistant. Beauty is something I have never had to worry about, but in difficult times, fine looks can be a sharp double-edged knife. You may get the best, or you may attract the worst. In any case, she will be leaving soon. At age sixteen, a girl has to leave here."

Anya stopped cutting the vegetables and looked at the knife in her hand. It did not have a sharp edge on each side, but it caused her to remember the director's glaring eyes at their meeting. A shiver went down her back. She began to chop rapidly, hoping her fingers would not become the main course in the orphanage's stew.

CHAPTER 40

On a special Sunday, all the staff were allowed a holiday, including the head matron, who wanted to sell finished garments on the black market. Sister Elena volunteered to remain at the orphanage and supervise the girls; the other supervisors quickly agreed.

Sister Elena saw an opportunity to let the girls just be children instead of sewing and cleaning. Elena decided to have a picnic with games for the children afterwards. She recruited Sergei to cut the grass around the courtyard, Anya and Ursula to prepare extra food on Saturday, and Esmeralda to organize entertaining games.

Sunday arrived with glorious sunshine in a clear blue sky. The children spread their woolen blankets on the ground, ate their simple meal, and chatted freely with one another. Other than Elena, there were no adults present ordering them to work or to be quiet. They could just be little girls having a wonderful time on a beautiful Sunday morning.

Esmeralda was an apt ringmaster: delegating the various activities to the older girls, visiting each group, making sure everyone was having a good time.

Anya sat next to Elena on a brown woolen blanket. She asked Elena, "Ursula told me that you have been here a long time. Did you ever have picnics when it was a convent?"

"Oh yes, Anya. The nuns were very kind and fun-loving in their own way. After my father passed away, I decided to join the order.

They were the only family I had. When the nuns were sent to the work camps, I felt very alone and afraid."

"Can you leave here if you want?" Anya asked.

"Yes, I could leave. On several occasions, when I was angry about the unfair treatment of the girls, I prepared to do so. After I cooled down, I always reflected, Who will watch over the children when I am gone? What if my replacement is even more hardened than the current matrons? Who will take care of their medical needs? So I stayed. We all have our special gifts, blessings, and even trials… perhaps this is mine."

"Esmeralda and I noticed a small tower on the other side of the convent. We never saw it before because we were not allowed in that area past the courtyard except for today. Do they still use it for anything?"

Elena's eyes brightened, and she replied, "You girls have keen eyes. It is an old bell tower." Elena looked around, and with a mischievous grin, she inquired, "How would you and Esmeralda like to go into the tower? It would be your reward for helping me today! The other children are busy and well supervised. We won't be gone long." Putting her finger to her lips, Elena whispered, "It will be our secret. No one is supposed to go there."

At the mention of a forbidden, secret hideaway, Anya jumped to her feet and motioned for Esmeralda to join them. Their faces beamed with the joy of a new adventure. Elena extended her hands, and the girls helped her to her feet. Elena had as big a smile as her two co-conspirators. She winked at them and said, "Follow me. We will take the back way—unnoticed." The three explorers went to a partition and disappeared around a corner of the courtyard.

When they reached the tower, Elena approached the oval doorway, which was recessed a short distance from the entry to avoid the rain. Elena looked around to make sure no one was watching, and she removed an old stone in the dark corner of the entryway. Behind the stone, she retrieved a large rusty key and quickly unlocked the tower door.

Elena cautioned, "Don't tell anyone about the key, or we will all be in trouble. The door used to be unlocked when I was a girl. One of my duties was to come here several times a day and ring the bell for mealtimes and for worship services. The nuns knew that I loved to ring the bell, so they always allowed me the honors. There used to be a long rope near this doorway that extended up to the bell. I would run, leap as high as I could, and grab the rope. It carried me up and down like a circus ride. It was quite fun."

Elena looked upward into the tower and gently ran her hand along the stone wall. "I had many happy moments here. Let's go see the bell. The tower allows for a great view. Use the rail and don't tumble down the stairs. I'll bet I can beat both of you up the stairs. Get ready. Go!"

Elena ran up the wooden staircase two steps at a time. Anya and Esmeralda giggled and enjoyed watching the "little girl" emerge from Elena—flowing on the warm memories of a young child's past.

Elena breathlessly called to the girls, "Isn't the view beautiful? You can see clear to the ocean on bright days like this. Oh, I spent many hours here! This was my secret place to think, to breathe fresh air, to explore the world from my little tower." Elena's face radiated her shared joy, and her eyes danced with the recognition of old things, old friends, old memories.

The three were quiet for a moment. They just circled the bell tower and breathed the fresh air that came from the sea. Elena was right—even on this orphanage island, the ocean and a very large world lay just beyond.

Ever observant, Esmeralda noticed that the bell did not have a clapper inside the bell and that a short segment of the old rope had been cut and left on the floor. She asked, "Sister, how can the bell ring without the iron clapper and a rope to pull the bell?"

Elena laughed and touched the bell. "Girls, look to your left. See that old field? Russian soldiers camped there. I loved ringing the bell, but the soldiers did not love hearing it, especially early in the morning. The nuns started the day before dawn for a morning Mass and for prayer. Finally, the soldiers forced their way into the convent, marched up here where we are standing, detached the clapper, and cut the rope."

Anya held the frayed ends of a short old rope and said, "I can see the marks on the floor where they cut it."

"Yes," Elena continued. "They used their bayonets to cut the rope and to dismantle the insides of the bell. They took everything with them except the bell. It was too heavy and too dangerous to remove. I imagine they sold the long rope and the valuable metal for vodka."

Elena fixed her eyes on the distant ocean and its restless waves crashing onto the shore. "I still come here at night when there is a full moon, or just before dawn when everything is so still and quiet. Few people even know the tower is here. Most fix their eyes on the elegant dome or the large red star. My little tower, like most of us in this life, remains unnoticed."

Elena walked to the center of the room and touched the bell. "Whenever I come here, I recite a poem the nuns taught me. It is a poem by John Donne, written in 1624. Let me teach it to you:

> No man is an island
> Entire of itself
> Every man is a piece of the continent
> A part of the main.
> If a clod be washed away by the sea,
> Europe is the less,
> As well as if a promontory were,
> As well as if a manor of thy friend's or of
thine were;
> Any man's death diminishes me,
> Because I am involved in mankind.
> And therefore never send to know for whom
the bell tolls;
> It tolls for thee."

When Elena finished the poem, she softly stroked the bell. Anya and Esmeralda were deeply moved. Each woman looked solemnly at the view from the tower extending to the sea. Everyone in the tower seemed to sense her own island beckoning, heard her own bell tolling, felt her own heart longing.

As if the bell rang in their minds, all three knew it was time to leave. They quietly descended the steep staircase to the door below, leaving behind a frayed rope, a forgotten tower, and a silent bell that no longer "tolls for thee"—except through a hidden key that opens the longing heart and the dusty storerooms of the mind.

CHAPTER 41

On Monday when the staff returned from their holiday, most seemed tired and agitated whereas Sister Elena and the children were rested and quite content. The head matron had a new, expensive brooch on her dress. Svelte had red eyes and a severe headache. The director and his comely assistant were arguing, and Ursula drove the head matron from her kitchen with a rolling pin when the matron complained about her wasting food on Sunday.

Old Sergei wisely hid in his workshop and sharpened the cook's knives until the storm passed. He also felt that it was best to keep the knives with him for the time being, lest the womenfolk organized a massacre upon themselves. Meanwhile the children watched the Monday mayhem with glee—for when the adults were picking on one another, they were not picking on them.

The head matron was particularly agitated. Things were just spiraling out of control: Elena went over her head asking the director for an assistant. She also organized an event without permission. The mountain girl and the little gypsy were getting way ahead of their stations in life. The cook was not cutting food rations as ordered, and Svelte was increasingly coming to work slightly drunk or with a terrible hangover. Something had to be done.

The cook had to stay. The head matron despised her impudence, but if she left, it only meant more work for the matrons until a compliant replacement could be found. Esmeralda was the finest seamstress at the orphanage, and her garments always brought the highest prices (the new brooch was evidence of that). The head matron could cover for Svelte; at least she was loyal and did what she was told. Quiet old Sergei knew enough to mind his own business.

The head matron heard a door slam, and the director's assistant stormed out of his office and entered her own apartment. The matron smirked and looked up at the office door overhead. "So Queen Sofia and the director are having difficulties," she murmured to herself. "She will soon be leaving our little establishment. Then there will be new openings—and vast changes. I wonder who will be the director's new assistant? Perhaps I can help with a few suggestions for Uncle K."

The head matron walked by the infirmary and heard Anya and Elena laughing while they rolled bandages. The matron smiled and kept walking, "Yes, changes indeed." She stared at them as she passed by while tapping her yellow stick against her leg—synchronized motion that matched each clicking step on the stone floor—as she marched passed the bubbling fountain and out of sight.

****

Anya finished rolling the bandages and walked toward the kitchen to help Ursula. She saw Esmeralda standing in an alcove outside the sewing room. It was a favorite place to talk since it was recessed so that two people could not be seen or heard. Esmeralda looked around and motioned for Anya to join her.

"Sister Elena gave us a break. I want to ask you a question. Anya, since the picnic, does it seem strange around here to you?"

"Esmeralda, this place has always been strange to me. I'll never understand it or the people who run it. I came from a place with solid, straightforward people who said what they meant, whether for good or for bad. I just try to survive one day at a time."

"Well, my people are good at survival," Esmeralda replied. "We have had to be, or we would have been finished long ago. My instincts tell me that the head matron is up to no good. Normally she would be ordering people around, swatting people who walked too slowly with her vile stick and just being a general nuisance. Now she just circles like a buzzard in her black dress, watching everyone and everything. I like it better when she screams at everyone. At least the poison fills the air. When she prowls and gets quiet, the poison drips into her heart. Something is wrong, Anya. I can sense it."

"You mentioned 'your people.' Is that why the matron calls you the little gypsy?"

"Yes, *gypsy* is the short way of saying 'Egyptian.' They should really call us Indians or Indo-Europeans. My father told me our people migrated from India to Europe several centuries ago. We call ourselves *Romany*."

"How did you get here in Eastern Russia all the way from Europe?"

"The Germans, Anya. Hitler hated Jews and Russians, but most of all, he loathed us—'the worst of the undesirables.' Hitler said that we were a mongrel race with no roots or county. He referred to us as 'antisocial vermin.' My family and our small group were driven from Eastern Europe. My father was very wise. Maybe that is where I get my instincts. We left early when my father heard about the attack on Poland. Those who stayed behind were either immediately executed or sent to work camps in Southern Poland. Many of our clan were taken to a place called Auschwitz. They were never seen again."

"But, Esmeralda, why Vladivostok? It's such a long way."

"My father heard that this area was a major escape route for anyone wanting to go to America, either legally or by other means. Many Jews had already done so. My father left our group and proceeded this way. One night, four drunken Russians who hated both the Jews and the Romany attacked our camp. My father shot two with his shotgun, my mother stabbed one in the neck with a knife. The fourth man shot my parents in the back during the struggle with his pistol. I was hiding in the bushes near our wagon. The last man stole everything and left in our wagon. He even looted his old friends before he left. Initially, I think they just wanted to steal our horse. They were not expecting a fight. I dug two shallow graves with a metal plate and buried my parents. I stacked rocks on top to keep animals away from them. It was all I could do. I left the other men to rot. Several days later, a village policeman found me. Since I was near Vladivostok, they sent me here."

"Esmeralda, I'm sorry about your parents. I didn't know."

Esmeralda wiped her eyes on the short sleeve of her brown dress and said, "My parents had such lovely voices. We always sang together. I miss them terribly. Now, Anya, when I sing, I sing for all of us—my parents, the Romany, all who are no more—for when I sing with all my heart, I know their voices are heard."

Esmeralda saw two black shapes emerging around a corner. It was the head matron and Comrade Matron Svelte.

"Time to go, Anya. Hitler and Stalin are coming this way. As I said, the buzzards are circling."

Chapter 42

Sofia closed the door of her apartment while clutching her new suitcase and a small handbag. She walked over to the balustrade and looked over the railing to the fountain below. She smiled and thought, *The fountain is a nice touch. Too bad it wasn't flowing two years ago.*

She glanced to her left at the director's door. There would be no fond farewell, nor did she desire it. Sofia reasoned that two years in this miserable place was enough. But considering the alternatives, she could have been scrubbing floors on her hands and knees and eating mush like the other poor inmates of this kiddy prison. Even worse, she could have joined her father by being executed or have been sent to the gulag with her mother. Both were dead. That was that.

She was walking away with two leather cases, a new set of clothes, and a university placement for mathematics at Moscow University. All in all, not bad. A secret letter and photograph to a general (an old friend of her father's) had certainly helped. Welcoming her as his new assistant, the general cleared the way with the university's officials.

"Well, Sofia," she murmured to herself, "you have had to crawl for two years—time to walk upright again. Better fountains are waiting."

As Sofia walked down the staircase to the portico, she noticed how quiet it was around the courtyard. She had planned it that way for her departure. At this time of day, the children were studying, the laborers were working, and the insignificant matrons were scheming. She had always enjoyed handing down directives to the old maids. What were they going to do, complain to Uncle K? She despised them—the feeling mutual.

Still, proceeding down the hallway of the portico, the sound of her steps sounded a bit hollow. Sofia would never admit it to anyone, but she felt a tinge of loneliness. She hid it well with her imperious bearing and demeanor, but as she approached the massive wooden door and her exit to freedom, a small knot twisted in her stomach, knowing she was a lost young woman, grasping in the darkness, fearing the unknown. Alone and vulnerable, she was afraid.

Elena heard Sofia's footsteps, and she greeted Sofia just outside the infirmary's doorway.

"Good morning, Sofia, I thought that might be you. I just want to say goodbye and to wish you the best of luck. Someone mentioned that you may get an opportunity to attend college. I am so proud and happy for you. I know you will do well. If your parents were here, I know they would feel the same."

Sofia smiled and caught her emotions before her eyes filled with tears. She was touched that anyone would express kind words at her departure. She slightly lowered her head and replied, "You are very kind, Matron. I will not forget this gesture."

Elena was a little hurt that Sofia did not remember her name, but she continued, "Ursula made this bundle of food for you, and Sergei offered to carry your luggage to the train station and to wait with you until your train leaves for Moscow." Elena saw the hesitation in Sofia's face and added, "Ursula is the cook, and Sergei helps with the maintenance here."

"Yes, yes, of course." Sofia blushed. "The cook and the elderly gentleman. Please thank both of them, but I have already eaten, and a car will be waiting for me outside in just a few minutes."

Elena nodded her head and stepped toward her. "Very well, Sofia, let me give you a hug goodbye." Elena hugged her and kissed her cheek. It so surprised Sofia that anyone would want to do so, untypically, she did not know how to react. She stood perfectly still with her luggage in each hand.

Sofia's voice broke, and she turned her head away quickly. "Thank you, Matron…bless you."

Sofia hurried through the main door and stepped toward the curb. Just as predicted, a car with a red star on the side of the door was waiting for her. Sofia walked to the vehicle, never looking back.

Elena waived goodbye as the car pulled away, watching until it disappeared down the tree-lined street. Elena slowly closed the old wooden door, her heart feeling as heavy as the door. "There she goes," whispered Elena, "a lonely girl with the finest luggage money can buy."

Chapter 43

The head matron knocked firmly on the director's door. She heard a loud voice call out, "Enter." Entering the office, she found the director seated behind his large polished desk. He did not rise to greet her.

"Thank you, Comrade Director, for this meeting. I know how busy you are. With Sofia just leaving, I knew you would be needing a new assistant as soon as possible. But first, a little business matter for you."

The matron slid a sealed envelope across the desk to the director. Without looking inside, he placed the envelope in his top right-hand drawer. The head matron smiled and continued, "We did quite well boosting the orphanage's fund this month."

The director folded his hands on top of his desk and said, "Thank you for your extended efforts to help the orphanage. Now about my assistant, I have been looking over the files, and I think one of the new girls might do nicely. Where did I put their files? Oh yes, an Esmeralda and the Anya girl who came here recently with Comrade Matron Elena. What do you think?"

The head matron could barely contain her excitement. She exclaimed, "My thoughts exactly! The girl named Anya would be perfect as your assistant. She likes new challenges, she works hard, and she's quite pretty, in a natural sort of way—the perfect choice!"

"Actually, Head Matron, I am so busy I think that I need two assistants. Both of these girls seem suitable."

"Comrade Director, I know how busy you are, but this Esmeralda is the finest seamstress we have ever had. Much of the orphanage's increase in funds are because of her garments. Surely the Anya girl can work hard enough to replace Sofia."

"Head Matron, that is part of the problem. Sofia was an excellent assistant, but toward the end of her stay, she became, shall we say, a little too self-important for her own good. With two assistants sharing duties, I think everyone will be happier, and more will be accomplished."

The head matron frowned. Things were not going as she had planned. Esmeralda was a gold mine.

"Comrade Director, perhaps a compromise would be helpful. Why not rotate your new assistants each month? One month Esmeralda can work for you, and the next month she can continue her sewing. Anya can take her place for that month and still help Matron Elena in the infirmary when it is Esmeralda's turn. This way, they can share the work as your assistants and still fulfill their current duties. They can live together next to you in Sofia's old quarters and be available, when needed, to complete their new duties."

"An excellent idea, Head Matron—the perfect solution! Today is Friday. I must be gone the entire weekend. Have them begin Monday. We will start with Esmeralda for this month. I need some new suits and shirts. Send her to my office Monday morning, and I will explain her duties to her. This Anya girl can begin next month. Well, that's settled. Please see that everything is arranged as soon as possible."

The head matron quietly closed the office door behind her. She walked past Sofia's old room with a smug smile. The meeting did not go exactly as she had planned, but she salvaged it in the end. Money would continue to flow, people would be humbled, everyone would know her place—not a bad exchange overall. The matron was eager to tell the two girls of their "promotion" and to rub Matron Elena's face into the stark reality of who was in charge. Descending the staircase, a sudden wind caused her stiff black dress to flow on each side like gigantic wings. Esmeralda was correct: finally the buzzards had landed.

****

Rumors spread quickly in any institution, especially in an orphanage where life is spent more intimately and in such close proximity. The other girls were beginning to distance themselves from Anya and Esmeralda. Change and the unknown often press not only wild creatures but people into faraway corners.

The new estrangement affected Esmeralda more than Anya since Esmeralda was always in close contact with the girls in the sewing room, especially the younger children. When she was showing them how to sew, some of the little ones would pat her hand, look into her face, and call her "mommy." It never failed to bring tears to her eyes.

Anya and Esmeralda agreed to meet at the fountain to discuss the situation. It was an opportune time since all the staff planned to be gone for the weekend in their quest for buying, selling, and escaping. Sister Elena and Ursula remained to care for the children. There would be no picnic this Sunday; no one had the heart for it.

Esmeralda loved the fountain as much as Anya. Esmeralda often exclaimed, "Listening to its happy voice makes me happy as well!" For Anya, the fountain represented kindness and a new life, a flowing inner strength.

Esmeralda spoke first, "Sister Elena is beside herself. She and the head matron had a fierce argument. It almost came to blows. Sister Elena said that she would report everything, regardless of the consequences, if the decisions were not canceled. The head matron was so furious she raised her stick to strike Elena. The director came down the stairs to leave for the weekend, so they both settled down and went their separate ways. I sense bad things are about to happen."

"Let's just take new clothes from the sewing room and leave," suggested Anya. "We both know how to live off the land."

"Anya, how far do you think two well-dressed, barefooted girls with no money are going to get before the authorities arrest us. We would be lucky to escape for even a few days before being captured. Our next stop would be to the local jail, followed by prison or a work camp. Let's not leap from a hot pan into the fire."

"All right, we decline the position—and if forced, we refuse to work. We take the stick until they play out. They aren't going to kill us. I have a few scars. I can take a few more."

Esmeralda smiled and took Anya's hand. "My brave and fearless Anya. You look life in the face and charge straight at it. You would make an incredible soldier but a poor politician. Perhaps you can endure the stick and carry the scars, but most of us cannot. You are fiercely loyal but innocently naïve. You have not seen much of the world. Perhaps I have seen too much, always one group trying to force its will on another. There has to be a better way—in this life or in the life to come."

"Well, we still have two days, Esmeralda. We can talk to Sister Elena and ask her advice. The three of us can form some sort of a plan. I just know it."

Esmeralda lowered her eyes and said, "All we would do is to destroy Elena, along with ourselves. Then where would the children be without her? It will take something dramatic to bring about any change—of what, I do not know."

"In any case, Esmeralda, let's meet here tomorrow morning at dawn before everyone rises. Sister Elena won't mind, and we will find a way. Don't be discouraged. We will think of something."

Esmeralda gently kissed Anya's cheek and walked down the long portico. Anya faced the fountain and touched the water cascading into the basin. She watched Esmeralda turn a corner and disappear. Sergei's "little bird" had lost her song.

*****

That night, Esmeralda awoke from her sleep and saw a ray of moonlight shining through a small window. She sat up in bed and watched the blue-white light edge toward her bed. It was as if it were calling her.

Esmeralda quietly left her room and went to the fountain courtyard to better witness a full moon rising. She enjoyed watching the soft light dance among the water droplets of the fountain. As the great moon climbed higher, Esmeralda remembered the splendid view from the tower. She slowly strolled across the courtyard toward the tower, allowing the light of the moon to be her guide.

The key was in its hidden compartment, exactly where Sister Elena had left it. Esmeralda opened the door, and a stream of soft light filled the entryway. She felt her heart beat faster in anticipation of the wonderful sight that awaited her as she ascended step by step to reach the tower.

Such a beautiful, clear night! The autumnal air was crisp and delicious, as if it were being served at an elegant banquet. Every breath was invigorating and precious.

The moon was above the horizon spreading its glowing wings in every direction. Esmeralda reflected how important the full moon was to the Romany people. It was more than an atmospheric wonder. To them, it was a guide and a friend. Every full moon ushered a new celebration of life: a festival, a wedding, a dance, a song, even a move to a new location in the heat of the summer—always with its gentle guiding hand.

The moonlight was spreading from the east and crossing the vast sea, one delicate step at a time, as if it were dancing on the waves. Every crest it touched sparkled like diamonds thrown before its feet.

The new light eventually reached the tower, as if the heavens had placed a deliberate spotlight to reach Esmeralda and the large bell beside her. Esmeralda lifted her chin and bathed in the moonlight. A sudden warmth flooded her body. She had not felt warm in a long time.

Wouldn't it be wonderful to walk upon this beam of light, a moonbeam leading across the sea, across the sky, across the moon itself, where her parents were already celebrating, waiting, beckoning?

Esmeralda touched the old bell and remembered the last words of the poem that Sister Elena had recited on that special day in this special tower: "for whom the bell tolls…it tolls for thee." The moon, the bell, the tower—yes, each "tolled" for her.

The moon was calling. It shone forth a clear, new path. Esmeralda removed her dirty brown smock and tossed it under the bell. Her body glowed in the moonlight. She closed her eyes and felt the sea breeze caress her face. Lifting her arms straight to the sky, she dove from the tower into the waiting arms of the moon—to enter a new world, a different planet, an old life once left behind. Once again, Sergei's little bird found her voice—and her wings.

CHAPTER 44

Sunday morning at dawn, Anya waited for Esmeralda at the fountain, as agreed. It was a beautiful, crisp morning with a spectacular sunrise, fingers of gold and red spread across the sky. Anya thought it to be a good sign, the herald of a new day—a new beginning.

Anya still believed that with Sister Elena's support and Esmeralda's cooperation, a firm stance could be taken and a solution to their situation finalized. All that was needed was a united front.

When the sun peered over the horizon, Anya became concerned. It wasn't like Esmeralda to be late, especially for something as important as this. Anya did not see her in the dormitory when she left, so Esmeralda must be in some room nearby.

After an hour of searching each wing of the facility, Anya finally found Sister Elena and reported, "Esmeralda is missing. The front gate is locked, and the walls are too high to climb. She must be here somewhere. I feel something is wrong."

Sister Elena thought a moment and asked, "Did you check the bell tower? Esmeralda loved the view from up there. It's a quiet place to go and think. She knows where the key is hidden. Don't worry, we will find her."

Anya and Elena hurried across the courtyard lawn and turned the corner to the bell tower. The oval door was slightly ajar, with the key still in the lock. Anya called for Esmeralda, but there was no answer.

"Anya, check the tower. I will search the east side where there is a small spring covered with wildflowers. It's a lovely spot. Perhaps she is there?"

When Anya entered the bell tower and saw Esmeralda's dress crumpled underneath the bell, she knew something dreadful had happened. At the same time, she heard a sound below that resembled the cry of a wounded animal: a rumbling moan that slowly increased until it reached its full crescendo.

Anya looked down from the tower and saw Esmeralda lying facedown in a grove of thick grass and wildflowers beside a trickling spring. Sister Elena was sitting beside her, gently rocking back and forth, holding Esmeralda's hand, beseeching the silent form to emerge from her deep slumber.

The tallgrass and spongy ground had cushioned Esmeralda's flight for freedom, but it also snapped her neck. Looking down from the tower, it appeared as though someone had laced a garland of red wildflowers in Esmeralda's pretty brown hair. Occasionally, a breeze moved the long soft hair across her still back. Anya thought she looked like a resting nymph next to a flowing spring, something from one of Vladimir's books—books from another lifetime, feelings expended long ago.

Sister Elena carefully placed Esmeralda's hand on the ground, and she rushed across the courtyard out of sight. Anya remained in the tower looking down at her lovely friend. The realization struck her that this would be the only true sister she would ever know. For just a few moments longer, Anya wanted to embrace the beauty of the tower rather than the ugly reality that awaited below.

Sister Elena returned with an armful of clothes. She looked up at the tower and said, "Anya, if you can hear me, come down and help me. There is one last kindness we can do for her." Elena unfolded a beautiful white dress with red roses embroidered throughout the white fabric. Esmeralda had just finished sewing it on Friday. She was its maker. Now she was its owner.

Elena and Anya reverently dressed Esmeralda in her beautiful creation. The white background, the roses, the wildflowers in a framework of lush green—it almost seemed like a fairy-tale dream.

Elena took off her shoes and placed them on Esmeralda's shapely feet. She wiped a tear off her cheek and exclaimed, "I won't have this young girl leave here barefooted in a brown stained flour-sack rag...never, never, never!" Kind and loving Sister Elena smoothed the lovely dress, stroked Esmeralda's hair one last time, and began to weep.

****

Three men came around the corner. A tall, slender man with silver-gray hair carried a black leather satchel. The doctor leaned down and touched Esmeralda's neck. He sadly shook his head and motioned for the other two men carrying a stretcher to come forward. The two men lowered the stretcher, and one reached for a coarse green blanket to cover the young girl. Sister Elena touched his arm and gave him a fine linen sheet. Some of the stitching wasn't quite straight along the hem; nevertheless, it was pure linen, one of Esmeralda's training projects—teaching the little ones to sew. Now it was her shroud.

Anya could not bear anymore. As they unfolded the sheet, Anya walked away and returned to the top of the tower. She needed a view, something beyond walls and sorrow. She needed answers. Before the men had arrived, Elena had asked her, "Why, Anya? Why would she do this?"

Anya had replied, "To save you, to save me, to save the children. She knew this would cause an investigation from the authorities. She wanted all of our voices to be heard. In her own way, she sang for us all."

Anya looked south from the tower and witnessed the three men crossing the courtyard lawn, proceeding toward the fountain. Elena walked slowly behind the linen-draped stretcher; her bare feet made small indentions in the grass.

Anya angrily snatched the brown smock from under the bell and easily ripped the threadbare dress down the center. In her frustration, she shoved the bell; and as it swung back and forth, she heard a faint metallic click coming from inside the bell. The Russian soldiers had removed the iron clapper. What could make that sound?

Looking inside the bell, she saw an iron bar at the top which once held the clapper. In the top corner above the bar, she discovered a broken bayonet that had snapped in two when they had used it to pry the clapper from the bell. She centered herself inside the bell, leaped up, and grabbed the iron bar with both hands. Carefully twisting the bayonet with Esmeralda's tattered dress wrapped around her hand, she finally wrenched it loose. Rubbing her thumb across the pointed tip and the two edges of the blade, Anya found it still remarkably sharp.

Anya looked down and saw the scratch marks where the Russian soldiers had cut the bell rope to carry it away. She took the brown dress and placed it along the same edges so as not to produce any new marks. Slowly, she trimmed the lower hem from the dress using the sharp bayonet. She tied the wide strip of cloth around her upper-right thigh. The broken bayonet fit perfectly in her homemade sheath; her formless brown smock concealed it perfectly.

Anya practiced drawing the bayonet from its cloth holster as fast as she could—flashing iron emerged in the blink of an eye. The blade required only a small handle to be complete. Anya placed her new weapon back into its sheath, raised Esmeralda's torn dress above her head, and said with determination, "Esmeralda, Monday morning we will both meet the director and the wretched head matron. Trust me, dear sister, both our voices *will* be heard—one way or another."

Anya walked to the northern edge of the tower to take one last view of the vista that Esmeralda loved to ponder. She threw the remainder of the brown dress as far as she could. A crosswind carried it, like a kite, across the wildflowers and the spring, over the wall, and into the rushing river below that flowed to the sea.

Chapter 45

Monday morning arrived gray and cloudy with a light drizzling rain. It was as if even the heavens were mourning the loss of Esmeralda. Anya's mood matched the day. She looked across the room and just stared at Esmeralda's empty bed. It seemed so cold and lonely.

She walked over and sat down on the bed. There was Esmeralda's number etched into the frame. Anya thought, *A number attached to a name. Is that all we are in this place?* She ran her hand along the mattress and lifted the pillow to her face. The pillow still retained Esmeralda's fragrance: warm and clean.

The entire orphanage was subdued over the loss of Esmeralda. There was no happy chatter, especially among the younger children. Esmeralda had been their entire world. All they could say was, "We've lost again."

Anya needed some fresh air, so she walked to the fountain and dipped her hands into the water. She touched her face, and the refreshing water ran down her arms onto her stained dress. Across the fountain, she saw a light in Sergei's workshop. The door was slightly open. Yes, wise old Sergei was just the comfort she needed.

"Sergei, may I come in?"

"Yes, of course, child. Enter Santa's workshop. I just finished this carving on Friday. It was to be a Christmas gift for our little bird…who sings no more."

Sergei handed Anya a wooden figurine that was a tree with intricate branches and a lovely songbird resting on a limb with its small beak open, as if it were singing. On the trunk of the tree, Sergei had delicately carved the name *Esmeralda*.

"As I told you on the day we fixed the fountain, I always try to have a little gift for all the girls at Christmastime. I don't have much money, so I carve little animals from bits of wood that I find here and there. They're not much, but everyone enjoys a little gift now and then. The carvings for the little children don't take much time. They are happy with anything. I try to do something special for the older girls since they have so much more required of them. Christmas is just around the corner. It's still autumn, but winter is coming."

Anya held the pretty figurine in the palm of her hand. She asked, "Sergei, would you mind if I kept this for a few days? It is beautiful, and it reminds me of her."

"Keep it forever. I think she would want you to have it." With misty eyes, Sergei quickly turned his head and looked away. He became silent and continued carving on his next gift.

Anya left the workshop. She could tell that Sergei needed to be alone. She returned to the fountain, where she and Esmeralda had met for the last time. She looked at the figurine with Esmeralda's name on it. Anya placed her hand over the trunk of the tree. It lay perfectly across the palm of her hand. She had found the handle for her bayonet. She slowly opened her fingers and looked down at Esmeralda's name etched in the wood. Listening to the falling water, she turned toward the fountain and said, "Esmeralda, when I meet with the director and the head matron today, you will be with me. Sergei was right—winter is coming."

Walking to the empty infirmary to get some medical tape to attach her new handle onto the bayonet, Anya could not have known that old Sergei was working on her wood carving. Sergei knew her past. He was making a crouching tiger.

****

Anya left the infirmary without being seen. She felt the bayonet with its new handle next to her leg. It made her smile. She encountered the head matron descending the staircase, who was just leaving the director's office. The matron was livid.

"Mountain girl, wait right there. The director wants to see you in thirty minutes. I just don't believe this. I leave for two days, and this place falls apart. Because of your little friend's dramatic farewell, an investigator from Child Services will be making an inquiry this afternoon. You and precious Elena will have a great deal to answer for—about this...this...gypsy-girl thing. If I have my way, darling Elena will be dismissed and transferred to a rough little place down the road, and you, my troublemaker, will be sent to a work camp for criminal delinquents." The matron smirked and continued, "Until then, you will have to be the director's only assistant, and you will be required to complete your other duties as well. That should keep your hands busy. Thirty minutes. We don't want to keep the director waiting, now do we?"

Anya glared at the matron with artic eyes and asked, "Will you also be there, Head Matron? I know the director will want to ask for your advice."

The matron ignored her and walked away.

Anya knew that the matron's fury was not about the loss of a young girl's life but the loss of profits from the young girl's life. Anya looked up at the director's door and said, "Don't worry, Mr. and Mrs. *Krokodile*, I won't be late." Anya returned to Esmeralda's bed and hugged the stiff pillow. She buried her face into the pillow and softly repeated, "Time to go, Esmeralda. Time for you to sing once again."

****

Anya firmly knocked on the director's door. She did not wait for an answer but immediately entered the office. It surprised the director. He momentarily frowned but recovered quickly and, with a sloppy smile, motioned for Anya to come near his desk.

"Well, well, you are early—always a nice trait. I see you brought your pillow. Your room, next door, should be ready this afternoon."

"It's not my pillow. It belonged to Esmeralda."

"Oh yes. Poor thing. Such a tragedy! She must have been very depressed. Well, these things happen. We just have to move on, don't we?"

Anya could barely control her anger. His flippant words and eager smile made her blood boil. She felt the hair on her arms and head beginning to rise. She realized that this was a time to be calm, but her sense of justice compelled her to proceed.

"I thought the head matron was to join us. I know she has much to say."

"I told her that her services would not be needed. We have much to do in the next few days. Don't you agree?"

"I'm glad you said that, Director. As your new assistant, I have prepared a list of recommendations to improve the orphanage. I think the head matron calls it 'initiative.'"

Anya tossed the sheet onto the wide desk, and it slid in front of the director's chest. The director's smile was beginning to fade.

"Very well, let's see what you have here:

- —Better food with more protein
- —Warm uniforms for each child
- —Year-round footwear, appropriate for the season
- —Fresh towels, sheets, and pillowcases for each bed."

The director's smile was gone, but he continued:

"—A raise for Matron Elena, Sergei, and Ursula since they truly run the place
- —The termination of Matron Svelte for drunkenness
- —The termination of the head matron for cruelty to children and the theft of orphanage funds

—The installation of Matron Elena as the new overall supervisor
　　　—The hiring of adult assistants who actually know how to type."

The director lowered the sheet of paper and glared at his new assistant. The muscles on both sides of his neck began to flex as he clenched his jaws. Tossing the paper into his wastebasket, he said, "Very interesting, Assistant Anya. Please tell me why I would want to do this."

Anya returned his stare and replied, "Because it is the right thing to do, because there will be an investigation this afternoon, and because of this."

Anya took the pillow and located a hidden zipper. She opened the fabric and removed a classroom notebook.

"Your haughty head matron thought Esmeralda was a backward 'little gypsy girl' that she could use in order to make money. Esmeralda was actually smarter than all of you. This notebook lists every piece of clothing that left this place. The head matron was so greedy that she never let Esmeralda leave the sewing room. Esmeralda saw it all and secretly recorded everything: item, date removed, black-market value. Esmeralda's people bought, sold, and bartered every day. Knowing the price of something was a matter of survival for them. When the inspector comes this afternoon, acting as the new assistant, I will give him this book and request a full investigation as to the money received but not listed in the orphanage's account. I will also ask him to review the treatment of the children, along with my own statement of why a young girl would rather take her own life than to be your assistant."

The director slowly raised himself and walked to the right of his desk. Anya placed the notebook back into the pillow and zipped it shut. She kept the desk between herself and the director.

The director ignored her and walked over to his office door. He removed a skeleton key from his pocket and calmly locked the door. He then took his time and opened a large window which faced the opposite of the courtyard to an empty space near the gray wall.

"Of course, my clever assistant, without your little book, it would be your word and the tragic accident of a homeless orphan against that of a director and an officer of the state."

The director's huge form was edging closer with each step around the room. Anya could see the anger building in his red cheeks and pulsating neck. If he ever got his massive arms around her, he would crush her to death. Anya positioned herself much like when she had fought another beast long ago. She kept the stone wall to her left and the wide desk to her right. This two-legged beast would have to attack from the right to reach her. The charge would come soon.

"Of course, it will be hard to explain why another poor girl leaped to her death so soon after one did so yesterday. But I am sure that I can convince the Child Services that you, Anya, being such a close friend, could not stand the loss and so you chose to join her. Since we are only two stories high in this office, it will be essential for you to also have a broken neck before you leap from that window." The director looked at his massive hands and nodded, "Yes, I think the edge of this desk will do nicely…and then, I'll help you through the window."

The director made his charge with savage swiftness. He knew how to use his bulk and strength to trap a foe. He had done it many times to other victims. This young girl would snap like a willow, he thought.

Anya crouched down on her left knee and raised the pillow with her left hand. In all the commotion, she heard a faint voice echoing in her mind, *Anya, wait for the charge. Be calm. When he is upon you, aim for his left eye. You have only one shot. You will know when it is the time.*

The director smiled when he witnessed the young girl cringing on the floor. He lunged at her with both hands, curled like claws, ready to seize and crush her. She had even raised the pillow and notebook as an offering of peace. "Too late, clever girl, too late!" he roared.

When the director made his mad charge, something overcame Anya: a fierce desire, longing for battle; memories of Esmeralda lying naked on the ground, wildflowers laced in her lovely brown hair, a purple ring around her broken neck—death's necklace, the orphanage's collar; a bell ringing, "tolling for thee"; an executioner's broken blade, a beast that must be destroyed. Just as the director leaned over to grab her, Anya tossed the pillow into his face. He momentarily lost his concentration when he caught the pillow, containing the incriminating evidence, now in his hands. Anya saw the hesitation, and with lightning speed, she rose from her crouched position and thrust the bayonet with all her force from her right side—straight into his face. An explosion of hot blood and eye fluid sprayed into her face and blonde hair. The bayonet was lodged in the director's left eye. Only Esmeralda's figurine handle could be seen writhing in the air. It appeared as though a tree was swaying in the wind with a small bird singing its song—while a shower of red rain covered them both.

The stunned director staggered and fell beside the desk. He touched the wooden handle, but the blade was lodged underneath his eye socket. Already, his brain was preparing to die.

Anya looked down at her red hands as the blood dripped down her face and arms onto her loathsome dress. She thought the running stains made her look as if she were wearing the red stripes of a tiger. She glanced at the director lying on his back on the hardwood floor. His heart was still beating; she could see a little red fountain of blood squirt around the bayonet with each beat. She would let him bleed to death. Anya had learned from bitter experience that a wounded beast in its death throes can still be dangerous. She had four red scars on her side to prove it.

While Anya waited for the head matron to arrive, she opened the windows that viewed the courtyard. The fountain displayed clear water instead of blood. A thick red puddle slowly expanded around the director. Soon that would end. She calmly rested her bloodstained hands on the window ledge. She remembered Esmeralda at the fountain, the beautiful white dress and the red wildflowers in her friend's lovely soft hair. She glanced at the director's still body and smiled. Esmeralda's figurine looked as if it had grown straight out of his eye. The little carved bird was now a blood-red cardinal—its beak still open for its song.

Anya walked toward the director. He was barely breathing. She knelt over him and spoke into the red bird's ear, "Esmeralda, they will hear your voice. I will make sure of it. Now it's time to punish the beast. Won't the head matron be surprised?"

CHAPTER 46

Late that afternoon, the head matron and an inspector from the Soviet State Children's Bureau came to the director's office. The head matron knocked several times, but there was no answer. Finally, she used her own key to unlock the door and enter the sanctum. They took only a few steps when the head matron shrieked, and the dazed inspector stumbled backward in shock.

Anya sat behind the director's desk calmly leafing through a stack of files. She was covered with dried blood from head to toe. It was difficult to even distinguish the color of her hair. Her blue eyes blazed at them behind a red mask. The director's mutilated body lay in front of the desk in a pool of black blood. Flies were already gathering around the man's face in what looked to be a pile of dark pudding.

Anya motioned with her black hand for them to come closer and, with a cheerful voice, announced, "Welcome! I've been waiting for both of you. You will have to excuse my appearance. The director was still alive when I began removing his claws. It created quite a stir, as you can imagine. I was going to wait until he bled to death, but I became impatient. His fingers were very thick. I think I have ruined my dress.

"Head Matron, I was very disappointed when you did not attend the meeting. I so wanted to ask you about a few things that I have found in these files. Perhaps this comrade can extract that information when he puts you in prison. As you can see, I have been very busy on my first day as the new assistant. There will be new leadership here at the orphanage. I convinced the director to retire. In fact, he is quite dead. I would also like to permanently retire the head matron, but I think being treated like a slave and receiving a good beating every day in prison is a more appropriate justice for her."

The head matron and the inspector were so stunned by the macabre setting and Anya's appearance that they were unable to move or speak. Anya's calm monotone delivery was even more frightening than if she had been screaming at them. Anya sensed their absolute shock. She was pleased and decided to continue.

"Comrade Inspector, I have some files that will help you with your investigation. The head matron thought I was only an ignorant girl from the mountains. I am actually quite good in science, mathematics, and as you can see, anatomy. In another life, I had a medical book. I studied it every night."

Anya picked up two files in manila folders and tossed them to the front of the desk. She pointed at the files with a bloodstained finger and said, "These files show the income and expenses of the orphanage. You will find that there is very little left in the income column at the end of each month. The small notebook beside them is the actual income listed by date, item, and price that was recorded by one called Esmeralda before the late director and our head matron coerced her, which resulted in her death. I do not know how the additional money was spent. However, I imagine the director lying before you and the head matron standing beside you received most of it. What we have here, Comrade Inspector, are predators in a den of thieves. Esmeralda died because of it, and I have killed in spite of it. We both did so to get your attention. Now—what are you going to do about it?"

A deafening silence reigned over the room. The shock of it all and the stark effrontery of the accusations silenced everyone. The head matron's survival instincts rushed to the surface, and she spoke first, "Inspector, come with me. This girl is a mad cold-blooded killer. We are going to call the police." She grabbed the inspector's arm and almost pushed him out of the doorway. The matron stopped for just a moment and stared at Esmeralda's notebook on the desk. Anya slowly shook her head and essentially dared her to try and reach for the book. The matron glanced at the director's body and realized that if she tried, she would most certainly join him. Better to risk losing the record than losing her life, better to retreat to fight another day.

Just like an animal in the wild, after making its selection, Anya's intense gaze never left the matron: following her across the room, beckoning with her encrusted black hand for the skittish, frightened woman to come closer—hoping, dreaming, craving for that moment of the quick kill. The matron slammed the door behind her, and with trembling hands, she frantically locked the door, as if a dangerous creature might escape from its cage. She ran after the inspector with an anxious ashen face, sensing that she had caused something primordial and terrifying to be unleashed, realizing that born out of that black pool of blood, a new predator had emerged—measuring, stalking, patiently waiting—and that she was marked forever as its prey.

****

The Vladivostok chief of police decided his presence was warranted for the unusual call that was placed at Vladivostok Central: a state employee, a director, had been viciously killed and mutilated. The inspector of Child Services had seemed rather frantic. The chief believed that most crime reports were exaggerated. He would soon learn—this one was not.

Anya heard the sirens as the cars approached the orphanage. It sounded as if there were two cars. They did not need the show of force. She was not going anywhere: no place to escape, no desire to leave. The most important items for the investigation were on the desk in front of her: the files and Esmeralda's notebook. If she left, both would be destroyed by the head matron. No, the die was cast. Time to see it through to the bitter end.

The head matron greeted the chief and three additional police officers. She gave the chief her key to the office and said, "I'm not going back in there until you have captured that wild animal!"

The chief handed the key to his lieutenant and replied, "Don't worry. According to the inspector, it is just a young girl. She won't be hard to handle."

The head matron shook her head and pointed to the second floor. She nervously exclaimed, "I wouldn't be so sure of that, Comrade Chief! She has a knife, and she knows how to use it! It's good you and your men are armed! My advice is to just storm the room and shoot her!"

The lieutenant unlocked the door and shoved it open as quickly as possible. Two police officers rushed through the door with their pistols drawn. The chief and the lieutenant followed them once the room was secured.

The chief was a hardened twenty-year veteran of the police force, but even he was shocked at the sight before him. The young girl was calmly sitting behind a large desk completely covered in dried blood. In front of the desk, the ex-director was indeed very dead, and certain body parts were missing. Pooled blood encircled the desk, as if the desk were an island surrounded by a black sea. The air was rancid, even with all the windows open.

The chief turned his head and whispered to the lieutenant, "Once she is handcuffed, send one man down to get the camera. Photograph everything. You and the other officer will collect evidence. I want every file and piece of paper in this office. Call in extra help if you need it. Let me see if she will come quietly. If not, shoot her."

The chief walked two steps toward the desk and asked in a fatherly manner, "Can you speak? Would you tell me your name?"

"Yes, comrade, I can talk. My name is Anya. Since you have come to investigate, I have a gift for you: these two files and this little book. They will show you everything you need to know. The other files are just employees' and orphans' personal records. These two are evidence. I've been guarding them for you."

"Thank you, Anya. I will certainly place them in evidence." The chief cautiously took another step toward her. "What is that necklace you're wearing? It is most unusual."

"It is the director's eight fingers and two thumbs. I tied them with a strip of this pitiful flour-sack rag that they make us wear. I once did this to a four-legged animal who attacked me. I decided to do the same to this two-legged beast who did the same."

"Anya, do you mind just placing your necklace on the desk in front of you and then slowly walk to the side of the desk, always showing us your hands. You seem like a smart girl. You know you have to come with us, don't you?"

Anya removed the bloody trophy from her neck. She carefully arranged the left digits to rest on top of the two orphanage files, which revealed all the financial records for the orphanage and a list of all proceeds from the black-market scheme. The right digits were placed on Esmeralda's notebook.

"There, comrade, the fingers point the way! I don't want you to miss the evidence. It probably won't make any difference, but he tried to kill me. He didn't want his crimes known. He told me that once he had broken my neck, he was going to throw my body through that window behind you. He mentioned all this with a smile. You judge which of us had the better reason to kill."

"And this butchery, young lady, how do justify that?"

"Unnecessary but fulfilling," Anya coldly replied.

Two officers handcuffed Anya's hands behind her back. The lieutenant put on his leather gloves and firmly squeezed Anya's left arm. Another officer took hold of her right arm, and they proceeded through the door to a police car waiting for them on the street.

An officer photographed the macabre crime scene from every possible angle. When he reached the desk, he paused in disbelief and said, "Chief, I think you should come and see this." The photographer stepped back for the chief to view the top of the desk. Carved in large deep block letters on the fine teak desk was one word: *B-E-A-S-T!* Each letter of the word was hyphenated with one of the director's four white incisor teeth. Anya's homemade dagger was stabbed into the desk next to the last letter to make a definite exclamation point for her statement. The chief had never witnessed anything like this. He muttered to himself, "What kind of creature would do this? What happened to this girl to make her do these things?"

The photographer nervously called out again, "Chief, one other thing." The officer pointed to the head of the corpse. "Chief, look closely at the bloody wound in the left eye. It's hard to see."

The chief placed a white handkerchief over his nose, leaned down, and examined the ragged flesh. Lodged in the eye socket, there was a small wooden bird with its beak open—as if it were about to sing.

CHAPTER 47

KGB Colonel Viktor Kurgan entered his private office at Moscow Center. He had just returned from an early morning briefing. His desk sergeant (and acting assistant) followed him into the office and handed him a folder with a broad red stripe slanted over the front cover.

"Colonel, I think you should see this. It just arrived from Vladivostok. It is in regard to one Anya Ruslanova. You had her name red-flagged some time ago."

The colonel took the file and asked, "Briefly, Sergeant, what is the situation?"

"It involves mutilation and murder, sir. It appears that she practically butchered the director of the orphanage where she resided. The mutilation occurred while the director was still alive. I'm afraid it gets even worse: she made his body parts into a necklace."

The colonel scanned the crime report and ordered, "Sergeant, contact the Vladivostok chief of police. Inform him that the KGB is going to take over this case. I will meet with him this afternoon. I want the accused placed into an isolation cell, and no one is to talk to her without my permission. Arrange air transport to Vladivostok and have my driver here in twenty minutes."

"Yes, Colonel, I'll make those calls right now. By the way, what do you think will happen to her?"

The colonel continued reading the file and replied, "Well, Sergeant, if you must know, she will probably be interrogated, tried, and shot. No more questions. Get things moving."

When the sergeant left, the colonel muttered to himself, "Vladimir, old friend, your little girl has gotten herself into a lot of trouble."

****

The chief of police met the colonel at a private airstrip just outside Vladivostok. A green sedan waited by the hangar. Both men shook hands and entered the backseat of the car.

"You are certainly a man of your word, Colonel. I didn't expect to see you for a couple of days. Your sergeant said that you would arrive this afternoon, but I didn't believe him."

"This is an unusual case, and I have some interest in it. Has she been isolated?"

"Everything has been done as you requested. No one has spoken to her or to the staff of the orphanage. I was going to do that today, until I received the call from your sergeant. You mentioned 'an unusual case.' I've never seen anything quite like it. However, it seems to be an open-and-shut case. She freely admits that she did it."

"Chief, I thought you said she was not questioned."

"Colonel, we found her next to a dead man with his severed fingers draped around her neck, and she stated clearly that she had killed him in self-defense—all this before she was even arrested. She said that she wanted to get everyone's attention. She certainly got mine."

"What evidence did you gather?"

"We found the murder weapon, fingerprints, body parts, and several boxes of files. We thoroughly photographed the crime scene, the victim, and the accused. Everything is waiting for you at the station."

"Thank you, Chief. It does appear to be a straightforward case. I will review the evidence first, then question her."

"Will the interrogation be hard or soft, Comrade Colonel?"

"That will depend upon her attitude... Comrade Chief."

The chief had no more questions. He didn't really want to know what would happen to this troubled girl once the KGB was finished with her. The chief quickly glanced at the colonel. The KGB officer had a faraway look in his steel-gray eyes. His hand rested on a black leather holster. Both men stared straight ahead, thinking their own thoughts as they passed through the countryside. The remainder of the journey was met with silence.

****

It took the colonel only a few hours to go over the files and evidence to obtain a clear picture of the recent events, the staff, and the occupants in the orphanage. He was gifted with the ability to accurately read people and to separate the "wheat from the chaff" from their words and actions. It was one of the many reasons he was considered a "rising star" in the KGB.

"Comrade Chief, thank you for your assistance. I've kept the most essential files and photographs. You may return the remaining files to the orphanage. After I question the accused, I will make a final report and a recommendation. The case will be closed by the end of the day."

"Colonel, I appreciate your efficiency, but how can the murder of a state employee, a director, be closed in one afternoon?"

"The girl in custody may be insane, but she is not stupid." The colonel removed three bloodstained documents from his black briefcase and placed them on the chief's desk. "It's all right there. I just don't know how they split the money."

"I've met the supervising matron, Colonel. She is a clever old witch. She will contend that she turned over all the money that she received to the director for the upkeep of the orphanage. The director did all the accounting. She will maintain her innocence, and essentially, it will be the presence of a dead man, the record of a suicidal girl, and the word of a murderer in our cell that the old matron was involved. The matron and the director were up to their ears in graft, and probably abuse, but it will be hard to prove."

The colonel replaced the stained files back into his briefcase. He looked intensely at the chief and replied, "I'm going pay a visit to this matron at the orphanage before I leave for Moscow. I feel certain that we will reach an understanding."

"Fine, Colonel. This is your investigation. May I ask when I will receive the final report so that I can close the case?"

"Good question! Why not now? No need to procrastinate. The report for your file will be as follows: 'The director of the orphanage was distraught over the suicide of one of the children in his care. He knew that an inspector from Child Services was about to make an inquiry regarding the incident. He became depressed, feeling responsible that he should have prevented the tragedy. In the end, he chose to take his life. Finding: death by suicide. Case closed.'"

The chief sprang to his feet and angrily retorted, "Colonel, you can't be serious. You want a report that states a man made a homemade dagger, stabbed the blade into his eye and, while he was bleeding to death, proceeded to cut off his fingers while placing a wooden bird into his eye socket? This is preposterous."

"Yes, Chief, that's about it. Dramatic, isn't it?"

The chief looked out of his window onto the street. It was another gray sky that matched his mood. He knew he was defeated, but he had to ask, "Colonel, in your scenario, when the sad director sliced off his own fingers, did he wrap them and present them as a gift?"

"Really, Chief! Sarcasm does not become you. As I said, this was a very troubled man. What is your point?"

"My point, Comrade Colonel, is that how does one adequately explain how his fingers came to be dangling from the neck of the bloodstained girl we currently have locked in a cage downstairs? We have photographs."

"Actually, Comrade Chief of Police of Vladivostok—you don't. Any pictures of her are locked in this briefcase. I took the liberty of burning any matching negatives."

The colonel walked toward the window and stiffly pointed at the chief's cluttered desk.

"Sit down, Chief of Police—do it now. Listen carefully. The niceties are over. You will write that report exactly as I stated. The inspector of Child Services will sign the report, just as you will. The inspector will deliver any documents in Child Services referring to the accused to me, personally, within the hour. I have the files from the orphanage. This girl does not have a birth certificate. There is not even an exact birthdate. I have come to the conclusion that she was never born. Thus, she never entered an orphanage. She never was here in this fair city. Consequentially, she could not have committed said crime. As far as the world is concerned—she never existed."

The chief sat bewildered at his desk. Only the KGB could make a hideous crime and a person disappear in one afternoon.

"When the inspector arrives, receive his documents, and I expect both of your signatures to be on the crime report upon my returning from my little chat with the supervising matron. I just know you will not disappoint me."

"Yes, Colonel, I understand. A suicide—case closed."

Since the whipping was over, the colonel changed his tone, smiled, and announced, "Comrade, it is time to meet your distinguished guest. If you would please assign a guard to lead the way to her abode, I will be forever in your debt."

The chief watched the colonel and a guard, who carried a large ring of keys, as they walked toward the hallway and disappeared down the concrete steps that led to the cells below. The jingling of the keys soon faded away.

The young girl was also going to fade away. The chief wondered which person was the most insane and who should be locked in an isolation cell with the key thrown away: the KGB officer or the one who never existed—the girl who had never been born.

****

Anya heard him coming before she saw him. An empty cell, except for a waste bucket in the corner, amplifies any new sound. His footsteps reminded her of the best predators in the forest: quick, quiet, deadly.

Anya covered her eyes when the heavy iron door creaked open. The light outside was dim but blinding in her dark cell. She slowly raised her hand to allow her eyes to adjust to the invading light. As she sat on the concrete floor, the first thing she noticed was the toe of his polished black boot. The guards did not possess fine boots. She realized that "authority" had just entered her dark corner of the world, and he would probably determine her destiny.

She had come too far to be afraid. She defiantly assessed the tall man standing in the doorway. His crisp black uniform with gold braid fit him perfectly. She had sewn enough at the orphanage to recognize that it was expertly tailored. His premature gray hair made it hard to determine his age—salt-and-pepper, but more salt than pepper. It made him look distinguished. He had that aristocratic "Sofia look" in his bearing. This was not just some desk officer. The tanned face, the faint wrinkles near his temples, like small crow's feet, told a different story. But it was his eyes that revealed the most: steel-gray eyes, piercing eyes, eyes that missed nothing, eyes without mercy—wolf's eyes.

Colonel Viktor Kurgan had seen his share of bloodshed over the years, but the black-and-brown creature sitting in a shaft of light before him made him feel uneasy. Her mantle of dried blood gave off a cordite smell: the scent of gunpowder. Perhaps he was looking at a keg of gunpowder sitting in the corner, just waiting to explode.

Most prisoners would have been afraid. The colonel noticed that this one was not. She dared to stare at his face. He decided it was time to test the mettle. "Prisoner, get up," ordered the colonel. "I wish to question you. Get to your feet."

Anya just remained in the corner, silently staring at him. What could he do, she thought, kill her? She felt that her heart was dead already.

The guard could not restrain himself. He raised his wooden truncheon, walked toward her, and said, "Get up when told, or you'll have more dried blood on you when I'm finished."

The man with the wolf's eyes never stopped looking at Anya; he just firmly gripped the guard's wrist and said, "Get a bucket of water, a large towel, and a female prison uniform. Do it now."

The colonel used his gifted skills to read people. Force was not the answer. An animal trapped in a corner has only two options: cringe or attack. This one would fight to the death. Time for more choices.

"The file lists your name as Anya. Anya, you can either come with me, or when I leave, three guards will return and beat you until you are unconscious. If we leave together, you will be able to say goodbye to your friends, if you have any, at the orphanage. I want to question the senior matron about certain matters I discovered from the files that you gave to the chief of police. I would like to hear your side of the story, describing recent events, as well as the matron's account. Only then will I be able to get a true picture of what occurred. Will you help me?"

The colonel perceived a slight reaction when he mentioned returning to the orphanage. He decided to test his theory. Walking forward, he extended his right hand to help the prisoner to her feet. He could not help but smile when she finally took his hand and clawed with her sharp fingernails into the palm of his hand.

****

The guard returned to Anya's cell with a bucket of water, a towel, and a fresh uniform as ordered. He threw the uniform at Anya with a hateful scowl on his face. He also carried two sets of handcuffs and a chain in his hands.

The colonel picked up the uniform off the cold floor and politely handed it to Anya. He looked into her face completely caked with blood and said, "Anya, it is time for another agreement. As you can see, our efficient guard has two restraining devices and a length of chain. Normally, when a prisoner is transported, her hands and feet are secured and attached together with the chain." The colonel lifted the chain and continued, "When secured, it is difficult to walk, impossible to run. The chaffing around the joints can become raw and painful. Give me your word that you will not run and that you will do as ordered, and we can forego this clumsy procedure."

The colonel tossed the chain to the guard while expertly drawing his pistol from his black holster, chambering a round, and aiming it at Anya's face. The ratcheting sound of the pistol echoed in the small concrete cell. In a calm voice, he said, "Break your word to me, and I will shoot you in the spine, with a concluding shot into your head—without hesitation. The choice is yours."

"Dearest captor, I have no intention of running. Where would I go? As for obeying orders, that will depend on the order. Now the choice is yours…captor."

The colonel smiled and dismissed the guard with his chains. He was pleased with her response. It was exactly what he had expected. He put the safety on the pistol and returned it to his holster. He turned his back to Anya and said, "Be ready in twenty minutes. I'm going to make arrangements for a car and a driver. We still have business to attend to at the orphanage."

Anya began splashing water from the bucket onto her face and hair. The dissolved blood dripped down her arms in long red stripes, forming dark pools on the slick floor. The red stains running down her face made her look like an Amazon warrior wearing fresh war paint, preparing for battle. She glared at the man with the wolf's eyes and fiercely replied to him as he walked away, "Hurry and get your car, comrade—I can't wait!"

CHAPTER 48

When the head matron opened the heavy door at the entrance of the orphanage, she was shocked to see a tall man in a black KGB uniform and Anya wearing drab prison garb. The KGB officer brushed past her without a word. At first, the matron thought he carried a rifle on a sling over his shoulder, but she quickly surmised that it was a long round map carrier with leather caps on each end.

The colonel coolly looked over the premises and addressed the matron, "Are you in charge here?"

"Yes, I am the new acting director. I contacted Child Services, and they told me to carry on."

"Well, Acting Director, I will require a small meeting room with a table and four chairs. We have much to discuss, and I have brought this criminal of the state to face all charges and accusations."

The matron smiled when she heard Anya described as a "criminal of the state." She recommended to the officer, "The chapel, with its long tables for your map, or my new office might please you." The matron looked directly at Anya and continued, "The fine desk has been ruined, but it might do for a short meeting."

The colonel looked to his left and pointed to a small room next to the infirmary. He asked, "How about this room? It is smaller and less intimidating. It also has a stout wooden door. We don't want anyone to escape, now do we? I will speak with you and the other matrons first, and then I will interview the remainder of your staff."

The head matron was not sure of her footing with this heavy-handed officer, but she plunged ahead and reported, "I regret that one matron is not feeling well, a Comrade Matron Svelte, and the other matron is supervising the children. The older maintenance man, Sergei, will be leaving us at the end of the week. He is becoming quite feeble and very absentminded. I have decided to let him go. The older girls can perform his tasks. It will also save a great deal of money. The cook, Ursula, could not obey my orders regarding food preparation, and she will also be leaving of her own accord."

Anya seethed with the realization that Sergei was being fired so that the head matron could steal his wages, and Ursula was being forced to leave because she would not starve the children. Her arms trembled as she stood beside the colonel. A volcano inside her was about to erupt.

"Ah, new changes—always a new director's prerogative," retorted the colonel. The colonel took two steps and looked down into the head matron's smiling face. He crisply ordered, "You have five minutes to gather yourself and the other matrons into the room that I have chosen. If all are not there in the allotted time, I will arrest you and your entire staff, and we will be going to the KGB interrogation center in downtown Vladivostok. You now have four minutes."

The head matron's smile instantly vanished. She hurried from room to room frantically screaming the other matrons' names.

The colonel grinned as he watched her erratic behavior. He gallantly swept his arm toward the small meeting room and said to Anya, "Dear heart, ladies first. I expect more company in, let's say, two minutes. Shall we?"

Anya felt that she could easily stab a bayonet into this officer's eyes, but as she walked into the meeting room, she had to admit—the Gray Wolf had style.

****

The "meeting of the matrons" created more tension than if all were waiting for a firing squad. It was exactly the atmosphere the colonel desired. He placed the head matron at the end of the table away from the door. Svelte was next to her against a wall. Anya sat at the other end of the table closest to the entryway, and Elena was to have the final chair directly to the right of the head matron. He wanted it to appear that the three matrons were facing Anya and that she was sitting in the "inquisitor's chair." What he really created was a cage, where he alone could ominously stand to tower over them and guard the door. He hoped the pressure would cause a nervous explosion. He got his wish.

Elena was the last to arrive. When she sat in her chair, Anya and the colonel could see that her right eye was black-and-blue and almost swollen shut. Anya's volcano finally blew. She lunged across the table and tried to reach the head matron's throat. The colonel allowed Anya to rip the collar off the head matron's dress before he grabbed Anya's thick hair and slammed her back into her seat. He walked over to Elena and leaned down to inspect her injury. He asked her, "What happened to your face, Matron?"

Elena glanced at the head matron and quietly replied, "I was required to clean the former director's office. It was quite, well, messy. Perhaps I slipped and hit the edge of his desk."

"Matron, your wound is narrow and deep. I have seen this many times. It results from being struck by a stick or a baton. You won't lose your eye, but it will take some time to heal." The man with the wolf's eyes stared directly at the head matron and said, "So the evidence in the office has been wiped away. That's a pity. It's also a crime."

While he let his last words soak into all of their minds, he reached into his briefcase and tossed Esmeralda's record onto the middle of the table. Everyone's attention was centered on the bloodstained book. The director's red fingerprints on the front cover seemed to shout, *It's all right here.*

"Now, Matron, as the new acting director, it appears your staff is abused, and your accounting is not accurate. Can you explain these discrepancies to me?"

The head matron was ready to roll the dice. She had attained the position that she had always wanted—and deserved. She was not going to back down from this cocky bureaucrat, KGB or not. The position was hers, and she intended to keep it.

"Yes, Colonel, I can. Comrade Matron Elena slipped as she said. Her injury will soon heal. The director received all the funds and did his own accounting. He was murdered by the monster seated in front of you, or he could answer your questions himself. Now we will never know."

The colonel paced back and forth across the room with his fingertips pressed together as if her were offering a little prayer. He raised his head and replied, "I'm afraid I must disagree, dear matrons. I believe the truth is just below the surface and aching to reveal itself. However, I think I have found a solution to our problem. Matron Elena, please wait for me outside, and if you would be so good as to close the door behind you."

The colonel went to the doorway and retrieved his map case, which he had leaned against the wall. He flipped the leather top of the canister and dramatically withdrew a long rawhide whip with a narrow frazzled tip.

"Ladies, I'm sorry to disappoint you. No maps—just this little item from Egypt. It's a camel whip with a few helpful modifications. I borrowed it from our quaint little interrogation center downtown. Now I am going to leave for a little while, and when I return, I just know we will have another discussion about the importance of telling the truth."

The colonel handed the whip to Anya and said, "Anya, I told you that you could come back and say goodbye. You have seventeen minutes to say farewell to these lovely matrons. Avoid the face, if possible. This thing often leaves scars. Try not to kill them. The paperwork is so tedious. I'll be waiting just outside the door. Well, ladies...let the games begin."

The two frightened matrons grabbed their short wooden sticks and held them above their heads, as if they were magic wands that could make this unleashed tigress disappear. Anya's first powerful stroke slashed across the head matron's face, slicing her right ear and knocking out one of her front teeth. Svelte made a piercing scream when the lash brought a squirt of blood down the side of her neck.

The colonel leaned back against the doorframe and lit a cigarette. When he heard the table and chairs fall over, he could not help but smile.

Elena pleaded, "Colonel, how can you let this happen? Someone could get killed in there. Please do something."

The colonel's smile vanished, and Elena felt a chill run down her spine when his cold glacial eyes seemed to pierce through her. He threw his cigarette down on the stone floor and mashed it with the toe of his boot. His words cut as much as the whip being used in the adjoining room: "Hard times breed hard men, Matron." The colonel pointed toward the kitchen and ordered, "Go make yourself useful. Have the cook prepare two lunches. Anya and I have not eaten all day. Also, bring Anya some new clothes from your sewing center. I have to say, that girl ruins clothing faster than anyone I've ever seen. She has a long journey ahead. Help her by helping me. Go now—do as I say."

The colonel heard a sobbing cry for help and the sickening thud of rawhide against flesh. He glanced at his watch and decided that he had time for one more cigarette. The smoke, along with another scream, drifted into the air and faded away.

****

The colonel finished his cigarette. He looked down at his watch and decided that everyone should have had enough time to say "goodbye." When he entered the room, he mused that it looked as if an earthquake had just struck: the table and chairs were overturned, and blood-red dots arched across the dull-colored walls and low ceiling, as if a crimson comet had streaked across a gray sky.

Bleeding Svelte cringed and whimpered in a corner. The head matron gasped for air and tried to crawl against the table for some protection. Anya beat her back and legs with the camel whip as the woman struggled to curl herself into a tight ball. Her black dress was cut into dark-red pieces.

"Anya, that is enough. Give me the whip. Listen to me. I said that is enough."

Anya ignored the colonel and continued her thrashing. She was beyond fury. All the wrongs she had endured since Vladimir's Store poured forth with each lash of the whip: the death of her beloved parents, the loss of her only home and the land she loved, orphanage cruelty, greedy men and women who caused pain and even death without a care, hateful people in uniforms, incompetent bureaucrats, paper eunuchs, lost years, wasted lives—every injustice brought to the surface with each red stroke of the whip, running down the tip and over the handle to cover and caress her bloodstained hand.

The colonel fired his pistol into the low ceiling just above Anya's head. Plaster rained down on Anya's head and shoulders in a cascade of gray snow. As she stood over the matron, her arms trembling, her chest heaving to gather more air in order to continue, even the colonel was unsettled by the look of pure hatred when Anya turned to face him.

The colonel pointed the pistol at Anya's face and exclaimed, "That's a good girl. Toss the whip over to my side. Try not to let it touch me. It's so hard to get blood out of a uniform. Do it now. If you kill her, I will have to kill you. I can't imagine the paperwork for two dead bodies in one afternoon. Including the rotting director, make that three." Anya threw the whip in the colonel's direction. It landed in front of him next to his boot.

Elena arrived with food and fresh clothing for Anya. When she saw Anya covered with blood and the condition of the room, she placed her hand over her mouth and closed her eyes.

The colonel holstered his pistol and grinned as he gazed at the carnage. He cleared his voice and said, "Well, ladies, since we are all here together, I have a few announcements. Comrade Elena is the new permanent director of this darling institution. Child Services will readily agree, especially when I threaten to arrest them for fraud and criminal conspiracy if they don't follow my wise decisions. Director Elena, you will also receive adequate funding. Make a list of the items that you need. Child Services will meet *all* your obligations, I assure you. The cook and maintenance man seem quite capable. I would retain them, but that is your decision."

The colonel turned to the two matrons bleeding on the floor and told them, "As for our two lovely matrons stretched out before us, listen carefully. I will only say this once: you are going to leave this facility and never—I repeat—never be around children again. I will red-flag your names. This means I will know every place you work, live, and even the activities you attend. If children are anywhere in the vicinity, you had better run to the nearest exit. If you violate these conditions, you will be arrested for crimes against the state, and I will have you transferred to an interesting little asylum just outside Moscow. It is reserved for the criminally insane. Your roommate will be a clever fellow who hates women. I should have executed him a year ago, but he has proven to be quite useful with men or women who don't want to cooperate with me. After a few days with him, they simply can't wait to see things my way. The last woman I placed in his care unfortunately died when he ripped out all her hair and gouged out her eyes with his fingers. Odd creature. She looked much like a plucked chicken. Am I getting your attention?"

The room was totally silent. The colonel's ruthless comments stunned everyone; his flippant descriptions about life and death were unnerving. Even Anya wondered, who was this man with the wolf's eyes?

The colonel turned toward Anya. It was time for her final test: would she feel remorse for the violent beatings she had committed, or would she continue on his command?

"Anya, these ex-matrons won't give me an answer. Perhaps you can assist them. Start with the drunk sobbing in the corner."

The colonel kicked the camel whip with the toe of his boot toward Anya. She gripped the whip and hovered over Svelte. The colonel noticed the flame in her eyes. He was very pleased. After the third strike, Svelte cried out, "Yes, yes, I understand, no more children! Stop—please, no more."

The colonel motioned with his head toward the former head matron. The terrified woman tried to hide underneath the overturned furniture. Anya grabbed her by the tight bun in her hair and dragged her away from the table. Anya raised the whip and noticed the round rawhide knot on the handle. She reversed the whip and struck the woman across her lower jaw. Everyone in the room heard the distinct snap of the bone. The victim groaned and passed out beneath Anya's feet.

The colonel lightly clapped his hands and remarked, "Well done, Anya. A little hard for them to answer when you break their jaw, but such is life. I think we now have an understanding. I noticed a fountain outside. Go wash yourself and the whip. I want it returned in pristine condition. I don't want to tarnish my reputation. Director Elena has some new clothes for you. I swear, there are so many directors in this place I sometimes get confused. Change your clothing in the infirmary. Hurry, we will have an airplane waiting for us in an hour."

Anya and Elena left the room. The colonel scanned the debris and the bleeding prostrate bodies in the broken assembly. The girl showed no remorse, no pity. Yes, she passed the test. There was real potential here, if she were not executed. Time would tell.

The colonel stood in the doorway to have his last cigarette for the day. He watched Anya at the fountain. The matrons' blood ran down her face and arms. As he lit the match, he smiled and whispered to himself, "Yes, indeed—my kind of girl!"

****

Anya stood by the fountain enjoying the sound of its running water. It gave her a sense of peace in the aftermath of the violence in which she had just participated—a quiet in the eye of the storm. She remembered when she and Sergei had repaired the forsaken fountain and brought it back to life. She thought fondly of the times that Esmeralda had talked with her at this exact spot. So much had happened since then. Anya wondered if she would ever be the same.

Anya placed the camel whip into the water. Blood swirled around the basin. It seemed like such a sacrilege to taint the water. However, she knew that the man with the wolf's eyes would just as readily use the whip on her if she didn't; he was used to being obeyed. The water felt refreshing on her face and running through her hair.

She looked up into the sky. Yes, for a little while longer, this was still the center of the universe where some sanity remained.

Elena approached her and waited until Anya had finished. She also had stood at that exact spot, next to the fountain, when they took the nuns away. Elena sensed that once again there would be a loss in her life: she would never see Anya again.

"Anya, I have some clothes for you. These are the last items Esmeralda made. I think she would be pleased for you to have them. I also want to share something with you. When the men came to take the nuns away, the Mother Superior saw that I was sad and afraid. She came to me by this fountain, hugged me, and told me something I have never forgotten: 'Elena, always remember, sometimes in the process of forgiving another's life—we save our own.' I pass these words on to you, Anya. Take them with you, no matter where you are required to go."

Anya said nothing. She touched Elena's arm and gently kissed her cheek. Anya noticed that the key Elena always carried around her neck had flipped over. On the back of the silver key, Elena had etched the markings of a cross.

Anya stroked the clothes, pleased that they were Esmeralda's last kind gesture to her. She walked toward the infirmary to change into the fine garments. Ursula emerged from the kitchen doorway and waved goodbye while dabbing her eyes with the end of her white apron. It was obvious that she was afraid of the KGB man and that she simply would not venture any closer.

Sergei approached the doorway of the infirmary, and with pleading eyes, he looked at the colonel and motioned with his hand toward Anya. The colonel nodded his head, granting permission.

"Anya, I finished your Christmas present the day the police took you away. I didn't think I would ever see you again. It is a tiger, a story from your past. May it give you courage for the days ahead, whatever they may be."

Anya was so touched that she could not speak. She just rushed and held Sergei as tightly as possible. He had been her anchor in this sea of change in her life—the grandfather she had never known. She did not want to let him go.

The colonel brought stark reality back to all. He cleared his throat and said, "Anya, where is the whip? Let's get moving. You have ten minutes. Director Elena, please bring me the whip while Anya changes. We need to have a final chat before I go."

Elena picked up the whip from the basin of the fountain with her thumb and index finger, as if it were contaminated. She wondered just how much sorrow this piece of twisted rawhide had witnessed.

"Thank you, Director. Just put it in this case so that it can be returned. There is one last item that I must stringently mention. Hear me well: Anya Ruslanova was never at this facility. No crime ever occurred here. The former director committed suicide over the loss of the young girl in his care. Tell your entire staff, including the two creatures in that room next door, the same thing. If you or your staff ever mention the name Anya Ruslanova to anyone, that unlucky individual will get to spend time with my ape-man at the insane asylum outside Moscow. Make sure everyone understands. There won't be a second chance—and certainly no mercy. I hope that I am clear on this point."

"Colonel, will we ever see her again? What will happen to her?"

"No, Director, you will never see her again—because she doesn't exist. She was never here. She must answer for her crimes to my superiors in Moscow. I will try to convince them not to execute her. I make no promises. Best of luck in your new position. I know you will do well."

The colonel pounded on the door of the infirmary and commanded, "Anya, get out now. It is time."

Anya and the colonel walked down the portico toward the ancient door of the former convent, current orphanage, exit to unknown worlds—the door the nuns went through, the door Sofia left open, the door to a reprieve or an execution.

Elena, Ursula, and Sergei openly wept. They knew in their hearts, when the massive door closed, they would never see again the "mountain girl" with the long blonde hair and the sparkling blue eyes.

Colonel Kurgan and Anya walked past her beloved fountain, her center of a fleeting world; and the blood in the fountain circled around the basin like a crimson river current, becoming a dark-red maelstrom, ever spiraling downward, pulled, drained into the bowels of the system against its will—rising again from its throbbing, pumping heart through the ever-flowing spout, spewing scarlet, as if from the mouth of a wounded animal, suddenly christening the sky with a spray of newly shed blood.

The splintered wooden door slowly closed behind the child of the forest and locked in its place forever.

CHAPTER 49

The car rolled to a stop near a gray airplane. Anya marveled that since leaving Vladimir's Store, she had been in a train, four times in a car, and now in an airplane. Life in a mountain cabin seemed far away, in a different world—an aching memory.

The driver opened the door for the colonel. Kurgan stood on the tarmac and looked at the airplane and then at Anya, who was waiting by the car. *Time for another test*, the colonel thought.

"Anya, carry my briefcase. I'm going to talk with the pilot."

Anya walked past the colonel and replied, "You look strong. I may be your prisoner, but I'm not your slave. Carry it yourself... comrade." She kept walking and never looked back.

The driver nervously darted his eyes back and forth between the colonel and the young woman who dared to speak to a colonel of the KGB with such defiance. The driver reached for the briefcase.

"No, that's fine, Sergeant. She is right. I am quite capable. It's going to be very easy to shoot this one."

The driver shut the car door and watched the two passengers walk toward the airplane. The colonel was actually chuckling to himself. The driver shook his head and started the engine. *These people from Moscow are an odd bunch*, he thought. *I wish they would all stay there—especially the KGB.*

As Anya prepared to enter the airplane, a green sedan with a red star on the door stopped near the tail section of the airplane.

Two burly men in black KGB uniforms escorted a woman wearing a beautiful white fur coat with a matching fur hat. Each man held one of her arms as they escorted her to the doorway of the aircraft.

The colonel signed a paper, and the two men left in the same sedan. When the woman turned, Anya discovered, in utter amazement, that it was Sofia. Both girls just stared at each other, not quite believing their eyes. Anya said, "I thought you worked as an assistant for a general and were enrolled at a university. I don't understand why you're here."

Sofia rolled her pretty eyes and replied, "Neither do I. Less than an hour ago, those two gorillas pounded on my door and informed me that I was under arrest. They barely allowed me to get my new coat and hat before shuffling me into a car. The signature on the arrest warrant was a Colonel Viktor Kurgan."

Anya looked over her shoulder and whispered, "The KGB officer talking to the pilot, he's the man. Beware what you say or do. He misses nothing."

Sofia looked anxiously about her. She rested her eyes on Anya and asked, "Well, my fellow orphan, what brings you into the clutches of our KGB friends? I would think that orphanage would be prison enough for anyone. How is our resourceful director managing without me?"

Anya stared at the elegant Sofia for a moment and coldly replied, "I killed him. That's why I'm here. I guess I did not appreciate him the way you did."

Sofia placed an expensive lambskin glove near her mouth to hide her smile. "My, my, aren't you the brave one!" she retorted. "I wanted to do the same thing but lacked the courage, or the opportunity, or so I told myself. Actually, the best thing for him—truly a bore. When are we going to leave this dreadful place?"

The colonel motioned with his hand to the doorway of the airplane and said, "Ladies, your chariot awaits you."

The airplane's metal interior was drab with single row seats on each side. The colonel placed the two passengers across from each other. Once the door was closed and locked, he handcuffed Anya and Sofia to their seats. A section of chain attached to each handcuff allowed them to raise their arm, but nothing more.

Anya raised the chain and angrily shouted, "We made an agreement—no running, no chains! What is this?"

"My little prisoner, it is called security. Our deal was in the jail, not in an airplane. You may find it hard to believe, but some people don't want to travel with me. They actually try to jump out of the airplane. Silly but true. Here, both of you have some lunch. Who says there is no free lunch? I'm told your cook at the orphanage makes splendid meals. It was prepared with love. Enjoy. It will be several hours before we reach Moscow. Try to get some sleep."

For the first time, Anya saw real fear in Sofia's eyes. Sofia's haughty bearing had been shaken: the sudden departure, the handcuffs, the destination of Moscow brought the castle down.

"Sofia, are you all right? You're very pale. What's the matter?"

Sophia stared at the colonel near the front of the airplane. Her voice cracked when she spoke, "The matter, my fellow inmate, is that you are a murderer, and I am the daughter of a man who was considered, in Stalin's paranoid mind, as a traitor. My father was executed, my mother died in a prison camp, and now the traitor's daughter is of age. No more orphanages for either of us."

"Sofia, what will they do to us?"

"If they follow their normal agenda, we will be tried in a KGB's 'guilty until proven guilty' court, be taken to a dreadful cell with a very large drain, and then be shot in the back of the head. Please, no more questions."

The airplane revved its engines and proceeded down the runway. The colonel was already asleep. Sofia just stared at the floor. Anya raised her arm and felt the handcuff bite her wrist. Anya looked out of the small scratched window next to her. It was late autumn, and the colorful leaves were beginning to fall in preparation for winter. All of nature seemed to be whispering into the wind, *Winter is coming. Get ready—winter is coming.*

For Anya, winter had come already—not in falling leaves but in chains. The airplane banked to the right and headed west. Anya watched the lovely trees disappear. The child of the forest was leaving the fading earth into an uncertain sky. The coming darkness surrounded the sun to force it down into another night. To her young and lonely heart, it appeared that the fiery sun was also slowly dying in the direction of the west—toward a place they called *Moscow Center*.

PART 3

The Center

Take firm hold of instruction, do not let go; keep her, for she is your life. Do not enter the path of the wicked, and do not walk in the way of evil… For they eat the bread of wickedness, and drink the wine of violence.
—Proverbs 4

CHAPTER 50

Moscow at night from the air, to Anya, seemed like a city of lights reaching to the horizon. She did not know places like this existed. The rumors she had heard were true. Sofia, being a Muscovite and the daughter of a former diplomat, was simply bored. She had traveled extensively with her parents, certainly not chained to a small uncomfortable seat. This city brought her only painful memories. The colonel looked down and saw a place of work, bureaucracy, and politics. To him, Moscow was just a second-rate town compared to the elegance of his birthplace, Saint Petersburg, now called Leningrad. Three weary travels with three different views: wonder, woe, and work. Yes, Moscow was all of these.

Moscow Center was a sprawling complex with many divisions. One of its least known was its training grounds and orphanage. It was believed that orphans made some of the best agents. They had nothing to fall back on, and in time, many could be trained to think of the state as their mother and the KGB as their surrogate father. The KGB constantly monitored orphanages and juvenile facilities to find those children gifted in science, mathematics, athletics, foreign-language skills, and those with aggressive but controllable natures. Sofia had several of these qualities; Anya had them all.

The colonel assigned Anya and Sophia to a special dormitory under his complete control. Each room held two children, generally of the same age and gender. Sometimes allowances were made for siblings, but rarely, unless they were quite young. The colonel decided to keep his two new charges as roommates. They already knew each other, and he hoped each could learn from the other's strengths: Anya's tough survival instincts; Sofia's cool, sophisticated bearing—fire and ice.

Sofia considered the room Spartan but much better than she had expected. Anya had never had this much space to herself. Both were relieved that it was not a prison cell.

"Colonel, what is going to happen to us?" Sofia asked.

"Your future will depend upon my superiors and your attitude. They will probably follow my recommendation. If I see potential in you, you will live. If I do not, you will die. Don't disappoint me."

The colonel walked to the door and turned to leave. He glanced back at them and said, "One last thing: to your instructors, you will just be a number. They are never to know your names. Sofia, you are number twenty-one. Anya, number twenty-two. You will receive your uniforms and living essentials this afternoon. For now, just rest and settle yourselves. Training begins tomorrow at dawn. Remember my warning, ladies. I can be your best friend or your worst enemy—it's up to you."

The colonel left and walked down the hallway. They could hear his boots marking time with each quick step down the dingy tile floor fading to silence. Sofia went to their only window and looked out upon the bleak surroundings. Anya remained staring at the doorway and imagined shooting the colonel, her Gray Wolf, in his left eye. Anya and Sofia would indeed learn from each other—*fire and ice.*

****

"Twenty-One, try harder. Twenty-Two, slow down. Precision is more important than strength," said the martial arts instructor. Both recruits looked at him: one with disdain, the other with fierce determination.

Colonel Kurgan entered the gray gymnasium to inspect his two latest recruits. He nodded to the instructor and asked, "Good morning, how are those two working out, the one with dark hair and the blonde? Do they have potential?"

"Well, Colonel, Twenty-One with the dark hair learns quickly and knows what to do. She just has no heart for it. Twenty-Two is as strong as a horse and as fierce as a tiger. I make her spar with me. She is too rough for the other girls. Even when I throw her on the mat and knock the wind out of her, she stands, takes a breath, and comes back at me. I've never seen such intensity. Whether it comes from natural desire or complete hatred, I don't know at this point."

The colonel glanced at the two girls standing next to each other. He replied, "I like your choice of words. That is exactly what I want. Make Twenty-One, the dark-haired girl, into a black leopard. They do exist, and they excel at stalking and fading into the night to find their prey. Teach her the basics to defend herself, but don't injure her hands or face. Make Twenty-Two, the one with the blonde hair, exactly as you described her—a tiger. I want her to be able to attack anything and destroy it on the spot—without hesitation, without mercy. Drive her to the edge."

"What about their probations, Colonel? How do I proceed?"

"Their probations have been lifted. Don't tell them. I want to keep them off balance awhile and totally dependent upon me. Let them think a sword hangs over their heads by a thin thread and that I alone can cut that thread whenever I desire. I'll wean them slowly. They both have special assignments. They belong to me."

Both men turned to look at the "black leopard" and the "tiger." Sofia was standing with her hands on her hips looking around the dingy gym with a scornful smirk on her face. Anya stood facing the men in the martial arts horse stance that she had just learned: legs, shoulder-width apart; knees, slightly bent; clenched fists, down in front of her torso.

"See what I mean, Colonel? Look at them. It says it all."

"Just remember my instructions: basic for one and very, very advanced for the other."

"As you wish, Colonel. Teach one to disappear, the other to kill."

As Colonel Kurgan walked to the door, the instructor shouted, "Twenty-One, follow the colonel. He has another class for you to attend. Twenty-Two, front and center. Face me and listen. This is how you break a man's neck."

Chapter 51

The sergeant lightly tapped on the office door and just placed his head inside to say, "Colonel, recruit number Twenty-Two would like to make an appointment to see you. She is at my desk. I can give her a date and time."

"No, Sergeant, send her in. I'm at a good stopping point."

The colonel left his desk and greeted Anya with a pleasant smile. He graciously motioned for her to take a chair in front of his desk. Anya gazed at the large office and nervously tugged at the bottom of her jacket as she sat in front of the colonel.

"Good to see you, Anya. Your instructors tell me that Sofia and you are doing extremely well and that both of you are at the head of your classes. Job well done! How is Sofia?"

"She seems fine. I only see her in the evening after classes. We sat together through all the tradecraft and communication courses, but now she spends most of her time in the science and mathematics section or in the English language department."

"Yes, Sofia is being trained for a special assignment. She must be fluent in English. I am not at liberty to say more. As for you, let me review your file. Yes, you have become an expert in weaponry, you have excellent working knowledge in four languages, and your martial arts instructor says that if you do not slow down, he fears you will be more proficient than he—very, very impressive!"

"Thank you, Colonel." Staring at a picture of Stalin mounted high on the wall, as if Stalin were looking over the colonel's shoulder and his desk, she built her courage. "Regarding another matter, may I ask how you came to know Vladimir, my friend back home? He said that he has known you for many years."

"Yes, we are friends. We were in the army together. We both fought at Stalingrad. In fact, he saved my life."

"Do you mind telling me how?" Anya asked.

"No, not at all. I joined the army when I was about your age. It was either that or starvation. I don't care to go into the details. Let's just say that after the revolution, some families suffered more than others. In any case, I worked my way through the ranks. When Comrade Stalin decided to purge certain high-ranking officers, I was just a noncommissioned officer not worthy of his attention.

"When the war with Germany came, I was a low-ranking officer and sent to Stalingrad. Vladimir was a sergeant. During a battle at the tractor factory, I was wounded. Vladimir found me and carried me on his shoulder to a hospital. His bravery gained him a medal and gave me my life. While I recovered, Vladimir marched west toward Berlin. I never saw him again, but we have always kept in touch. Vladimir is a remarkable man whose actions have allowed me to sit before you today."

Anya hesitated, but asked, "How did you come to be in the KGB? Why didn't you just remain in the army?"

"When I left the hospital, I was reassigned to the Army Intelligence Division. I knew several languages, including German, so it was only logical to use those skills. After the war, I was assigned to the KGB. It seemed a natural fit. Is this why you came to see me?"

Anya raised her head and looked into the colonel's eyes. "No, Colonel, but I do have a request related to Vladimir. Now that I am here in Moscow, may I write to Vladimir and Dmitri to let them know where I am and that I am all right? I have never asked for anything. Please allow me this courtesy."

Kurgan admired her concern for her friends and replied, "Excellent idea, Anya. However, I have already taken the initiative to let him know that you are safe and sound and in my care. I'm afraid direct contact is not allowed at this stage in your training. However, you have been doing well—time for a little privilege. In the future, give me your correspondence, and I will ensure its prompt delivery. Please don't tell anyone. It will be our little secret."

"Oh, thank you, Colonel! I won't forget this!" Anya left with the first smile the colonel had seen from her. The colonel patted her shoulder and returned to his desk. He took a sheet of his personal stationery and wrote:

>Dear Vladimir:
>
>>Upon your request, I have been monitoring the matter regarding Anya Ruslanova. Unfortunately, she has recently contacted typhus from one of the other children at the orphanage in Vladivostok. Both were taken to the local hospital and placed in an isolation ward to avert any spread of the disease.
>>
>>I regret to inform you that your friend Anya has died. Because of the contagious nature of this illness, she was cremated the same day. I have pushed through the paperwork to have her remains sent to you once the state gives its approval. You must be patient. This could take some time.
>>
>>Please relay this information to any of her friends who share your concern. I will notify your district commissar, Comrade Lepan, so that he can close his files.
>
>>>You have my deepest sympathy,
>>>Colonel Viktor Kurgan

Kurgan pushed the button on his intercom. "Sergeant, in my office please." Kurgan ordered, "Send this letter through normal channels to the address listed on this card. Tomorrow you are to have the psychopath Sobelev taken from the asylum and executed. Here is his signed execution order. He is too expensive to maintain, and he has served his purpose. Have his corpse cremated. He is a big man, so take half of his ashes and place them in a sealed box. Wait two months and send the box to the same address as the letter that I just gave you. Flush the remainder of Sobelev's ashes into the sewer."

"Yes, Colonel. Is there anything else?"

"Sergeant, while we are at it, write Sobelev's family and tell them that he made a full recovery and was sent to a work camp in Northern Siberia. Six months from now, notify them that he died in a camp accident, and because of the distances involved, he was buried at the camp cemetery. Enclose a death certificate with the corresponding date to match his accident and forge the camp doctor's signature on the document."

"Very well. Anything else, Colonel?"

"One more item: any correspondence relating to the recruits numbers twenty-one and twenty-two are to come directly to me and to no one else. That is all."

When the sergeant closed the door, Colonel Kurgan walked over to his office window, which overlooked the training ground below. He spotted Anya with four trainees on the pistol firing range. He took his large black binoculars, which always rested on the windowsill, and focused on Anya's target. Every shot was dead-center. He lowered the binoculars and whispered to himself, "Well, Anya, your letter is on its way. Welcome home."

Chapter 52

KGB colonel Viktor Kurgan continued to stare at Anya from his office window. Anya's questions had stirred emotions and images that he had tried to distance from himself long ago. The past was the past, but sometimes it lifted its tormented head and called out, *I'm still here.*

Viktor understood Anya's situation more than she realized. He had faced a similar life decision but followed a different path.

Viktor Kurgan came from an aristocratic family that had thrived throughout the centuries. They had landholdings not far from Saint Petersburg, now renamed Leningrad. The Kurgan estate was large and elegant. The family was honored by the czars; it was devoured by the Bolsheviks.

The Communists seized the Kurgan home and stripped it bare. That which was not confiscated was looted or spitefully destroyed. The vast rooms were partitioned, and several families were assigned to each room. The land and its production was claimed by the People of the Union of Soviet Socialist Republics. The plunder was now complete. Viktor was fifteen years old.

Before the revolution, like Anya, he was an only child, and he had studied at home. Unlike Anya, he had been blessed with the finest of tutors, and he had access to an enormous library to advance his education. He spent his days reading, riding, and exploring the vast family estate. All that he had ever dreamed was simply to work the land that he loved and to see it prosper for generations to come. He wanted to be a farmer.

When the estate was seized, life became a matter of survival. The Communists allowed the Kurgans to live in a rustic hut at the northern edge of the property. It was formerly a caretaker's cabin, small but sturdy. Viktor did not mind: his family was together, his family still lived on their ancestral land, his family had not been executed by the Bolsheviks. Other noble families had simply disappeared.

The new collective-farm manager told the Kurgans that they could work or starve; he did not care which they chose. The family worked in a nearby field by day, and Viktor tended their garden every evening. Viktor was big for his age, and he enjoyed working outdoors. He worked heartily, and the other field hands came to admire his positive outlook and cheerful smile. Viktor sang Russian folksongs during their afternoon breaks, and soon the other workers accepted him as one of their own.

Viktor's parents did not fare so well. The labor and sparse diet was difficult for them. Viktor's mother had never been in the best of health. She sometimes suffered a shortness of breath because of her asthma. Viktor struggled to complete the work for all three of them. He watched his mother slowly fade each day. She died before the fall harvest.

Viktor's mother was buried by a stream near the hut. The family cemetery near their handsome estate home no longer existed. The tombstones of generations had been removed and used as weights for planting cultivators so they could dig deeper into the soil.

Viktor's father lost his will to live. He felt that he had lost everything: his land, his wife, his future. To comfort himself, he took a long walk to a special pond on the estate. He and his family had enjoyed many leisurely picnics and quiet, wonderful moments by this idyllic pond. There was always a rowboat at the dock, and white swans gracefully glided upon the water. Mr. Kurgan started to walk faster. He smiled with the anticipation of renewing a fond memory—something to cherish, something to embrace.

When Mr. Kurgan arrived at the pond, the grass had been churned into black mud; deep tracks were everywhere. Two men were fixing an engine and washing the parts in the pond. The water had an oily sheen that spread as the men continued to work. Dead fish floated on the surface, creating a putrid smell. The rowboat had been used as firewood to roast the swans that glided no more. The pond was dead, and so were his memories. That evening, while Viktor tended the garden, Papa Kurgan shot himself with the caretaker's old rusty shotgun. He was buried next to his wife by a stream, where black oil slowly flowed past them on its way to Leningrad.

****

The collective-farm manager had liked neither Viktor nor his family. He felt that the Kurgan family and all aristocracy had ruined Russia and enslaved people such as himself. It did not matter to him that the Kurgans, for generations, had always opposed serfdom and paid their workers excellent wages to reward them for their hard work and years of loyal service to the family. After the death of Viktor's parents, the hateful manager gave Viktor two spiteful choices: go to a state orphanage or lie about his age and join the army. Like Anya, Viktor had also reached a crossroad in his life. Anya was forced into an orphanage; Viktor chose the army.

Leaving the familiar for the unknown is always difficult. The sights, the fragrances, the sense of belonging—all seem to slip away. Viktor knew this banishment would be a turning point in his life, never to be the same. So on that crisp, beautiful autumnal morning, Viktor left the only world he had ever known and walked down the road toward Leningrad.

When Viktor used to travel with his parents to Saint Petersburg in a carriage, it took half a day. Viktor estimated it would take him a very long day of walking to reach the outskirts of the same city the Communists had renamed Leningrad. Viktor thought it a sacrilege to replace the namesake and the creation of Peter the Great with some obscure rebel called Lenin. Saint Petersburg, with its lovely architecture, its magnificent Hermitage Museum, and its grand ballrooms, seemed the epitome of culture and intellect to Viktor. Moscow rated a far second place as the "older sister" to Viktor's way of thinking.

Perhaps that was why Stalin always resented the elegant city named after a czar.

Passing his ancestral home, Viktor saw the towers of his family's mansion in the distance. A red hammer-and-sickle banner hung from the second-story balustrade, where he and his parents had enjoyed the fresh air on such a day as this.

Watching the red banner flutter in the cool breeze, Viktor sensed that his dreams were also passing away: his parents, his property, his past all gone, swept away by the fierce winds of revolution.

Viktor realized that if he were to survive, he would have to leave his former life behind. He began to run with all his might down the hard dusty road, never looking back, fleeing the warm memories of a treasured past into the cold embrace of an uncertain future.

As he fled his past, the farm manager's pass rustled in his shirt pocket, begrudging permission for him to forsake all that he had loved, now his ticked into oblivion. Viktor Kurgan, the son of aristocracy, never saw his home again.

****

The military enlistment station emerged from the outskirts of Leningrad. The dingy makeshift barracks were a far cry from the elegant city center with its European architecture and the glittering ballrooms Viktor and his parents frequented in his youth. When he stepped through the narrow doorway and slowly walked toward a heavyset man behind a worn desk, Viktor sensed that his days as a carefree boy were to end in front of that scarred desk.

He stood in front of the desk and was finally greeted with a gruff, "What do you want, boy?"

"I have come to join the service and to become a soldier."

"Oh, you want to be a soldier? You look to be smarter than that. You could work in a factory, but you would rather get a medal, maybe Hero of the Soviet Union, eh?"

Viktor said nothing. He could smell the alcohol reeking from the man's breath, the man's brown tobacco-stained fingers gripped around a cheap black pen. Viktor vowed to himself that no matter what lay in store for him, once he walked away from that desk, he would never become the jaded, cynical man who sat before him in a stained uniform with bloodshot eyes. Better to be dead on the battlefield than to slowly rot behind a bottle and a desk.

"Welcome to the army, 'Hero of the Soviet Union.' Go through that door on the right. Someone will get you a uniform."

Not once did the drunken sergeant ask for Viktor's name or his age. Exodus complete.

Chapter 53

Every week, Anya went to the postal clerk to see if she had any mail from her friends. She was always disappointed when there was never any word from Vladimir or Dmitri. Perhaps the resident censor was holding her letters until she completed her training, she thought. In any case, she did not feel too sorry for herself, for at least she knew that she had friends back home who cared for her.

Sofia had no one. All her family and friends were destroyed or deported by Stalin's regime. She found a world inside herself: "trust no one, watch out for yourself." Sofia had reached a point in life of never hoping too much for anything.

When Anya reached her dormitory for the evening, Sofia was closing a new leather suitcase. Another smaller case was on her bed, her closet empty.

"Sofia, where are you going? We have not graduated yet."

"It appears that I have. My training here is over. I have been promised a university degree, but I have heard that before."

"Do you know where? Maybe I can write to you?"

Sofia looked at Anya as if she were a naive little girl. In many ways, Anya was still the simple girl from Siberia: loyal, straightforward, uncomplicated.

"Anya, the only person who gets less mail than you is little old me. Thank you for the thought, but they will never allow it. I don't even know the city. They just told me 'the West.'"

"I know you are fluent in English. Doesn't that mean Britain or the USA?"

"I'm not a complete fool. They made me spend hours learning American slang and idioms. America is a good guess."

"Do you know what you will do there? Is it just for education?" Anya asked.

"No, no, my dear. That would be much too simple. I not only have a new location and university, I have new parents, a new surname, and a new case officer. Your Gray Wolf will still be in charge, but I will report to a resident officer. I know that my new parents are diplomats who want their promising daughter to get a degree in physics. I will live near the campus and try to get close to a young professor who teaches physics and does research on missile guidance systems. That's all I know."

Sofia looked at Anya, and her voice softened, "Please don't mention any of this to anyone. I should not have said anything. If they were to find out, we would both be in serious trouble. I told you because it would be nice to know that there is, perhaps, someone on this earth who cares for me just a little and who occasionally keeps me in their thoughts."

Anya had never seen Sofia allow herself to be so vulnerable. She walked to Sofia and hugged her. Anya felt a single tear fall on her neck.

"Anya, I used to travel with my parents, but this is different. I'm a little bit afraid. The world seems awfully big right now. I don't know what they will do to me if I fail."

Anya handed her a handkerchief and retorted, "That's not the Sofia I know: head of the class, smartest person in the room, leader of all snobs. You'll take America by storm."

Sofia dabbed her eyes, and she had to laugh. "Yes, my cocky ambition should fit in rather well with the Americans, if that is the destination." She took Anya's hand and said, "I doubt that I will ever see you again. Think of me sometimes when you have a chance."

"Sofia, something tells me that I will see you again. I don't know how or when. Just remember, we Siberians are a hard bunch to get rid of. I don't know much about religion, but I will say a little prayer for you every day. If things get tough, think about that and know someone cares."

"I will. I will," Sofia replied. "You can't imagine how much that means to me! Now stop it, before I cry again and ruin the KGB's expensive makeup."

A KGB officer came to the doorway and looked at their room number. With a firm but polite voice, he said, "I've come for number twenty-one. A car is waiting downstairs to take you to the airport. At Berlin, another man will escort you for the remainder of your journey. He will give you your new documents for your final destination."

The officer politely took the largest suitcase and headed for the door. Sofia smiled and blew Anya a kiss. Anya called out, "See you soon." The large man, followed by the elegant dark-haired beauty, walked down the hallway, turned left, and disappeared out of sight.

The empty room, the lack of letters from her friends, the loss of her only confidant—all felt like open wounds to Anya, making Moscow even more lonely. Lying on her bed, Anya stared at the ceiling and, with a renewed sense of loss, said her first prayer for Sofia.

CHAPTER 54

The chemist was dressed in the traditional long white coat. His white springy hair only emphasized his small stature. He rested his hand on a full-sized rubber mannequin which had been placed facedown on a wooden table. Several syringes were lined on a stainless steel tray. Anya stood with the other recruits listening to the strange little man.

"As most of you know, this will be your last class before graduation tomorrow. You have all been trained in interrogation techniques, both in physical and psychological methodologies. Today we will explore chemical aides to interrogation: truth serums, pain enhancers, and a new drug which causes paralysis but all other senses remain active and functional."

A trainee asked, "How is this new drug best used?"

"Excellent question! It was designed to immobilize a target for transfer and then have him remain conscious for continued interrogation, with no side effects. His mind and speech faculties will be clear. Another advantage is that it will not numb his pain threshold. However, you should note that large dosages cause instantaneous death, with no detectible residue. It will appear as if the target had a massive heart attack.

"Everyone take a syringe and fill it with water. Each of you will practice on the rubber body. Observe! Optimal placement is here at the base of the skull and the top vertebrae. It will also take effect if injected in the side of the neck or underneath the jaw, but with a shorter period of paralysis."

The chemist expertly injected the mannequin in the three different areas that he had mentioned. He continued his instruction, "Since you may inject the target with several devices besides a syringe, the dosage is as follows: For transport or interrogation, use one finger-width of serum. This will cause paralysis for six hours when applied at the base of the skull, and for four hours if injected in the neck or jaw. A dosage of two finger-widths will cause death, either for assassination or for execution after an interrogation."

Anya inquired, "What is the name of the drug? May we see it?"

The instructor went to a locked cabinet and removed a small bottle of clear liquid. He held the vial above his head for all to see and said, "The drug is so new that it does not have a name. Observe the dosage when in a syringe: one finger-width, paralysis. Now two-fingers, paralysis and death. Line up and begin practicing with your water solution."

Anya watched the chemist replace the serum back into the bottle. He returned the bottle to the medicine chest and locked the cabinet before he proceeded to evaluate the students. Anya went to the back of the line and leaned against the windowsill. While everyone was looking at the mannequin, she unlocked the bottom window directly behind her.

After four hours, the chemist gave each recruit a passing grade, and he congratulated them for completing their courses for the next day's graduation ceremony. When Anya left the room, she mentally measured the distance between the window and the locked cabinet.

At 2:00 a.m. on the day of her graduation, Anya, dressed in a black KGB fatigue uniform, quietly made her way to the laboratory. The armory was always well guarded, but the classrooms were only locked at the end of each day with no additional supervision. Anya crawled through the unlatched window and opened the locked cabinet in a matter of seconds (just as she had been trained). She took a small brown vial that had been discarded in the wastebasket. In the medicine chest, she discovered one bottle of the new drug that had already been partially used. Using a syringe from the classroom, she filed the brown vial with the new drug. So little was taken it would never be detected. She cleaned the syringe and placed it exactly as she had found it.

Anya locked the cabinet and made her way back to her dormitory. In seven hours, Anya would officially become a member of the KGB. Obtaining a sample of the new drug became her first successful mission.

CHAPTER 55

Some students study four years and receive a scholastic diploma. Anya spent four years training at Moscow Center's "University of Espionage" and learned how to kill.

Upon completing the graduation ceremony, Anya met with Colonel Kurgan at his request. Her KGB dress uniform displayed a medal with a brass star topped by a red ribbon, honoring her for graduating at the head of the class. When she closed the office door, Kurgan rushed to greet her. He kissed her on each cheek and shook her hand.

"Well done, Anya! Congratulations! I knew you could do it! It is a shame Sofia could not be here to receive her award, but I will keep it for her for the time being. My two recruits earning the highest positions—seldom accomplished.

"I have also received a little recognition." The colonel lifted a paper off his desk and handed it to Anya. "This is a letter of commendation and a promotion. I will be assigned to the Intelligence Operations Division here at Moscow Center. It places me one more rung on the ladder to becoming a general. Good news for everyone!"

Anya returned the letter to the colonel and asked, "You wanted to see me?"

"Yes, for being the first in your class, it is customary to allow the recipient the opportunity to request a preferred assignment. It is just a request, mind you, not a guarantee. It also has to match the needs of the service. Have you any particular interests in this regard?"

Anya walked over to the window and viewed the training ground below, where she had spent many hours on the firing range. She noticed the black binoculars resting on the windowsill. She thought to herself, "The Gray Wolf has been watching me every day from his den." She turned to the colonel and replied, "I would like to be on the KGB Border Guard Patrol near the border of Manchuria."

The colonel was a hard man to surprise, but this revelation floored him. He raised his hands and exclaimed, "You can't be serious! That is where we send KGB personnel to punish them, not as a reward. It is mainly tromping around the mountains catching illegal aliens who are trying to escape a dreadful life in China by entering the Siberian fur trade. We interrogate them, send them back to China, and Mao's Red Guard executes them. The other criminals you will encounter are smugglers and poachers from both sides of the border. They can be very dangerous. They know, if detected, they will be shot on sight. They have nothing to lose by killing you and trying to flee. Please reconsider!"

"Colonel, you asked for my request. I have given it. I guess that I just miss the wilderness and the mountains."

"Another reason I foresee that your request will be denied," continued the exasperated colonel, "is that it is KGB policy not to assign new personnel in a region near their hometown or village. It produces a tendency for leniency and a conflict of interest. Absolutely not! I won't even process your request."

Anya turned her back to the colonel and once again stared out of the window. She offered, "Well, Colonel, do you have any suggestions?"

"I do indeed! The Intelligence Division is where the most activity, budgets, and promotions are offered. That is where you need to be. We didn't spend thousands of rubles and four years of training on you for you to chase illegal aliens or to get shot by criminals in the mountains. You have earned an opportunity—use it wisely."

"One last question, Colonel. Who would be my supervisor?"

"I would," the colonel replied. "With my new promotion, I can select anyone I desire."

"Well, you are probably correct. I could learn more here in Moscow in one year than six or seven years in the mountains. I suppose that is what I will do."

The colonel smiled and nodded his head. "Wise choice! I will make the transfer today."

Anya left the office and quietly closed the door. As she walked down the corridor toward the exit of the building, she had a slight smirk on her face—the Gray Wolf had given her exactly what she wanted.

Chapter 56

Sofia arrived in Berlin, along with her escort. They were ushered through the diplomatic line without delay. Her escort left her with the closing words, "Good luck," as he walked away.

A slender man in a gray suit approached Sofia. He wore round black spectacles that were tinted about the color of his suit. His hands were scarred, looking as if they had been burned. He motioned with his fish-scaled hand for Sofia to follow him and said, "Come with me. We have much to do in the next few days. Welcome to Berlin."

Sofia's days in Berlin were a whirlwind of activity. Her stern supervisor did not allow her to sleep except for a few hours each day. Every day she received special equipment and was taught how to use it, even when blindfolded.

Her "dark lord," as she tended to think of him, gave her a folder regarding her target. He required her to memorize even the smallest details. The dark man with the dark glasses told her, "You will learn, Sofia, that every detail is important. The chink in a knight's armor is often just a small seam. Observe everything as if you are looking at nothing. Know every coded dead drop and signal without even thinking about it. Store them clearly in your mind. They are your line of communication, your voice—possibly your very life. I will be your resident agent. We will never meet in public, but I will know your every move. Review your escape-route procedure again and hope that you never need it."

Sofia did as she was told. She never spoke to this matter-of-fact instructor unless he asked her a question. The experience of being the daughter of a diplomat had taught her to be a good judge of character. She sensed that this "dark lord" carried scars not only on his hands but in his soul. When she bravely asked his name, he grimly replied, "They call me the Raven."

CHAPTER 57

At the Intelligence Division, Anya worked at her small desk in a very large room surrounded by other small desks. There was no privacy; it was intended that way.

Like most new agents, she was assigned to be a "watcher." She spent most of her days following foreign diplomats around Moscow, observing their contacts and activities. This was standard new duty since it was felt that it helped refine tradecraft skills: shadowing others, disguising oneself, establishing listening posts.

Anya actually enjoyed getting out of the office and being on her own. The weather never bothered her; it seemed tame compared to Siberia. She did detest the tedious contact and observation reports filed at the end of each day for her supervisor's examination. She understood their importance but dreaded doing them anyway.

Today's report would raise eyebrows. Her assignment for the day was to shadow a new American diplomat. Watchers were constantly changed to avoid detection. When she had changed to a new location, the diplomat unexpectedly entered a new restaurant. There was no time to set up a team or a listening post, so Anya followed him into the restaurant and chose a table within clear sight of the target.

She ordered a light meal and paid for it in advance, just in case the target suddenly changed his mind and left. The diplomat ate by himself and made no contact with anyone. Apparently, he was just hungry and wanted to try a new restaurant.

He noticed the pretty Russian woman eating by herself. Diplomats were warned about the dangers of outside contacts, but a pretty woman is a pretty woman. He asked to join her, and she readily agreed. He introduced himself as Paul Adams.

Anya was eager to use her English-language skills. She was not as fluent as Sofia but still quite good. The American was pleasant, and the conversation centered on places to go, things to see, and local restaurants around Moscow. Between the smiles and kind suggestions, Anya made a mental note of each location that he seemed interested to visit. That would be the bulk of her contact report.

They left the restaurant, and he walked with her to the metro. She did not want to be seen at the American embassy. She told him that she worked at a book depository and gave him a telephone number in case he had other questions. He thanked her, and she descended into the metro.

If the diplomat called her, he would indeed get a book depository, but the number would be rerouted to KGB Moscow Center. There, Operations would decide what to do next. Anya knew the colonel would be ecstatic about this chance encounter. She also wondered what he would do with this opportunity. She did not trust Kurgan. Why was she given such extensive training in weaponry and martial arts? Why did he insist on being her supervisor? The Gray Wolf had plans beyond the horizon. In any case, the lengthy report had to be finished.

Anya had to stay late to finish her report. When the last person left for the evening, she looked around just to make sure she was alone. In the quiet, empty office, she opened the main drawer of her desk and retrieved four folders: a KGB census report for Vladivostok, an area census report submitted by District Commissar Lepan, and two red-flagged files with a broad red stripe across their front covers.

Anya had manipulated the colonel to get into the Intelligence Division for this very moment. It allowed her extensive access to all records relating to Soviet citizens and to foreigners. She had to have this access in order to do her job. After years of waiting and extensive planning, her reward was now within her reach, beckoning to her heart, mind, and soul: life-changing information just resting on her small desk—four files, four lives, four enemies, four debts to be paid.

In the silent building with her small desk lamp bent low, she opened the first document: District Commissar Lepan's report. She looked at the names listed alphabetically until she came to an old acquaintance: *Chekov*. He was listed as living in Anya's old family residence, deep in the forest. Anya slammed the folder shut and seethed, "My, my, Chekov, aren't you and the commissar clever boys!"

The Vladivostok census report and the two red-flagged files delivered additional information. Anya placed the red-flagged files side by side and looked at the photographs attached on the first page of each document. Anya memorized the addresses of the two subjects and smiled. In the dark, quiet room, under the harsh glow of her lamp, Anya stared at the two photographs and muttered, "Head Matron, Comrade Svelte—there you are!"

Anya slowly closed the folders and watched the cover obliterate their faces. She looked into the darkness and, with a cold voice, proclaimed, "My greetings, ladies. Now you are mine."

CHAPTER 58

Sofia's entry into the United States of America was efficient and carefully orchestrated. She spent a few weeks with her new "parents" in New York City to establish her cover. Funds were channeled through the parents to pay for her many expenses. It was natural and undetectable since the father's status at the United Nations allowed for a variety of budgets and expenditures.

Sofia spent most of her time in New York shopping for a college wardrobe. This, she thoroughly enjoyed, to the point that her local supervisor asked her to curb the expenses. She didn't, and she knew that they would let her get by with it. At this point, there was no one to replace her, and the mission was too important. As usual, she got her way. Later, when the resident agent saw pictures of her walking on the campus, he decided it was worth the expense.

Sofia's freshman status lasted only one week. She was so advanced that she passed all of her preliminary placement tests in science and mathematics. She requested permission to begin graduate-level courses in physics, and it was granted. When she subtly mentioned that she planned to get her doctorate at the university and hoped to teach there one day, the doors flew open: she received a prestigious scholarship and a recommendation for a research fellowship. Yes, Sofia had arrived.

Sofia lived off campus in a small bungalow. This privacy was essential to perform her mission. Most new students were required to live in the campus dormitories, unless a relative lived nearby. The KGB provided a very tough "aunt" who inspected the house, kept it stocked with food and supplies, and tested all the cameras and sound equipment, strategically located throughout the bungalow. Sofia firmly insisted that the bathroom was "off-limits" to their technology. Begrudgingly, this privacy was granted.

Sofia discovered that she had more freedom and privacy at the university's library than in her own "home." When the doors opened in the morning, she was the first to enter the library, and except for classes and office visits with professors, she remained there, until the library closed at night. This was noticed by many and admired by all, especially in the Physics Department. She returned to her bungalow only to sleep, bathe, and eat one meal a day, much to the annoyance of her watchers. They could not stop her from studying without blowing her established schedule and cover, and Sofia knew it. "Let them suffer in silence," became her motto.

The Dark Lord had instructed Sofia, "Cast your net far and wide." Her main target was a young single physics professor named Leslie Price. Few people knew of Professor Price's extensive research for the American military regarding missile guidance systems. The KGB only became aware of Price because an informant saw Price's signature on a schematic that had been placed on another absent-minded professor's desk, who also worked on the same project. Genius professors of all nations (including the USSR) were notorious about these lapses in security. The KGB planned to capitalize on the careless nature of these professors, and Sofia was the key to unlocking their secrets.

Within two months, Sofia had visited every professor within the Physics Department during his office hours. She always carried her black designer purse with the thin strap over her shoulder. Enclosed in the clasp of the purse was a wide-angle lens that took exceptionally clear pictures. While speaking with professors, she would merely direct the lens and press the clasp. The camera operated silently, and within a short time, she could photograph every paper on his desk, book titles on his shelves, and every lock in his office. The film was placed in a dead drop and developed at a secret dark room.

Sofia's main dead drop was a bench at a beautiful city park near the campus. The bench had two vertical pipes to which the *L*-shaped bench was attached. The caps at each end of the two pipes appeared to be attached by a simple screw. The KGB had arranged that only a special tool could release the caps on either end. Sofia always purchased some seeds and scattered them around the bench. When several pigeons had gathered, she stood at the back of the bench and dropped the bag of seeds next to the bottom of the bench. The sudden influx of birds provided a steady distraction to cover her hand movements, inserting a slender key into the screw. The cap slid to the left, allowing her to drop her film into the pipe while bumping the spring-loaded cap back into its place. The entire process took less than three seconds. She then stood with her hands on the back of the bench for another thirty seconds, as if she were gazing at the pretty pond in front of her. Glancing at her watch signaled her quiet departure.

Sofia's next stop was to a streetlight outside a popular campus coffee shop. The lamppost constantly had notices (usually a lost pet or a current student activity) taped on it. Sofia would place a slender strip of masking tape, the tip colored in light yellow, as high as she could reach. The subtle vertical marker could be seen by someone on the street, whether from a car, a motorcycle, or a bicycle.

She had four similar dead-drop sites and four signal posts in various areas within walking distance of the campus. Watchers drove by each signal post each day to see if a dead drop had been made. Sofia never used the same dead drop twice in a row. Randomness was her ally against detection.

When the film had been retrieved, a watcher would return to the lamppost and place the tape horizontally to let Sofia know that the dead drop was empty. If instructions were left for Sofia at the same dead drop, the strip of tape was turned diagonally. However, an *X* mark meant possible danger: "Go to the prearranged meeting point for possible extraction." The entire process was simple, and no one was seen meeting another agent. If one agent was being watched, it would not "contaminate" the other networks of agents working in the area.

Sofia strolled into the coffee shop and ordered her usual café au lait. Her elegant black purse was placed across her front and rested on her lap against the table. The purse never left her possession—anytime, anywhere. The thin strap was actually a steel cable covered in fine leather. A slash-and-grab purse thief would leave empty-handed.

Today she slowly drank her hot coffee and reflected that within a few hours, a man in green City Park overalls carrying a garbage bag and a collection stick would pick up some trash at the base of her bench and reverse the process with the pipe cap. It would take him a little bit longer since he had to kneel down to retrieve the film—maybe four seconds. Then he would continue gathering trash and walk away.

Sofia finished her coffee and walked by the pretty row of flowers lining the sidewalk toward the library. She would be there the rest of the day until it closed at 11:00 p.m. She planned to visit Professor Price the following morning and, with a winsome smile, photograph the papers on his desk. All in all, just another day at the university—just another coed who lives as a spy.

CHAPTER 59

"Come in, Anya. Any word from the American diplomat that you encountered?"

"No, Colonel. It has only been a week," Anya replied.

"Perhaps you are right. What did you want to see me about?"

"Colonel, I've never had a vacation in my life. I would like to request one at this time."

"You have never had a vacation? Didn't your family ever go anywhere together?"

"No, sir. I was young, and life was hard. I have lived in a Siberian cabin, a state orphanage, a KGB dormitory, and now a government apartment here in Moscow. All I know about our Soviet Union is from a map. I would like some time to explore. I think I've earned it."

It never occurred to Colonel Kurgan that Anya had never traveled anywhere other than Vladivostok and Moscow. Neither could be considered vacation destinations under the circumstances. He had traveled extensively with his family at her age, but he and Anya came from very different circles.

"Yes, I see your point." Kurgan walked over to a large map on his office wall and asked, "Where would you like to go?"

"Outside Moscow. Maybe somewhere I can hike and be around nature. I miss it. I just want time to read, relax, and think."

The colonel pointed on his map to some woodlands not far from Moscow and suggested, "How about this area? Some party officials have nice dachas there, and several inns are nearby. I can give you a list, if you are interested?"

Anya walked over to get a better look at the map and replied, "Thank you. That would be nice."

"How much time do you need?" Kurgan asked.

"I'm requesting two weeks. It takes time to travel in our large country, and this is my first vacation."

The colonel was not pleased to give her the full two weeks, especially if the diplomat were to call. He inquired, "And what do I say if your new acquaintance from the American embassy wants to contact you?"

"Perhaps for once, Colonel, we could just tell the truth: 'The employee is gone for two weeks on holiday, and she will return your telephone call when she returns.' Surely even American capitalists understand the concept of a vacation."

The colonel smiled. He knew that he had lost the battle, but perhaps not the war. He cautioned, "You realize, Anya, that new agents are not to go near their previous domiciles or other areas where they might be known. The penalties can be rather severe."

"I understand, sir. There is nothing for me back there anyway. It's all gone. If you will give me that list of inns you mentioned, I will trouble you no further. Thank you, and I will see you in two weeks."

When Anya left, Colonel Kurgan summoned his assistant and ordered, "Sergeant, for the next two weeks, I want you to monitor all bus, train, and airline manifests departing from Moscow. Also include hotel registrations for this immediate area."

"Any particular person for the inquiry?" the sergeant asked.

"Yes, Sergeant, Agent Anya Ruslanova. That will be all."

The sergeant raised his eyebrows, but he knew better than to ask too many questions. As he turned to leave, he mentioned, "If you desire, I will have her followed. It would be difficult for two weeks, but it could be done."

"No, Sergeant. She shadows people for a living. She knows every street and alley in this city and every tree in the forest. A team would not last an hour before she lost them, either in the city or in the woods. Good suggestion though. Carry on."

Anya went back to her desk and placed a small map under her lamp. She had no intention of using the inns the colonel recommended. She planned to hike and camp far away from the Gray Wolf's prying eyes. Running her finger along the map, the tip of her finger stopped on her desired destination: the city of Vladivostok.

PART 4

The Return

*Whoever digs a pit will fall into it; and he who
rolls a stone will have it roll back on him.*
—Proverbs 26:27

CHAPTER 60

Anya arrived at the train station at a strategic time when the guards and watchers made their shift change. Within thirty minutes, the new security personnel would be in place to observe the crowds at the busy station. Anya's timing coincided with the arrival of a specific clerk, just coming on duty. Anya's position in the Intelligence Division made this exact planning possible.

Dressed in a nondescript beige outfit with a tan overcoat, Anya wore a dark shoulder-length wig, her eyes now dark brown because of contact lenses. Special makeup gave her a soft olive complexion. She wore this disguise in her shadowing operations of foreign dignitaries, but not enough to be recognized by another member of the KGB.

Seeing the clerk walking down the sidewalk, Anya walked beside her, looked straight ahead, and began her interrogation.

"Comrade Clerk, just keep walking. I know who you are and where you live. I know your work schedule. I also know of an arrangement you have with a certain conductor: you arrange specific compartments to be empty, and the conductor sells them to wealthy businessmen and tourists, whereby you both split the profits. I am with the KGB on a special mission. You are going to assign me one of those compartments, and no one will be the wiser. If you do not help me, you and the conductor will be arrested, interrogated, and sent to a gulag near the Arctic Circle for capitalist crimes against the state. I now require your cooperation and your silence."

The clerk, terrified and with trembling hands, shook her head and exclaimed, "There must be some mistake. I'm just a simple ticket clerk. I'm not clever enough for such things!"

Anya tersely replied, "Don't look at me and keep walking. Listen carefully to your instructions. You will go to your work station as usual. I will be the third person in line. You will give me compartment number 112, which is directly beside the lavatory and the train's exit doors. I will give you a card with the name of Olivia Gabrilova—Textiles, Moscow. This person does exist. Use this information on your manifest for the name, business, and residence. Say nothing. Just write it down and hand me the ticket."

"But I don't even know where you want to go!" the clerk pleaded.

"You know very well that compartment is on the train to Vladivostok. You are beginning to annoy me."

"Yes, all right, I'll do exactly as you say. You have my cooperation. You have my silence."

"Thank you, comrade. This mission is not to be revealed to anyone regardless of their credentials. I may just send someone to test you. All you will do is to show them the manifest, as you are legally required. If they ask for a description, you will say that you have so many customers that you don't remember exactly, but perhaps middle-aged, dark hair, average height—nothing else. I know you won't fail me."

Later, Anya found the conductor, who was looking over the passengers' list for the day. Anya passed him and began to enter the train. "Just a moment, miss." The conductor stepped toward her. "The train doesn't board for another hour."

Anya approached him with a pretty smile. She gently placed her tan suitcase on the platform. With her left hand, she showed him her KGB credentials, and with her right hand, she grabbed him above the elbow and pressed a nerve that made his arm go limp. With a pleasant smile, she whispered in his ear, "Don't talk. Escort me to compartment 112 right now if you ever want to use that arm again."

Anya glanced carefully over her shoulder to make sure that no one saw them together, and they entered the train. Once inside, she ordered the conductor, "Lock the door behind you. Tell me everything you know about a small station, number 934."

The conductor rubbed his arm and said, "It's not a manned station, just a short stop for the rare passenger, or to collect and leave mail."

"What is the procedure?" Anya asked.

"It's pretty simple: an electric red light is turned on before a part-time clerk leaves for the day. The red light means to stop for a passenger, or they have outgoing mail. If we have incoming mail, we stop and place it in the building. Most of the time, there is neither a passenger nor any mail, so we just continue without stopping."

"What time does the train arrive at this crossing?"

"We arrive at approximately 3:00 a.m., depending on the weather. It's just a little hut in the middle of nowhere. Why do you want to stop there? Your ticket is for Vladivostok."

Anya grabbed the man's arm again, and he flinched. She glared at him and said, "Listen carefully. If you want to continue selling these compartments to the wealthy when high-ranking officials are not present, if you want to breathe without pain, if you want to live—do as I say. Tell the engineer to stop at crossing 934, whether there is a red light or not. Take a mailbag, place it in the hut, and relock the door. The clerk will think it is just an extra bag left for him for future deliveries. Can you see the date on this card?"

The conductor nodded his head and leaned away from her.

"Memorize the date on this card. On that date, you will reserve this same compartment for me from Vladivostok to Moscow. I know your schedule. You will escort me into the train early, just like today. No one is to know about my leaving the train at crossing 934 or anything we have discussed. Do you understand?"

The conductor slowly pulled his arm away and said, "Yes, I understand completely. One last thing: when you leave the train at crossing 934, go to the right. There are no lights there, and you can go to the back of the station. No one will see you."

"Excellent suggestion, comrade! Please tell the stewards not to come to my cabin. Explain that you have a high-ranking official who wants privacy. I brought my own food and water."

"May I leave now? I need to make arrangements to begin boarding the other passengers. My absence will be missed."

"Please do. And, conductor, remember this date." Anya took the white card, struck a match, and held the burning card near the conductor's nose. The conductor saw the flames reflecting in her eyes. She dropped the card onto an ashtray and continued, "Thank you for your cooperation, comrade. I'll see you soon. We have a slogan: 'the KGB never forgets.' I suggest that you do the same. Please lock the door behind you."

The conductor hurriedly left and locked the cabin door. He went to the lavatory and splashed water onto his face. As he dried his face, he looked into the mirror and spoke to his reflection, "God have mercy upon the person she's after, for truly, this creature will have none."

The train arrived at crossing 934 on time at two forty-five in the morning. The conductor did as he was told, and he carried a few empty mail sacks with him. He unlocked the tiny station and left the sacks inside the door. Locking the door, he signaled the engineer with his lantern to proceed. As the train slowly gained speed, the conductor looked to his right but saw only darkness. *Whoever she is*, he thought, *good riddance*. But with a sinking feeling, he knew they would meet again.

****

Anya left the train just as it began to move. She was dressed entirely in black; her fatigues and field boots were designed to blend with the night. Following the conductor's advice, she turned to the right to avoid any lights and waited behind the station, until the red caboose light faded into a small speck, swaying in the night.

Anya was pleased to get out of her small quarters on the train and to stretch her legs. Time to begin the second leg of her journey. The old wagon track that Dmitri, Petrov, and she had traveled several years ago was now a wide two-track dirt road made by truck tires. It was still very basic and probably impassable with deep snow or heavy rains, yet it was progress of some sort for the sparse population in the area.

She stored the black wig and the brown-colored eye contacts in the suitcase. The wig was no longer needed, and she could see better without the lenses. She attached two straps to the suitcase and slung it onto her back. A large web belt secured the suitcase against her. Her field compass showed that the road went north and then curved slightly to the west to reach Vladimir's Store. By going cross-country, she could eliminate several kilometers. No need for her small flashlight; the bright full moon shone with soft, clear light.

Once her eyes adjusted to the moonlight, she ran down the road for a short distance to limber her legs from the long train ride. She was in perfect condition, and the crisp autumnal air refreshed her. Running, smiling, following the old road, it seemed like a lifetime ago since she had been in this wild country. In many ways, it was another life—lost in time. She had left as a frightened young girl; she now returned as a determined young woman, an agent of the KGB.

Anya left the road and increased her speed. She wanted to reach Vladimir's Store before dawn and enter the village unnoticed. There was plenty of time. She checked her compass one last time—north by northwest—and ran with unbridled freedom by the lantern of the moon.

CHAPTER 61

It was still dark when Vladimir approached his store. He had to stock some shelves with newly arrived goods before the day began. As he approached the front of the store, he detected a faint whiff of smoke. At first, he thought his store was on fire; but as he rushed toward the door, he noticed a thin line of smoke rising from the chimney. This was odd since he never left a fire in the stove when he closed at night.

He cautiously inserted his large skeleton key into the latch but found it was already unlocked. Standing in the doorway, he quietly pushed the door open with his foot. Cautiously, he advanced utilizing the hard lessons learned from the fierce fighting at Stalingrad: approach, wait, listen. Next to the stove, he saw a figure sitting in the shadows, drinking a cup of tea.

"Who are you?" Vladimir called out. "Why are you breaking into my store like this? Answer me."

The intruder said nothing but slid a pistol, which Vladimir kept in his desk, down the long counter toward him. Vladimir stared at the revolver and heard a voice, "Come now, Vladimir. Is that any way to greet an old friend?" The stranger struck a match, lit a candle, and placed the flame near her face.

"Hello, Vladimir. It's Anya. I've come home."

Vladimir was so shaken that he had to grab the counter to steady himself. With a trembling voice, he whispered, "No, it can't be… I was notified of your death. How is this possible?"

"In many ways, I was dead, my friend. But here I am—alive and in the flesh. Please shut the door. Let's talk."

Vladimir's hand was shaking so badly that he had difficulty lighting a lantern. Finally, he made his way to his desk and sat down. Tears sprang to his eyes, and he covered his face with his hands. Anya never anticipated the shock that her presence would bring upon her friend, nor was she aware of the death notification that he had received. It was beginning to make sense: no letters, no contact of any kind, being forbidden to ever come home. She felt the presence of the Gray Wolf.

Anya knelt beside Vladimir and hugged his shoulders. "I'm all right, Vladimir, and so are you. Who told you that I was dead?"

Wiping his eyes, opening his desk drawer, offering the notice of death with a trembling hand, Vladimir gave Anya the ominous letter. When she reached the ending where it said, "You have my deepest sympathy," signed by Colonel Viktor Kurgan, she clenched her fist to control her rage. Looking at her troubled friend, seething with pain and indignation, reading the deceitful letter by the light of a lantern, Anya determined that the Gray Wolf must pay for his treachery.

"I'm sorry, Anya. I asked for his help to release you. We were comrades in arms. I thought he was my friend. Why would he do this?"

"Don't worry, Vladimir. You did your best. Your old friend betrayed both of us. I appreciate all that you tried to do for me. Now get up and be the shrewd businessman that I have always known you to be. I need to purchase a few supplies before I go to see Dimitri. Up now—on your feet."

Anya reached out and took Vladimir's hand to help him out of his chair. Touching her cheek, stroking her long soft hair, he exclaimed, "I can't believe it, but I am overjoyed! It really is you—my long-lost daughter of the forest! Here you are in front of me!" Smiling, regaining his composure, winking at Anya, his intelligent eyes glistening with happiness, he retorted, "Very well. Since you broke into my store and almost gave me a heart attack rising from the grave, I'm going to have to skin you alive in trade. What do you need, dear?"

Anya was relieved. The old Vladimir was back, and as feisty as ever. Smiling, patting his hand, winking at him with her crystal-blue eyes, she tartly said, "First things first, Vladimir. Do you still have my father's old rifle, or did you trade it for some pots and pans?"

"Oh, you are terrible, dear girl, and certainly your father's daughter—weapons and ammunition first, then all else. Yes, of course, I have his rifle. It is in the backroom, oiled and wrapped in a blanket. Your father would also return to haunt me if I had neglected his precious rifle. I'll get it shortly. What else do you need?"

"Yes, well, Papa was right. I need a box of cartridges, those tall black boots with the leather soles, two pairs of thick socks, and that large pack to hold everything."

Vladimir hesitated and turned toward Anya. He was no fool; Anya's selections puzzled him. He inquired, "Anya, this is a very strange order for a simple trip to see Dimitri, especially the men's boots that are two sizes too large for you. I know equipment. The boots that you are wearing are some of the best. The average citizen cannot even buy them. Your black fatigues are government-issued. What are you up to, my little *Krokodile*?"

Anya had to smile at the mention of *Krokodile*, the title of a book he had given her when she was a young girl. Yes, Vladimir was just as astute as ever.

"Vladimir, you have become entirely suspicious with growing age. It does not become you. I just want to see Dimitri and to do a little hunting before I have to leave. Surely, that is innocent enough."

Vladimir gathered her request and placed the items on his counter. Handing her the boots, he said, "Try these. I'll get your father's rifle." Anya put on the tall leather boots wearing two socks; they fit snugly. She returned to her comfortable field boots and placed all the other items into the pack. Vladimir handed her Sasha's rifle and a small canteen. He advised, "For a hunting expedition, you'll need these."

Anya checked the chamber of the rifle, and it was as clean as the day that she had left it before going to the orphanage. She put on the pack and slipped the rifle sling over her shoulder. It was almost dawn, and she did not want to be seen with Vladimir at his store. Time to depart.

"Vladimir, I left a tan suitcase behind your desk. May I leave it here until I get back from hunting? About Colonel Kurgan, let's just keep that between ourselves and Dimitri for right now. I'll take care of it later."

Vladimir had a look of surprise on his face. He exclaimed, "Are you telling me that you know this man?"

"Vladimir, I work for him."

Vladimir once again sat down at his desk. Shaking his head, he replied, "Anya, this is too much. You return from the dead, and now you work for the man who told me this—the same man who was my friend and my ranking officer in the army. I can't take much more. Go! Go shock poor Dimitri. Maybe the old buzzard will croak when he sees you. Too much, child, just too much!"

Anya pulled some cash from her front pocket and mentioned, "I almost forgot, how much do I owe you?"

Vladimir quickly replied, "For all the agony you have caused me, a fortune! But I guess I will settle for a small kiss on the cheek from a pretty girl that I've always loved as my own."

Anya kissed Vladimir and playfully ran her fingers through his hair. As she turned to leave, she said, "I'll see you soon, grouchy old man. Thank you for helping me. I love you, Vladimir."

"Oh, get out of here and pester Dmitri. Tell him hello for me. By the way, Anya, what are you going to hunt?"

Anya stood at the doorway and turned toward Vladimir. The happy grin was gone, and Vladimir saw the face of a young woman he did not recognize: fierce and threatening. She coldly replied, "I'll be hunting weasels!" Anya quietly closed the door and vanished into the blue gray before dawn.

Vladimir sat at his desk for a long time, reading and rereading the colonel's letter. Looking at the empty doorway, the sun's rays streaming through the storefront windows, lifting his eyes to an unseen heaven, softly he whispered, "My dear child…what have they done to you?"

****

Vladimir wisely sent a message to Dmitri briefly describing the situation and that Anya was on her way to see him. He sent the letter with Mischa, a handsome, easygoing young dark-haired man who owned a salvaged World War II motorcycle that he treasured. It was in constant need of repair, but Mischa could fix anything—one of the many reasons Vladimir hired him part-time for various duties.

The colonel's letter had been particularly cruel to Dmitri since Dmitri had been Anya's protector and escort to Vladivostok and was the last person to see her before she entered the orphanage. He had blamed himself when he was told that she had died of typhus at the very place that he had left her. Vladimir tried to reassure him that there was nothing he could have done; even so, Dmitri fell into a deep depression for several months. Dmitri often referred to himself during that dark period of his life as "Anya's executioner."

Dmitri stood for several hours scanning the horizon, like a faithful watchdog waiting for its master's return. When he finally glimpsed Anya coming down the road, he could not contain himself, and he rushed to greet her. Anya smiled when she saw him running toward her. With his portly figure and awkward gait, he reminded her of a T-34 tank coming down the road on a collision course. When he finally reached her, he almost knocked her down in his excitement and with his crushing bear hug. With tears in his eyes, he kept holding her while repeating, "Forgive me, Anya, forgive me. I'm sorry I failed you."

Anya held Dmitri closely and allowed him to weep. She suddenly realized that Dimitri had suffered more than she. The orphanage had been a lonely struggle for her, but it had been a prison of sorrow and regret for her poor friend. It was an important life lesson for her: she now understood that those in the heat of life's battles often suffer less than those loved ones who must stand by and dread the carnage. With one hand, she patted Dmitri on the shoulder; with the other, she clenched her fist and swore revenge. Those responsible would severely suffer for this ordeal of agony.

Anya broke the tension using Napoleon's strategy of "divide and conquer." She whispered into Dmitri's ear, "Vladimir sends his warmest greetings and asked me to remind you that you need to pay your bill."

Dmitri immediately released Anya and jumped back as if she had applied electric shock. "Why that wretched, conniving scoundrel! I paid him a month ago! He needs to get off his lazy duff and update his accounting! Anya, I pay my bills. The very nerve of that man to tell you such hogwash! What he needs is a good lashing with a horsewhip to help his memory!"

Anya calmed the volcano by slipping her arm through his and suggesting, "Come, show me your farm. I haven't been here for years. Everything looks so neat and clean." Anya took off her pack and rested her rifle against it to begin her tour.

Dmitri walked beside her, beaming with pride. He loved his farm and loved even more to talk about all his new improvements. Anya just nodded her head and complimented him profusely. Dmitri could not keep his eyes off her for very long. He held her arm tightly, perhaps secretly fearing she would once again vanish before him. Kind and emotional Dmitri decided that this was the happiest day of his life.

They passed a lovely orchard and a large pine tree that stood alone near the center of the farm. Dmitri took Anya's hand and quietly said, "Come, Anya. I need to show you something." Under the spreading boughs of the pine tree, there was a little mound covered with pine needles. At the head of the mound, Dmitri had chiseled into a half-dome rock the following: "Anya Ruslanova—Beloved Friend, Faithful Daughter, Child of the Forest." Dmitri continued, "When the ashes arrived, Vladimir and I decided that this would be a good resting place for you. We wanted to bury you next to your parents, but we were denied permission."

Anya looked at the small graveside and tried to control her anger. "And who would deny such a thing?" she asked.

Dmitri turned away and said, "Chekov! The district commissar assigned him the property once you were recorded as an orphan. I'm sorry to tell you…he now lives in your cabin. I thought you should know."

"Thank you, Dmitri, for all that you have done. This is a lovely spot, but someday I hope to rejoin my parents. When that day comes, would you make sure this lovely headstone rests with me?"

Dmitri was very touched but exclaimed, "Of course, I would do that, but let's not talk about the impossible! I am much older. You will probably have to bury me. I certainly don't trust that crooked Vladimir. He would probably just clean out my pockets and toss me into a ditch. Come to the house. Let's eat! Let's celebrate!"

Anya replied, "I agree. Come over to my pack. I have a gift for you." Anya opened her pack and retrieved a bottle of vodka stored inside one of the black boots that she had received from Vladimir. Dmitri was impressed. This was one of the best brands of vodka. Dimitri could also see that another bottle remained protected in the other boot.

"Dmitri, this may seem odd, but I need to keep this bottle—let's just say for a keepsake—to remember this moment. Do you have an empty bottle I may use?"

Dmitri decided not to ask any questions. He retrieved another bottle and watched Anya transfer the expensive vodka into his old green bottle. Mysteriously, she walked to Dmitri's well and filled the empty vodka bottle full of water and firmly sealed the cap. Once again, she placed the bottle back into the boot and secured the flap of her pack. She could tell that Dmitri was baffled by her behavior.

Anya explained, "I have a canteen, but you can never have too much water on hand when traveling."

Dmitri was not convinced, so he carefully probed further, "Where did you get such fine vodka? This must have cost you a fortune."

Anya mischievously grinned and replied, "Oh, I stole it from Vladimir. I broke into his store and helped myself to his storage area next to the bar before he arrived in the morning. I left money where the bottles were stacked. It should take him all of ten minutes to figure out who took them. I thought that I might blame it on you. I hope you don't mind?"

"No, no, Anya, that's my girl—anything to annoy our dear Vladimir. However, you won't get away with it. Vladimir knows that I am too cheap to buy this quality. He will catch you in the end."

Anya looked at Dmitri and considered how profound his last comment applied to her at this moment in her life. She followed Dmitri into his house and ruefully replied, "Yes, Dmitri, you are probably right…they will catch me before it ends."

Chapter 62

Dmitri tried to convince Anya to stay longer. She told him that she just wanted to hunt for a few days and that she would see him soon. Dmitri helped her strap on her pack and handed her Sasha's rifle. He also handed her the tiger-claw necklace that she had given him at the door of the orphanage for safekeeping. Anya held the claws in her hand momentarily before placing the necklace around her neck. Her father's rifle and this token of her past were her most treasured possessions. She was touched by her friend's dedication to preserve them for her. Dmitri was indeed a man of his word.

"Remember, a few days, and then I will come to look for you," Dmitri cautioned.

"You worry too much, old friend. Besides, you wouldn't find me anyway. You're not that good of a tracker."

Anya kissed his cheek and began the next leg of her journey. Dmitri saw that she was heading up the valley toward the mountain where her parents' cabin remained. He had an uneasy feeling, but there was nothing he could do. He watched her until she faded from his sight.

On the evening of the second day, Anya saw her cabin from a distance. She was shocked to find it in such disarray: several shingles were missing from the roof, all her mother's flowerbeds were brown with neglect and decay, the door to her father's work shed was hanging crookedly on one hinge, and several animal hides lay rotting on the ground. She changed into her large black boots with the new leather soles and poured some dust over the tops of the boots. Cautiously, she approached the cabin and called out, "Hello, anyone home?"

After a short time, the cabin door opened slightly, and Chekov came out with a rifle in his hands. He shouted, "Who are you? What do you want?"

Anya was repelled by his appearance: his dirty shirt stained down the front, several weeks of gray-brown stubble on his face, yellow tobacco-stained fingers and teeth—the dried, rancid look of a vulture that had been feasting on bloated carrion.

"Just passing through. I'm with the Wildlife Service. We are checking animal populations in this area for a government survey. I thought I might camp outside your cabin for the night, if that's all right? Besides, I have a couple of bottles of vodka to break the chill. I hate to drink alone."

Chekov grinned and lowered his rifle. She looked harmless enough. Vodka and a pretty inspector might be a welcome diversion for the evening. He had not talked to anyone for a month. Any conversation was better than none.

"Come in. Bring your vodka. I hope you brought some food. I'm a little short of grub right now."

Anya opened the chamber of her rifle to let Chekov know that it was empty and that she was not a threat. She walked into the cabin and set her pack on a broken chair. The cabin was in such a wretched state that she had to turn her back away from him to not reveal her anger. Chekov smiled with anticipation when he saw her produce two bottles of very fine vodka, a loaf of bread, and a small round of cheese that Dmitri had given her for her "hunting expedition." She held the two bottles in the air and, with a forced smile, exclaimed, "I'm hungry, let's eat!"

Chekov motioned for her to sit down. Anya slung her rifle on the back of her chair as she watched Chekov's eyes glance at the empty chamber—his making sure it was indeed empty. She brushed dried food to the side of the table and opened both bottles of vodka, tossing both caps over her shoulder to signify the Russian custom that the caps would no longer be needed: they would drink until both bottles were empty.

"A bottle for you and a bottle for me, comrade. *Vashe zdorovye*—to your health." Anya saluted Chekov. She tipped her bottle back and drank a quarter of the bottle. Chekov was not about to let a woman outdrink him, and so he did the same. His eyes suddenly brightened. Great vodka and this woman could really drink—a promising evening was in store.

Anya cut the bread and cheese and asked, "Comrade, I don't mind drinking out of a bottle, but do you have a couple of glasses?"

Chekov nodded, and with a goofy grin on his face, he slightly weaved while walking to get two glasses from a cabinet behind him. The alcohol on an empty stomach was already beginning to take effect. He placed a dirty glass in front of Anya. She smiled and filled her glass to the top from her bottle of water. Chekov marveled at how this pretty city girl could really drink vodka. He did the same from another chipped glass; he would show this city girl how a trapper could match anyone.

Anya had no intention of drinking out of his nasty glass. She smiled and waited until Chekov slammed his vodka down in one swift gulp. She guided the conversation by asking, "And what is your name, comrade?"

"Chekov," he replied. "And yours, honey?"

Anya coyly smiled and said, "My name is Andrea. I work in Vladivostok."

When Chekov heard the word *Vladivostok*, a warning signal came to him even in his drunken state: the sudden visitor, the blonde hair, an old rifle. "Odd choice of rifle that you carry," retorted Chekov. "I would have guessed that a wildlife inspector would want something more modern. I once knew a fellow who had a rifle just like that. Great shot, old Sasha. Don't guess you knew him?"

Chekov poured himself another glass. Anya noticed that this time, he took it in his left hand and that his right hand was slowly dropping under the table. She knew that he had a pistol hidden in his belt under his shirt. Chekov smiled and raised his glass in the air in an attempt to draw the imposter's eyes away from the table, "*Vashe zdorovye* to you, Andrea."

Just as the glass touched his lips, he pulled the pistol from his belt. Anya was ready. She whirled the rifle next to her forward, smashing the butt of the rifle into the glass when it reached Chekov's mouth. The glass shattered, and Chekov fell out of his chair onto the floor, dropping the pistol.

Anya was on top of him before he could regain his senses. The alcohol had slowed his reactions and weakened his strength. She rolled him over on his stomach and pinned both of his arms with her knees. At the base of his neck she inserted a needle with a syringe of serum measured one finger in width. Chekov's body went limp instantly. When Anya rolled him onto his back, she saw with satisfaction that his lips were shredded, and two yellow bloody teeth lay scattered on the floor.

"Come, Comrade Chekov, you seem tired. Let's get you to bed!"

In a moment of rage, Anya threw Chekov across the room, where he hit the wall and landed on her parents' old bed. She quickly tied his hands and feet to the bedstead, just in case the serum wore off too soon. She leaned into Chekov's terrified face and taunted him, "Comrade, you just rest awhile. I have a few errands to tend to, but don't worry, I'm coming back for you."

Anya went to the toolshed. Many of her father's tools were broken or scattered. He took such pride in his workshop—now this. She eventually found enough tools to work with. She went to her mother's flower bed. A few of the yellow Siberian tulips her mother had cheerfully planted still had some green shoots. Anya dug up the bulbs and proceeded toward her parents' graves.

In short order, she transplanted the bulbs with the hope that they might bloom again. The soil was better here, and the nearby stream provided more moisture. She stood over her parents' graves that were now covered with a blanket of grass. She felt their loss, but there were no tears—a deep rage had replaced them.

Anya took a pick and shovel and began to dig on the small mound between her parents. She had to hurry since the serum would be diminishing in a few hours. The trunk that she had buried so long ago was still in good condition. The thick waxed oilskin had protected it. The oilskin was ruined, but the trunk was not. She took a small chisel and hammered away the wax seal and lead solder around the lid. Opening the lid, she was relieved to find that everything inside was perfectly dry.

She quickly retrieved the contents and left the closed trunk behind. Refilling the hole took only a short time. She then cut a branch and brushed away all her footprints around the graves, all the way to the flower beds. It would take an expert tracker to find any prints. The next rain would erase any traces of the large man-sized boots with new unmarked soles.

Returning to the cabin, she cleaned the table with an old rag and placed three items on the table. She rechecked Chekov's bindings and told him, "Chekov, I know you can see and hear me—you just can't move. I think you have figured out that I am the little girl that you sold out to our beloved Commissar Lepan. Well, comrade, the little girl grew up and decided to pay you a visit.

"You may be wondering where I found these three things. They were buried not far from here. Now in this canvas is a tiger's fur. The tiger killed my father, and I killed the tiger. I can see the greed in your eyes from here. Yes, if you had found it, you would be a wealthy man today. The next item is my mother's Bible. You probably would have used its pages to roll tobacco into them and smoke your cigarettes. The last item is of particular interest to you: a jar of tiger claws. This slightly bent one is for you."

Anya took a hand drill that she had retrieved from the shed and made a small hole near the top of each claw. She untied her necklace and put Chekov's designated claw alongside the three existing claws. She walked over to Chekov and dangled the necklace in front of his face. Chekov was clearly terrified, and his eyes darted back and forth from the necklace to Anya's hateful face. She then did something even more frightening: Clutching the necklace in her right palm, Anya squeezed until drops of blood formed on the base of her hand. She forced Chekov's mouth open and watched as rivulets of blood dripped into his mouth. She gripped Chekov's designated claw with her bloody hand and raked it across his left eye, smiling as she heard Chekov wail with pain.

"You wanted to consume me—have your fill. But know this—today I will consume you. You sold me for vodka. Let's wash down that blood with what's left." Taking the bottle of vodka, she rammed the neck of the bottle into his mouth. Several more teeth were broken, and blood poured out of his mouth. The blood from his eye and mouth formed a steady stream that mingled together and rained on the wooden floor.

Anya put her retrieved possessions into the pack, placing the pack and rifle near the cabin door. She removed Chekov's bindings and strategically placed the two vodka bottles just below his bed. The fireplace already had a small fire, so she stuffed as many logs into the pit as it would hold. Taking a kerosene lamp, she opened its reservoir and poured a thin line from the edge of the fireplace to Chekov, lying paralyzed on the bed. Spitefully, Anya splashed the remainder of the kerosene onto Chekov's face and chest. The lantern was placed between the two bottles and the bedsheets draped on the floor.

The scene was set: a known drunk who drank two bottles of vodka, the expensive labels burned off in the fire, a lamp too close to a bed in a living area full of trash. The solid wood cabin would do the rest. There would not even be an inquiry.

"One last thing, Chekov, before I go. I need your thumbprint on this piece of paper. It's a transfer of assignment to this cabin, valley, mountainside, and hunting rights to our old friends Vladimir and Dmitri. You generously gave them an equal share before your demise. I would have, but then I don't officially exist. I took the liberty of forging your signature and backdating this a month ago. Hold still. This is the only part that will be painless."

Anya folded the document and placed it inside her jacket. Chekov shouted, "You'll never get away with this. Commissar Lepan will have to sign and approve it as well. He will never do it."

Anya spoke in a deliberately chilling voice, "Oh, he will, Chekov. Believe me—he will."

Amidst Chekov's sobbing cries for mercy and bleak bargaining against death, Anya shouldered her now heavy pack, which contained almost all of her worldly possessions: a tiger robe, a jar of tiger claws, and her mother's Bible. Her father's rifle, the tiger-claw necklace around her neck, and Sergei's crouched-tiger carving on her desk at Moscow completed the collection. She breeched a shell into her rifle and placed the sling on her shoulder. Time to gather another signature.

She stood in the doorway of the cabin for one final look and only saw a mirage. This was no longer her home. The temple had been defiled. Her inner sanctum of love, joy, and a future with hope lay in dust and ashes. The temple robbers had done their work well. The commissar, Chekov, the orphanage, and Kurgan had not only stolen her land and home, marked her body with scars, as if using a hot branding iron, and taken the most promising years of her life, they had committed the unforgivable sin: murdering her memories, slashing the throat of joy, searing her soul.

Sadly, she realized that once leaving or losing the connection, there really was no "coming back." One returns home to die, if not physically, then emotionally and spiritually. This was no longer her home; it was a mausoleum—a place of dried bones, a past covered in dust.

She blew on the firebrand in her hand until it produced a small flame. As she tossed it into the pool of kerosene next to the fireplace, the combustion boomed like a muffled cannon. The fire slowly crawled toward Chekov and his flowing bedsheets. When she heard Chekov screaming, she slowly closed the door. The mausoleum was sealed, the funeral pyre lit—the death rite of her past life finished.

As she walked down the mountain trail, the screaming rose to a shrill crescendo: an opera of death. Already, black smoke and licking flames were billowing out of the windows. Walking by the light of Chekov's burning coffin, proceeding down the steep and winding path to the world below, never looking back, she disappeared like the black smoke rising behind her—into oblivion, the silence of the night.

Chapter 63

Anya waited in the woods near the quiet pond. She knew it would not be long. District Commissar Lepan always liked to fish here every Saturday morning. His unvarying schedule was very helpful to her.

The commissar liked this pond because it was not very large but very deep. The fish would surface to feed, and in his trusty rowboat, he could catch them not far from the shore. Lepan could not swim, but he always knew he could thrash his way to shallower water and wade to the nearby bank if necessary. He never ventured to the center of the pond, where its depth unnerved him.

It was a beautiful morning, and Lepan happily placed his bait and fishing rod into the rowboat. He was about to push the boat off a grassy knoll into the water when Anya came into the clearing and called out to him.

"Commissar, I hate to spoil your morning, but I need to ask your opinion on a simple matter." She held a paper and her credentials in her left hand, and her right hand was tucked into her jacket.

The commissar saw her tall black boots and assumed that she must be a government official of some kind.

"How may I help you?" the commissar cautiously inquired.

"Oh, it is a simple assignment, but it seemed rather suspicious. I thought you might be of assistance."

Anya held out the paper and closed her KGB credentials before the commissar could read her name. The commissar leaned forward to read the small print and exclaimed, "This is suspicious, indeed! Chekov would never sign—"

Before he finished his comment, Anya grabbed his hair and twisted his head around, exposing the back of his skull. With her right hand, she drove the needle of the syringe into the base of his neck just below his shirt collar. She held him tightly until his body became limp.

Anya lowered Lepan onto the grass and quickly placed his thumb on an inkpad and pressed it next to his forged signature—mission accomplished. After the thumbprint dried, she placed the commissar into the rowboat and tightly wound the stout fishing line around his left leg to the bench seat where he lay. She lowered the sharp fishhook in front of his face and dangled a tiger claw beside it.

"Commissar, look a little closer at my identification papers. Does the name look familiar to you?" When the commissar recognized her name, he immediately cried out, "It was Chekov's idea. He...he blackmailed me! Yes, that's it—it was blackmail. I had no choice."

Anya shook her head and placed the tiger claw next to the others on her necklace. Lepan watched in horror as she gripped the claws until a drop of blood oozed from her hand. She fiercely squeezed his mouth until he squealed, and she let the blood drop into his mouth. Leering into his face, she coldly said, "You buried me in an orphanage. Now I'm going to bury you in the deep."

She took a large limb and rammed it into the side of the rowboat just above the watermark stain. In a final act of revenge, she raked the designated claw for the commissar across his left eye and drove the fish hook underneath the same eye socket, firmly jerking it into the bone.

Disregarding the commissar's wailing, she pushed the boat into the water and let a steady breeze and the gentle current drift the rowboat toward the center of the pond. Like a giant broom, the limb still remained lodged in the bow of the boat, stroking the surface of the water.

Returning to the woods, pushing the safety off her rifle, carefully aiming just below the jutting limb, she expertly fired a round into the boat. Water began to slowly seep into the craft. As the water rose toward Lepan's bloodstained chest, he cried out, "You can't do this to me! I'm the commissar!"

When the bow of the boat slowly sank into the center of the pond, she watched Lepan's terrified face contort amidst his shrill, staccato screams. The stern followed the bow of the boat into a steep, pitched dive, as if an unseen hand had seized its throat, dragging it into the deep. Anya waited on the bank and listened as the commissar frantically cried for help. His paralyzed body was soon covered in water; the fishing line held him fast. He and the boat made excellent weights to keep each underwater, never to be seen again. Then there was silence. Concentric rings from Lepan's watery grave radiated toward the shore.

Anya watched the water return to its serene, idyllic setting, peacefully covering the murder below. She made sure that she stayed on the grass so that there would be no footprints. If anyone thought to drag the pond, the boat would have settled to a depth beyond discovery. Even if found, the commissar's decomposed body would indicate a fishing accident, where he ran into a limb; and in the confusion, he carelessly wrapped himself into his line, hooking himself in the process. It was common knowledge that Lepan could not swim. Anya felt that little effort would be made and no tears shed for a missing crooked commissar.

Anya glanced back to view the tranquil pond before walking into the dark woods to change her oversized boots. It was a short walk to the village, where she hoped to see Vladimir and Dmitri one last time. Vladivostok was waiting.

*****

Anya arrived at Vladimir's Store just before closing time. She had waited near the pond for the remainder of the day to make sure none of Lepan's equipment floated to the surface. When she left, his hidden burial site would reveal no secrets.

Vladimir was happy to see her, but he frowned and scolded, "I seem to be missing two bottles of my best vodka. You wouldn't know anything about that, would you?"

Anya sweetly replied, "You know that I don't care for vodka. Dmitri must have taken it."

"Not on your life! That cheapskate would never pay the price. In any case, the thief left money behind. Oh well, a sell is a sell."

"Spoken like a true businessman," Anya retorted. "Vladimir, do you think that early tomorrow morning Mischa might bring Dmitri here to your store? I'm going to have to leave sooner than I had originally planned."

"That is a sight I would like to see." Vladimir chuckled. "Farmer Dmitri riding in the sidecar of a motorcycle. The old rascal won't even get into a car or truck. He thinks that they are nothing but death traps. However, he might do it for you."

"Vladimir, you seem to know everyone in this area. Do you know anyone who will be traveling toward Vladivostok in the near future, perhaps tomorrow?"

Vladimir squinted his eyes and looked sternly at Anya. "Why would you want to go to that place after all you were forced to endure there? What do you have up your sleeve, Anya?"

"Nothing, Vladimir. You are so suspicious these days. At the orphanage, there were a few people who treated me kindly. Since I am this close, I just want to visit them."

"It just so happens that our popular Mischa is taking my truck next week to Vladivostok to bring back some perishable and fragile goods. I use the train crossing for heavier sealed items, but I had to buy a truck for smaller goods because of breakage and theft, particularly cases marked 'vodka.' One week earlier won't make any difference to Mischa, and I am sure that he would enjoy the company. I warn you, it is not for the faint of heart. It is a two-day journey."

"Thank you, Vladimir. I too am fragile, but I think I can manage."

"We both know that you are anything but 'fragile.' But I have to ask, why not just take the train? It is much quicker and certainly more comfortable than a stuffy old truck."

Anya walked over to Vladimir and squeezed his shoulder. "Vladimir, you worry about me too much. I just want to see some new country. I've never really traveled extensively. New sights, new experiences—what's wrong with that?"

"There's nothing wrong with that. There are also no passenger lists and no records of entry and exit, eh, my little *Krokodile*?"

Anya smiled and opened her pack. Vladimir was just as sharp as ever. Anya thought that he should be in the KGB rather than herself. "One more request, and I will leave you alone. I need to purchase a small trunk and a padlock. I have to be able to lift it on my own, yet it must be large enough to hold these items on your counter. You can resell the pack. I no longer need it."

"Let's see what you have here: a very large square canvas package, two tall black boots that don't fit you, one box of ammunition, a small leather pouch, and a leather Bible."

"The Bible was my mother's. It is dear to me."

Vladimir held the Bible in both hands and pressed the black leather cover to his lips. "Anya, I adored your mother. She was a jewel. You remind me of her. I miss both of your parents terribly, as I know you must." Vladimir looked at the counter and broke his spell. "Yes, yes, I have everything stuffed in some corner around this place. I have a small trunk at my house. It already has a lock and key."

"Oh, Vladimir, I forgot. There is one more item." Anya reached into her pack and retrieved Sasha's old rifle. She had disassembled it and wrapped it in a piece of canvas.

"And where did you learn to do this, my clever child?"

"Papa taught me well," she replied.

"Yes, Anya, and it appears—so did Colonel Kurgan."

****

The next morning, Vladimir stood on the porch of his store and anxiously anticipated Dmitri's arrival—this he had to see. He knew that Dmitri would come for Anya's sake. Anya remained in the store in order not to be seen by anyone who happened to come early to the village.

She heard the motorcycle approach and then a sharp, tinkling sound when the hot motor was turned off. Vladimir entered the store, laughing with unconcealed pleasure. "Now I have seen it all: old Dmitri riding a motorcycle, straddling the sidecar with one foot hanging down nearly scraping the ground, just in case he needs to escape, as if that would help! Now I can die and hopefully go to heaven!"

Dmitri stormed through the door madder than a rousted rooster. His face was covered with dust, and he still had a pair of goggles over his eyes. His wiry red hair and beard stuck out in every direction, looking much like a red squirrel that dared to face a hurricane. Mischa followed sheepishly behind him with a shy grin on his face.

"*Never! Never again* will I ride with this maniac!" Dmitri pointed at Mischa and erupted, "Twice, I tell you, he almost killed us! I know we must have been going at least two hundred kilometers an hour! The human body was never meant to go that fast!"

Mischa shrugged his shoulders and said, "We never got out of the second gear, maybe forty kilometers an hour at most. He tried to jump out of the sidecar twice."

Anya entered the room with two wet towels. She handed one to Mischa and used the other to gently remove the dirt from Dmitri's face. Dmitri was not use to being pampered in such a way, and his hot lava soon ceased to flow. Anya was dressed in her beige outfit, and her feminine presence settled the tension in the room. When she finished, Dmitri took her hand and squeezed it affectionately to express his thanks. He noticed that she winced.

"Anya, let me see your hand. It seems a bit red and swollen," Dmitri observed.

"Oh, it is nothing—just a little scrape while hunting."

Dmitri looked at Vladimir with an accusatory stare and exclaimed, "I leave her with you for only a few days, and you let the girl perish with gangrene! I just can't believe it!"

"Get out of the way, old fool!" Vladimir carried a small medical kit, and he examined her hand. "This is not a scrape. These are puncture wounds. What have you been up to, young lady?"

"Oh, you two. Just a thorn bush," Anya retorted. "Now put some ointment on it and leave it at that. Where is Mischa? We really need to get started."

Vladimir expertly treated her with antiseptic and carefully bandaged her hand. His army training was not wasted. "Keep this clean, Anya, if you don't want an infected hand. I sent Mischa for the truck."

Anya heard the truck arrive, the metallic ringing of a slammed door, and heavy footsteps. Mischa came into the store and placed a small trunk on the counter. She quickly packed the trunk and retrieved her tan suitcase. Vladimir and Dmitri carried the trunk and loaded it into the back of the truck. Mischa quietly carried the suitcase and secured the luggage with a short rope near the cab of the truck.

Mischa thoughtfully got into the driver's seat to give Vladimir and Dmitri a few moments alone with Anya to say goodbye. Anya hugged and kissed both of her dearest friends. She knew it might be a long time before she would be able to arrange the circumstances to see them again.

"Now, you two boys don't fight and be good. I'll see you soon."

Vladimir and Dmitri helped her into the truck. For once, words escaped them both. She blew them a kiss as Mischa slowly drove away. Waving goodbye, they watched the truck go down the dirt road until it faded from sight.

"Vladimir, do you think we will ever see her again?"

"I don't know, old friend," Vladimir replied. "I fear for her. Vladivostok offers nothing good—a spider waiting in the web—but I think she knows that." Vladimir firmly took Dmitri's arm and complained, "Come inside, my wayward thief. I'll let you steal some more of my best vodka. Anya told me about your wicked deeds."

Both men walked into the store and made several toasts to the young blonde-haired girl they loved and treasured and hoped that she was not lost to them forever.

****

Mischa and Anya arrived at Vladivostok in the early evening. It had indeed been a long trip, yet they had enjoyed each other's company. Anya was pretty and easy to talk to, and Mischa had a quiet, unassuming way about him that Anya appreciated. He took a task, did his best, and enjoyed himself along the way. His simple, uncomplicated life was just the opposite of what Anya daily experienced. In many ways, she envied him.

"I'll drop you off in front of the train station before I go to the warehouse. It will be easier for you with that trunk," Mischa said.

"That's not necessary, Mischa. The station is hectic and full of people. The parking in front is too difficult, especially with this large truck. The trunk is not heavy, just awkward. I'll get a porter to help me."

Anya directed Mischa to a side street just around the corner from the station. She could not afford someone seeing her leave the truck as a blonde and later reappear with dark hair and brown eyes. She also needed some privacy to change into her wig and contacts. Mischa would not understand, and it would alarm Vladimir and Dmitri if Mischa spoke to them about her sudden change of appearance.

Mischa did as she asked and helped her unload the small trunk and suitcase. Anya opened the trunk and called to him, "Mischa, come here, please. I have a gift for you." She retrieved the tall black boots and handed them to him. His face lit up as if it were Christmas.

"This is to thank you for helping me. They are just the right size for you and much too big for me. Here is a pair of thick socks to keep you warm in the winter. You will look grand in these boots on your motorcycle!"

Mischa quickly removed his old scuffed shoes and tried on his new footwear. "Anya, they fit perfectly! I've looked at them many times in the store, but I could not afford them."

Anya kissed his forehead and enjoyed watching Mischa blush. He had probably never had a person outside his family show him such affection.

Mischa returned to the truck, and with a happy smile, he waved goodbye. Anya watched the truck until it disappeared around the corner. She quickly changed into her wig and contacts. The special makeup would not be needed for her nighttime mission. She tied a leather strap to the handle of the suitcase and slipped it over her shoulder like a rifle sling. Both hands could easily carry the small trunk the short distance to the train station.

She saw a water drain a few meters to her left. Being an expert in the art of following people, she knew the secret was to never wear, do, or say anything that brought attention or that could be remembered. The white bandage protecting her wounded right hand floated down the drain.

As Anya rounded the corner, a kind porter saw her and came to her rescue. "May I help you? Which train will it be for you this evening?" he inquired.

"Just to the stored-luggage area for right now," Anya replied. "I still have a few errands before the train leaves."

Anya tipped the porter and subtly discovered that he would not be working for the next few days, the exact time when she planned to be leaving. She wanted no one to recognize her when she boarded the train. Taking the storage ticket for the suitcase and the trunk, she thanked the porter and went outside to the taxi ranks in front of the station.

It was dark now, and the station lights were coming on one by one. At the taxi stand, she selected an older driver. They usually were more helpful, were safer, and were not as prone to ask personal questions as younger drivers who flirted and were full of themselves. He asked, "Where to, ma'am?"

"There is a restaurant just a few blocks away from where the large red star is located outside the city."

"You mean the star over the People's Orphanage?"

"Yes, that's the one. No need to hurry, sir. I have plenty of time for this appointment."

Chapter 64

Anya walked up the steps to the old massive door. It seemed like a lifetime ago that she and Dmitri had parted company at this exact spot. Much had changed. She had changed.

It only took a matter of seconds to pick the lock and to enter the orphanage. All was quiet. Everyone had gone to bed hours ago. Anya's first stop was to the flowing fountain. It never failed to lift her spirit. She stayed in its shadow and washed her face and hands as she used to as a young girl. The splashing water brought memories of her talks with Sergei, Elena, and pretty Esmeralda—talking by the fountain, planning what to do next, surviving another day.

Anya was amazed at the abundance of flowers; they were everywhere. It gave the facility a light, beautiful atmosphere, making the air fragrant and refreshing.

She backtracked to Sergei's workshop. The door was unlocked. Using her small flashlight to scan the room, she saw dozens of small wooden figurines scattered in every corner. Good old Sergei was already preparing his Christmas presents for the orphanage's girls.

Walking down the portico of the courtyard, she found the infirmary stocked full of medicine and supplies, with a new examination table centered in the room. Everything was so neat and clean.

Anya cut across the courtyard to the back door of the kitchen. She unlocked the door and merely poked her head inside. The kitchen larder was completely full. The smell of potato soup still lingered in the air. Ursula must be extremely happy to be able to feed "her girls" without worrying about provisions for the next meal.

It was risky, but Anya had to inspect the girls' dormitory; she had spent many days living in fear and agony in her small corner of the world, with only a number stenciled on her bed frame. She stood behind a wooden beam and peered at the peaceful, sleeping children. Every bed had new blankets, pillows, and linens. Nice-looking, clean uniforms hung on a stand, which contained a few shelves for personal items. Shoes were at the bottom of the stand: one pair for summer, another pair for winter; light and heavy socks accompanied each.

She told herself that she was not going to make the next stop, but she felt compelled to do so. She crossed the courtyard, staying in the shadows next to the wall, until she came to the bell tower. She had no desire to enter the tall tower. The view would hold no charm—just painful memories. Instead, as if drawn by an unseen hand, she walked around the corner of the tower to a grassy spot she knew too well: Esmeralda's final resting place.

Anya stood over the spot and remembered Esmeralda with flowers in her hair. Her leap for freedom produced a chain of events that were still unfolding. She cut several flowers and made a bouquet. Placing the colorful flowers where Esmeralda fell so long ago, she whispered softly, "Rest now, Esmeralda. I have not forgotten you, and I will make sure that others do not as well."

Anya sadly retraced her steps and returned to the fountain. She needed to think a moment before proceeding. She had promised Sister Elena that she would return someday. The flowers on Esmeralda's death site would probably give her presence away, but others at the orphanage also loved Esmeralda. Anya was so pleased with all that Elena had accomplished she wanted Elena to know how she felt.

She took off her shoes and quietly walked up the staircase to the director's apartment. Silently, she slid a note under Elena's door using a piece of paper she had found in the infirmary. It read:

Beloved Elena,

    I have returned as promised. Everything is so lovely. The nuns who had to leave you behind would be so proud of you—as I am. I am well. Don't worry about me. Continue your good work by helping those who cannot help themselves. I will never forget you. God bless you always.

All my love,
Anya

Anya had one more stop before leaving the orphanage: the chapel.

The shabby tables were gone. In their place were chairs arranged in a semicircle facing a small stage at the front of the chapel. Now the chapel was used for assemblies, lectures, and theatrical performances. On the stage, there was a pretty homemade theater curtain and a few props in the corner from a recent play.

Anya sat down and looked up at the stained glass windows. A bright full moon made each panel come alive in a soft, quiet way. She just closed her eyes and absorbed the peace. She thought of the men and women in those pretty windows, of Esmeralda, of Elena, of Ursula, and of Sergei—how just one person could make a difference in the lives of so many, often in a world gone awry.

She began to doze in her chair. This was dangerous; she had to remain vigilant. It had been three days, and she desperately needed sleep, even if for a few hours. A hotel, with its government registration requirements, was out of the question. It was a calculated risk, but Anya decided to "hide in plain sight." She locked the chapel doors and braced the back of a chair under each door handle. She left one side door unlocked for a quick escape, if needed.

It would be several hours before the orphanage came to life. Anya had to regain her strength, for dawn would bring a very busy day. She still had two more appointments and then a long train ride to Moscow. She reclined on a fabric used in the previous play and used a prop as a pillow. Resting in the shadow of the theater curtain in a far corner of the stage, she could still see every door in the chapel. Her KGB wristwatch had a silent vibrating alarm with an illuminated dial. She set the alarm for 4:00 a.m. The nearby restaurant would be open at 5:00 a.m. for a hearty meal, and she could continue with her "Operation Reunion."

She smoothed her jacket and skirt to avoid wrinkles and looked up at the beautiful chapel dome. The moon shone like a celestial theater light displaying an array of colors which spread over the stage. In this rainbow performance, Anya's last thought before drifting off to sleep was, *Esmeralda, your voice was heard. Truly, you made a difference.*

The moon slowly passed over the chapel dome, and so did the restless dreams of the "mountain girl." Once again, she was "on stage"—one more outcast moment in yet the latest orphanage of her life.

****

When Anya heard the solid *click* of the heavy wooden door at the orphanage closing behind her, she knew that sound would remain within her for the rest of her life. Never again would she pass through this door—that chapter of her life locked and closed forever.

Upon leaving the orphanage, she spent the morning consuming food to regain her strength and surveying a typical Soviet apartment block in central Vladivostok: squat, drab, concrete. She entered the complex and memorized every entrance and exit, watched the traffic patterns of cars and pedestrians, and mentally recorded the faces of the residents coming and going, particularly near apartment block 11, floor 3, room 323.

The former head matron led a meager life upon being dismissed from the orphanage. There were no more jewelry purchases since the cash provided by the sale of garments from the orphanage's sweatshop to the black market was also gone. Her old jewelry had been pawned long ago to keep food on the table and a roof over her head.

Eventually, she found a job at a local factory. The pay was modest but adequate. She loathed the work and hated the routine. It never occurred to her that she had implemented the same drudgery on the girls at the orphanage; her mind did not work like that. It was late afternoon. Soon it would be evening, and then the prospect of enduring another boring day at the factory the next morning.

Trudging up the stairs with heavy footsteps, she once again cursed the fact that she lived on the third floor. There were no rooms available below that level when the factory assigned the small apartment to her. The inefficient elevator seldom worked, and the staircase was always dim regardless of the hour—a marvel of Soviet construction. She was a little out of breath as she approached the third-floor landing: turn to the left, then to the right, down the hall, enter room 323, and then collapse on an old worn sofa. The two sacks of groceries in her arms were beginning to feel like lead weights. "Oh, why do I have to live on the third floor?" She groaned.

As she was about to step upon the landing, a person holding a small bouquet of red roses appeared from the left and faced her. It was an elegant woman dressed in a nice beige outfit. *It is doubtful that she lives in this dump*, thought the matron. *At least I've never seen her.* However, something seemed familiar about her, even though she looked almost Mediterranean with her dark hair and olive complexion.

The unfamiliar woman stood on the landing looking down upon the matron. She blocked the matron's path and spoke in a clear tone, "Good afternoon, ex-Head Matron. So good to see you again."

The matron remained still and became alarmed. She did not recognize this woman, but somehow the voice seemed familiar.

"No, I don't know you—nor do I care," the matron spitefully replied. "Get out of my way. Can't you see that I'm struggling with these groceries? If you are an inspector, why don't you ever fix the elevator? It's always broken."

The tall woman never moved. "Oh, I'm certainly an inspector. I have inspected many things: greed, cruelty, sadism, and even murder."

"You're mad! What are you talking about?" the matron shouted nervously. "I'm a simple factory worker. What would I know about those things? Who sent you?"

Anya pulled off her black wig and allowed her long blonde hair to flow over her shoulders. "Esmeralda sent me—remember her? Remember me?"

"The mountain girl!" the shocked matron exclaimed. "I thought you were dead!"

"I was dead, Head Matron, and you were the chief gravedigger. However, I have come back to life, and I came to pay a visit for old times' sake. I left a scar across your face with a whip. You left a scar across my heart, mind, and soul."

The matron bent down to lower the groceries onto the step. Her arms ached, and she planned to use the sacks to block the staircase while she ran for help. She was one second too late.

Anya placed a side kick straight into the matron's chest. The heavy blow sent the matron tumbling down the long staircase, the food items scattered beside her. Anya dodged the debris, being careful not to squash an item or to leave a shoeprint. She grabbed the matron's thick hair, jerked it to the side until she found her mark, and injected the matron at the base of her skull. The matron's eyes grew wide, and her body went limp.

Anya stood still and listened; it was an old KGB trick. Most people hurry or make unnecessary noises, drawing attention to themselves; but for the experienced agent: wait, listen, walk—never run, never look back. The KGB way. There was not a sound. Anya's surveillance had paid rich dividends; it was as quiet as a mausoleum. People were shopping or still on their way from work. There would be plenty of time.

Anya carefully positioned the matron's neck on the edge of a step. The matron became even more frightened when Anya removed her shoe and put on two heavy socks on her right foot. She tried to scream when Anya pulled out a necklace of large claws and dangled one claw in front of her face.

"This claw is for you to add to my private collection. I also bring you flowers from the orphanage. Some I put where Esmeralda died. These are for you, where you will die."

Before the matron could utter a sound, Anya squeezed the matron's mouth open, being careful not to bruise her cheeks, which might alert a potential medical examiner. She slowly removed the glove on her right hand and repeated her blood ritual by pressing the new claw against her flesh until blood seeped down her fist.

"You always wanted my blood, cruel woman. Be careful what you ask for—now drink it."

Anya watched the woman choke and gasp, and then took the sharp tip of the bloody claw and pierced the matron's left eye. The matron cried out, but there was no one to hear her. She pleaded as Anya grabbed her hair and raised her head, placing the stem of the red roses underneath the left side of her face. The thorn marks would cover the injection point and the puncture of the matron's left eye: injuries incurred during the fall, or so it would be assumed.

"Enjoy the flowers," Anya taunted. As Anya slowly raised her right foot, the matron tried to lift her head, but her paralysis made this impossible. With one quick movement, Anya smashed the side of the matron's neck against the step: the sickening sound of snapped bone, then silence. A thin trickle of blood dripped out of the matron's mouth onto the fresh red roses, a crushed rose petal mingling with the red-brown stream slowly oozing down the staircase, like a broken canoe cascading over a jagged waterfall. Step by step, the golden eagle struck with her talons, the dark vulture circling no more.

Anya carefully inspected the bruise across the matron's neck. There was no sign of a heel-mark; the socks had done their duty. She replaced her glove and shoe and made sure none of the matron's blood touched her clothing. The protective thick socks and the matron's saliva would conceal any trace of Anya's blood: blood she felt compelled to force into the matron's mouth, blood consumed for the grave. The lazy authorities would probably not perform an autopsy. Even if they did, the serum could not be detected. A lack of evidence, a clumsy woman falling down the stairs, an unmarked grave—mission accomplished.

Anya stood over the corpse and felt nothing; it was as if she had put down a rabid dog. This lack of feeling actually alarmed her. Shouldn't she feel relief, rage, revenge—something? But there was nothing, just emptiness.

Anya walked several blocks away from the apartment block and boarded a bus to go to the other side of the city, far away from the murder scene. She planned to find a quiet restaurant and have a leisurely dinner until certain bars closed at midnight along the waterfront. Comrade Svelte lived, drank, socialized, and would die there. Time for her to join the "Vladivostok reunion."

As the bus rumbled along, Anya looked out of the window. Most of the trees had lost their leaves, which lay haphazardly on the ground. The stark scene reminded her of the now cold corpse and two sacks of food scattered down a poorly lit staircase. She watched another leaf fall in front of the headlights of the bus. Anya decided that autumn was a good season in which to kill, or to be killed: falling leaves, falling memories, falling enemies—a falling empty soul. Anya continued to look out of the stained window solemnly as the gray dented bus plunged ahead, grinding, roaring, carrying her down the steep twisting road, descending to destroy yet another falling leaf waiting at the waterfront.

****

Anya sat in the darkness of a marine supply shop which faced the street and three rough waterfront bars. It was a bit of a risk breaking and entering a private business, but less so than a pretty girl wandering the streets for several hours in elegant clothing drawing attention to herself. The large shop windows and its exact location made it a perfect observation post.

The bars closed earlier on weekdays. About 12:30 a.m., several people stumbled out of the bars and staggered in various directions, generally toward their ships. Svelte struggled out of a bar and proceeded down the wooden sidewalk for a short distance, until she tripped and fell into the shallow street gutter.

Anya quickly relocked the marine shop and walked in the shadows across the street from Svelte. She thought to herself, *This may be the easiest one yet!* She crossed the street with a new tiger's claw in one hand and the syringe in the other. Just as she was approaching Svelte, two drunken sailors noticed her, and they eagerly weaved in her direction. One called out, "I'll take the one standing up, and you can have the one in the gutter." Both laughed loudly and separated slightly to trap Anya between them.

Anya stood still and slightly raised her skirt, revealing her shapely legs. Both sailors smiled, lowering their guards, not realizing that her actions were only to get the skirt out of the way for freedom of movement. The sailors winked at each other and held out their hands for her to come to them. She did. The first victim received a roundhouse kick to the side of his bearded face. The second sailor caught a hammer-fist blow to his right temple. Both fell as if struck by an axe. Dragging them by their hair, she placed them side by side and tightly wrapped their arms around each other. Sweetly she said to the two unconscious figures, "Sleep tight, lover boys."

Svelte was lying on her back, so inebriated that she could not move. Anya leaned down with the claw and syringe but stepped back when she saw Svelte's face: Large sores protruded around her mouth and in the corner of her eyes. Her skin was a sickly greenish-yellow color, and her thick flaming-red hair was now burnt-orange with several bald spots exposing her scalp. This woman, who once gloried in her new dresses obtained from orphanage funds, now wallowed in a threadbare garment barely held together by a series of patches. Anya estimated that she would be dead within a few months, either from disease or from hypothermia, shivering to death, when the first hard frost or freezing rains struck the city.

It was obvious to Anya that this pathetic woman was slowly dying of cirrhosis of the liver and of syphilis. No man in his right mind would now have intimate relations with her, so she must be begging on the street to obtain her alcohol. Anya thought, *How could someone fall so far, so fast?*

Svelte tried to lift her head. She did not recognize Anya, disguised in her dark wig. Seeing the syringe in Anya's hand, she called out, "Oh, thank you, Doctor! I'm in such pain! Please, kill me! Please, end all of this—I want to die! Thank you. Thank you—let me die!"

Anya put the claw in her pocket and carefully put a safety cap on the needle of the syringe. Shaking her head in disgust, Anya turned and walked away from the repulsive creature in the gutter.

"Doctor, where are you going?" Svelte asked. "Won't you help me?"

Never looking back, Anya answered, "There is no need to kill you. You're already dead. Ending your wretched existence would be an act of mercy. May you live a long and miserable life, Comrade Matron."

Anya walked past the two prostrate sailors toward a taxi stand two blocks away, next to the wharf. Her mood was such that she actually hoped someone would try to bother her, heaven help them. She threaded the claw designated for Svelte onto the necklace and placed her war trophies back under her blouse. Enough of Vladivostok. Time to return for one last target. Colonel Kurgan was waiting in Moscow. "Operation Reunion" was over. "Operation Gray Wolf" was about to begin.

"Taxi, to the train station."

CHAPTER 65

When Anya reached Moscow, she hurriedly placed her trunk at the foot of her bed and the tan suitcase into her closet. The helpful conductor at Vladivostok and the express train to Moscow cut the travel time in half, but her scheduled vacation would soon end. Time was of the essence.

Anya measured the bottle of serum. There were two finger-widths left, just enough to put the Gray Wolf asleep—forever. She placed the lethal dosage and the syringe into a hollowed-out bedpost where she also kept her cash. A KGB search team might find it, but it was secure from any common thief.

Within minutes, she had removed the makeup and changed into some hiking clothes. A worn backpack with an old pup tent attached to it had already been placed next to the door. The pack and the tent had been purchased months ago at a local flea market.

Anya walked a few blocks to the metro where she would not be noticed among the crowd, who were racing about trying to make their next connection. At the taxi stand outside the metro, she selected an older driver to assist her. When the driver asked for her destination, Anya showed him the address to one of the resort inns recommended by Colonel Kurgan located near Moscow.

"Miss, for any ride outside of the Moscow city limits, I have to record your name, address, and occupation."

CHILD OF THE FOREST

Anya smiled and handed him a bottle of superb vodka and a wad of cash. "I was so hoping you could help me, comrade," she cooed. "I have a little dilemma. I have a rendezvous, and well, sometimes a girl needs a little privacy."

"This is double the fare, and this vodka is only available to high-ranking officials," the driver observed. "Where did you get this? You must have some good connections!"

Anya blushed coyly and retorted, "Well, yes, but a girl never tells."

The taxi driver winked and said, "Oooh, that kind of rendezvous. I understand. He sure is a lucky man. All right, let's forget the paperwork, but this has to be a secret."

Anya patted the kind man on his shoulder and leaned forward to whisper in his ear, "Trust me, I'm very good with secrets."

The driver pulled away from the curb and sighed. "I'll bet you are."

Forty-five minutes later, the taxi reached a pleasant alpine area. Anya directed the driver to stop at a corner on the opposite side of the inn; she did not want anyone at the inn to see her leave the taxi. The taxi driver waved goodbye, and Anya blew him a kiss as he drove by her.

She walked across a lush green lawn to a flower bed, away from the entrance of the inn. Looking over each shoulder to ensure that no one was watching, she knelt down next to the flower bed. Driving her hands deep into the soil, she rubbed the dark earth on each side of her neck and around the collar of her shirt, making sure her fingernails were lined with dirt. She rubbed her knees back and forth on the lawn until her trousers were stained a pale green. Her final deception was to tease her hair with her fingertips until it stood out in the back and from the sides of her head.

The innkeeper was a pleasant plump woman wearing a navy-blue dress. She welcomed Anya and asked if she had a reservation.

"I don't have a reservation, but you come highly recommended," Anya replied. "I do hope you have a room left. I've been out camping for some time. I really could use a bath." Anya smiled and showed the kind lady her soiled hands.

"Well, not to worry, young lady. It is the off-season, and we have several nice rooms left. I just need you to write your name, address, and occupation here on the register, as the government requires."

Anya listed her correct name and address and wrote "civil servant" as her occupation. The trusting lady did not even check her identification papers. She handed Anya a key and directed her, "Second floor, last room on the right. I hope you enjoy your stay. Will you be dining with us this evening?"

Anya quickly replied, "Oh yes. I've heard the food here is wonderful. I'm just going to eat, read, rest, and pamper myself until I have to return to dreary old Moscow. While I am thinking of it, I noticed that there is a bus stop across the street. Does a bus run every day?"

"Yes, it does. Old Vasily or his son arrives there every day at 9:00 a.m. They make several stops before reaching Moscow, but the fare is quite reasonable. You will have to fill in your personal information on Vasily's clipboard, but it only takes a few moments."

Anya was very pleased. Now she would have two official records to establish that she had been in this area. No one would be the wiser that she had not camped here in the woods her entire vacation. Good luck to the colonel's henchmen to prove otherwise.

Anya thanked the helpful lady and put her backpack on her right shoulder. As she turned to leave, the innkeeper asked, "By the way, did you enjoy our beautiful forest? The air is so fresh and invigorating this time of the year!"

Anya flashed through her mind all the things that had occurred over the past few weeks: the blood, the terror, the lives poured out like sand through a bottle into the hourglass of her life. She inadvertently touched the tiger claws resting hidden beneath her shirt. She also thought about her coming showdown with Colonel Kurgan.

Anya forced a smile, but her eyes spoke otherwise. She faced the innkeeper and complimented the kind woman, "You chose the exact word. It has been very *invigorating*—invigorating, indeed."

PART 5

The Decision

Multitudes, multitudes, in the valley of decision!
—Joel 3:14

CHAPTER 66

The year 1953 was a momentous year for Sofia and for all in the Soviet Union: Joseph Stalin died of a cerebral hemorrhage, and a power vacuum descended upon the country. The question on everyone's mind and whispered in every corner: "Who will be next?"

Sofia did not care who would be the next leader of the Soviet Union. She assumed it would be another Communist Party tyrant like Stalin, although she believed few could ever match his paranoia and ruthless tactics. Sofia hated Stalin and all of his henchmen; they had destroyed her family and taken away her youth. The only question in her mind was if it would be possible to measure the heat in centigrade where Stalin simply had to reside in hell.

The KGB was also in flux. They were "testing the water" in every direction at the same time. The next leader could become their best friend or worst enemy. They were going to manipulate the system as much as possible for a favorable outcome. Stalin had made many enemies. The KGB did not want to become "Stalin's scapegoat" when the dust settled.

Sofia's resident agent, codenamed the Raven, had been temporarily recalled to Moscow to help sort out the "Stalin mess." She knew that this hiatus was the moment that she had been waiting for: now was the time to apply for admission to begin her doctoral program. Her master's thesis was finished. All she lacked was to pass her oral board to receive her degree. Once accepted, the KGB could not suddenly withdraw her without breaking her cover and arousing suspicion.

Wasting no time, she immediately met with the chairman of the Physics Department and outlined her desired course of study. She conveniently requested that Professor Leslie Price be her program counselor and for him to supervise her progress. Once again, the KGB could not complain about her degree if it brought her closer to the target.

The old director of the Physics Department was putty in Sofia's hands, and they both knew it. He looked over the top of his reading glasses and commented, "Sofia, it is most unusual to admit a student into a doctoral program before they have technically received their master's degree. Although, I must admit, I see nothing to indicate that your thesis and oral boards will not be accepted. You are one of the brightest students that we have ever had."

Sofia rushed in for the kill. "Sir, I told you when I was a freshman that all I desired was to receive my degrees and to teach here at this fine university. That dream has never changed." She leaned closer and met his glance with her hazel eyes, pleading, "Won't you help me fulfill that dream—to teach under your direction, to make a difference in the lives of others?"

The old professor did not stand a chance. He sighed and remarked, "I suspect that you have the admission form in that fancy purse of yours. All right, young lady, hand it over." Sofia shot him her killer smile and handed him the papers. With a shy grin, he shook his head and signed the acceptance sheet. Sofia was so thrilled that she ran to the side of his desk and planted a firm kiss on his cheek. She exclaimed, "You won't regret this. Someday I will make you proud!"

The old professor rolled his eyes and cajoled, "If you keep that up, you already have! Now off with you. I have work to finish—and, Sofia, good luck, dear."

Sofia's pleadings were actually true; she had always wanted this opportunity to receive an advanced degree and to teach at the university level. It would never have happened under Stalin's regime, especially under the cloud of suspicion regarding her father's trial and summary execution. But Stalin was dead, and the Raven had "flown the coop" to attend Stalin's funeral. In Sofia's mind, it was RIP—may they both *rot* in place.

Sofia went to her house to celebrate Stalin's death, the Raven's departure, and her new opportunities to gain her doctoral degree. She had saved a bottle of champagne (appropriated from her designated parents' wine cellar in New York City) for such an occasion. Looking around the sterile house, she realized that she had no one with whom to celebrate; no one who could also share in her joy, her excitement, her new accomplishment; no one, except a hidden camera in the ceiling and those who viewed it, who even knew where she was or that she existed. It seemed to her the story of her life: always alone.

Ever resilient, throwing self-pity aside, Sofia popped the cork, poured the golden nectar into a very expensive crystal flute, and reflected, "Today is indeed the day. Stalin is dead, a doctoral degree is launched, and the KGB is in turmoil—not bad for a day's work!"

In the full view of her watchers, she stood at attention and slowly raised her sparkling glass toward the ceiling. Lifting her chin, she solemnly proclaimed, "A toast to Comrade Stalin!"

Chapter 67

Anya prepared for her showdown with Colonel Kurgan. She made a hidden cloth holster in the lining of her uniform jacket to hold the steel syringe with its safety cap and the last lethal dosage of the serum. The syringe was full, and it could be retrieved in a matter of seconds. She knew that her window of opportunity to catch the ever-watchful Gray Wolf would be brief. There would only be one chance. From now on, the deadly syringe would be with her at all times at the office. Since she never removed her uniform jacket, hiding in plain sight seemed her best option.

The night before she was to return to work, she walked several blocks away from her apartment to a location near the metro station. Crushing the empty serum bottle into small slivers, she dumped the remains into a storm drain, thus eliminating any residual evidence that could be traced back to her. The stage was set.

When Anya returned to work, she found several reports stacked on her desk and a note directing her to see Colonel Kurgan in his office immediately upon her return. She touched the syringe hidden in her jacket and breathed deeply. Perhaps this was the day.

The colonel was as friendly as ever, and he motioned for Anya to take a seat in front of his desk. Another man whom she had never met was seated by the window. She noticed that the visitor was strategically positioned so that he could see her face and hand gestures. He was also making sure that she could see a folder with a large red stripe across it, which had "Vladivostok" written in large letters across the top. Anya suddenly realized that this was not a "How was your vacation?" chat. It was an interrogation.

The colonel smiled pleasantly and asked, "Anya, how was the vacation? Tell me all about it, spare no details. You know how I love details. I hope you are rested."

"Yes, Colonel, quite rested. It was perfect—camping in the woods, reading by the campfire, relaxing at the inn that you suggested, all of it lovely. Thank you for *your* assistance."

Anya wanted to make sure the "witness" knew that the colonel was involved. If she went down, she wanted to drag the pleasant colonel along with her. Doubt and the colonel's instinct for self-preservation were her best allies for this little inquisition.

"You didn't stay very long at the inn, just three days," added the colonel. "You must really love camping. Did you have any trouble getting there? I hope my directions were adequate. You probably just took the bus back. It arrives just across the street. That is one reason why I recommended that particular inn."

Touché, wiley wolf, thought Anya, *but I won't take the bait.* She smiled and replied, "No trouble at all, Colonel. I made a few purchases at a kiosk near the metro, just a few food items. A man mentioned that he was heading in that direction, so I offered to pay for half of the fuel. You know us Siberian girls, always thrifty. He was glad to have the company and for someone to share the expenses. He said that his name was Ivan, nothing more."

Both men looked at each other. It would be impossible to verify. There were hundreds of kiosks selling food, especially near the metros, and finding one "Ivan" would be the equivalent of tracing "John Smith" in America. The car would be of no value without a license number, for cars were often shared by many or rented to others for the weekend.

"Well, the important thing is that you had an enjoyable time," the colonel replied. The colonel thought, *Time to change tactics.*

"Anya, I need your opinion on something. Strange things occurred while you were away on vacation, particularly at your old stomping grounds. Since you know the area and people so well, this gentleman and I seek your advice. A trapper discovered a burned cabin—oddly enough, where you use to live. Two charred vodka bottles and a few bones were all that remained. The property is listed to one Chekov, but the body was so cremated that it was impossible to identify. Chekov frequently worked as an informer for the district commissar.

"It just so happens that the commissar is also missing. He left early one morning and just vanished. There has not been a single clue as to his whereabouts or regarding what happened to him. Another old acquaintance of yours, the old head matron of the orphanage, was found dead on her apartment staircase. Apparently, she fell down the steps and broke her neck. It just seems strange that three people, whom you knew and terribly disliked, suddenly died within one week and during your vacation. How does one explain such a coincidence?"

Anya calmly folded her hands on her lap and replied, "Since you both desire my regional experience and my opinion, I would suggest the following: Chekov was a known alcoholic and an informer—both are dangerous habits in Siberia. After drinking two bottles of vodka, I'm surprised that he did not go up in flames due to spontaneous combustion. As for the commissar, we have several complaints on file against him for bribery, blackmail, and fraud. Perhaps he demanded a bit too much once too often. Colonel, you said yourself that the smugglers were a dangerous lot who shot first and asked questions later. A poacher or smuggler knows how to hide a body in the woods. We both know that. You mentioned the old head matron. The key word is *old*. We have elderly people here in Moscow who regularly fall and injure themselves. There is nothing odd about that, except that it happens way too often because of poor maintenance.

"You both are inquiring about a large area with a small population. Everyone knows everyone else. You have to, if you want to survive. Speaking of 'acquaintances,' how is the—as you put it, Colonel—'charming and lovely' Comrade Svelte? Did she also have an untimely demise during my absence?"

The colonel went to the officer by the window; the investigator handed him an updated folder. The colonel stated, "According to this recent report, our dear Comrade Svelte is alive but not well. She seems to be suffering from a liver problem and from advanced mental difficulties after contracting a social disease."

Anya stared coldly at the colonel. She spoke to him in crisp, determined terms, "Colonel, you know me very well and that I am an extremely thorough person, just as you are. Do you really believe that I would leave anyone alive, especially a person like Svelte, if I really wanted to repay her in full? Would you, Colonel?"

The colonel returned her gaze and replied, "Yes, I see your point. You, of all people, would certainly not leave her untouched. Well, enough of these pleasantries. Back to work. Anya, is there anything else you would like to add?"

"One final comment, Colonel. What you have is a careless drunk, a compulsive crook, and a clumsy sociopath. All three led high-risk lives. Their absence, by whatever means, seems of no great loss to our Soviet state. That is my professional opinion."

"Fine. We have spent enough time on this matter. Anya, the American called while you were gone. Make it your first priority. Call him and arrange a meeting."

Anya quickly stood and said, "I will get to that right now. Good day, gentlemen."

When Anya left the office, the colonel looked over at the plainclothes KGB officer. The officer did not say anything but just shrugged his shoulders.

"That's what I thought," the colonel said. "Just leave the file on my desk. I will take it from here."

There was no proof, but the Gray Wolf's instincts told him otherwise. As an intelligence officer, he did not believe in coincidences, but Anya's logic prevailed. The colonel was not going to jeopardize an upcoming mission with this American by losing a top agent because of innuendo regarding "a careless drunk, a compulsive crook, and a clumsy sociopath."

After the agent left, the colonel returned to his desk. He took out a handstamp, pressed it on an inkpad, and marked in large red letters across the cover of the file: "Case Closed."

****

Anya returned the American's telephone call. He seemed genuinely pleased to hear from her. He agreed to meet her for lunch at the same restaurant where they originally met since both knew the address.

Her next call was to organize a surveillance team for the meeting. A listening device would be attached to a table near the window. A team across the street would record their conversation while watching the table and the restaurant entrance. Another couple would be strategically placed in the restaurant to have a leisurely lunch but within listening distance. A watcher would act as their waiter and reserve the selected table with the receiver. The stage was set.

Anya rushed to her apartment and changed from her uniform to a casual dress. Once again, she hid the syringe in her bedpost. Her rendezvous with the colonel would have to wait for a more opportune moment, when he was alone and vulnerable.

A taxi driven by a KGB driver got her to the restaurant early, but much to her surprise, the American was already waiting outside the restaurant entrance. The baffled taxi driver had to leave so as not to arouse suspicion. The American approached her only after the taxi was several blocks away.

"Anya, so good of you to come, especially on such short notice. I found a new restaurant on the way over here. It's only a couple of blocks away. Let's try someplace new."

Anya wanted to persuade him otherwise, but before she could speak, he politely extended his arm, and they walked down the sidewalk, much to the disgust of the various surveillance teams.

At the new restaurant, the American helped her remove her coat and briefly touched Anya's back as he draped her coat over his arm near their table. He turned his back and quickly ran his hand over her coat when he placed it on a rack behind her. A warning light registered in Anya's mind. Was all this a coincidence, or was this true tradecraft: changing to a new location, approaching her only when the taxi was beyond the distance for an electronic listening device, searching very subtly to discover if she had a recorder or a small microphone on her person or in her clothing? She concluded that this was going to be an interesting meal.

He courteously seated her and inquired, "So, Anya, when I called the book depository, they said that you had taken a short vacation. I hope you had a splendid time!"

"Yes, Mr. Adams, a lovely time—hiking, reading, relaxing. You should try it sometime."

"Please, call me Paul."

The waiter arrived and handed them a menu. Anya carefully observed the American to see how much Russian he understood. He glanced at the menu and sheepishly asked her to order for both of them. She did so, but noticed that his eyes followed every item that she ordered on the menu. Mr. Adams knew more Russian than he pretended. Time to enter the fray.

"Paul, what brings you to Moscow? Is it business or pleasure, perhaps both? You never mentioned your profession when we first met." Anya had a file five centimeters thick on Mr. Adams. She knew where he walked, where he shopped, what he purchased, what he ate. She wanted to test his answers against her file.

"Oh, I'm just a lowly clerk at this stage. My official title is economic specialist. I think my real specialty is getting lost on the underground metro and trying not to look like a fool around Moscow."

"In that case, Paul, you are almost a Russian. We, of course, do the same." (Anya knew every street, alley, and sewer cover in Moscow.) "Tell me, Paul, what is it you do for—what is the word?—pastime, to entertain yourself when not working?"

"I like to read, to visit museums, and to ride horses, but there aren't too many opportunities to ride here in Moscow."

"Paul, you might be surprised. I will contact a few friends. I would also like to learn how to ride. Perhaps you could teach me?"

"Anya, if you were to provide the horses, I would be honored to provide my humble instruction."

Anya had found her way into this man's inner sanctum. Libraries, restaurants, and museums provided little opportunity for gathering information or for his recruitment. Riding horses, being alone with him, choosing her own settings on her own terms was exactly what she needed. The hook was set—if only she could reel him into the KGB's boat.

The waiter arrived with their food and poured a glass of vodka for each. Anya smiled and said, "*Vashe zdorovye!*" They touched glasses and began their meal. Anya wanted to see how well the American could handle liquor. She noticed that he only brought the beverage to his lips; most of the vodka raced down his chin onto a cloth serviette. He smiled and apologized profusely for his clumsiness while patting his chin. Not a drop went down his throat. *Very clever, Mr. Adams*, Anya thought.

Anya determined that Mr. Paul Adams of America was going to be a challenge. So be it. This was her Rome, and she was raised in its coliseum. *Let the games begin.*

CHAPTER 68

During the same week that Anya met with the American, Sofia also had a meeting, but of a very different sort.

After the library closed, Sofia walked down the sidewalk, and as she prepared to cross the street to go to her house a few blocks away, a black car with dark-shaded windows pulled up next to her. The back-seat door swung open, and a voice commanded her, "Get in—quickly." Sofia peered into the car to find that the voice was the Raven's.

As soon as she closed the door, the sedan quickly pulled away from the curb into the sparse night traffic. Sofia spoke first to relieve the tension and to satisfy her curiosity.

"I see you are back from Moscow. How are things shaping up there?"

"It's a madhouse," he replied. "Everyone is jockeying for power. It appears Nikita Khrushchev is slowly edging ahead. He is not the KGB's first choice, but he will do. He fought in the war, especially at Stalingrad. Anyone who survived that is no wallflower. Khrushchev is also not given to the whimsical purges that Stalin ordered. He does not blame the KGB for Stalin's excesses. We will do all right."

"I'm surprised to see you," Sofia continued. "You said that we would never meet in public due to the danger of exposure."

"Yes, I did say that, but tonight we will make an exception. Extraordinary times require extraordinary measures."

The Raven's tone did not comfort Sofia, but as a case officer, he never did. She began mentally to prepare for the worst.

"When I returned, I was rather surprised to see that you were already admitted into a doctoral program. I suppose congratulations are in order. However, it does limit our options, doesn't it, comrade?"

"On the contrary, sir, the target is supervising my program. I meet with him two or three times a week. It is the perfect cover for my being in his office so frequently. I wrote that in my report."

"Yes, our good professor is exactly what our little meeting concerns tonight. How is he? What progress have you made?" The Raven turned and faced her with his round dark glasses. "Specifically, have you found his research papers?"

Sofia knew her next words would be crucial; she chose them carefully. "His research material must be either in his home or in his office. "He never takes vacations, and his entire life revolves around his research and his teaching duties at the university. I have never been invited to his home. He would find that inappropriate since I am a student. It could also get him dismissed from the university, and that would end his top-security clearance. I have taken hundreds of photos of his office. Has anyone searched his home in the same dedicated manner?"

The Raven admired her courage and logic in speaking to him so directly. He replied, "The house has been thoroughly examined. A team posing as gas repairmen photographed every inch of the house before searching it to make sure everything was placed back into its original position. They even photographed the outside of each drawer, making sure the absent-minded professor did not leave a thread or hair, which might drop to the floor, when the drawer was opened. They need not have bothered. Every floorboard was checked for a hidden safe. Even the walls were x-rayed. Nothing. The papers must be somewhere in his office. That is your domain. Find them."

"If I may suggest," asked Sofia, "why don't you send the same team to his office after hours? Surely they will discover more than I can by simply sitting in front of his desk."

The Raven looked at her as if she were a child. "Sofia, perhaps we require a little refresher course on your tradecraft. Begin by explaining the mystery of how one eccentric professor can have a house as neat as an old maid's, and yet his office looks as if a bomb went off in it. There are papers stacked everywhere. I know his type. He seems disorganized, but he knows exactly where he has placed specific files or papers, even in the midst of his landfill. It would be almost impossible to put them back in the same order, at night, without causing an avalanche of paper or alerting your odd professor."

Sofia had to smile. The office did seem a disorganized mess, but the Raven was correct in his analysis. She replied, "His house is neat, and his office is cluttered, comrade, because he lives in his office, and he only visits his house to meet his basic needs. I know this man. Please be patient."

"Sofia, look at me and listen carefully. You are not here to become an amateur photographer or to receive multiple degrees at the expense of the Soviet state. Your mission is either to find the research material or to recruit the professor to work for us—by any means necessary. At the risk of sounding like a capitalist, I want more productivity and results. Do I make myself clear?"

"Yes, sir, very clear. I will try to visit his office more and to inspect it closely. However, I must report to you that he seldom leaves his office when anyone is there. I hope you will reconsider my suggestion for a trained search team. I'll do my best."

"Sofia, allow me to tell you why my code name is the Raven. Some colleagues think my thin frame, my long nose, and my odd round glasses make me appear birdlike, along with my habit of turning my head to the left when others speak. I acquired these unusual features and habits after the Battle of Berlin on the Eastern Front. A German soldier threw a phosphorous grenade that exploded next to my platoon. My comrades died in flames, but I survived. The bright flash and explosion damaged by eyes, and I was temporarily blinded. The hearing in my left ear never returned. Even today, any bright light clouds my vision and causes me great pain behind my eyes, thus the dark glasses.

But the main reason I am called the Raven is that after I recovered from my wounds, I could not see clearly to shoot a rifle or to hear a necessary command. So I was placed in an interrogation unit with the NKVD. One does not need perfect vision to gain information from a prisoner, and a lack of hearing is actually a benefit—especially when they begin to scream. The NKVD became the KGB, so here we are—two birds in the same nest. I should point out to you that they also gave me my nickname because ravens have no qualms about eating the wounded and dying, generally starting with their eyes and face. Sofia, you have a lovely face and beautiful eyes. Don't make me consume you down to the bone."

To illustrate his point, he removed his glasses and squinted at her. Even in the dim light, she could see his seared, scarred eyes with smudges of embedded black gunpowder completely encompassing them.

"Our meeting is over, Sofia. If we have to meet again, the 'pecking' begins. Remember that."

The car pulled over to the curb a block away from Sofia's house. When it left, Sofia noticed that her hands were shaking. She had seen hard men and hard times, but not until this moment had she ever been truly afraid. Never had she met with absolute evil.

Still shaken, as she walked toward her house, Sofia remembered the last refrain from Edgar Allen Poe's "The Raven": "Quoth the Raven… 'Nevermore.'"

CHAPTER 69

Anya arranged for the American's equestrian event at a large dacha just thirty minutes outside Moscow. The dacha belonged to the KGB, holding enough electronic equipment to rival any television station. The horses were provided by an army general who was convinced by the KGB that it would be in his best interest to "loan" the horses to their organization for a short time.

Anya knew this was going to be an important meeting. Her first objective was to determine just who was this Paul Adams and what were his exact duties at the embassy. Her second priority was to record some statement or action that might later incriminate him. Blackmail and subtle recruitment would then follow.

The Adams mission puzzled her. Colonel Kurgan was making it a top priority. Adams only mentioned that he was a "lowly clerk" dealing with minor economic issues. There was a missing link in all of this. She hoped today's excursion would answer some of those questions.

Paul had access to an automobile, so he met Anya outside of a metro station. She had no intention of letting him know where she lived. He opened the car door for her, and they proceeded down the wide boulevards of Moscow toward the countryside. Both enjoyed the scenery during the short drive to the dacha.

The American liked the dacha and its adjoining pastures. He immediately saddled the horses in a small corral (hastily built by the

KGB) in preparation for Anya's first lesson. He was not aware that she had already had several lessons from KGB personnel at a local stable before this orchestrated event. He tested the horses and found that they were gentle and well trained. He offered Anya the most gentle horse, and her lesson began.

Anya was a natural horsewoman: her athletic abilities gave her excellent balance, and she quickly learned to move as one with the horse. Her hand movements were light, and she had the golden touch: slight signal, then release.

Paul was impressed, and within an hour, they were riding through the countryside. It was the perfect day for a ride: a leisurely Saturday, the bright leaves of autumn surrounding them, crisp, autumnal air—"sweater weather."

While they were riding, Anya glanced at Paul. He reminded her of her father, Sasha. He was not as tall and lean as her father, but he had the similar brown hair with auburn highlights and the keen blue eyes. His quiet, polite manners also brought welcome memories of the relationship between her mother and her father. Anya determined that riding in the countryside with a polite, handsome man on a beautiful autumn day was very nice duty. It beat shadowing people on a cold day in Moscow or sitting behind a desk.

They came to a natural spring. It was not wide but very pretty and clear. Paul stopped his horse, looked around, and declared, "This is the spot! Yes, right here—perfect for a picnic!"

Anya was surprised and said, "Paul, the dacha has much food. I thought we might eat there after our ride."

"No need, Anya. A picnic with a beautiful woman on a beautiful day—what could be better?" He took her hand and helped her dismount from the horse.

Anya held the reins and retorted, "What are we going to eat, leaves and grass? Although, the spring does seem inviting."

Paul answered her question by reaching for a large coat that he had tied behind his saddle. "Never fear, milady, your knight shall provide it all." With a flair, he unfolded the coat and began pulling out food items left and right. Anya had never seen a coat with so many pockets. She had to laugh at this impromptu magical act: a wedge of cheese, several sausages, half a loaf of bread (slightly squashed), two apples, and a small bottle of champagne with two glasses tied around the bottle by a navy-blue ribbon.

He chose a spot near the stream and, with a flourish, spread the large coat onto the grass. He placed the champagne in the cold stream and asked Anya, "Would you be so kind as to organize our feast? I must tend to our steeds. It's an old cowboy rule: horses always come first."

Anya smiled and began placing items on the coat while Paul watered the horses and then placed their saddles and blankets next to his coat so that they could be a backrest for Anya. He gently wiped the horses' backs with a cloth taken from his coat pocket after being soaked in the cool stream. Anya watched with amazement as he took two soft ropes from his saddle, tied each horse's two front legs together, and attached the same rope to one back leg. He called it "hobbling." He removed the headstalls and stepped back toward Anya. The horses were not used to the ropes and jumped around for a short time, but they quickly became accustomed to taking small steps and quietly grazed next to the stream.

Paul found some late-blooming wildflowers and presented them to Anya, proclaiming, "What a bounty. Let the feast begin!" He plopped down and leaned against a saddle next to her. Pouring a glass of champagne for both of them, he toasted her, "*Vashe zdorovye!*" She smiled and touched her glass to his. The stream, the warm sun, the flowers, the sound of happy conversation—Anya could not help but reflect about that special day when her mother planted the Siberian tulips. Her father was quietly cleaning his treasured rifle while she read her new book from Vladimir, *The Krokodile*, by their own stream next to their home. A perfect day then, a perfect day now.

They talked the entire afternoon about whatever interested them. Economics, electronic devices, and blackmail were left behind. Anya had already surmised he was not going to say anything in the dacha. The eagle was going to soar, and for one afternoon, she was going to soar with him. Her superiors would be furious with her, but that storm would pass. She knew that after today's special connection, there would be no one who could take her place. Let them stew!

As Anya sipped her champagne and watched the horses graze peacefully by the stream, she could not help feeling the irony: that the most pleasant time that she had ever had since leaving her family was with a polite, handsome man who was classified as "an enemy of the people."

CHAPTER 70

Sofia increased her efforts to be around Professor Price. Anytime he had office hours for students, she was there. At least twice a week, she found an excuse to ask his opinion about some matter relating to her doctoral program.

She tried several of her old tricks to get him out of his office: When she suggested that they take a break and get a cup of coffee together, the professor produced a thermos and offered her some of his own coffee, which he had brewed at home. He informed her that it saved time and money. When she offered to treat him to lunch to thank him for all his work on her behalf, he took a small paper bag from his weathered briefcase and offered her a sandwich. When she suggested that maybe he would like to come to her bungalow and have tea, he looked at her like a deer in a car's headlights and remarked, "Why would I want to do that? I have plenty of tea at home, but nice of you to offer."

Sofia came to the conclusion that she had never met a more amiable, pragmatic, and totally clueless man in her life. She often wondered that if she were to stand in front of his desk without a stitch of clothing, would he even notice, or would he simply hand her his tweed jacket and calmly comment, "Here, Sofia, you must be chilly."

The anticipated day came unforeseen, without her planning and scheming. She arrived to ask him about suggestions for her doctoral thesis. It was a pleasant day, and the office windows were open. His office door was always left open when a student was present to ensure that no one would question his integrity when alone with students. A colleague asked to see him for just a moment. While they were talking in the hallway, a gust of wind produced a sudden draft through the windows and doorway. A wooden panel behind the professor's desk blew open about halfway.

Sofia saw a sturdy American safe that had two dials and a large keyhole under an *L*-shaped handle. She centered her purse and quickly took as many pictures as possible, making sure that she captured the name of the safe and the dial readings in each picture. Apparently, the professor neglected to push the panel hard enough to make it latch the last time he closed it. It also meant that his most recent research was still there.

When the professor returned, Sofia had her head down and acted as if she were reading a folder on her lap. The professor noticed the slightly opened panel and crossed between Sofia and his desk to block her view. He gently closed the panel while taking a book from a shelf directly overhead. Sofia never looked up, but she heard the quiet *click* of the latch when it locked in place.

Sofia lingered in the office for another thirty minutes so as not to arouse his suspicion and excused herself to attend an afternoon class. Once outside, she sat on a bench and quickly made a diagram of the safe and its location while it was fresh on her mind. This was double insurance in the rare event that the camera or the film did not function properly.

She marked a drainpipe with her tape, which indicated that there was a message and film at her closest dead drop. After depositing the diagram and film at the secret location, she hurried to attend her class. To preserve her cover, she never missed a lecture.

After the class, she went to her favorite coffee shop to celebrate her discovery. The watchers must have seen her walking in that direction, for on the lamppost outside the coffee shop, there was a signal for her. She ordered her usual café au lait and headed for the park.

While feeding the pigeons gathered around her, she quickly leaned down and retrieved her message at the base of the park bench. It was from the Raven, containing only two words: "Well done."

Sofia broke protocol: instead of leaving immediately, she sat on the bench and watched two white swans floating like feathery clouds on the still surface of the pond in front of her. She wanted to be one of those swans—floating with the current without a care in the world. While sitting at that peaceful setting, Sofia swore that never again would she allow the Raven or any of his evil flock make her live in fear and terror. She also determined that she was going to finish her doctoral degree, no matter the risk or cost.

She returned to the coffee shop and turned the signal tape horizontally, to indicate that she had received the message. Tossing the remainder of her coffee onto the signal and fiercely throwing her paper cup into the trash bin, she made her way toward the library, where she would study until they turned off the lights.

****

A week after Sofia's discovery, on a quiet Sunday morning at 2:00 a.m., a three-man team entered the back of the Physics Department to photograph the contents inside the hidden safe. These men specialized in opening American safes. They had waited a week so that there would not be any connection to Sofia if things went wrong.

Upon entering the building, they changed into the janitorial coveralls used by the campus cleaning service. Two men obtained a service cart from the custodial closet while the third man watched the front of the building. Because of Sofia's extensive surveillance, they knew the schedule of each custodian and the route taken by the campus security police. At 2:00 a.m. on a Sunday morning, they knew that the campus would be deserted and the security extremely lax.

The two men placed the service cart in the men's restroom and spread a tube of brown foul-smelling gel on the floor and around a toilet. If discovered by a security officer, their cover story would be that they were called in to clean the mess before classes began on Monday. Upon leaving the building, another compound would be spread on the brown gel, which would turn the alcohol-based material into a clear liquid that would look like water and then quickly evaporate.

If a security guard still did not believe them, the men would seize the unfortunate guard, and the third man would inject him with a serum that caused instant heart failure. The body would be left on the bathroom floor with his hat on the countertop, and a few wet towels would be placed in his dominate hand, which could be determined by the placement of his holster on the right or left side. It would appear that the man felt ill and entered the building to wash his hands and face before suddenly dying of a heart attack.

The two men left the cart and proceeded into the professor's office. Sofia's surveillance had revealed there were no alarms on any windows or doors in the entire building. "No one would want to break into the dreary old physics building," seemed to be the university's attitude.

The latch hiding the safe was released within seconds, and the safe stood before them. One man was designated to open the safe while the other handed him special tools and directed a low-beamed red light. Since they could not drill the safe, the dials had to be manually aligned using an instrument which looked much like a large stethoscope that doctors placed in their ears to listen to a heartbeat.

Before touching the safe, the team checked the edges of the panel and the safe for any thread, hair, or small pieces of paper that might fall unnoticed onto the floor if either door was opened. They also recorded the exact numerical setting of the two dials on the safe. It was an old trick to always leave a dial on a certain number. If the number was different upon his return, the owner would know the safe had been compromised.

It took the team only thirty minutes to align the dials and to insert their own key, made according to the images from Sofia's pictures. When the door of the safe swung open and there was no alarm system, the team breathed a sigh of relief.

There were five folders in the safe. The team used a special camera that was designed for low-light exposure. The interior of the safe was first photographed with a polaroid camera so that each file could be replaced in its exact angle and position. The stack would be neither too neat nor too messy—just exactly as it was, without arousing suspicion. Even the folders were measured from the inside wall of the safe to the edges of the folder to match the polaroid picture and to ensure that no one could tell they had been moved.

The file that they desired was in the middle of the stack. Both men worked rapidly: one turned a page while the other photographed each side of the paper with the special camera. The watcher reported to them that only one security vehicle had driven by the entire time; it never even slowed as it passed the building.

The files were replaced according to the polaroid photograph and their measurements. The dials were reset to their original numbers while the two men were careful not to touch any folders on the professor's desk and cause a disastrous avalanche of papers just before they left. All the team wore elastic gloves, but every item they had touched was still wiped down with a special compound designed to eliminate the salt and oils that left fingerprints. Spreading the alcohol-based compound on the brown gel in the lavatory and replacing the cart to the custodial closet took less than one minute.

Each man left the building one at a time at ten-minute intervals. Traveling in different directions, a car was waiting for each of them two blocks from the campus. The first man to leave carried the film since he had the best chance of not being seen. The lookout was the last to leave. He carried the satchel with their tools and a large book in his hand. He looked young, and he was dressed like any ordinary college student. If stopped, he was to explain that he had been studying with a friend for an important exam; he was just cutting across the campus to save time. If forced to provide an address, he would mention the location of an expendable KGB safe house four blocks from the campus. He also carried a .22 caliber automatic pistol with a silencer in his waistband. He was authorized to use it. The weapon was to be used only as a last resort; but whatever was required, the equipment must not be discovered, nor the mission compromised. Too much was at stake. A "cleanup" van was waiting nearby in case a body needed to be whisked away. The team hoped it would not be needed.

The last man to leave the building received the signal, "All is clear." The young agent looked at his watch when he left the doorway: 3:15 a.m.: one hour and fifteen minutes. *Not bad!* he thought. *The Raven will be pleased.* As he slowly walked away from the deserted campus, the man with tools in his satchel, a book under his arm, and a gun in his waistband disappeared into the darkness, thus allowing Sofia to survive, to study in the same building, to spy another day. Mission accomplished.

CHAPTER 71

Paul Adams, special agent of the Central Intelligence Agency, was treading on a very dangerous path, and he knew it. The CIA and the KGB had a tacit understanding that they would not assassinate the other's agents, but if one were to cross a tenuous line—all bets were off. Agent Adams was approaching that line.

He had diplomatic immunity working at the US embassy in Moscow as an economic specialist. His cover was that he sought to increase trade in various grains and other US agricultural products to the Soviet Union and other Eastern Bloc countries. Like all good cover stories, there was an element of truth to his: an agricultural background, being raised in the American Southwest, and an acquired understanding of import-export commodities, courtesy of the CIA.

Under normal circumstances, if he violated Soviet law, he would be declared *persona non grata* and asked to leave the country; but his undertakings were far from "normal," and all the "immunity" in the world would not prevent a hit-and-run accident or a knifing from a supposedly botched robbery on an isolated street. Soviet authorities would simply explain, "These kind of things happen in every large city, even in America. You have our condolences—so sorry." Immunity or not, Paul Adams would still be quite dead.

Paul's real mission was to get a nuclear scientist, Dr. Yuri Yegorov, his wife, Lyola, and his young daughter, Tanya safely out of the Soviet

Union and onto the shores of the United States of America. The main difficulty was the isolated location where the scientist lived: Central Russia.

The Russian scientist was of Jewish origin. He changed his family name from Yegevi to Yegorov when he applied to enter the University of Moscow, hoping to gain more opportunity and less discrimination. He had been recruited by US agents during a scientific conference in East Berlin. A year before the conference, his Jewish identity had been revealed, and although quite talented, his promotions ceased. There was also a different feeling in the air at his workplace. He sensed danger. It was time to leave.

It was easier and safer to bring a defector westward across Russia through Finland. Because of this, it was also more closely watched by the KGB Border Patrol. Since the scientist and his family lived in Central Russia, it seemed that the better option was to go east and reach the Pacific coast just above the city of Vladivostok. It was the least expected route, and it was closer to transportation that could take them to the United States. The problem was that one section of the journey passed through a secluded and uncharted woodland. Because of isolation, death, and attrition, this region was now known by only one person: Anya Ruslanova of the KGB.

In previous years, a Jewish escape route had been established, crossing Eastern Russia to the port city of Vladivostok. At the docks, Jewish shippers had boats waiting to transport the refugees to America. During the Second World War, the route had to be changed, hence the wooded detour through Anya's family property. Although only a handful of people knew it, this new route led directly to Vladimir's Store.

Vladimir's great secret was that he was Jewish, and his family had helped Jewish refugees to escape Russia for several decades. It actually began when he was a small boy.

The Symann family left Russia during the Russian Civil War after a pogrom destroyed their village. Vladimir's parents, grandparents, and several extended family members used the originally established route in order to reach Vladivostok. When they arrived at the present location of Vladimir's Store, it was open land with a spring which never ran dry, thus the reason for its importance on the route.

At this spring, the young boy Vladimir became quite ill, and he could not continue. His father made a heroic decision and told the others to proceed. He would stay with his son and try to find them later in America when the boy recovered. Vladimir eventually regained his health, but his father realized that the boy could never survive the long trip to the United States. Another life-changing decision was made: father and son would stay in Russia to help others gain their freedom.

Father Symann was a self-taught engineer; he could build anything. He recognized the importance of the springs and its location for refugees to rest before the final push to Vladivostok. The springs flowed from a rock formation inside a large depression. Vladimir's father cut timber and made a warehouse over the depression and attached the current store to the warehouse.

The area had no facilities, and Soviet authorities were anxious to settle this region of Siberia to expand their lucrative fur trade. They encouraged the operation and gave Mr. Symann (now changed to Simonov) permission to bring in supplies to entice others to settle near his establishment. What the authorities never learned was that the springs underneath the warehouse provided water and living quarters for Jewish refugees wanting to leave their country. The various supplies could not be traced and, in turn, fed hundreds of needy people on their way to Vladivostok and to a new life.

When his father died, Vladimir Symann-Simonov continued the operation. The warehouse was still functional, but only Vladimir and his extended family in America knew this. The once sick boy carried on the family tradition of offering freedom to others.

Before leaving for his assignment to Moscow, Paul Adams approached an old rabbi of Russian descent in Brooklyn, New York. A large number of Russian Jewish families lived in Brooklyn at that time. He told the rabbi about his dilemma and asked for the rabbi's assistance and advice. The rabbi swore him to secrecy and directed him to Vladimir's family.

Vladimir was secretly contacted, and he agreed to help—if, and only if, they could safely and discreetly reach his store. He would not jeopardize his life nor the future of others for just one family, no matter how important they were. The line had to remain open. Before Stalin's death, there were rumors of yet another bloody pogrom that Stalin had been considering. Adams reassured all the parties involved that he would never compromise this vital lifeline to accomplish his mission. Vladimir knew nothing of Adams's hope to recruit Anya as their guide, or he would never have agreed—it was simply too dangerous.

Paul Adams sat at his desk in the embassy and pondered the situation: How does one convince an active agent of the KGB to help establish a route that could cost the agent her life for the treasonous possibility of saving others? How could he place a woman in mortal danger whom he was becoming quite fond of and whom he could hardly wait to see again? Agency dictum stated, "The mission always comes first." Paul Adams, the man, wondered if he would lose his way in life if he convinced himself that by betraying and sacrificing this rare woman, the ends justified the means.

At two o'clock in the morning, Agent Adams of the CIA was still at his desk, wrestling with his soul.

****

On the other side of Moscow, far removed from the American embassy, Anya was also working well into the night. She was completing the tedious task required of all intelligence operatives: the Foreign Contact Report. The KGB went even further than most agencies by requiring as much detail as possible. It was not only time-consuming but mentally fatiguing.

She tried to summarize the past months with Paul Adams. The horseback riding and picnic outings were finished because of the onset of winter. The horses had been returned to the general since the KGB did not want to feed them throughout the winter. The general did not appreciate the KGB's frugality.

Anya could not make up her mind about this American. He remained a man of mystery to her: the outings had been quite enjoyable, but not once would Adams venture into the dacha. He described his work in abstract, almost guarded terms. He was an excellent listener, sometimes too good, since she frequently did most of the talking. Was this just basic embassy training, or was it real tradecraft? Was this man as nice as he seemed to be, or was it all an act?

Anya was not naive. Most Russian officials and embassy employees in foreign posts were either KGB trained or had some link to an intelligence wing of the Soviet state. She knew the Americans often did the same.

She was about to conclude her report on Paul Adams by suggesting that, in all likelihood, he might be affiliated with a United States intelligence agency. However, she decided to wait and try to discover which intelligence unit he represented, if any.

She also hesitated to make a hasty conclusion regarding his possible intelligence background, for she knew that additional personnel would be assigned to the case. She and Paul would then never be able to talk freely or to be entirely alone again. Colonel Kurgan would "turn loose the dogs" to try to expose or compromise the American.

Allowing her private feelings to cloud her thinking was not professional, but she could not help herself; she was enjoying his company. She just wasn't ready to let him go. Nothing permanent could ever happen between them; the KGB would never allow it. Still, for a woman who had never even had a boyfriend, it was nice for someone, even a mysterious foreigner, to treat her in a kind, romantic way.

Anya wrote at the bottom of her report: "Paul Adams, Embassy of the United States of America, Economic Specialist—High Priority, More research required."

Locking Paul's file in her desk, she turned off her desk lamp and made her way toward the exit at the end of the office. When she left the doorway of Moscow Center and walked on the wet sidewalk next to the quiet street, Anya smiled as she proceeded toward the metro—with warm memories of beautiful horses, of carefree picnics, and of a handsome man laughing by a flowing stream.

CHAPTER 72

Sofia's operation was going so well that her resident case officer, the Raven, was already considering plans to recall her to Moscow to utilize her upcoming doctoral degree in the Soviet Union or to use her on a new personal assignment. Sofia had no intention of submitting to either one.

She knew the KGB would not jeopardize her current mission with a sudden recall, if it would cause unnecessary questions and damage to her cover story. Her advanced doctoral program was proceeding rapidly, and it was assured. Sofia planned to use her academic cover to gain additional opportunities.

Under the principle "It is easier to ask for forgiveness than for permission," she decided to find a new project that would make her indispensable in the United States. Her new "project": Congressman Thomas Stevens—currently running for the United States Senate.

She purchased an elegant evening gown (her Russian "bean counters" went crazy) and proceeded to a United Nations function in which she knew Congressman Stevens would be present. She did not have an invitation, but this did not trouble her. When she arrived and kissed her new diplomatic parents on each cheek, admission was assured. When asked by her surprised parents as to why she was there, she simply explained that it was to protect her cover since she had not seen them for several months. They had no choice but to smile and introduce her throughout the crowd as the proud parents of their very charming and educated daughter. Sofia subtly directed them to Congressman Thomas Stevens.

Congressman Stevens was everything a promising politician needed to be: handsome, loquacious, a winsome smile, extremely likeable, and possessing the rare political commodity of being quite intelligent. He was noted as an "up-and-coming" legislator, and if he could win the senate race, he was almost guaranteed a new position on the Senate Intelligence Oversight Committee. He was also the most eligible bachelor in Washington, DC.

When Sofia was introduced to him, she immediately saw the sparkle in his eyes. Throughout the evening, they talked and danced together. Several remarked, "What a lovely couple!" These remarks were not missed by her cover parents and would be reported to her case officer, just as Sofia had hoped.

Congressman Stevens also noted that when Sofia was next to him, more people relaxed and instantly approached him. Charm, elegant beauty, and extreme intelligence—what more could a rising political star desire in another standing beside him?

Before the evening ended, Stevens and Sofia made arrangements to meet again the next weekend at one of Washington's most famous restaurants—and a fertile reservoir for politicians of every stripe who wanted to be noticed. *Let the games begin.*

As Sofia left the party, she placed her hand on Stevens's shoulder and kissed him softly on his lips. Her final *coup de théâtre* was when she whispered into his ear, "See you soon, Thomas." Senate hopeful Thomas Stevens was smitten, hook, line, and sinker.

Stevens helped her get into a taxi and waved goodbye. As the cab pulled away from the curb, he placed his hands on his hips and said to himself, "What a lucky guy I am!" Sofia smiled, blew him a kiss, and softly voiced to herself, "You're my ticket."

****

When the Raven heard of Sofia's exploits in New York City over the weekend, he was absolutely livid. It was terrible tradecraft; he could already see gossip column photos and headlines, "Who is the rare beauty with senatorial candidate Congressman Stevens?" The photos and publicity could draw unwanted attention and blow the current mission with Professor Price at its most crucial stage.

The research gathered from the professor's safe was impressive, and they found new material each week. This was the highest priority. The Raven could not believe his privileged "upstart" would pull such a stunt and possibly jeopardize such an important operation. However, the Raven had survived this long by being realistic and practical: the damage was done; it could not be recalled. The professor had no love except for his work, so he would not be offended. If the congressman entered the senate and especially if he became a member of the Intelligence Oversight Committee, the rewards could be substantial. Also, if elected, women would come flocking around the new senator; at least Sofia already had her elegant foot in the door.

When he cooled down, he realized that he objected more to the timing than the target she had selected. He would have preferred an approach to Stevens after the guidance system mission was over and Stevens had actually won the election and obtained the committee position.

The election was only one month away. The Raven understood the value of planning and patience. Since the die was cast, he would roll with it. He also decided to jerk the chain on his presumptuous agent.

The Raven sent Sofia a signal for her to check drop box number 3 for a message. His ominous note read:

> Proceed with new target. Know this: if we lose old target or if new target loses position, we lose You.
>
> —R

CHAPTER 73

Upon completing her reports, Anya walked down the wet sidewalk toward her apartment, hoping for at least a few hours of sleep before starting another day at the center. A fine mist hovered over the dark empty streets, not cold enough to snow yet not warm enough to rain. A rising ground fog made it difficult to see to the end of each corner. It didn't matter to Anya. She could navigate these streets practically blindfolded. It did matter to the man who was following her.

Anya heard him before she saw him. Footsteps have a distinct echo and pattern on a quiet street in dense air. Anya recognized that her stalker was well trained. He knew how to match her pace and when to lengthen or shorten his stride to keep a certain distance—not too long, not too short.

She abruptly turned a corner, which led to a labyrinth of side streets and dark allies. If the man followed her into the darkness, he would meet his end. She always carried a custom-made stiletto switchblade knife in her jacket just for these moments.

The man briefly silhouetted himself when he turned the corner, entering the dark side street. Anya measured him for the kill: above-average height; wearing a hat, an overcoat, a tie; tilt of the head—aim high just below the jaw to hit the jugular and slice left. She took a few deep breaths to slow her heartbeat. Timing and motor control were essential for a silent kill. Move too soon, and the target might see the movement and possibly deflect the blow. Move too late, and the blade might strike the jawbone or the large muscle at the back of the neck—both painful but not necessarily fatal.

Anya braced her left foot against the brick wall of the alley to support herself. She would have to pivot with her opposite leg and right arm to quickly strike the victim when he walked into her thrusting zone. She counted his steps: three, two, one—silence.

The stranger stood perfectly still. He instinctively knew that he was in a kill zone. He slowly took two steps back away from the shadow of the alley and quietly called out into the still night air, "Anya, show yourself. I have a message for you."

Anya stepped to the edge of the shadow with the switchblade concealed next to her thigh. The man slowly raised his right hand so that she could see it, and he carefully removed his hat. Anya expertly closed the knife blade against her leg and exclaimed, "Paul, what in the world are you doing here?"

****

Paul Adams put his hat back on his head and pulled it quite low. "Let's keep walking," he suggested. "The walls of Moscow always seem to have ears not far away. Let's stay in the shadows."

Anya walked closely to him and instinctively stayed in the darkest areas next to the red-brick walls of the alley. If anyone saw her in her uniform while talking to an American without authorization, it could be her death knell.

She quickly overcame her surprise and said, "So you knew whom I worked for from the beginning. How else would you have known where to follow me?"

"Not at first," Paul replied, "but we have our informers as well. It only made sense to investigate any contacts, just as you do."

"We are supposed to meet in two days. Why this emergency meeting? That's what it is, isn't it?" Anya inquired.

"Yes, it is exactly that, and our next meeting will be our last, unless I can convince you to help me."

"Help you? How can a KGB officer help an American embassy's employee, if that is what you are?"

CHILD OF THE FOREST

"Anya, you don't work at a book depository, and I don't work for the embassy. I think you surmised that after just a few meetings. I'm going to be leaving the Soviet Union very soon, and I...well, I hope you will come with me."

They continued walking, but a deep silence engulfed them. Paul Adams had never spoken like this, and it took her by surprise: recruitment, defection, assistance, a relationship—what was behind this awkward situation and request?

"Paul, we Siberians are noted for being straightforward. We don't play games. Say what you mean before we reach the end of this alley or walk away before we both end up in the Lubyanka Prison."

"Anya, when I leave, I will be escorting three Soviet citizens who have decided to leave this country and start anew: a man, his wife, and their ten-year-old daughter. Unfortunately, the odds are against us. You know what will happen to the four of us if we are captured. With your help, I think we will make it."

Anya was becoming angry and replied, "Help, assistance, danger—get to the point! We are almost to the end of the alley. What is the plan? I won't commit suicide for anyone. Either you trust me or you don't. You have five seconds—make up your mind!"

Proceeding against every intelligence protocol, disregarding every principle of his training, and risking arrest by either the Soviets for espionage or by the American government for treason, CIA agent Paul Adams stopped and made a small sketch on an onion-skin paper in the faint light and handed it to KGB agent Anya Ruslanova. He quietly remarked, "Now, Anya, you hold all our lives in your hands."

****

Anya held the transparent paper and took a small worn pencil from her shirt pocket. Placing it next to her mouth, she said, "Paul, turn your back and touch the end of this pencil with a match. Cup your hand and make it look like you are lighting a cigarette for me. Open your coat to shield the light."

Anya glanced at the drawing and quickly blew out the match. She instantly recognized a crude map that went through her family's land, which led directly to Vladimir's Store and ended at the coast above Vladivostok.

"Paul, you are mad! You will all be captured or killed, and you will take Vladimir with you. Does Vladimir know that you have involved him in this escape, this mission into a maelstrom?"

Paul chose his words carefully. The moment of crisis had come. With her assistance, there was a chance of success; without it, as she had said—a possible journey into "a maelstrom," or even death.

"Anya, Vladimir volunteered. So did I. I'm praying, so will you.

"Who is this man and his family that you would risk all of our lives to flee this country?"

"It is top secret. I have already revealed too much. I could be tried for treason. Let's just say that he is very important."

"He is a scientist, isn't he? Your map is close to a location where only scientists live. They do that for a reason. It is so that they can watch them. Once your scientist does not show up for his work or appointments, a general alert will go to every transportation center and port. You will have twenty-four hours, maybe forty-eight at best, to get to the coast. You also do not understand the terrain. The woods are so thick and the ground is so broken that even a compass is of limited use. If you follow animal trails, many only lead to steep cliffs or deep ravines. Do you really believe that a pampered scientist, a woman, and a young child can scramble up and down these obstacles? If you make even one wrong detour, they will have the time needed to catch you.

"You should also be aware that they use special tracker dogs who are trained exactly for this type of search. Even when young, they are trained to track for their food. If they don't find it, they starve. Only the best survive. The dogs won't make a mistake. If you do, you're doomed. There are also the unknown factors that cannot be anticipated: we are approaching winter. That area is notorious for early snowfall and even blizzards. If anyone becomes lost, slips down a ravine, or breaks an ankle or leg, it is the same as a death sentence. My mother died exactly that way, and she was born and raised in those mountains.

"Last but not least, if you are caught, the scientist will be tortured to find out who were his accomplices. The wife will be sent to the worst gulag up north. The girl will be sent to an orphanage for 'enemies of the people.' My orphanage was terrible. This orphanage is beyond description. Vladimir will be interrogated and shot. You will be dumped into a dark cell for the rest of your life or possibly traded ten years later for a Soviet spy held in the United States. I don't want to think what will happen to me. This is what you are facing. Know this before it is too late."

Paul hesitated, but the time had come—it was now or never. He turned to her, with her face covered by shadow, and said, "Anya, I don't want you to come with me as a guide. I want you to come with me…forever. I don't want to leave Russia without you. Your parents are gone, and so are mine. I was never an orphan. I just came to them late in life. You have no one. I have no one. Perhaps together we could start a new life of our own. I know we are taking a great risk and that I have no right to ask you, but this is the only chance we will ever have. The same system that took your land and your youth is now standing in our way. Don't let them take our future."

Anya was speechless. It was too much, too soon.

Paul continued, "In two days, we are to meet at the restaurant where I first saw you. I will bring a flower with me. A blue ribbon will be tied to the stem. Later, soak the ribbon in alcohol. Any form will do, even vodka. The date, time, and rendezvous point will be visible on the ribbon for exactly ten seconds. Then it will disappear. If you arrive on time at the rendezvous point, I will know your answer is yes. We cannot wait. If I don't see you, we must leave at once. Then I will never see you again. It is my fervent prayer that you will come."

Paul took a pouch of tobacco from his overcoat and rolled a cigarette using the onion-skin map that he had shown Anya. He wanted to take her hand, but that could get them both killed. Instead, he calmly turned up the collar of his coat to block his face, pulled down his hat, and walked to the end of the alley. He never looked back. He couldn't; his training and her safety would not allow it.

Anya watched him walk away with a wreath of smoke hovering over his head and a secret map disappearing with each puff. When he turned to the right at the end of the alley and vanished from her sight, she wondered if she would ever see him again.

****

Anya waited ten minutes and walked the opposite direction of Paul's exit. She followed several side streets that were different from the route she and Paul had come. The blue hues of dawn were present, and the city was already beginning to stir. The sun was ready to lift its head. There was no use going home, so she slowly made her way back to her office. A decision had to be made.

As she walked, she considered Paul's startling plan and proposal. Initially, it had struck her as foolhardy going east instead of west; but upon deeper reflection, its daring simplicity might just work.

The scientist lived next to a railway station. If he planned to take his entire family, it meant that he had a holiday pass. Those fortunate scientists who were allowed abroad for academic conferences or symposiums had to leave their family members behind to discourage their defections. Most scientists vacationing with their families left their isolated area and went to Moscow or to Leningrad to shop, to visit museums, and to eat at better restaurants. Since most were in a hurry, the vacationers normally bought express tickets to reach these major cities quickly. However, some took more local trains, which had cheaper fares and made more stops, so that they could visit a few friends along the way. They changed trains in Moscow for the night train to Leningrad. All of this took more time.

Eccentric scientists were always missing trains. It was a paradox that they could build something that might destroy the world, but they could not coordinate a standard rail schedule in their heads. Thus, a general alert was not issued until the next train arrived without them, and they failed to check in as they were required.

If Paul's scientist bought a family ticket for a local train heading west toward Leningrad and exited at the next sleepy country station, which generally had low security, and then headed east, he and his family would have at least a forty-eight-hour head start before anyone discovered their absence. The immediate search would begin toward the west since that was his ticket destination, and no one in their right mind would head east and risk cutting through the Siberian woods with winter so near. An early snowfall would trap them, especially when considering a wife and a young child wading through deep snow in their best clothes. They would be dead before the end of the day.

Anya still did not understand how Vladimir became involved in all this. There was a missing link somewhere. Paul must have convinced him that it was to give her the freedom of a new life in America. In any case, it was extremely dangerous, and she feared for Vladimir.

Paul's words about the Soviet system failing her were true. She detested the privileged Communist leaders' hypocrisy and their bureaucratic reach into every person's life. She loathed the government, yet she still loved her country. Would American bureaucracy be any different? Would they even allow a former KGB agent to have a meaningful life in their society?

If she were to leave, no one in Russia, except Vladimir and Dmitri, would understand her desire to study medicine and to be with a man who treated her as if she were a queen rather than "property of the state." Worst of all, she was not officially allowed to see Vladimir and Dmitri, the two people she truly loved.

Colonel Kurgan would certainly not understand nor forgive her. His opinion did not matter to her, but he was a danger. He liked to remind her of the refrain "The KGB never forgets!" He was also dangerous because of what he knew.

As she approached Moscow Center, an alarming thought came to her: Colonel Kurgan was someone Paul Adams had not factored into his escape plan. There was no way that Paul could have seen the danger. Colonel Kurgan was the only Soviet official who could immediately send all resources to the exact location of their escape: Only he knew that Anya's family once owned the woods for the shortcut to the coast. Only he could connect Anya's relationships to Vladimir and to Paul Adams. Only he could lead the KGB directly to Vladimir's Store. Kurgan was no fool. Once the watchers reported that Adams was no longer entering his embassy, Anya was missing from work, and there was a general alert for the scientist, he would immediately put all the pieces of the puzzle together. Where else would Anya go but to Vladimir and to the coast? Familiar people, familiar territory—a familiar fate for all.

Anya realized that Paul's decision to include her was the fatal flaw in his plan; it would lead Colonel Kurgan to Vladimir's front door. No one would be safe. A decision had to be made within the next two days: either she could keep the meeting with Paul at the restaurant and warn him of the danger—never leaving Russia for the rest of her life—or Colonel Viktor Kurgan had to be eliminated.

Anya opened the door to the Center and touched the syringe hidden in her jacket. There was still time to silence the Gray Wolf—perhaps today, perhaps tomorrow—perhaps forever.

****

Paul waited nervously at the restaurant for Anya. Normally, she was never late. True to his word, he had a flower with a blue ribbon resting on the table before him. If Anya had decided to turn him over to the KGB, the ribbon contained all the information necessary to have him arrested as a criminal against the Soviet Union, and the scientist and his family would suffer a fate worse than death.

He could not help but wonder whether his trust in her was based on realistic love and admiration or simply in a misplaced desire for something that was not really there. Better men than he had fallen for this oldest trick in the world, especially in Cold War espionage.

When Anya entered the restaurant, a flood of relief surged through him. He politely seated her and gave her the flower. She accepted it with a smile. Her smile was genuine, for it was a beautiful yellow rose, and she also felt close to him for trusting her. She glanced around the room and spotted two Soviet agents. This was not going to be an easy encounter.

Anya had decided not to tell Paul about Colonel Kurgan, his secret files, or his exclusive knowledge regarding her history. Paul might choose to hurriedly change his plans, and last-minute changes generally caused confusion and defeat. His timetable for the escape was already set with all the parties involved. The die was cast; it was now time for his operation to proceed with confidence, not nagging doubt.

The table conversation was pleasant, but an underlying tension was present. Both knew the stakes were high, and even one error would result in disaster. Watchers always looked for anomalies, and any suspicions were reported immediately.

When their meal was over and they parted company, Paul gave her the traditional light kiss on the cheek. As he did so, she whispered in his ear, "Yes." She shook his hand and took the rose with her.

Anya went to her apartment to change clothes so that she could return to the office to file her contact report. This was the normal procedure. She had not noticed anyone following her, but now was not the time to arouse suspicion of any kind.

She placed the blue ribbon in a bowl of alcohol and stepped into a ray of sunlight away from the window so that she could not be seen. The time, date, and location of the rendezvous magically appeared. She quickly memorized the information and watched it slowly fade away. She burned the ribbon in an ashtray next to the sink in her small kitchen, far away from any windows. The ashes were flushed down her toilet into secret oblivion.

Anya was not a smoker. However, when working undercover, she always tried to have a pack of cigarettes available, for purposes of tradecraft or to simply get closer to a target. She lit a cigarette and let it burn to cover the smell of the burnt ribbon. Sitting on her couch, she watched a small plume of smoke spiral from the ashtray toward the ceiling. It reminded her of how transitory life could be, like smoke rising, only to fade away, leaving but our fragrance and ashes behind.

The pretty blue ribbon had revealed everything that she needed to know. Next to an open window, seated on her couch, wreathed by sunlight and smoke, Anya calmly looked at a calendar hanging on her wall. Within six days, she must kill KGB Colonel Viktor Kurgan.

PART 6

The Exile

*And where is the fury of the oppressor?
The captive exile hastens, that he may be
loosed, that he should not die in the pit,
and that his bread should not fail.*
—Isaiah 51

CHAPTER 74

Paul Adams paced himself for the remaining two blocks that loomed ahead of him to reach the embassy compound. Two Soviet agents followed him, one on each side of the street. This was their normal procedure. Any time he left the embassy, he was followed until he returned, no matter where he went or the length of time required. Today he welcomed it. He stopped at a small kiosk and bought a newspaper so that he could momentarily look over his shoulder and make sure they saw him. This evening, he wanted his vigilante escorts to see him enter the gates of the embassy.

It would be dark in another hour. Adams wanted his watchers to witness his entrance, to record the time on their ledger, and then to sit at their safe house across the street from the American embassy with their cameras and binoculars, drinking hot tea and relaxing until the end of their shift. Paul estimated that he would gain seven days before someone compared notes and realized that he was never walking through those gates again.

He was pleased the way his lunch had gone with Anya. He had seen her only a few hours ago, but now he knew that he had to put her out of his mind. He felt certain that she would somehow manage to make the rendezvous on time. If she did not, perhaps she would meet them at Vladimir's home. In any case, his focus now had to be on a one-way journey out of Moscow.

Paul took a heavy work shirt out of his briefcase, the last garment of his travel wardrobe. Every day he had carried one item of clothing to the embassy so as not to attract attention. He quickly changed out of his overcoat and suit into a very worn workman's outfit with a brown leather cap. There was no time to lose. The night awaited him, whatever it might bring.

The dark night covered his escape as he entered a small tunnel, which, unknown to the Soviet government, led from the embassy grounds to a grove of trees not far from a city park. A rusty sedan with one side mirror missing was waiting one block from the park.

Paul Adams was a calm, courageous man, but his Achilles's heel was that he hated confined dark places. The tunnel was claustrophobic. What awaited him was little better than a tomb.

He reached the car safely and quickly proceeded down the dark streets to a warehouse district, where his "tomb" was waiting. A large jolly man, Piotr, slapped Paul on the back and motioned for him to get into a large truck with an olive-green canvas top. Piotr was a former smuggler, now employed as an asset for the CIA. Inside the cab of his truck, he had a hidden space that was lined with stainless steel and vacuum-sealed, much like an iron coffin. Once sealed, dogs could not smell the guns, explosives, radio equipment, or humans that he transported. A small oxygen bottle and mask were included in case there was a long delay at a border crossing.

Piotr had a license to be a long-distance truck driver. This license cost the CIA several thousand dollars given to a corrupt transportation official, but it allowed Piotr to drive almost anywhere with legitimate documents.

The long-distance drivers were a hardy breed, generally driving alone. Tonight's cargo, legally listed on his manifest, was a driver's dream: an entire load of expensive vodka for special government facilities. The CIA paid for several more cases (not listed on the manifest) to "reward" border guards for their hard work in serving the Soviet Union. For special shipments, it was not uncommon for there to be two drivers. This allowed the truck to constantly be moving, except for refueling.

Piotr opened the "tomb," and Paul slowly positioned himself into his stainless steel coffin. He was already drenched with sweat. There was an emergency release inside the box in case the oxygen bottle became empty, but the thought that the release might jam or not work properly terrorized Paul.

Piotr smiled at Paul's discomfort. Before he shut and sealed the lid, he said, "Okeydoke, comrade, it go like this: You stay in magic box very short time, just until out of Moscow. We stop and act like little doggie and wet on tire. You then ride up front with me, except for checkpoints. Like rabbit, you go back into hole while I show manifest and give a few rewards to official bandits. This takes them from cab and magic box toward back of truck. They get nice vodka. Don't sign my name on manifest to ledgers. Number of cases remains the same. They get no blame, bad boys stamp Road Authorization Pass, smoke cigarette with bandits. Off we go. Got it, okeydoke? Good night."

Piotr slammed the hidden door shut and sealed the compartment. Bathed in silent darkness, Paul lay on his back like a dead man and felt the beads of perspiration race down his ribs. When he heard the hiss of the airlock, blood began to pound inside the temples of his head. Gripped with nauseating fear, he struggled to put on the mask, his hands shaking so violently he could barely open the valve of the oxygen bottle.

As Piotr pulled away from the dock, he whistled a familiar jaunty tune. Paul Adams bit his lip until he tasted blood and stifled his desire to scream.

CHAPTER 75

Anya sat at her table next to the window of her small apartment. Dawn had arrived, and its soft light streamed through the window and onto the yellow rose Paul had given her. It had blossomed in the slender blue vase, and each delicate petal seemed as if it were spreading its arms to the sun.

Anya smelled the fragrant rose and felt an unnatural calmness. She was going to kill a man today, but life and fate marched hand in hand before her: by nightfall, she would either be free or sitting in a dark, musty cell waiting to be shot.

She was already dressed and ready for work. She just wanted to see her home one last time, bathed in light. The tiger-claw necklace fell over her neck and under her blouse. A single claw rested in her left pocket, and the syringe, like a sleeping cobra, held its single fang and deadly venom just within reach in her jacket.

Anya took one last look at her simple home and locked the door behind her. Destiny was drawing her, just like her yellow rose, both reaching for the sun.

****

Anya planned to work late and approach Colonel Kurgan in his office at the end of the day after everyone had left for the evening. She had overheard the colonel tell his assistant that he would be staying late and that he wanted no interruptions after 6:00 p.m. She looked at Kurgan's door and said to herself, *Finally, it comes. This is the day.*

If she could just inject Kurgan at the base of his neck without a struggle, an autopsy or an inquiry was unlikely when he was found dead the next morning. The serum was untraceable, and others would assume he simply died of a heart attack from the long hours and the stress of his work. Even if there were suspicions, she hoped to be far away.

Anya had a vacation form which listed Vladivostok as her destination. She expected the colonel to view the document and protest since he knew she would see Vladimir and Dmitri along the way. Angrily viewing the form with his head down, focusing on the paper, she hoped the momentary distraction would provide the time that she needed to inject him. However, he was an alert man and seemed to have a sixth sense about danger. Timing would be everything.

The vacation form to Vladivostok covered her absence, and since it was such a long journey, no one would be alarmed when she did not immediately return. By the time an investigation ensued, she planned to be with Paul and the scientist's family, beyond the borders of the Soviet Union. If Kurgan refused to sign the form, she already had another form ready with his forged signature. She had practiced for several days to make it look identical.

The clock seemed to barely move that day. Anya had plenty of work to do. Several files were stacked on her desk. It appeared normal for her to stay late and finish her work. One by one, the office cleared, until she was the only person left. She could see a light under the colonel's office door. At 6:10 p.m., she approached his office. It was time.

She tapped lightly on his door. There was no answer. Finally, she cracked the door open and said, "Colonel, sorry to bother. I just need your signature on a form, and I will be on my way." Kurgan still did not answer. Entering the doorway, she was startled by what she saw.

Kurgan was sitting in his chair with his back to the door. His feet were resting on another chair, and he was looking out of the window. His uniform jacket and tie were carelessly dangling off a chair, and a half-empty bottle of vodka was at the corner of his desk, near his left elbow. Kurgan merely glanced at her with glassy eyes and seemed to be in another world.

Anya realized that this was the moment she had been waiting for—never again would she find him alone and in such a vulnerable position. With her heart pounding, she slipped the cap off the syringe and hid the apparatus next to her leg in the fold of her skirt. The back of his neck was exposed, and he remained just looking out of the window.

As she made her final approach with the syringe in one hand and the vacation form in the other, Kurgan surprised her again by saying, "Sit down, Anya. Feel free to have a drink. Today is a special day for me. Let's celebrate together."

Anya had no choice but to sit down, but she positioned herself at a right angle to the desk, where the colonel could not see her hands and his back was still vulnerable.

"Anya, today is my parents' anniversary, or at least...it was. Both of my parents died within a day of each other. But in the old days, when I was a boy, oh, how we celebrated this day together!"

Anya knew that she should spring into action while he was still talking. A dark voice kept repeating deep within her, *Now, now! What are you waiting for? Do it! This will never occur again. You hate him—finish it!* His comments about his parents caught her off-guard. Her mind screamed for destruction, but her heart wanted to hear the rest of his story (the mind always seems quicker to reach a conclusion than the heart), so she waited.

Kurgan continued, "We owned an estate outside of Saint Petersburg, now Leningrad. Anya, you should have seen Saint Petersburg before the revolution: ballrooms, dancing, exquisite culture and taste—such a beautiful city, such sparkling times! The last time we celebrated this day in Saint Petersburg, my mother was wearing an elegant white floor-length gown. Her dark hair was lifted high on her lovely head. Sparkling jewels hung from her ears and across her pretty chest. She and my father glided across the ballroom in perfect unison. They were the loveliest couple at the ball. Everyone said so. I was so proud of them.

"Then came the revolution. The Bolshevists seized our property and forced us to live in a little cabin near the woods. I didn't mind. I just wanted to be with my parents. Everything else did not matter. My mother died first. Her health was always frail. The hard work and the meager food destroyed her. When she died, my father lost all interest in life. He killed himself the next day. I'm afraid that I became an orphan just like you. The manager of the collective farm hated my family, and he forced me to leave. I was not much older than you were when you had to enter the orphanage. No one wanted me. So I joined the Army—too young, but no one cared.

"The Civil War, Stalin's purges, the Second World War—I survived them all. So here I am with a half bottle of vodka and a half life of memories. I must admit, Anya, I still miss my lovely parents, and I would give anything to see them again, especially today. Anya, I never wanted to be a soldier. I just wanted to be with my family and to work the land. I always loved the land."

Viktor Kurgan's story unsettled Anya. She had never realized, until that moment, that they had traveled a parallel path that led to devastated destinies: both had lost their parents at approximately the same age and under tragic circumstances beyond their control; both had lost homes and lands that they had loved—forcefully and unjustly. Both had learned to survive in a ruthless system that they had never desired. Both had learned to kill and to justify each death, buried deeply within themselves. Both had become predators in the very system that had created them.

Sister Elena's words rang like the tower bell in Anya's soul: "Remember, Anya, sometimes we must forgive a life in order to save our own. Ask not for whom the bell tolls—it tolls for thee." Anya determined that she also had blood on her hands. Enough of death. It was time to begin to live. She carefully placed the safety cap on the syringe, and hid it in her uniform pocket. She then did something that she would have never dreamed: she walked over to Viktor, and instead of driving a needle into his exposed, unprotected neck, she gently placed her hand on his shoulder and quietly left the room. The roar of the tiger had ceased.

When Viktor saw the vacation form on his desk, he berated himself for the way that he had treated Vladimir, an old friend, a man who had saved his life. Anya wanted to go home and to see those she loved. Viktor, especially on this day, understood her desire. He leaned across the desk and signed the form. Tomorrow he would give it to his assistant and rearrange her schedule. It was the least he could do for her.

The last rays of the setting sun streamed through the office window. KGB Colonel Viktor Kurgan, son of Russian aristocracy, survivor of Stalingrad, rising star in the KGB, upcoming general, and alias "the Gray Wolf," poured himself another drink and stared beyond the window while thinking of ballrooms in Saint Petersburg, happy, laughing parents, and days of what might have been.

****

Anya was unaware of Kurgan's signed vacation request, allowing her two weeks to escape. Leaving Kurgan alive, not processing her forged vacation form, both were a risk, but she just could not kill him—not on that day, not at that moment. Even a wounded wolf deserves pity. Now, she reasoned that she had two days to reach the rendezvous with Paul. With the weekend free, she would not be expected back at the center until Monday. There was just enough time to get there, but not much.

She left Colonel Kurgan's office and immediately made her way to the train station. She had already purchased her ticket for the night train to Vladivostok. Fortunately, the rendezvous point was well before Vladivostok, thus saving valuable time. A large suitcase was waiting for her in the stored-luggage area at the rail terminal. She would use her KGB uniform and credentials, if needed, to thwart authorities, until she and the escape party reached the coast. For now, she covered her uniform with a long black overcoat.

Anya boarded the train, and when it moved, she felt as if she had stepped off a steep cliff into the deep darkness of a moonless night.

Chapter 76

When Paul reached the small railway village for the rendezvous, Piotr barely slowed the delivery truck so that Paul could leap from the vehicle and then cover the three blocks to the isolated station. Piotr was an old hand at this maneuver—never revving the engine, silently gliding forward, always looking straight ahead—as Paul rolled from the truck and lay still on the ground until the truck lights disappeared into the night.

Paul timed his arrival to meet the others just as the train pulled into the station. At this time of the evening, only a few passengers departed the train. The station office was already closed.

Paul looked down the platform and saw the scientist and his family walk slowly toward him. There were only two locals. Unfortunately, there was no Anya. He felt a heavy, sinking feeling in his chest. There was nothing that he could do but proceed without her.

Just as the train prepared to leave, Paul looked back and saw an image that brought him the greatest joy of his life: a tall blonde woman in a black overcoat left the train as it was pulling out. She had stayed on the train to see if any officers were lurking next to the station, leaving adequate space between herself and the scientist's family so as not to arouse suspicion that they had exited together. She walked erectly and at an even pace, never drawing anyone's attention.

Paul could not help but smile and admire her tradecraft. This was his Anya, and he loved her all the more for it.

Paul waited until the two local passengers left and then proceeded down the platform to the right side of the station. The scientist had been briefed to follow a man in a brown jacket wearing a leather cap. Anya, true to form, went to the left side of the station and disappeared into the darkness.

Paul waited until the area was completely quiet and approached both parties. A plain dark-colored car was parked one block from the station on a dark street. Taking Anya's suitcase and kissing her on her cheek, he remarked, "This is heavy. What do you have in here, a body?"

"Something like that," she replied. "Paul, let's get moving."

Anya surprised them all by handing three pairs of handcuffs to Paul. The scientist and his family feared that they had been betrayed. Anya calmed their fears by explaining, "Paul, I don't mean to take over your operation, but I know the country and KGB procedures. Please do as I ask. Place the family in the back seat with the child in the middle. Put the handcuffs on them loosely so that they can quickly slip out of them if necessary. I will drive, and you will sit in front next to the window on the passenger's side. I'll explain more later. We need to hurry. Small villages have big eyes and even bigger ears, especially late at night."

Three small satchels and Anya's large suitcase were quickly placed into the trunk of the car. The handcuffs were distributed as Anya suggested. She noticed the car had a full tank of fuel. It would be just enough. Paul had planned well.

After they had driven for thirty minutes, Anya broke their nervous silence by explaining, "I'm sorry that I alarmed you. The handcuffs are just in case there is a roadblock. It is unlikely to occur so soon in this remote area, but they sometimes have mobile squads for rapid deployment. Please listen carefully. If there is a checkpoint, say nothing and sit still. Make sure they can see your hands and, particularly, the shiny handcuffs. There are generally only two, but sometimes three, guards at a mobile roadblock. One will stand in front of the vehicle, and the other two will approach the car from each side.

"Just before we reach the checkpoint, Paul, you and I will roll down our windows. Paul, I noticed that you have a pistol with a silencer in the right pocket of your jacket. By the time we reach the roadblock, have your pistol ready and wait for my signal. Let me do the talking. They will defer to the driver. They will assume that Paul is an undercover officer. I will show my KGB credentials and announce to them that I have caught the traitors to the Motherland. They will see your handcuffs and relax. Paul, this is when we will strike.

"I will hold my credentials back toward myself so that the guard will have to lean his head inside to view them with his flashlight. When I say, 'Comrade, my credentials are in order,' that is the signal. Paul, shoot the officer near you in the face, then lean out of the window and shoot the guard in front of the vehicle. I will eliminate my target with my switchblade knife. The car will be in gear. I will run over the front guard in case your bullet did not kill him. When we stop, hand me your pistol and shine your flashlight into their faces to blind them. I will finish them with a shot to the forehead. If we break their legs with a tire tool, we can fold them into the trunk, and you can hold your luggage on your laps in the backseat. We will dispose of their bodies in a secure location down the road. Are there any questions?"

As the car rumbled down the empty dirt road, there was complete silence in the car. Finally, the realization about the stakes involved and the possible dangers that lay ahead struck all the occupants. Even Paul was amazed at Anya's cold, calculating plan. It made him wonder, who was this lovely Russian woman that he had asked to join him to live in America? Obviously, he had much more to learn about her. Nevertheless, he knew that her assessment was correct. He smiled and said, "Yes, dear. Onward and forward."

****

They drove several hours. At every crossroad, everyone seemed to hold his breath. Would a vehicle suddenly dart forward and block their path, with men toting machine guns pointed at their faces?

Would this be the end of a long chase and the beginning of a road to terror? The outcome was too terrible to contemplate. Silently, each person became lost in his thoughts and prayed for dawn to shed light on another day, but the night had just begun.

Eventually, Anya stopped the dusty sedan on a steep clearing, which descended to the edge of a deep ravine. The headlights displayed a forest of massive trees and thick woodlands spreading in every direction, as far as the eye could see. She exited the car and breathed the forest-scented air. This was life to her. Would America have forests like this? Would she ever see her country again? Would she ever have close friends such as Vladimir and Dmitri? She felt the answer would be no to each of these doubts, but with typical Siberian willpower, she knew the course was set. Time to press onward.

Paul and Anya put the luggage on the ground. Fortunately, there were no bodies in the trunk. Anya handed Paul a tire tool and said, "While I change into hiking boots, crawl under the vehicle and puncture the fuel tank. When it is drained, we will tie the steering wheel, put it in neutral, and push it over that ravine. Even if they come this way, it will take weeks to find it, if it does not catch fire."

Paul punched a hole in the tank at a right angle to ensure that he did not get gasoline in his face and thus blind him. When he emerged from under the car, he was surprised to see Anya's suitcase in the trunk of the car and a backpack on the ground. She was wearing black boots and a black fur KGB field hat with a large red hammer-and-sickle insignia on the front of the hat. She kneeled next to the pack and began putting an old rifle together. A leather cartridge belt hung across her chest, and a string of large claws draped the front of her neck. She stood and watched a pale moon rise slowly. A full moon would show them the way. Once again, Paul had planned wisely.

Letting her eyes adjust to the new light, she stood on a knoll and scanned the horizon. Paul saw the moonlight reflect off this Russian beauty as if she were a statue in Saint Petersburg: erect, with a pack over one shoulder, a rifle over the other. Her black KGB hat contrasted with her long blonde hair: a yellow wave flowing with the wind, away from her face and the back of her black coat. The moonbeam highlighted her upturned face, a face even Michelangelo could not have chiseled better. Paul looked at her with pride. This was Mother Russia in the flesh. This was Siberia at its best.

****

Anya and Paul pushed the car while the scientist and his family stood at a safe distance. The car gained speed down the steep slope. There was a momentary silence and finally an eerie sound, like rolling thunder. Silence again. The mountain had swallowed it whole.

Anya pocketed the handcuffs and lined everyone behind her. "Don't be afraid. Just stay on the trail behind me. I will be at the front. Paul will guard you from the back. We should not see anyone. Even trappers do not come here at night this late in the season. If they were injured, they could easily freeze to death. If we see someone, crouch low and hide in the brush next to the trail. Paul or I will deal with them.

"Don't talk, make noise, or light a match. A match or a cigarette is like a signal flare in the darkness. It momentarily takes away your night vision. It could also get us killed. We should reach the springs by dawn. The moonlight will help us. Stay together, and we will be all right."

Anya took a cartridge from her bandolier and placed it in the chamber of Sasha's rifle. With a tiger skin resting in her pack, with tiger claws draped around her neck, with her father's rifle in her hands, and with her beloved forest ahead of her, Anya felt a peace that she had not known for several years. The deceased head matron was correct about one thing: Anya Ruslanova was *indeed* the mountain girl.

When Anya slammed the bolt forward on her rifle, it made a powerful, solid sound that seemed to encircle the woods, a symbolic herald as old as Siberia—the hunter, the prey, the chase. The full harvest moon was up and waiting. Without looking back, like a goddess of the forest, a creation formed from these ancient mountains, Anya called to the others, "This is my country. Follow me."

CHAPTER 77

Odd how a piece of paper on a desk can be routine one moment and then, because of a certain day or a particular event, it becomes a revelation.

The notice placed on Colonel Kurgan's desk was a simple status report mentioning that Paul Adams had not left the American embassy for five days. Kurgan tossed the report into his file box. This was nothing new. Embassy employees throughout Moscow often lived at an embassy for extended periods of time when they were working on special projects or if they had several meetings to attend. On the other hand, almost a week was longer than usual. The colonel decided to ask Anya whether she had recently communicated with Adams when he recalled that she would not be coming in today since he had approved her vacation.

An hour later, an emergency general alert was issued for the immediate capture and arrest of the scientist and his family. In the field of intelligence, a coincidence doesn't just happen. There is always the calculation of cause and effect: Anya and Adams—both connected, both absent. A scientist and his family on the run.

Kurgan unlocked his safe and retrieved Anya's personal childhood files. The ex-district commissar had listed the names of her parents and a legal description of their property. Kurgan wrote down the coordinates and went to a large map that covered one wall of his office. Taking a long ruler, he drew a line from the scientist's workplace, pointing southeast, until it connected to Vladimir's trading post. The line went straight through the northern section of Anya's old homestead.

Kurgan had been made a colonel at an early age because he had an innate ability to read people, to accurately assess their strengths and weaknesses, but above all, to see things that others failed to notice. These skills always placed him at the head of the pack—advancements that some of the "pack" would never forgive.

The general alert was distributed throughout the Soviet Union. The main focus would begin at the scientist's home city, then toward Moscow, and up to Leningrad—everything moving west. It suddenly occurred to Colonel Kurgan that he was the only officer in the vast Soviet Union that had all the information at his fingertips. The escape party was going east.

Kurgan measured various distances from Vladimir's village. Vladimir's location was two days north of Vladivostok but less than a day east to the Pacific coast. His map showed several small inlets and bays fishermen used in this area. Analyzing various schedules, he estimated that there was still just enough time to capture the entire group before they could reach the coast. Still it would be a close-run thing.

This capture would ensure Kurgan's promotion to the rank of general and an advancement to becoming the director of the Intelligence Division. This would be his golden moment. He reached for the telephone. The search needed to be redirected at once to trap the party on or near Vladimir's home. Once they reached the coast, it would be very difficult to find the exact inlet. There simply was not enough personnel and soldiers in the vicinity to immediately cover this large coastal area on such short notice.

One thought troubled Kurgan: Why Anya? Yes, she would be their guide. Yes, she was probably enamored with Adams, but he also knew that she was no traitor. She loved Russia, Siberia, and her parents' land. These bonds were her fiber and being.

Kurgan put down the telephone and decided to think this through; there was still time. He reread the general alert: Scientist—Yuri Yegorov, below average height, dark hair and beard, brown eyes, glasses. Wife—Lyola Yegorova, average height, blonde hair, blue eyes. Daughter—Tanya Yegorova, blonde hair, blue eyes, ten years old.

Kurgan rubbed his forehead and looked out of the window. The last piece of the puzzle fell in place: it was the little girl. Young Tanya was almost the same age that Anya had been when she lost her parents. A blonde-haired girl who would never see her parents again and who would go to a very unpleasant orphanage for the sons and daughters of traitors. Anya could see herself in that little girl.

Viktor thought about his last meeting with Anya. He had been slightly drunk (a rarity for him), and he had talked too much about personal matters. He remembered that when he had finished his story, Anya had not said a word. She simply touched his shoulder and left. He had lied, manipulated, and used her, yet that gentle gesture seemed to represent her forgiveness for all that he had done to her.

Crossroads come at the most inopportune moments: one road led to advancement, status, and glory; the other road led to mending a life he had torn apart. Wolves can be fierce creatures, but they never desert the pack. Anya was now a member of that pack, even though she never desired it. He had made her run with them for the hunt. It was now time to let her go. He chose his road.

Viktor gathered all her files from the district commissar, the Soviet State Children's Bureau, the Vladivostok police reports, and all the paperwork from the orphanage. The vacation form had already been filed. He would try to deal with that later. He placed the files in a burn-bag container for secret documents. A special incinerator would reduce the incriminating evidence to untraceable ashes in a matter of seconds.

Colonel Kurgan's assistant saw him leave his office with the burn bag. This was not unusual. Senior officers often did this to ensure that prying eyes could not reveal secrets that would come back to haunt the officer for breaches of security. What was strange was that he did not sign a register for the time and date of the burning event. The assistant assumed that he had just forgotten. Being efficient, he wrote the required information in the register for the colonel. The colonel could sign the register later at his convenience.

Viktor walked down several flights of stairs to the basement. He was fortunate; the orderly for the incinerator was at lunch. He would not have to complete a document stating a vague reason for the burning, the exact time, the date, and his signature. With no record at his office nor at the incinerator, no one would ever know about the destruction of the files. This was his gift to Anya: at least two additional days of freedom, away from the hunters. He could do no more; the rest was up to her.

He quickly opened the door of the incinerator and stepped back, covering his face with his hand. The wave of heat rolled forward as it were crashing over him, surrounding him, reaching for him. He threw the burn bag at the mouth of the Soviet dragon as if it were a lance, much like a knight of old: to protect, to rescue, to safeguard hidden secrets nestled in ashes.

As he watched the flames consume Anya's past, he also believed that she, just like the phoenix, would rise from the ashes for a renewed future. He closed the door of the incinerator and whispered, "Good luck, Anya. Godspeed."

KGB Colonel Viktor Kurgan walked to the stairs with a clear conscience and a free heart, but his exceptional instincts gave him a sense of foreboding. Each step echoed like a pistol shot—a warning to beware, lest the Gray Wolf became the prey, to hunt no more.

CHAPTER 78

They heard the waterfall before they saw it. The little girl left her parents and ran to the front next to Anya. She reached up and took Anya's hand while Anya pointed off into the distance to a large outcropping of rocks. The moon was still high enough for its reflection to shine upon the rushing waters, giving the cascade a glittering effect before crashing to the pool below.

The waterfall was not at its zenith, which occurred during the summer snowmelt, but it was still refreshing on a crisp, late autumn day. The party carefully made their way to the inviting pool, where Anya instructed everyone to take a rest. It would be dawn in one hour.

Anya took some food out of her pack and encouraged the group to eat and renew their strength. The little girl excitedly took off her shoes and dipped her small feet into the cool water. Anya could not help but smile. She would like to do the same, but vigilance precluded that luxury. With the moon going down and the sun coming up, they would be conspicuous targets on the open plains leading to Vladimir's Store.

In the fading moonlight, Anya noticed a narrow car track that led to within fifty meters of the pool. Times had changed. When she was young, it was still a day's walk to Vladimir's outpost. Apparently, this was now a popular destination for picnics and a quiet getaway. Ironically, it was this location's isolation that had attracted Anya's father to come here on his way to sell his furs. He generally had it all to himself. Time marches on.

Paul stood next to Anya and handed her a canteen of water. She told him, "This was one of my father's favorite places. He loved it here. He said that it gave him peace. You would have liked my father. You remind me of him in many ways."

"I'll take that as a compliment," he replied. "I'm glad that I got to share his little oasis. Just so you know," he continued, "I expect transportation to arrive here just before dawn. That way, we will not need to use any headlights. These people are exhausted. They are not accustomed to hiking over rough terrain. We should be at Vladimir's warehouse by noon. We leave for the coast as soon as it gets dark, before the moon rises again this evening."

Anya was impressed with Paul's planning. She asked, "Who is the driver? Is he reliable? Can he keep our presence secret?"

"Vladimir organized the transportation," Paul replied. "It is one of his drivers. I think his name is Mischa, Mikael, something like that."

Anya flashed Paul an angry look and retorted, "Paul, you are endangering too many people—most of all, my friends. This house of cards could fall at any moment. The KGB's sweep for accomplices will be wide and without mercy. Your planning has been excellent, but just one error, and an avalanche of wrath will cover us."

Anya sat down and splashed some water on her face from the canteen. She did not mean to criticize Paul, but she was very concerned for her friends being so involved in such a dangerous enterprise. Looking up at the fading moon and listening to the music of the waterfall, she understood her father's sense of peace at this special place. Her father once told her, "Anya, I never worry about things of which I have no control. It is a waste of time. I direct my energy and tell myself, 'This is what I can do,' then I try to do it the best that I can." Following his advice, she checked the chamber of her father's rifle and prepared to advance toward the faint road to establish a hidden watch post.

As she gathered her pack, Paul sat down next to her and tried to ease the tension. He knew she was correct, but he also knew that there was no other viable way. Vladimir and his resources were their lifeline to freedom.

"Tell you what, Anya, I have been remiss. In all the excitement, I haven't even introduced you to everyone. Come, let's all get acquainted."

Anya looked down the direction of the car tracks and stoically replied, "I don't mean to be rude, but I don't want to know their names. It's easier that way."

"Easier! What do you mean?" he asked.

"Paul, there is an old Siberian saying: 'Never name anything you might have to shoot.' We are but a stone's throw away from death. We have been clever and lucky to stay ahead of the pack, but the wolves are closing in. I can feel it."

Anya reached into the inner pocket of her overcoat and removed a long gray cylinder. She held it for him to see. "Inside this tube is a syringe with a lethal dose of serum—"

Paul interrupted, "You would take your own life?"

"It's not for me. It's for the little girl. If we are captured, I know what awaits us. I will euthanize the girl and then shoot the mother in the back of the head when she is not looking. I will then turn the rifle on myself. You and the scientist concocted this little journey. Both of you are on your own. If you are wise, you will shoot the scientist and then kill yourself. If you don't, may God have mercy upon you, for the KGB won't. As for me, I won't be taken alive."

Paul looked away and said, "Anya, you seem rather hard."

"This is Siberia, Paul, and tough country breeds tough people. If we survive this, I will start a new life with you in America, but I will always be a Siberian. Don't ever forget that."

Before Paul could respond, Anya stood and saw the faint outline of a dark sedan making its way down the narrow track toward them. She took her rifle off its safety and moved next to a large tree. Sighting the rifle at the driver's window, she placed her finger on the trigger.

The car stopped with a lurch. Young Mischa got out of the car and wisely stood still, next to the driver's door. When he spotted the rifle pointing directly at his chest, instead of fear, he grinned from ear to ear and said, "Anya, what are you doing here?"

Anya lowered the rifle and put on the safety. "Hello, Mischa. Thank you for coming." She looked directly at Paul Adams. "Mischa, you're not the one I should be shooting."

****

It was late when Mischa drove the weary party to Vladimir's warehouse. He drove to the back of the immense building and opened the doors for the tired and hungry passengers. They emerged stiff and a bit nervous, but at least they were safely out of the forest.

Vladimir heard the motor of the car from his house. He entered the warehouse from a side door to greet his guests and to see to their comfort. Beside him was his friend (and "stone in his shoe") Dmitri.

Vladimir and Dmitri approached the huddle of dark figures, and Vladimir gave them a hearty welcome. "I'm glad everyone arrived safely. Mischa, let's get them below to their quarters so that they can rest out of sight." It was not until Mischa turned on the overhead lights that Vladimir and Dmitri noticed Anya near the dark sedan. Both men looked at each other in amazement and then rushed to embrace her.

"This is both wonderful and ominous!" Vladimir exclaimed. "Paul, you never mentioned that Anya would be in your party."

Paul cautiously replied, "In all fairness, I didn't know if she would come."

Mischa opened a hidden panel at the back of the warehouse. He pulled a lever, and counterweights hidden behind the walls creaked into action. A cleverly designed trapdoor in the southeast corner of the building slowly raised, revealing a staircase which led to an underground cellar. Mischa carried a lantern and called out, "Everyone, if you will please follow me." When the last person came down the steps, Mischa pulled another lever, and the trapdoor lowered itself into place. Once the door was firmly sealed, Mischa flipped a switch for the underground lights.

The large cavern was equipped with chairs, cots, food, a large stove, and enough firewood to last for months. A hand pump stood on a concrete platform off to the right. The cave could have easily held a hundred people.

Vladimir tried to make his guests feel at ease. "No one has been down here for years, so the air may seem a little musty. Don't worry, we have ventilation fans. Also, the stovepipe is connected to my house. Any smoke will draft through my chimney. Anyone passing by will think that old Vladimir is baking a lot of bread for the store."

"Or illegal vodka," Dmitri smirked.

"Please, ignore him. Everyone does," Vladimir retorted. "He's an imbecile, but relatively harmless. Paul, Anya, may I speak with you for a moment? Mischa, please seat the others over at that table near the stove. Slice them some bread, cheese, and sausages." Vladimir smiled and continued, "We will get the stove going and have some tea and hot food for you. Just relax and rest awhile."

Paul, Anya, Vladimir, and Dmitri gathered near the water pump. Vladimir spoke in hushed tones, "I'm afraid you may not be able to leave tonight as originally planned. Dmitri and Mischa made a trial run to the cove. It looks less suspicious with two people. They delivered some goods to the captain of the boat. The captain said a storm is rising over the Pacific. He feels it would be too dangerous to proceed, at least for tonight."

"It's true," Dmitri added. "I saw whitecaps already forming in the protected cove. I can't imagine what it would be like on the open sea at night."

Vladimir interjected, "The captain also said that the sea is not the only danger. No responsible boat would go out in this weather. If spotted, a coastal patrol boat would assume there was foul play. Smugglers often use bad weather to hide their movements, but even they would not go out in a storm this severe. If you try to outrun a patrol boat, they will shoot your vessel without warning. If they board your boat, we are all in danger. I assume you have a backup plan?"

Paul looked over at the scientist and his family, who were eagerly devouring their snack with Mischa. "Yes, there is a backup plan," he replied. "If we do not make the rendezvous point at the specified time, they will return exactly forty-eight hours later. If we do not make the second rendezvous, they will assume that we are either captured or dead. We then have to make contact in Vladivostok before they will return. There is no radio contact here, for fear of the signal being traced. I don't like it, but I guess we have no choice. We wait." Paul turned to Anya to gauge her reaction, "Anya, what do you think?"

Anya shrugged her shoulders. "We eat, we rest. There is nothing else to do. Have Mischa notify the captain of the delay. Why worry about things of which we have no control?"

The others walked away nodding their heads in agreement. But Anya did worry. She estimated that Colonel Kurgan had already put the pieces of the puzzle together. Their head start was perilously close to being nonexistent. Time was not on their side.

Perhaps by coming with them, she had inadvertently condemned them to their deaths. However, she reasoned, they would never have found their way through the forest without her. They would have been trapped and alone. It was all a calculated risk. The "risk" was closing in on all sides.

Anya looked around the massive cave. This was a good hiding place, but it would not last twenty-four hours once the KGB arrived. They would literally "turn loose the dogs." If necessary, they would tear down Vladimir's house, store, and warehouse piece by piece.

Anya transferred a cyanide capsule and one bullet to her left shirt pocket. From now on, both would never leave her person in case she became wounded or ran out of ammunition in the heat of battle. She turned her back to the others and subtly counted the cartridges for her rifle and pistol. She had just enough ammunition to delay an assault team in time to kill everyone in the group, including Vladimir, Dmitri, and young Mischa. She must not leave any alive. The outcome for anyone captured was unthinkable.

Anya shuddered contemplating what she might soon have to do. Kindhearted Mischa raised a teakettle and smiled in his innocent, boyish way. He called to her, "Anya…tea's up. I have a cup for you."

"Thank you, Mischa. I'll be right there."

Anya turned to the side and quietly chambered a shell into her pistol. She put on the safety and placed the weapon into a shoulder holster under her coat. Her hand slightly trembled. Glancing over her shoulder, gazing at Mischa's trusting smile, feeling as if a weight of hot lead rested on her heart, she softly spoke to him, "Coming, Mischa. Please pour me a cup. I'm coming."

CHAPTER 79

All powerful people have enemies; it is the nature of the beast. Colonel Viktor Kurgan was no exception. The Gray Wolf and the Raven had been circling each other for years.

The Raven had never liked Kurgan. Kurgan descended from aristocracy whereas the Raven came from a humble background, a factory worker's family. Both men had clawed their way through the ranks to be promoted, and both had suffered physically, being wounded in the war. But Kurgan's meteoric rise had left many behind—some who felt that they were more worthy. Essentially, the Raven wanted Kurgan's job. The Raven's Parthian shot was an arrow that would strike directly into Colonel Kurgan's heart.

The "arrow" that the Raven used was a formal request for a file on his agent, Sofia Karaleva-Borodina. As her supervisor, he had the right to review all her records to assess how to better utilize her skills for the Professor Price operation. Since the mission was going so well, he knew his request would be honored. He discovered that there was a secret file on his agent Sofia, and he wanted that file. The Raven learned early in life that information was power. He hoped this new information would serve two purposes: helping him transfer his arrogant, insubordinate agent off the professor's case while casting a shadow on Kurgan for not turning in all his files to Central Registry at Moscow Center.

Oddly enough, it was Sofia who innocently revealed the existence of these secret files. The Raven was indeed a skilled interrogator. When he debriefed Sofia after her first contact with the professor, he asked her some seemingly straightforward questions: her hobbies, her favorite books, her family background, her recruitment and training with the KGB.

Sofia guarded her answers, but she did mention that Kurgan had selected her and another girl who had been involved in some trouble at the state orphanage where both had attended. The Raven had smiled and asked, "How in the world did our clever Colonel Kurgan discover you? I understood that you had already left and that you were going to work for some general." Sofia shrugged her shoulders and replied, "I guess through the orphanage files. After reviewing them, he took us both by airplane to Moscow."

If Kurgan was keeping these files secret, the Raven concluded that there must be some piece of information that the colonel was hiding. The Raven wanted that information. The little upstart, Sofia, was going to pay for her high-handed effrontery, and she was not going to even remotely be allowed to inadvertently interfere with the Raven's second operation: his mole in the Senate Intelligence Oversight Committee. He had determined that she was going back to Moscow either by walking on an airplane or being delivered in a casket. Her secret file was the key.

The Raven made his request through an old friend, an agent in the Office of Internal Affairs for the KGB. He wrote to Captain Malenkov reporting the "missing secret files" on two female agents and that he needed Sofia's file for his vital operation in the United States. The Raven also suggested the file on the other agent should also be "strenuously assessed."

Malenkov sensed a juicy morsel of intrigue and, possibly, a promotion. Colonel Kurgan would be a formidable adversary. He decided the Kurgan investigation must proceed behind closed doors. As Malenkov raised the telephone, he thought, *How do you capture a wolf?* Smiling, he murmured, "Bait a trap and shoot it."

****

The hunt for the scientist was in its third day when Colonel Kurgan sensed there was danger in the air. He received a notice to attend a meeting that was "to assess the escape situation." The colonel was an officer of the Intelligence and Operations Division, so the request was not that unusual; the meeting location was—General Gurov's office.

When Colonel Kurgan entered the room, he immediately realized that trouble was brewing: Four men sat behind a long table. A single chair was empty in front of them. The colonel was invited to sit in the "execution chair." General Gurov, a heavyset white-haired man with a long array of medals across his chest, shuffled his papers and began:

> "Colonel Kurgan, there seem to be some irregularities in the search for the missing scientist. In over seventy-two hours, not one solid clue has emerged to find him. Comrade Khrushchev has taken a personal interest in this case. We are here to explore possibilities."

The general let the words hang in the air. Colonel Kurgan thought, *What you buzzards really want is a scapegoat to protect your own hides for a lapse in security.* Kurgan calmly replied, "Of course, General, I would be glad to help in any way."

The general looked to Captain Malenkov of Internal Affairs and nodded. The interrogation began:

> "Colonel, it has come to our attention that you have files on two of your agents that were never received by Central Registry. Why did you never turn them over to the proper bureau?"

The colonel chose his words carefully, "They were just odd forms and unrelated paperwork, not cogent to various recruits' status reports or to their training as agents. They seemed of no importance. I don't see how this helps us to find the traitorous scientist."

"Where are the files now, Colonel?"

"It was a few years ago. They are either in a storage box, or I had them destroyed in our normal way."

"Which brings us to another irregularity, Colonel. Twenty-four hours after the scientist was noted as missing, you personally burned some documents. Your efficient assistant recorded the date—*as required*. However, you never signed his record. The register in the Disposal Unit has no corresponding content or signature on its register, which as you know, is required for security purposes. Could you comment on this?"

"Perhaps I forgot to sign my assistant's register, and as I recall, there was no one on duty when I arrived at the burning station. I am also curious why the employee or his relief was not on duty."

"What was in the burning, Colonel?" General Gurov asked.

"Oh, nothing of great importance, just miscellaneous notations. However, according to regulations, they were not something to be absentmindedly discarded into a wastebasket."

All four men were staring at Colonel Kurgan. So far, he had fenced them off, but Malenkov was not finished.

"Colonel, another difficulty needs to be clarified. When I went to speak with one of the agents in your *withheld* files, she was not at her station. I checked the Records Department, and there was no vacation form, leave of absence, or other documentation for her to be absent. She is in your charge. You are supposed to be aware of an agent's location at all times. Where is she?"

Colonel Kurgan turned his head, looked Malenkov straight in the face, and replied, "She is, in fact, on vacation. I signed the form. The Records Department is notorious for misplacing items or not processing them in a timely fashion. She likes to hike and get away from the city. Her last vacation was just outside Moscow at a nice inn, which I recommended. That is also in the record, if you would like to verify it. She is most likely hiking as we speak. I wish more employees would follow her example instead of being drunk for most of their vacations and returning to work in need of more time to recover from their hangovers."

Malenkov had not scored any major points. The colonel's comments about the Records Department were valid, and a forgotten signature on a routine register was not uncommon among any of the four men facing him. Malenkov saved his trump card for the last.

"Well, Colonel, you certainly would not destroy any recruitment files, would you?"

"No, Captain, I certainly would not. Why do you ask?"

"I have in my hand a request for the recruitment file of Sofia Karaleva-Borodina. This woman is also one of your agents. It was requested for an important operation in the United States. You might as well turn in the same files for our missing Anya Ruslanova. It will simplify matters, don't you agree? I look forward to having those files by tomorrow morning. I have nothing further, General."

The general looked down at his notes without facing the colonel. "Thank you for coming, Colonel. You are dismissed."

As Colonel Kurgan left the room, he realized that he had walked into a trap. If he provided Sofia's files, they would ask why Anya's files were not present. If he withheld Sofia's files, he would be in violation of an operational order. He could not admit that he had burned Anya's files. If only his assistant had not been so efficient, no one would have been the wiser. He also did not know how Malenkov knew of the existence of the two files. There was a missing link.

Perhaps burning Anya's records was a mistake; but her files led to Vladimir, to the escapees, and to Anya's defection. Vladimir had once saved Viktor's life. Now it was time to save his old friend and several people who only wanted freedom. Memories of Saint Petersburg and his family still lingered.

He had no intention of being anyone's scapegoat. He had ridden out several storms in his life. It was still his word against theirs. He would delay; he would wait. The main battle was yet to come. Time to retreat to fight another day.

As he entered his office, he shook his head in amazement and looked out of his window. Who would have ever imagined that one thin file would lead the hounds to the Gray Wolf's door? He planned on finding whoever was the missing link, the betrayer on his own threshold. Looking at a barren tree from his window, he reminded himself, "The KGB never forgets."

When the Raven was cabled by Malenkov that Colonel Kurgan was under investigation, the Raven congratulated himself that his missile had struck home. Perhaps his celebration was a bit premature, for deadly arrows can fly both ways. All that is needed for a mortal wound is a small gap in the enemy's armor. The KGB never forgets—and neither do others.

CHAPTER 80

While Anya waited on a storm to pass over the Pacific Ocean and Colonel Kurgan weathered his own storm in a battle with Internal Affairs at Moscow Center, another storm brewed in the United States. The man waiting in the eye of this hurricane was the deputy director of operations of the CIA.

James Patrick Anderson sat on a blue plastic chair at the back of a red-brick warehouse. The faded white sign on the front read, "Simpson's Plumbing." He was used to waiting; his employment and ancestry made it a permanent fixture of his temperament.

He came from solid Scotch-Irish descendants who came to America in the early 1800's. President Andrew Jackson had just forced the Cherokee Nation to travel the infamous Trail of Tears from Georgia to the Indian Territory of Oklahoma. Unaware of the government's unfair resettlement of the Native Americans, the Andersons settled on their land. They held nothing against the Cherokee people or against anyone. They were just poor immigrants who were informed that there was free land, if one were willing to work hard and to start a new life. They were willing.

The first and second generations of Andersons basically worked themselves to death. They did so willingly, for it was their homestead, and they were building a future for themselves, opportunities the "old country" never offered. A few generations later, James Patrick Anderson was born.

James was raised as a good Southerner on a small Georgian farm. He had always been a tall, husky lad with quick reflexes and a farm boy's strength. A natural football player, his athletic prowess earned him a scholarship at the University of Georgia.

He wondered what he would do after obtaining his degree in history. The Japanese decided that for him when they bombed Pearl Harbor. He enlisted the next day.

The army discovered his aptitude for learning foreign languages. Lieutenant Anderson was immediately assigned to military intelligence.

When the promising lieutenant was the only one to survive from a platoon of soldiers on a reconnaissance mission, he captured the attention of "Wild Bill" Donovan, the head of the Office of Strategic Services, or OSS. Lieutenant Anderson was parachuted into occupied France to prepare for the D-Day Invasion.

His language and leadership abilities made him a natural foreign agent. He never asked the French Resistance fighters to do anything that he was not willing to do. He seldom used a firearm; his favorite weapons were the garrote and the knife. With speed and strength, he only needed one thrust. The French called him *La Lame* (the Blade).

After World War II, he left the OSS and joined the new Central Intelligence Agency. Working tirelessly through the ranks, he obtained the coveted position of deputy director of operations. His qualifications were never challenged—earned through bloodshed in the flaming crucible of war.

Most of his contemporaries thought of him as a typical, easygoing, good ole' Southern boy. He encouraged that assumption; a relaxed adversary often lowered his guard. Actually, his intense personality made his as tightly wound as one of the piano wires which he had used to garrote his enemies in France.

He slumped back in the blue chair with his legs crossed and his large hands folded behind his head. His chestnut hair was not as thick as in the "old days," and he combed it straight back. There were flecks of white mixed with the chestnut, making him look distinguished. His Scotch-Irish misty gray eyes missed nothing. If the KGB bragged about never forgetting anyone, James Anderson always remembered everything—even the smallest details. Today was no exception. He heard the faint sound of a car approaching. His "guest" had arrived.

The guest exited a taxi owned and operated by the CIA carpool. A heavy black industrial side door magically opened as the visitor approached the building. An agent dressed in a thick brown shawl-collared sweater quickly jumped into the back seat and the taxi sped away. The taxi's assignment, until the end of the meeting, was to cruise a five-block area. If it discovered a parked car with someone waiting in it at the curb, the taxi would radio the vehicle's description and the number of people in the car to spotters who were strategically located in each direction on the one-way street in front of the warehouse. If the marked vehicle later approached the frontage road near the warehouse, the taxi was to rear-end the automobile and cause an accident. The meeting would be quickly aborted. Nondescript getaway vehicles were already parked in the warehouse.

The guest surveyed the warehouse. Four men armed with Thompson machine guns guarded the premises, especially each exit. The visitor was impressed with the security arrangements. Agent Anderson smiled and put his hand in his pocket, as if he had all the time in the world. Showtime.

Mr. Anderson, in his best Southern tradition, offered his seat. He also wanted to stand so that he could tower over the visitor and intimidate with his size. Both looked at each other warily. The preliminaries before an execution carried more warmth than this gathering.

Anderson of the "prosecution" began the cross-examination:

"Business before pleasure, I always say. Where are your buddies, and where are you supposed to be?"

The visitor answered, "At the theater. They are waiting out front until the end of the performance. I bought tickets a month ago for the sell-out event so that they could not obtain tickets to get inside. My ticket selection was conveniently next to a side-door exit—not the best seats in the house but efficient. I left at the intermission. We have about an hour before the ending. I suggest we hurry with your 'inquisition.'"

Anderson smiled. He liked a keen adversary. "Well, you shot off the emergency signal flares for a crash meeting. What can I do for you, Sofia?"

"It seems, Mr. Anderson, that I am in a bit of a quandary."

"Darlin', I'm a little slow, but I figured that out since we're here in a damp warehouse eyeballin' each other. I suggest you get to the point before we both get shot."

Sofia crossed her long elegant legs and elevated her pretty oval face in preparation for the kill. She knew that she would have only one chance in this shaky encounter.

"I know that we were never to meet like this, unless it was an absolute emergency. You made that quite clear. However, do you recall when we first met at Saks on Fifth Avenue, in the fitting room, of all places, when I first arrived in the United States, when I supposedly went on a shopping spree for two weeks before beginning college?"

"Yes, dear, I vividly remember both the date and the arranged meeting. What of it?"

Sofia squirmed in her seat. She knew that Anderson was a hard sell and totally unaffected by her charm. "Well, I also *vividly* remember your promise that you would totally protect me and that I would never have to leave the United States. I now ask you to keep your word: Protect me and keep me, or I am doomed."

Anderson could tell this was not an act. She was nervous as a cat, and her left foot was shaking.

"Tell me, Sofia, has the operation with the professor gone south on us? So far, it has gone like clockwork. We give the professor the documents, he puts them in his safe, your friends steal them and scoot them off to dear old Moscow. You wrote in your last dead drop that all was well."

"Mr. Anderson, they are not my friends. They belong to the KGB—people I despise, people who destroyed my family, people who tried to make me a slave. The operation is going well, perhaps too smoothly! Since the professor is oblivious to anything except his work, my case officer thinks that my presence is no longer needed."

"Hold your horses, little lady. Which case officer: Moscow Center, your resident KGB master, or one of mine? You have so many that a fellow has to get a ticket and go to the back of the line just to get a debriefing from you."

Sofia had to smile. Anderson was an expert at slowing the pace and making a person feel that she could tell him her darkest secrets. She considered him a cunning professional.

"Yes, Mr. Anderson, I realize that I answer to a number of inquisitive gentlemen. However, the resident KGB case officer is, as you Americans say, the fly in the ointment. He plans to send me back to Moscow. I don't know whether it is pride or anger at my rather independent ways, but he is serious about it—deadly so. The threat is real to me."

"Missy, this is not quite making sense to me. I'm just an old country boy livin' in a big city. I thought you and the new senator from Virginia were a hot item around Washington. He has been appointed to the Senate Intelligence Oversight Committee. Did you drop him for another?"

"No, no, I did not. That is what is so mystifying. If I were to marry the senator, why would any logical mind want to interfere with a possible gold mine of information at their fingertips? It doesn't make sense. It has to be for spite…or worse."

Anderson gave Sofia his handkerchief. She was crying, and they were not crocodile tears. The girl was terribly afraid. Anderson called for another chair. The "inquisition" was over; time to regroup for a plan of action. James sat next to Sofia and took her delicate hand into his large bear paw. He let her regain her composure.

"Sofia, nothing is going to happen to you. I gave you my word, and to a Southern boy—your word, your honor, and your ability to save damsels in distress are a way of life." He was rewarded with an amused smile, which reflected, *Please go on, gallant knight, save me.*

"Missy, you hit the nail on the head. There is no logical reason to give up a gold mine, unless…unless you're *already* getting the gold."

Sofia wiped her eyes and said, "I still don't understand. How could I influence that situation?"

James did not want to alarm her. Her information was vital. If a mole existed within the Senate Intelligence Oversight Committee, he had to find it. He also knew that the KGB would do anything to prevent the mole's exposure—including sacrificing another KGB agent.

"Sofia, let's play the what-if game. What if you did marry the senator? What if you received information that somehow accidentally got leaked by another source? What if that caused a witch hunt in the committee to find the leak? What if the KGB already has a miner in the gold mine, a mole? The investigation could cause a cave-in, so to speak. Their agent might be discovered in the investigative process. If they are already getting the information, two chefs could spoil the broth. They won't let that happen."

"I see, Mr. Anderson. I'm a risk. Thank you, that makes sense."

James Anderson looked at Sofia, and he saw a remarkable transformation. No more the tears of a weepy girl—her hazel eyes were ablaze, the eyes he used to have before he plunged the blade into an unsuspecting sentry warring in France. She slowly released his hand and looked him squarely in the face.

"Mr. Anderson, you come from a solid Southern tradition. What would you do if a crow refused to stay out of your garden, ruining everything you worked so hard to grow and to prosper?"

"Simple as eatin' pie, darlin'. One twelve-gauge shotgun, one less crow!"

"Well, Mr. Anderson, I need you to shoot a crow for me, but this one is a bit larger. It's a raven."

CHAPTER 81

It was a beautiful Sunday morning. The Raven loved these late autumn days: the sky was clear; the air, crisp and inviting. The traffic was light, almost nonexistent. A perfect day to walk and enjoy a quiet moment. He had no idea that he was soon to die over a simple loaf of bread.

The Raven's tradecraft and security skills were finely honed after years of training and experience in hostile places. He never took the same route twice and seldom walked any distance in the open. He wore a bulletproof vest, and his chauffeur and bodyguards were the best. He never attended public events. To most of the world, he did not exist. Only a few people knew his actual name. He always went by his code name: the Raven.

The chink in this professional spy's armor was his absolute delight in purchasing a dark round loaf of black bread, the kind he loved to eat in Russia: a hard crust, soft interior, a little salt (but not too much)—just the way his mother used to make it. Every time he entered the bakery and smelled the heavenly aroma of fresh Russian black bread, he fondly remembered his days as a young boy anxiously waiting for his mother to bring out the loaves from the oven—warm, perfect memories.

The bakery belonged to a family of Russian Jews. They were first-generation Americans who had escaped one of Stalin's many pogroms just in time. The Raven discovered this bakery and their past, so in his typical, heavy-handed way, he made a deal with them: three loaves of Russian black bread made to his specifications, freshly baked every Sunday morning, available before their normal working hours. In return, he would help some of their relatives exit Russia to join them at an unspecified time. The bakers readily agreed. They were open on Sundays, after celebrating their Sabbath on Saturdays, and they always made extra for themselves and for other Russians in the area—small requirements for a possible reunion with their relatives.

The Raven usually had his chauffeur park next to the curb in front of the small bakery located on a one-way street. The Raven liked to make the purchase himself. He enjoyed the aroma and always selected a morning pastry from their wonderful showcase. It was a quiet moment he treasured every Sunday: no heavy traffic, no open stores with busy customers, no uncomfortable bulletproof vest, no bodyguard for a quick purchase among bakers who feared him. It was a nice way to begin the week: secure, private, satisfying, with enough bread to last until the next Sunday. He felt secure.

When the chauffeur prepared to turn right onto the one-way street to the bakery, the street was blocked by orange-and-white barriers with flashing orange lights. A sign in bold black letters read, "Closed for Repairs Until Monday." Tight orange netting blocked the sidewalk. A large sign with black arrows directed traffic to detour around the block.

Since the bakery was located near the southern end of the block, it made more sense just to follow the detour and approach it from the opposite intersection. Upon circling the block, most of the parking spaces were occupied on the opposite side of the street, so the Raven had the chauffeur park in a long red-marked fire zone, just ten meters from the intersection.

The chauffeur offered to walk to the bakery, but the Raven looked forward to his nostalgic moment. He directed his driver to stay with the car. The vehicle had diplomatic plates, but if it were towed, questions might be asked, bringing attention to the Raven and his presence in America. It was a nice day, no traffic, and most people were still asleep or getting dressed for church. He felt that the walk would be good for him—a little fresh air.

As the Raven approached the intersection, his "security antenna" still remained alert. He quickly scouted the area. The intersection would be busy on Monday, but today it was practically deserted. A yellow dump truck was idle in the left lane to the west. The traffic was funneled to one lane next to the truck. One workman standing in the intersection directed traffic for safety, and two more were working near an open sewer cover next to the truck. A workman wearing an orange vest looked to make sure there was no traffic and signaled with a simple round green disc for the Raven to cross the street. The efficient workman conscientiously watched the intersection and nodded in a friendly manner as the Raven passed him.

The bakery smelled as fragrant as ever to the Raven. He smiled when he received the three loaves of bread, carefully wrapped to ensure freshness. The Raven could feel the warmth of the bread against his chest. He slightly opened the sack and inhaled the luscious aroma—heavenly! He selected a fresh pastry and left without paying; he never did. He owed them nothing; they owed him everything—if they ever wanted to see their relatives again.

On his return to the car, the Raven stopped at the opposite curb to inspect the situation before crossing the intersection. The dump truck remained across the street in the left lane, exactly where it had been. There were still just three workmen. An elderly lady with a cane and a large shopping bag appeared to be window shopping across the street. All the businesses were closed. The Raven thought, *What a waste of time, old woman.*

The friendly traffic workman stopped a beige compact car next to the dump truck. Behind the car, there was a white panel van. The worker held the red side of this rustic handheld sign toward the two vehicles and motioned for the Raven to cross. When the Raven came next to him, he asked the Raven to stop in order to let the two cars safely proceed away from the dump truck and the two workmen. The beige car turned right, away from the intersection, and the white van proceeded slowly toward the helpful traffic controller and the Raven. When the van passed them, the Raven was allowed to cross.

As soon as the van cleared the intersection, it swerved into the left lane, stopped, and then slowly began to back up. The traffic worker stepped to the left and waved his arms to direct the van toward him. The back of the van carried the logo "Bering Pump Supplies." The Raven looked at the van and thought it must be a delivery. When he heard the shrill beeping sound of the van that was safely backing toward them with flashing taillights, not wanting to be bumped accidentally, he focused his attention on the van and stepped back out of its way toward the intersection. He never saw the black Mercedes down the block quickly gathering speed.

With the beige car and the white van making sure the right lane was open, a workman next to the tall dump truck signaled the black Mercedes. The Mercedes entered the intersection at an estimated speed of sixty-seven miles per hour. After gaining speed for over a block, it had the force as if it were shot from a cannon.

The Mercedes sedan is a heavy, well-centered car, often used for this type of operation. This Mercedes had been modified in important ways: the motor was quieter and more powerful, the front end was reinforced, the front bumper was larger and lower than most cars, the windshield was bulletproof and the driver was a professional. The perfect killing machine.

With his vision blocked by the beige car, the white van, and the tall yellow dump truck, his attention diverted by the loud beeping sound, and his desire not to be bumped by the backing delivery van, the Raven did not see the black streak of metal until it mowed him down. The impact threw him across the street onto the empty gray sidewalk not far from the elderly woman. His body was almost cut in half.

The white van quickly left the scene to chase the black Mercedes. One man leaned out of the passenger's side of the van with a clipboard in his hand, desperately trying to write down the tag number of the fleeing Mercedes. With their tires squealing, both vehicles turned right at the end of the block and headed south.

Once out of sight, the van slowed down and guarded the Mercedes's escape. It radioed the black car, "All is clear." Two blocks later, the Mercedes turned into an underground garage, which was closed for the day. A dark-green truck with a white stripe down each side and a decal which read "City Recycling" lowered its hydraulic bed and opened the back end of its trailer, like the monstrous jaws of a giant reptile. The Mercedes entered the mouth of the modified garbage truck, and the metal jaws closed over it. The truck bed, now containing the car, lifted again to its proper place above the wheels. The truck slowly left the garage and proceeded to a nicely arranged stack of cardboard at the corner of the block. The top of the truck opened, and two men in green overalls pushed the recycling containers in place. The cardboard floated down on top of the car and covered it completely. Any patrol car, or even a helicopter, looking for a hit-and-run black car would not be able to see it. The recycling crew made two more stops and left the area.

The chauffeur left his car and ran to the scene of the accident. He passed the elderly woman, who held a white handkerchief to her face, covering her mouth and nose. When he heard the sirens, the chauffeur quickly left before being identified. It was obvious that the Raven was dead. The driver was trained not to bring any attention to himself or to this resident agent. The Raven never carried any identification, and there was no record of him or fingerprints on file, except at Moscow Center.

The Raven had entered the United States from a Soviet freighter. No one, except a few officials at Moscow Center, even knew that he existed for the special operation involving the professor's papers. The Raven had his own special unit and safe houses. Even the chauffeur did not know his name. There could be no publicity, or any action taken, which might affect the current operation regarding Professor Price or his research. This accident would be secretly coded to Moscow Center, completely bypassing the Russian embassy. The missile-guidance project was too important for a clerk or a minor bureaucrat to inadvertently leak its existence.

The police arrived and questioned the three workmen and the elderly woman, who was quite upset and dabbed her eyes with her handkerchief. The two men by the yellow truck said that they were on the opposite side of the truck and only heard the sickening impact. The traffic signaler said that he had his back turned directing the delivery van and that the white van blocked his view when it chased the hit-and-run vehicle. He thought the van was chasing a black car. "It all happened so fast," he added. The elderly woman reported that it definitely was a long black car with dark-tinted windows. She did not know the make or model of cars, but she thought that she saw the letters *DC* on the license plate. She just wasn't sure.

The investigator thanked all four and called in an all-points bulletin for a "Hit-and-run—black sedan—tinted windows—possible DC tag." When finished, he shook his head in exasperation. That description in Washington, DC, would be about as helpful as telling a Texas Ranger to stop every white pickup truck in Dallas, Texas. The detective was also baffled that the victim had no wallet or identification of any kind. He wore nice brown slacks and an expensive tan sweater, but he did not even have a coin or a set of car keys in his pockets. How did he get to this location? Why was he downtown on a quiet Sunday morning? The workmen had no idea. However, they helpfully suggested that he seemed to be lost.

The workmen finished their project in forty-five minutes and removed all the barriers. The police were still measuring distances from the impact area to the covered body to estimate the car's speed. The police were now directing traffic.

The sweet elderly woman asked if she could leave. Her health was frail, and she was just visiting the DC area. She gave her name as Janice Browning from Lansing, Michigan. She was a retired school teacher, a widow with no children. She left her home telephone and address if further questions were needed. The police felt sorry for this upset, kind lady and offered to drive her to her hotel. She declined. The fresh air would help settle her after experiencing such a dreadful incident.

After poking along the sidewalk with her cane for three blocks, she turned right at the corner, out of sight from the flashing lights and the busy emergency personnel. A white sedan stopped for Mrs. Browning. She thanked the two men, delicately entered the backseat of the car, and the vehicle headed south. Its destination was a safe house in Arlington, Virginia. Janice Browning's real name was Jacqueline Bascoulard. She was retired CIA.

Jacqueline had known "Jimmy" (Deputy Director Anderson) since his OSS days in occupied France. He had been her colleague and a once-upon-a-time passionate lover. Earlier in the week, Jimmy had asked her to do him a "little favor" on an important "one op" that was off the record. She had been bored and had agreed to help. Her role was to be an eyewitness and to deflect the police investigation. Also, she was to be present to clean up any evidence that might connect the incident to the CIA or to the workmen at the work site.

She would remain at the safe house for the next week being wined, dined, and pampered by Jimmy. If the DC police called the number that she had given them, they would indeed reach the correct name, number, and address for Janice Browning, as listed in the telephone book of Lansing, Michigan. However, the Browning telephone number would be rerouted by the National Security Agency, or NSA, to Jacqueline's safe house in Arlington, Virginia. It was remote that the Washington police would telephone or travel to Lansing, Michigan, to question an elderly woman who had witnessed very little that would further their investigation.

Jacqueline's services would only be needed for one week since the real Janice Browning was in a cancer ward in a suburb of Lansing, Michigan, and who was expected to pass away in a matter of days. Any local police contact would soon find her house empty and her telephone disconnected.

Jacqueline removed her white wig, stripped away the artificial age lines around her eyes and neck, and allowed her beautiful brunette hair to rest on her shoulders. She unloaded the walking cane, which contained a row of .45 caliber bullets—backup in case the car missed the Raven or the target fled. She opened her shopping bag and removed three loaves of very flat Russian black bread. Being born in France, she appreciated fine bread. She was hungry; the early-morning operation had caused her to miss breakfast. Jacqueline handed the driver and her bodyguard a crushed loaf of bread. She cheerfully cajoled, "Enjoy it, boys. It's still warm!" She winked at them and exclaimed, "Oh, this is yummy. *Bon appétit!*"

****

James, JP, Jimmy, the Blade of France Anderson sat at his desk at the CIA headquarters in Langley, Virginia, with his morning newspaper and a large mug of coffee. He read that the police investigation of a hit-and-run accident involving an unidentified man last Sunday was still underway but with "no leads as to the culprit or to the identity of the victim at this time."

Turning from the crime section, he perused the local obituaries. There he found a picture of a rather plain-looking woman, thirty-two-year-old Samantha Goodman. The article listed her occupation as a "civil servant secretary." The FBI had insisted, for security purposes, that the newspaper did not reveal her former position as the secretary for the chairman of the United States Senate Intelligence Oversight Committee. The obituary stated that she died of carbon monoxide poisoning because of an accidental gas leak in her small apartment. What Deputy Director Anderson knew was that Samantha Goodman was a KGB mole.

The previous Friday evening, when Samantha Goodman arrived at her apartment after work, two men were waiting for her. As she stepped through the doorway, she was struck in the back with a high-voltage charge from a modified stun gun. They caught her before she hit the floor to avoid any scrapes or bruises and placed her on the sofa. Her shoes and purse were neatly placed beside the coffee table, and a red plaid blanket was draped over her. A mask attached to a small cylinder of carbon monoxide was gently placed over her face to ensure that there would be no facial marks. Within seventeen minutes, she was dead.

The team slightly opened a valve on the gas heater near her sofa. They extinguished the pilot light to ensure that there was no risk of an explosion. It would appear that Ms. Goodman failed to properly light her gas heater and unfortunately took a nap, leading to her demise.

Before leaving, they opened a kitchen window two inches to let any excess gas escape. A neighbor, while watering plants on her balcony, smelled the gas and spotted the open window adjoining her patio. She reported the gas leak to the apartment manager, and Samantha Goodman's body was discovered.

The FBI was also searching for Ms. Goodman's secret companion, a handsome KGB agent. The agent was already aboard a Soviet airliner headed for Moscow. Samantha had become a mole in the hopes of obtaining eternal love; the CIA team eliminated her in the hopes of obtaining eternal silence.

The attorney general of the Justice Department ordered that the Goodman case was to be closed by the end of the week. No autopsy would be required. No explanation was given; no questions were asked.

In his operations in-tray, Mr. Anderson had a photocopy of another obituary from a newspaper in Lansing, Michigan, stating that retired teacher and widow Janice Browning had died over the weekend after a long bout with cancer. Her funeral would be on Thursday.

Finally, he turned to the society section of the newspaper where he saw a large photo of a striking couple in the center of the page. The couple were affectionately holding hands with perfect smiles for the camera. The bold headlines announced the engagement of the newly elected Senator Thomas Stevens of Virginia to Dr. Sofia Karaleva-Borodina, an associate professor of physics, also residing in Virginia. Their wedding was planned after the senate retired at the end of the session. Deputy Director Anderson looked at Sofia's beautiful picture and said to himself, "Well, darlin', now you are indispensable to both sides, in two operations. Welcome to a brave New World."

James Patrick Anderson looked around his office. It was neat and Spartan: nothing was on his desk except the photocopy regarding Janice Browning, an open newspaper, and a cup of steaming coffee with a faint smoke-like trail of vapor rising into the air.

There were no family photos on the desk, for he had no family—all dead or scattered to the four winds. He had no vanity wall with pictures of himself shaking hands with people holding high positions, or diplomas and awards conspicuously displayed to impress others. He accepted that some leaders were noble and self-sacrificing, but many seemed to be cunning, power-hungry fools who would drown their own mothers to get what they wanted, or if the price were right. He knew from his war experiences in Europe that when bullets and shrapnel were flying, awards and diplomas meant nothing. Death cared not whether one possessed an advanced degree. The main objective was to simply survive the day and to protect those who had placed their lives in your leadership.

The only personal item in his office was a souvenir that he had brought back from the battlefields of war: a small reproduction of a painting that he had found discarded in some weeds outside a French village where everyone had been shot by the German SS as retribution for partisan activities. The edges of the picture were burned, but he liked it all the more because of that. It was a portrait of the biblical scene—Daniel in the lions' den.

The painting shows Daniel in a dark stone dungeon looking out of a small window. A ray of soft light shines on his face and chest in the midst of the gloomy darkness. Daniel is older, with his sparse hair combed back. He is wearing an elegant emerald-green robe that almost touches the stone floor. His hands are clasped behind his back. Behind him are seven hungry lions, intensely watching him. Daniel keeps his back to them, focusing on the window and the radiant light.

James had the picture framed with the burnt edges showing: a constant reminder from whence it came. At the bottom of the frame, he had attached a brass plate which read: "Know Thy Enemy—Know Thyself." Every day when he arrived for work, he placed his overcoat on a hook beside the picture. He read the brass plate and called out, "Bring on the lions." He then went to his desk and began the tasks before him. In the evening, he retrieved his coat, looked directly at Daniel, and quietly said, "I survived another day," a ritual he spoke every day in war-torn France as the sun went down.

Deputy Director of Operations James Anderson placed the photocopy regarding Janice Browning in a large burn-bag envelope and sealed it. He glanced one more time at Sofia's pretty smile in the newspaper and slowly folded it shut. Sadly, to most of the world, Samantha Goodman was already a faded memory.

Much like Daniel, he sat looking out of the window and watched the red, yellow, and orange leaves waver in the breeze. Autumn had come. It came for Daniel. It rested on James's shoulders in the autumn of his life. James ran his hand back through his thinning chestnut hair and sipped his strong black coffee. A solitary red leaf fell from a tree and floated toward the earth. James tossed the newspaper into his empty black wastebasket and watched the red leaf until it hit the ground. "Operation Blackbird" was over.

CHAPTER 82

The two days spent in Vladimir's hideaway were some of the most nerve-wracking in Anya's life. She knew that every hour of delay meant the difference between life and death for all of them. Time was now their greatest enemy. The hands of time were slowly carving away their hopes and liberty.

Anya looked at Paul. He was holding up well, and he constantly tried to encourage the others with, "It won't be long now." But Anya could tell that the strain was beginning to wear him down. *He must be feeling that the weight of the world rests upon his shoulders*, she reasoned. In many ways, it did.

Yuri, the scientist, spent most of his time resting on his cot. The strain exhausted and depressed him. Anya thought that at least he was wise enough to recognize this and to save his strength for the final strenuous push toward freedom.

His wife, Lyola, was taking it the worst. She was a bundle of nerves. She could not sleep, she ate very little, and she constantly worried, especially about her little girl. Anya felt sorry for Lyola, but there was little anyone could do to help her. Each person had to encounter fear on separate terms and in her own way.

The young girl was the bright flower in this bleak garden. To her, this was just another adventure. She explored the large cavern, sighing with disappointment when she could find no bats. Anya often walked with her hand in hand on her explorations. This blonde-haired, blue-eyed tomboy reminded Anya of herself and days long ago, that she had spent with her parents in the woods. Anya was in this refurbished cave because she loved Paul, but also to save this precious child from even worse horrors than Anya had experienced. Anya felt that she was going back in time—saving herself.

Paul made his rounds and checked on everyone. The critical hour had come. He had to decide whether to brave the storm or to wait and then make other arrangements at Vladivostok. The path he chose would either bring them freedom or a fate worse than death. He held their lives in his hands. Each anxious face wounded his heart. Although surrounded by others, he felt very alone.

The trap door slowly creaked open, and Vladimir, Dmitri, and Mischa clamored down the steps. All three wore wet raincoats—not a good sign. Everyone rushed to them—hoping, praying for good news.

Vladimir looked directly at Paul and reported, "The storm is still brewing, but the good news is that the sea is improving. It will pass in another day."

"Yes, Vladimir," Paul replied. "However, our transportation will have already left. This is our second attempt. Either we reach the rendezvous point tonight before the moon rises, or the others must plan on staying here until I can make other arrangements at Vladivostok. Either choice has its own special risks. I have to make the final decision, but I want everyone's opinion. It affects you all."

Vladimir declared, "You are welcome to stay here as long as you desire. However, each day brings the possibility of discovery. I will provide for you either way."

"The road is not that bad to the coast. I can get you there, if you wish to go," Mischa added.

Yuri was impatient. "My health cannot stand much more. This waiting and worrying is killing me. I want to go now."

Lyola complained, "I fear the sea. We have food and shelter. We are hidden. I think Vladivostok is safer."

Dmitri had to interject, "Better to drown in the sea than…well, you know the other. Take the boat. Get out while you can."

Anya seconded Dmitri's suggestion, "I agree with Dmitri. A net is closing around us. We don't have any more time. If the captain won't agree, leave me alone with him on the boat for ten minutes. When I am finished with him, he will volunteer to sail into a typhoon. Paul, now is the time."

Paul knelt down facing Tanya and asked, "What is your opinion? This involves you as much as anyone."

Young Tanya looked into Paul's face with her bright blue eyes and replied, "I'm going wherever Anya goes. She's smart, and besides, she has all the guns."

Everyone laughed, and the tension in the room began to fade. Paul looked at them and said, "I feel like General Eisenhower when he had to decide whether to proceed with the Normandy D-Day Invasion or to wait for better weather. I agree with Ike—we go."

CHAPTER 83

Officer Malenkov had been working like a bloodhound for the past twenty-four hours. His discoveries astonished even himself.

"General Gurov, please. This is Captain Malenkov. Tell him it is urgent!"

"Go ahead, Malenkov. What do you have?"

"General, since our last meeting with Colonel Kurgan, I have been working nonstop. I assigned a special team to research Kurgan's missing agent, Anya Ruslanova. General, on paper, she doesn't exist: no birth certificate, no school records, no record of her parents' deaths. There is no mention of her or her family in any current census surveys. We are researching old census material throughout the Soviet Union, but that will take some time. She does not have a file with the police nor with any state agency, including an orphanage. We only know that she was an orphan because of a statement made by an eyewitness who had lived at the same orphanage. Her life officially began when Kurgan brought her to Moscow for KGB training. She and Sofia Karaleva arrived here on the same day, escorted by Kurgan. I've never seen anything like this!"

"What does Colonel Kurgan have to say?" the general asked.

"Nothing, sir. He sent me a memorandum this morning stating that he has not found the files we requested, but he will continue searching for them in his long-term storage area. General, he's stalling, and I think for good reasons."

"Malenkov, what are you insinuating?"

"Sir, Kurgan may not be good with files, but Agent Ruslanova has very thorough records. Her case notes indicate that her major mission was an American target named Paul Adams. She was investigating whether he actually was a diplomat or an agent for the CIA, and if he was a possible candidate for recruitment. This Adams has not been seen for some time. Consider this: A Soviet scientist and his family go missing. Paul Adams is missing. The agent dealing with Adams is also missing. Her records, supposedly in Kurgan's possession, cannot be found, and Kurgan begins burning papers exactly twenty-four hours after all these people have disappeared.

"General, it appears that Colonel Kurgan is involved in this escape. He has possibly sold out to the Americans. He sets up a mysterious agent with no known background to be his go-between to the Americans. They pay him to prepare the escape and misdirect the search attempt. His female agent then defects with the US intelligence agent. Kurgan has carefully planned this for some time and is now quite rich. It is the only logical explanation. Nothing else even remotely makes sense."

"What is your recommendation, Captain?"

"General, with your permission, I want to distribute photographs of this Adams and Ruslanova to all agencies involved in the search. I would also like to expand the search to the eastern coast."

"Malenkov, every transportation center and port has been alerted. It seems unbelievable that a scientist with a wife and a young child could leap from a moving train and then hike hundreds of kilometers through forest or tundra to reach the eastern coast without dying or being discovered."

"I agree, General, but the only known location that Ruslanova can be traced to is Vladivostok, and even that comes from second-hand information. It's worth a try. Nothing has turned up from our search to the west."

"Go ahead, Captain. However, I think it is pointless. They are probably in Scandinavia. This is the fourth day."

"General, there is one way to find out. I request the authorization to immediately arrest Colonel Kurgan before he also defects.

He must be thoroughly interrogated to divulge where the scientist, Adams, and Ruslanova are at this time."

"Very well. I give my authorization for his arrest and interrogation, Malenkov. But you should know that if he does not confess, either you or I will be sitting on that solitary chair when the next board of inquiry meets, and I do not plan on being that person. Do you understand, Captain?"

"Don't worry, General. I will get the information and a confession. I was trained by one of the very best in these matters. He was rather brutal but *very* effective. After the war, he always went by the code name—the Raven."

Chapter 84

The delay gave Vladimir, Dmitri, and Mischa time to build a false backdrop inside the bed of the delivery truck. Although snug, the hideaway provided enough space to conceal four adults and a small child. Two large barrels of fuel lashed against the facade would deter close inspection. Two or three men might move the heavy barrels, but most roadblock guards were not that energetic. The ship captain had requested extra fuel because of the storm, so his order form was attached to each barrel. Some rope, netting, and food supplies completed the inventory.

Everyone proceeded to load into the truck inside the warehouse. Dmitri agreed to ride with Mischa to establish a cover and to help unload the supplies faster. Vladimir chose to stay at his store; his absence might attract attention and unwanted questions.

Vladimir always hated goodbyes, especially this one. He felt that he would never see Anya again; however, she never ceased to amaze him by showing up when least expected. He went to Anya and gently cupped her face with both his hands. He spoke softly to her, "You look so much like your mother. God bless you, my little *krokodile*. I hope to see you again."

Anya smiled at his reference to the book *The Krokodile*, which Vladimir had bought for her when she was about the age of little Tanya, who was also taking the most dangerous journey of her young life. Anya could not think of any words to say. None were needed.

She hugged Vladimir and kissed his cheek, tasting the salt of a tear coming from his tender eyes. As she turned to leave, Anya handed him a long white envelope with the words written on the outside: "Keep this in your safe. Love to you and to Dmitri."

Dmitri and Mischa helped everyone into the truck and closed the backdrop behind them. The heavy fuel drums were lashed into place. Vladimir opened the warehouse doors and watched the truck travel to the east until it faded from sight. He called out, "Farewell, my daughter, farewell," but only the afternoon sun heard him. Vladimir closed the large warehouse doors and walked to his store with his head down and with Anya's unopened white envelope in his hand, knowing he had done what was right—but a lonelier man all the same.

Mischa knew the road well. He planned to arrive at the cove just before sunset, enabling him to proceed without headlights, which might alert a random patrol. If they met a roadblock, it would appear as a normal delivery running slightly behind schedule because of the muddy roads. The captain knew they were coming, and the boat was ready to leave once the people and sparse supplies were onboard.

By the time they reached the cove, everyone was ready to leave the truck. The journey had been long and rough, but because of the weather, there were no roadblocks or delays. With perfect timing, Mischa had arrived just as the sun dipped below the horizon, with fading sunlight and deepening shadows forming on the shore. The scientist and his family were quickly escorted below to the galley of the boat while the captain and the other members of the party hurriedly unloaded the truck and secured everything onboard.

Dmitri and Mischa stood with a light mist dripping off their dark raincoats. Anya hugged and kissed both. She never expected to see them again. Dmitri, never a loss for words, said, "Well, that vile Vladimir has left me to say goodbye again in the worst circumstances. This is almost as heartbreaking as when I left you at the orphanage. Now you are leaving me."

Anya touched his wet cheek and told him, "No matter where I go or what I do, I will never leave you, Vladimir, or Mischa behind. The three of you will be with me—always."

The captain called out, "Young lady, we have to shove-off—please come aboard!"

Anya boarded the vessel while Dmitri and Mischa tossed the lines to Paul. The old scarred fishing boat slowly pulled away from the oval cove. The last thing Dmitri saw was Anya's long blonde hair fluttering in the wind before the night enclosed her.

****

The captain was an old salt, and he knew these waters like the back of his hand. His background came from the migrating strong-willed independent Cossacks, and he looked the part. He had white hair and a long drooping mustache, which highlighted his brown leathery skin. He could have been just as easily riding on a horse, wearing tall boots, a pistol, and a saber as sailing on a ship. He used his dark, well-used pipe much like a saber—stabbing it in the air when he gave directions or when he wished to make a specific point.

The captain turned the large wheel of the boat with ease, even in the choppy water. Steering a new course with his short stubby pipe fixed in his teeth, there was a smile on his face. Paul watched him and wondered if the old sailor was not enjoying himself.

The skipper motioned for Paul to come near the wheel and said, "This weather is a blessing and a curse. This mist and cloud cover will help us, even if the moon rises before your other transportation arrives. The difficulty is that legally we have to have running lights on in this kind of darkness or weather. But if a patrol boat sees our lights, it is bound to check on us. I'm not going to use the lights and gamble that no smaller patrol boat will be out in this weather. The larger boats will be closer to Vladivostok, for that is the better harbor and the place where most people would try to escape the country.

"I know the delay was hard on your group, but it would have been too dangerous to attempt this two days ago. The weather is going to clear hour by hour. The sea will be a little rough at first, but it will slowly get better—take my word on it. We will navigate by compass and a little guesswork with the wind and currents. Don't worry. I know my way around here."

"You come highly recommended, Captain," Paul replied. "Vladimir said that you are the best. I trust you both."

The captain smiled and said, "Good to hear, mate. Do you mind going below and checking on the others? They may be feeling a little green around the gills. Give them a little tea and some of those soda crackers. It will settle their stomachs. Tell them to come up and get some fresh air on occasion but to stay away from the edge of the boat—one hand on the boat at all times. They'll get their sea legs before it's over."

Paul left the bridge and found Anya near the stern looking back at the churning water and a small white streak of water caused by the propeller. Every turn of the propeller was taking her farther and farther from home. He touched her shoulder and asked her, "Any regrets, Anya?"

Anya continued to look in the direction of the cove, now engulfed in darkness. "No, Paul, I don't live with regret. We make decisions, and then we live with them, for better or for worse. Back there is my homeland, but it also meant death. This boat is heading to the unknown—but also to life. I've found that choices are never simple. At least this time, *I* made the decision. Someone did not force it upon me. I'm beginning to think that is the essence of truly being alive—of being free."

Paul left her so as not to invade her private thoughts any further. He walked down the stairs to the galley and left a woman without a country to quietly say goodbye to her past.

****

Paul kept looking impatiently at his watch. It was imperative that they make the rendezvous at the specified time. Since this was their second attempt to make the rescue, the submarine would stay for exactly twenty minutes and then submerge, never to return.

Paul went to the bridge to assess the situation and to drive away some of his nervous energy. The captain was humming a sailor's tune and carefully watching his compass.

"Ahoy, mate. Glad you came up. I was about to call you. We are almost at the meeting point. I had to estimate the drift and current, but we're close enough. I want to give a little room for your submarine. He will be using his periscope, but since we have no lights in this darkness, he might not see us. I don't think any of us want a sudden piggyback ride on a sub when it comes up. We'll hear it before we see it. The sea is getting smother, and the moon is still asleep—perfect timing."

"You seem to know a great deal about submarines," Paul observed. "Did you ever serve on one?"

"Just the opposite, my boy." The captain smiled with a twinkle in his eyes. "I used to try and sink them. I was a captain on a destroyer. I helped protect American cowboys bringing in lend-lease material from your country. Those supplies and equipment helped us to win the war."

"What made you decide to become a fisherman? I would think that the Russian Navy would want to keep you."

The captain tapped out the ashes in his pipe and glanced at the compass before answering. "The navy did not get rid of me—I got rid of the navy. After the war, I was assigned to bring home some of our soldiers who had been captured as prisoners of war. I was proud to do it. The boys—and they were mostly boys—were so happy to be finally coming home. They were a starved, unsightly lot. Many of their comrades had died in the concentration camps.

"When we docked, the boys let out a cheer. As they left the ship, the NKVD henchmen held firearms on them and loaded them into trucks. Later, I found out that some were shot and others were sent to work camps in Siberia. Stalin considered them either cowards or traitors. It made me sick to my stomach that I had unknowingly been a part of it. I've hated Stalin and his regime ever since that treacherous day. The boys weren't cowards or traitors. Most had become prisoners of war because of Stalin's ignorant tactics or from the boot-licking generals he left in charge after he had killed the best of the officer corps years before the war began.

"I left the navy and bought this fishing boat and nets that one man could handle. I'm not a traitor, son, but any person who wants freedom—I'll captain them part of the way. Stalin may be dead, but I'm sure he's watching from hell." The captain thrust his pipe into the air, as if it were his saber, and called out, "In your eye, Stalin, in your eye!"

Paul watched the captain reload his pipe, and with a puff of gray smoke, the captain slightly turned the wheel and began humming again.

"Captain, I'm going below to get everyone ready. I will signal the submarine with only one quick flash of light. They will return my signal with a single red light. Get as close as you can, safely. They will send a rubber raft to get us."

"Sounds like a good plan. I'm going to throttle the engines to keep us from drifting, but low enough so that we can hear them surface. Get the others ready. We're at your coordinates."

Paul looked at his watch and exclaimed, "Captain, we are right on time! You amaze me! We went through a storm, rough and heavy seas, in pitch-darkness, yet we arrived at the exact spot at the specified time. The Russian Navy lost one of their best!"

"That they did, my boy." The captain smiled at him and gave his orders, "Get 'em ready, sailor, hop to it! That's from the bridge. Proud to sail with you, young man. May your bowline never break."

The United States Navy also has good captains, and they pride themselves on never being late. The Russian captain was correct: they heard the submarine before they saw it. A massive stream of bubbling water gushed to the surface, as if an underwater volcano had just erupted. The Russian captain heard and saw it first. He called down below, "Thar she blows. Move toward the stern, but stay near the middle of the boat. Always keep one hand steady on something. I'll ease to them once signals are made."

The submarine rose to the surface. Sheets of water drained over the structure. Anya had never seen a submarine. It reminded her of a mighty beast, a dragon of the sea—a modern-day *Krokodile* from her storybook—now rising into the air. Truly it was an awesome sight.

Paul signaled with his large flashlight, and the submarine responded with a quick red beam. The Russian boat slowly advanced toward the US vessel, rocking a little from the wake the submarine had created upon the water's surface.

"This is as close as I can safely approach them," the captain yelled to the group, each person struggling to keep his balance. "The waves are still strong enough to push us into the sub. We'll wait here."

The scientist was not a brave man, and he knew it. Still, one task needed to be done before the raft arrived. Clinging to the ladder on the rocking boat, he lifted his daughter up to the bridge and followed after her. The captain started to correct them and order them below for their safety; then he saw the little girl. She was not afraid, and she rushed to the captain and held his waist. The old salty captain expertly steered the boat with one hand and stroked the girl's pretty hair with the other.

The scientist said, "We owe you our lives. We will never forget you!"

Even old weathered sea captains cannot resist a tender farewell. He leaned down and kissed the child on the top of her head and shook the scientist's hand. The captain replied, "May the Good Lord bless ya and keep ya. Now get below with the others. I hear the raft coming. Off ya go!"

The captain steadied the boat as the passengers boarded the black rubber raft. Everyone waved to him as he carefully made a safe exit away from the submarine. Several sailors waited on the deck of the US vessel, ready to assist the boarding party.

An orange moon was just beginning to rise. A break in the clouds momentarily allowed a soft moonbeam to rest on the tall conning tower and along the slender sides of the submarine. As quickly as it had surfaced upon the waters, so it sank into the dark restless sea. Anya's *Krokodile* left only a momentary gasp of air as it closed its jaws from below.

The captain watched the submarine in the moonlight. When the tower disappeared under the water, one of the Russian Navy's finest captains stabbed the stem of his pipe in the direction of the sinking submarine and proclaimed, "This is for my boys, Bloody Stalin—my innocent boys—and right under your ugly nose! In your eye, Stalin—in your eye!"

The captain headed south. The weather was breaking. It was going to be a pleasant, starry night with a nice moon to keep him company. He lowered his nets for cover and for profit. "A sailor might as well use his time wisely." He chuckled. As the old boat chugged along, he thought about the young girl hugging his waist and her fearful father trying to be brave—trying to be free. "God preserve 'em," he whispered.

Within forty-five minutes, a lone patrol boat approached his port side. A searchlight on the bow of the vessel bathed the captain in blinding light. He stuck his head out of a side window on the bridge and waved at them. They could see his nets, so they gave him distance to avoid tangling their propeller.

The three patrolmen decided it was pointless to search the old wreck of a fishing boat. Only a fool would go out in that hulk into a storm. He was just an old fisherman, and a crazy one at that—the storm was just ending. Besides, he was heading the wrong direction down the coast toward Vladivostok. The guards hoped the old seabird would not run into another boat with his rust bucket and sink both boats. The patrol continued north while constantly shining its bright spotlight across the water and into each cove along the coast.

The captain smoked his pipe and sang a new tune:

> Oh, come now, lads and sing me a shanty.
> Sail away, sail away.
> I've got lots of sail, and the sea is calling.
> Sail away to the Northland.

Looking up at the moon, he stabbed his pipe into the air and finished the song with his favorite refrain: "In your eye, Stalin, in your eye!"

When the captain docked at Vladivostok, he estimated that it was one of the largest loads of fish that he had ever caught.

Sail away to the Northland.

Chapter 85

Colonel Viktor Kurgan heard the closing thunder of heavy footsteps echoing down the hallway—a rising storm coming his way. Within a few minutes, they would breach his locked office door and make their arrest. He knew the darkness that awaited him.

He had helped Anya gain her freedom and a new life, at the expense of his own. He did not regret his actions, only the consequences: the arrest, the shame, the interrogation, the torture—the execution. There would be no trial. Just a dark cell, a forced confession, and a sudden bullet.

Oddly, he felt at peace—a quiet before the storm. Life now seemed simple and clarified: no planning, no scheming, no betrayals, no self-promotion, no fear of being left behind. He thought, *Life becomes quite precious when there is only one spoonful left of golden honey at the bottom of the jar.* He knew his "spoonful" was about to be consumed.

Viktor sat looking out of the window as the knocking on the door grew louder. He held his old, scarred binoculars, a keepsake from Stalingrad which he always kept on the windowsill. He thought of all the recruits that he had observed on the training ground below him. Anya had been one of his best.

The wood frame around the lock of his door began to splinter; thunder had become lightning. He returned the binoculars to their place and opened the window to feel the breeze on his face. The wind stirred the curtains as he sat down at his desk. His last thoughts were of elegant ballrooms in Saint Petersburg, his beautiful parents, and Anya holding the arm of a good man.

The pistol shot stopped the assault. There was a momentary silence, for the thunder and lightning knew the earth was now receiving its crimson rain.

A single drop of blood ran down the lens of the scarred binoculars belonging to one Viktor Kurgan, formerly of Saint Petersburg, formerly of the Soviet Army, formerly a colonel of the KGB. The red stain would not cloud his vision; he was beyond that. Like Anya—now he was free.

There is an old Siberian proverb: "A wolf cannot live chained to a tree." Viktor Kurgan gave Anya a mission with Paul Adams, which changed her life; two additional days, which saved her life; and a future in another country, which would begin a new life. It cost him everything, but he could live no longer "chained to a tree." The revolution took the boy, but not the man. It was time to leave the chains behind, time to return to noble ideas and noble ways, time to return to Saint Petersburg with his parents.

When Malenkov and his assault team knocked down the door, they found Viktor at his desk, a pistol on the floor and a pair of old binoculars by an open window, the curtains flowing in the breeze. Viktor held in his hand a small golden ring which carried the Kurgan crest. Captain Malenkov would become Major Malenkov, but Viktor Kurgan ran ahead of the pack. He was the alpha who came to realize that what we treasure in life either makes us a slave or sets us free. The Gray Wolf was free.

CHAPTER 86

Anya went down the conning tower first. She helped Tanya, Yuri, and Lyola off the steep ladder. Paul and the executive officer, or XO, came last. As soon as the XO entered, he reported, "Captain, all is clear. We are prepared to dive."

"Very well, XO," the captain replied. "Commence our dive—as deeply and quietly as possible. Let's get out of here."

The crew stole furtive glances at the five new civilian passengers, particularly at the tall blonde woman who had a weathered backpack on one shoulder and an old rifle slung on her other shoulder. Her black field uniform, complete with a crimson hammer-and-sickle crest wreathed in gold on the front of her black fur hat, surprised several sailors. Her shoulder patch bearing the sword-and-shield insignia of the KGB surprised them all.

Lieutenant Jones, who was in charge of the armory, wanted to make a good impression on everyone, especially the captain. He proudly strolled over to Anya, and utilizing his self-important initiative, he reached for her rifle while proclaiming, "I'll take that weapon, ma'am. Sorry, navy regulations."

Anya grabbed Jones's wrist and twisted it into an odd angle high into the air while simultaneously sweeping his feet out from underneath him with the side of her boot. Lieutenant Jones, keeper of the armory, ingloriously went facedown onto the floor, as if he had been struck by a pile driver. Anya continued to hold his hand in what is often called "the gooseneck configuration." Only a very silly goose would continue to resist the quite extensive pain. Lieutenant Jones was a smart gander, and he quietly remained with his nose pressed against the floor.

The entire incident and martial movement occurred so rapidly, and it was executed in such a nonchalant, professional manner, that everyone just stared in silence. Anya broke the tension by looking directly at the captain and stated, "Captain, I respect you and your vessel, but I ask for your respect as well. I wear the uniform of your enemy, but today I am your guest, and I will act accordingly. However, everything I own in this world is in this pack. This old single-shot rifle was my father's. It is all that I have in which to remember him."

Anya reached inside her coat and removed her service weapon from her shoulder holster. The crew did not know whether to try and stop her or just to leave her alone. Most, very wisely, decided to stand back and wait—good luck to the haughty Lieutenant Jones.

"However, Captain," Anya continued, "in good faith, I will surrender this Soviet pistol and two clips of ammunition as a demonstration of goodwill and respect for your navy's regulations." She expertly unloaded the pistol with one hand and placed it with both clips on the navigator's table next to her.

"I insist that my father's rifle and my few possessions are to remain with me at all times. I give you my word that the rifle will be unloaded, that I will not walk about your vessel, and that I will stay confined to my quarters for the entire voyage. No one will enter my room except for your food steward. A sentry may escort me to the lavatory every morning and every evening. If this is not agreeable to you, let us begin World War III immediately."

The captain wryly observed that the "surrendered" pistol was still easily within her reach. There is the "letter of the law" and the "spirit of the law." The captain decided that the "spirit" should prevail for the day. The captain looked at Paul, who slightly nodded his head, as if to say, *She means it, Captain. Please, no World War III.*

"Very well, ma'am. I accept your terms. My crew will respect you and your property. You will remain confined in your quarters for the entire journey. Now if you will release my lieutenant, I have other duties for him."

Anya released the officer's numb arm, and it fell to the floor like a clubbed fish. Two sailors helped the lieutenant to his feet and escorted him to the infirmary so that a medical officer could tape his broken nose.

"Chief," ordered the captain, "place this gentleman with his wife and child into my quarters. It is the largest that we have. Have someone place a cot in there for the little girl. Check to make sure that my desk is locked and that all files are stored securely. I will share the XO's quarters. Either the XO or I will be on duty at all times. I estimate that there will be very little sleep on this boat for anyone for the next few days. Find a berth for the other fellow with one of the officers. Clear out the berth of our beleaguered Lieutenant Jones and his roommate Lieutenant Peterson for the young lady—and her rifle. Post a guard in front of her door. No one—I repeat, no one—is to enter her room or to have contact with her without my express consent. Is that clear?"

"Aye, aye, sir," the chief said. "If all of you will please follow me. Please be careful ducking your heads through each entryway."

As Anya turned to follow the amiable older chief into the bowels of the submarine, she called back to the captain, "Oh, Captain, one last item." Anya forcefully drew back the bolt on her rifle and ejected the single shell from its chamber. The cartridge spiraled into the air and landed on the navigator's charts, spinning in a clockwise motion until the tip of the bullet just happened to point north by northeast.

The captain watched her leave his bridge, relieved that World War III would have to wait until another day—hopefully never and not with that agent. He looked at the cartridge on the map and said to his navigator, "Looks as if the lady's bullet is pointing the way. Let's move like a bullet, north by northeast."

"Aye, aye, sir—north by northeast," the navigator repeated.

The captain collected the shell and observed it. He decided to keep it as a souvenir. He could never talk about this top-secret mission, but perhaps one day he might be able to show his grandchildren the bullet and tell them about its remarkable owner, who was willing "to go to war" to honor her father.

"Captain, we are approaching cruising depth. No contacts and heading north by northeast."

"Very well, XO." The captain put the long bullet into his pocket. "Take us home."

Chapter 87

Anya entered the small room assigned to her. She placed her pack next to a narrow bunk, a pack that contained a tiger skin, a claw necklace, a wooden figurine of a crouching tiger, and a Bible that belonged to her mother—the remnants of her entire life. Each treasure harbored a memory with its own story to tell. Leaning against the pack was her father's rifle—the last emblem of the Ruslanov family in Russia.

She placed her black fur KGB hat on a desk adjoining the bunk. Looking at the blood-red hammer-and-sickle crest, she pondered the twisted journey that had brought her from a cabin in the mountains of Siberia to a submarine of the United States Navy in the Pacific Ocean.

She was bone-tired, not so much from the finale of the escape to this submarine but from the gnawing reach of the unknown. She loved Paul, but she also loved her country and all the familiar sights, sounds, and friendships that define a life.

The tiny room seemed to capsulate how she felt about her new life. Everything seemed to be closing in on her. Would she ever see her old friends again? How would she cope with the American culture? Could she start over again and feel connected to a country which she had been taught from her youth was the "enemy." If she could not adjust, would Paul tire of her; and if he did, what next? There was no going back.

She felt adrift—a person without a country. The past was cast aside, the future wrought with uncertainty. All these emotions seemed like a heavy hand pressing down upon her. Even when her parents died, there were friends. Even at the orphanage, there was a common culture. Even at Moscow Center, there was a sense of purpose. Now sitting in the jaws of an enemy's submarine, everything seemed stripped away and empty. Never had she felt so alone.

Anya sat on the hard bunk and noticed her hat move slightly toward the edge of the desk. The submarine was going down and turning. As the vessel plunged into the dark depths, it also carried a child of the forest to a new life, a new wilderness, a new world—*America*.

ACKNOWLEDGMENT

The dews of heaven fall thick in blessings upon her.
—William Shakespeare

Blessings upon Holly Kibel and Tina McIntrye—my editors, my friends.

ABOUT THE AUTHOR

S. D. Shadden is a former law enforcement officer and professor of international affairs. He received his advanced degree from the Monterey Institute of International Studies in Monterey, California. While completing his studies, he worked at the Center for Nonproliferation, which tracks weapons of mass destruction throughout the world.

He has spent time in Bosnia, Afghanistan, Pakistan, Outer Mongolia, China, and Russia. After the fall of the Soviet Union, he lived and taught in Katowice, Poland, and in the drug capital of Culiacán, Mexico. He currently resides in the American Southwest.

CPSIA information can be obtained
at www.ICGtesting.com
Printed in the USA
JSHW030813310722
28652JS00001B/24